HASTENING

BOOK *ONE* OF

Steve Smith

VENTURES

104 Mowad Drive
Oakdale, LA 71463

2414 Ventures
104 Mowad Drive
Oakdale, LA 71463
2414Ventures.com

Publisher's Note: This is a work of fiction. Names, characters, places, and incidents are a product of the author's imagination. Locales and public names are sometimes used for atmospheric purposes. Any resemblance to actual people, living or dead, or to businesses, companies, events, institutions, or locales is completely coincidental.

Most Scripture quotations are taken from The Holy Bible, New International Version®, NIV® Copyright © 1973, 1978, 1984, 2011 by Biblica, Inc.® Used by permission. All rights reserved worldwide.

Book Layout © 2015 BookDesignTemplates.com

Cover Design: Jason Subers — RainShineGraphics.com

Hastening/Steve Smith — 1st ed.
ISBN: 978-0-9969652-0-0

Dedicated to my three sons,

Cris, Josh, and David,

whose passion for the King and His King-reign surpass mine.

May theirs be the generation that fulfills Psalm 110:3!

Acknowledgments

This book has been in process for over twenty years. Many people have believed in the mission of this book and its sequel, *Rebirth*. My wife Laura has spurred me on at each stage.

The amazing members of our church plant in Los Angeles inspired me to set this book in a church similar to ours. They have had the nations in their hearts and now live among the nations.

Robby Butler encouraged me to pull my initial e-book version out of publication to get it cleaned up as a first-rate novel. He has worked hard to get the book edited, formatted, published, and out to the world.

Many have helped with the editing process: a huge community of missional readers who plowed through the first version of this book, my mother Jean Smith, Laurie Ann Powell, Nancy Hoke, Elaine Colvin, Fred Campbell, Brian Rodriguez, Don Visser, Lorena Wood, David Seibert, and Rick Shear. Julie Gwinn lent her expertise for a final fiction edit and added confirmation to all of our prior edits. Valery Gresham did the final copy editing, and Jason Subers designed our covers.

Thank you, everyone!

PROLOGUE

I was a privileged Orange County co-ed on the math track at the rich kid's university.

Family? Well-positioned.

Test scores? Off the charts.

Resume? Increasingly marketable.

Good looks? Sure, if I tried.

Inside? Insecurity gnawed at my psyche.

The nerd on the front row of Calc II.

First to answer the prof's questions but last to strike up a conversation with the student in the next seat.

High school's most likely to ace college, but least likely to succeed in *life*.

A second grade math student could count the number of words I spoke socially my first semester.

Despite my best efforts to change, insecurity eroded everything going for me. No one believed in me, least of all myself.

Wasted. Hopeless. Broken. Lost.

Then YOU came and wrecked my brokenness.

I was loved—truly loved—for the first time. Not loved for my potential. Not loved for my performance. Not loved for my looks. Not loved for my connections.

Just loved.

Hope stepped out of the wreckage of our collision.

How do I explain the miracle of that day? These once-tight lips now gaping like a chasm, chattering incessantly about You. I still chuckle at wide-eyed responses: "Ruth Grant? You're *talking* to me?"

You daily speak words of renewal and destiny to me.

Destiny.

Destined to fulfill that final great task of life—of history. Not a vain American dream, or empty causes either.

Destined for something grander.

It's settled; You've spoken. This nerdy, broken-restored, Orange County girl was destined—*is* destined—for a globe-shaking endeavor.

Misunderstood by my church and by my parents but finally applauded by Christopher and Chara Owen.

And knowing *You*, You'll turn impossibility into a reality.

I'm stepping into the light-edged darkness with goose bumps and knocking knees.

And I couldn't be happier.

Stepping into my destiny.

—From the journal of Ruth Grant

ONE

The cool moonlight washing through the gothic windows competed with dancing shadows from the fire in the hearth. The effect on the walls was sinister—shifting, gargoylish silhouettes of the nine men sitting around the triangular table.

"Number Three, you asked for this meeting," a raspy voice said from the front.

While a clerk in the shadowy corner recorded every word, a British baritone replied, "Gentlemen, we have a rapidly developing anomaly on the Rebirth timeline."

"What sort of anomaly?" the raspy voice asked.

"In the past we have kept the Christian church at bay through a combination of time-tested strategies."

"Such as?" A query came from across the table.

"Late 1800s," a rapid-fire Korean voice answered, "when they became a threat, we 'blessed' them with prosperity. As they grew rich, they also grew apathetic and gave up their mission."

"And in the early and mid-twentieth century," a lilting Indian voice added, "we sowed discord that divided denominations with debate and left many impotent against our agenda. Then finally in the late twentieth century, we introduced enough New Age thinking and political correctness that another large swath of churches adopted a doctrine that all roads lead to the same place." Number Eight smiled smugly, pleased with the success of these strategies. "Thus they lost their evangelistic fervor."

"The prosperity strategy is also still working," the Korean said. "Preoccupation with buildings, salaries, and programs has removed many from our opposition—unwilling to risk what they have gained materially to challenge us."

The raspy voice grew impatient.

"So what is the issue, Number Three?"

"An anomaly," the Englishman answered. "A combination of factors—generational values, economic downturn, the rise of a new cadre of pastors—have coalesced to produce a breed of

Christians and even church leaders who are breaking out of their lethargy. They are ignoring materialism, numerical success, and religious pluralism. They are looking for a new mission and a new modus operandi."

He took a deep breath before delivering the dreaded news. "This could interrupt our plans for the Rebirth."

"What?" Number One's eyes narrowed menacingly. "It is your job to be three steps ahead at all times!"

"That is why we asked for this meeting," Number Three said boldly. "In order to stay three steps ahead, we must better coordinate the strategies of all three departments. This aberration is unusually resistant to the normal strategies of our Religion and Education Department. We must involve the Politics Department and the Science and Economics Department as well."

"Surely you are not talking persecution, are you?" a Chinese voice protested. "You see what good that did for us in China."

"Do not worry, Number Two. Though we misjudged the effect of religious persecution on the church in China, we are increasingly neutralizing it through economic prosperity. The growth has slowed dramatically. The new Chinese nationalist agenda should take care of the rest."

"What are you planning?" the raspy voice asked. "What do you need from this group?"

The Englishman surveyed the room and leaned forward, eager to reveal the simple brilliance of the plan.

"We shall let these new 'Jesus-followers'"—he sneered at the term—"move forward, but on the path of our choosing. Together we shall direct them through a variety of means—from character assassination to subtly redirecting their true mission. If necessary we will also add political repression."

"So you are advocating persecution!" the Chinese voice retorted.

"Yes, but not like you are thinking. We shall attack in such a way that the world will see the church and Christians as the enemies of tolerance, political correctness, and everything decent. *They* will become the bad guys."

The room fell silent.

"This will work," the raspy voice finally affirmed. Then, as an afterthought, "And the militaristic propaganda pieces remain repressed?"

Questioning looks swept the room.

"Absolutely. No one will ever find them," the Englishman replied.

The clerk looked up but continued typing.

Number One stood, signifying the end of the meeting. "So be it. Number Three, convey to each department leader what is needed from his section."

Slowly he wagged his finger at each man around the table. "Let this be a lesson to each of you. We must act swiftly and ruthlessly. Nothing must stand in our way. We hold the advantage, for we realize this is war. As long as they do not, we win. Nothing must awaken the church to this reality!"

TWO

Michael Wroth **stormed out** of the Senate Chamber, his aides scurrying behind in fear. The striking redhead Marlene Hayes was alone at his side.

"Marlene! Call Hansen's and Spears's offices and find out what happened! Check with their assistants. They should know."

"Got it."

"We had that bill blocked yesterday, and those guys wouldn't dare cross me. Someone powerful had to strong-arm them, and I want to know who it was! If their assistants won't talk, get the senators on the line directly. In fact, catch their assistants before they leave this building. Now, do it!"

Senator Wroth dashed down the steps of Capitol Hill into his waiting limo. He was furious that someone had outmaneuvered him. But he was also intrigued that this unknown opponent could have such influence.

It must be some lobbyist. But who? Who is strong enough to turn these men against me?

* * *

Marlene Hayes, Senator Wroth's administrative assistant, would normally have accompanied him in the limo. But not today. She soon had Senator Spears's AA cornered.

"What happened, Harold? Who got Senator Spears to swing his vote in favor of the Free Trade bill?"

"What are you talking about, Marlene? Senator Spears is free to change his vote as he thinks through the issues."

"Harold, someone talked with him since yesterday morning, and I want to know who it was. Either you tell me, or Senator Wroth will talk to Senator Spears. Do you want to break the news to Senator Spears that Senator Wroth insists on speaking with him today?"

Harold's eyes shifted nervously. He hated that Marlene could make him feel so spineless. "Okay. But you didn't get it from me.

Some call came in late yesterday."

"What call, Harold? What time?"

"I don't know, around quitting time. But I remembered hearing the same voice say the exact same thing fourteen years ago, and it made my skin crawl. Creepy. The last time I almost lost my job for refusing to put the call through. Somehow the man broke through on another line. The senator went berserk afterward, telling me if I ever had someone tell me 'code ten' again I was to connect him, even if I had to find him in Antarctica. I was as surprised as you were when Senator Spears swung his vote to support the bill. That phone call is the only thing I know that could have influenced him."

"That's it? There's got to be more to it. Cough it up, Harold. Who is this mysterious caller, and what does 'code ten' mean?"

"I don't know, Marlene. I've told you everything."

"There must be something more.... What do you know about the caller?"

"Nothing except his voice. It was quiet, a little hoarse, like he might be an elderly gentleman. Maybe a slight European accent. Marlene, the senator's going to be upset if I don't hurry along."

"Thanks for nothing, Harold. If you hear anything more, let me know. I expect Senator Wroth will still want to talk with Senator Spears personally. He won't be satisfied with the information you've given me."

"Tell him not to push too hard, Marlene. I know Senator Spears. It would take a lot to pit him against Senator Wroth. He must fear this mysterious caller more than he fears your boss, and there's got to be a reason. If Senator Wroth meddles, he may be picking a fight too big even for him. Tell him to lick his wounds and aim to win the next time."

"Senator Michael Wroth back down?" Marlene scoffed. "He lives for the fight, Harold! He won't drop this until he understands what happened and how to win next time."

"This is one fight he won't win," Harold said with growing assurance. He rushed off to find his boss, leaving Marlene feeling strangely unsettled.

She headed toward the Rotunda, deep in thought. Then her phone rang.

"Marlene, this is Jessica. We've got Hansen's AA. She nearly got away from us, but Meg caught her on the east-side steps. I don't think we can occupy her for long."

"Good work, Jessica. I'm on my way."

Marlene tried to process everything she had just heard, resisting the little voice telling her that Harold might be right. *What could be too big for Senator Wroth?*

Quickly Marlene's attention turned to Senator Hansen's AA, Anita Burdette. The sixty-four-year-old woman was widely seen as the queen of Capitol Hill's AAs. She had held her role for the last thirty-nine years, and had the clout to go with it. Facing her was difficult, even for Marlene. If Harold was putty, Anita was granite.

At least I have a little ammunition in my arsenal, thanks to Harold. I'm glad I ran into him first.

She was almost too late. Jessica had been unable to detain Anita any longer, and she had turned to leave.

"Anita! May I have a word with you?" Marlene shouted after her. "Anita Burdette!"

Much as Marlene suspected Anita wanted to, she knew that Anita could not simply ignore her in public. Anita stopped and turned. There was rancor in her eyes, but she replied with a controlled voice.

"Why, Marlene, how good to see you. What might I be able to help you with?" As they drew near each other, she murmured, "Loyally running secret missions for Der Fuhrer?"

"Funny, Anita. I won't mince words. Senator Wroth wants to know why Senator Hansen switched his vote on the Free Trade bill. Senator Wroth had understood that Senator Hansen opposed the bill."

"Senator Hansen isn't your boss's puppet, Marlene. He doesn't answer to anyone but his constituency. Understood?"

She really is made of steel, thought Marlene. But she spied a crack in Anita's demeanor. Anita's voice exuded confidence, but her eyes weren't quite so firm.

"Not even when it's a 'code ten'?"

Anita's hesitation told Marlene all she could hope to learn.

"What are you talking about? Senator Hansen weighed the

issues and voted his conscience. Now, unless you have something substantive to talk about, I must be going."

"No, that's it. But I don't expect that Senator Hansen will be so defiant when Senator Wroth has him in a corner. Please inform the esteemed Senator Hansen that Senator Wroth will be talking with him today."

"Senator Hansen is a busy man with a full schedule. Don't assume he has time to burn for Senator Wroth."

Anita clipped a defiant "Good day" and left.

* * *

Senator Wroth paced the floor. "'Code ten'? What foolishness is this? I've never heard anything so preposterous! Spears's AA is feeding you a bunch of hot air, Marlene."

"Harold's afraid to lie to me, sir. And Anita practically cringed when I said 'code ten.' It may not sound credible, but I believe Harold's story to be true."

Senator Wroth took a deep breath, accepted Marlene's assessment, and settled in at his desk to ponder it.

Marlene waited. She knew not to bother Senator Wroth at such moments. She found it fascinating—almost exhilarating—to watch how quickly he could compose himself, think through a situation, and propose a course of action. It was this quality and his ability to get things done that had inspired her loyalty to him through his meteoric rise from local California politics.

Five minutes later Senator Wroth looked up to let Marlene know he had mapped out his strategy. Slowly and methodically, he outlined his plan.

"Get Spears on the phone first. While I'm on the phone with him, get Hansen on standby."

"Yes, Senator."

A moment later Marlene notified him that Senator Spears was on the phone.

"Marty! How are you? You can't imagine how shocked I was when you voted for today's bill. I thought you had agreed to oppose it."

"Sorry, Michael, but I had a change of heart."

"Marty, you know how many thousands of American jobs

hung in the balance with that vote. How could you have had such a fundamental change of heart in twenty-four hours? Is there more to this?"

Though Senator Wroth spoke cordially, Senator Spears was clearly uneasy.

"Michael, I can't explain why my decision changed, but it did. You're going to have to accept it. It was only one bill, okay?"

"Listen, Marty," Senator Wroth said, keeping his growing rage in check. "I don't care if it was a bill on the production of clothespins. Something bigger is going on. You and I agreed we would vote against the bill. You betrayed my trust. Someone has scared you or manipulated you, and I want to know who it is!"

"I can't tell you anything, Michael. Let's just drop this."

"Marty, my sources tell me you received an unusual phone call yesterday afternoon, a 'code ten'? What is this all about?"

"Michael, this is one issue I can't discuss. If you know what's good for you, you'll stop. This is too big even for you. Good night!"

The phone went dead, and Senator Wroth knew it was useless to call Senator Spears back. He was clearly scared, and he wasn't going to talk.

"Senator," Marlene announced over the intercom, "I have Senator Hansen on the line when you're ready." Senator Wroth collected his thoughts and picked up the phone.

"Sam, how are you?"

Senator Sam Hansen was a senior senator from the Midwest. He didn't aspire to much and generally got along well with his colleagues. When Senator Wroth arrived in Washington, Senator Hansen had given him informal mentoring, and they had grown close. Normally he would listen to Senator Wroth, and often he went along with him. His response this time was out of form.

"Michael, I'm not going to play games with you. I know you're mad that I changed my vote today, and you are trying to find out why. I'll only tell you one thing. In my forty-three years in Washington, I have encountered a 'code ten' only four times. I have learned never to argue with it, and you will do well not to probe any further.

"And let your AA know if she ever tries to pry information

from my AA again, heads will roll."

He paused to let his words sink in. "Do you understand me, Michael?"

Senator Wroth was dumbfounded. "I understand, Sam. I've just never heard you talk this way before. You're usually so ... congenial."

"Michael, you have never encountered me under a 'code ten.' I like you, son. I know you will go a long way. You're only forty-nine, and you've got time. Skip this one for your own sake and forget it. I'm sorry. Good night."

"Good night, Senator."

Senator Wroth sat again in silence—this time thirty minutes. Finally, he called Marlene in.

"These guys are unbelievable. As tight-lipped as clams. Something big is up. Someone powerful, I mean really powerful, is in the game. Call Jake Simmons at the CIA and ask for a list of all the calls these senators received late yesterday afternoon. Find the numbers common to both offices and trace the owners. I want a name on my desk by seven tomorrow morning."

CIA? List of calls? Marlene hesitated a moment in disbelief.

"You realize that what you're asking is illegal, right?"

"Marlene, do I ever ask you to do something before I have weighed the risks? Just don't get caught."

Marlene's thoughts raced.

"I'll have it to you in the morning, sir."

THREE

Perhaps I have never put myself in a place where I need a miracle.
Obediently I enter that place now.

—Ruth Grant

The chilly night air rushed through the door as Christopher Owen closed it quickly and approached the pair awaiting him in the dimly lit corner of Common Grounds, a coffee shop near the university.

"Ah! Our diminutive leader, faithful chum, and stalwart co-collaborator graces us with his presence!" A growingly rotund John Steward stood and wrapped Christopher in a massive bear hug, lifting him off the ground.

Lanky Nicolas Fernandez arose and repeated the gesture. "Hey, buddy!"

Safely back on the ground, Christopher poked playfully at each of the men. The well-built, sandy-haired man could clearly hold his own.

"All right, guys ... make fun of my height. Have I ever told you Napoleon was only five-foot-six?"

"About a million times!" John laughed. "Do you need to compensate like he did by conquering the world?"

"Well, John," Nic said, smiling, "Christopher is always telling us how he plans to see the Kingdom spread throughout the whole world!"

"Peacefully, guys, peacefully!" Christopher laughed. "Gandhi changed India as a pacifist. A five-foot-three pacifist, at that!"

"O esteemed one, do you keep a list of history's greatest short people in your pocket?" John asked. "If I wrote down the names you've quoted since we were in college, they'd fill a notebook."

Christopher grinned at his two best friends as he grabbed the cup of decaf they'd purchased for him. His blue eyes glistened. *Friends don't come any better than this.*

"What's wrong with you, Christopher, that you can't handle real coffee at night?" John teased.

"Give it time, bro. You reach your thirties and things change. Caffeine insomnia's gonna hit you just like it did Nic and me. When it does, we'll see who's laughing. I see that Nic is drinking decaf, but you haven't said anything to him."

"I chided him for his ignoble choice before you arrived," John said. "By the way, O faithless one, did I tell you I found another famous five-foot-five person the other day? Curly Howard of the Three Stooges!"

"Woo-woo-woo-woo-woo!" Christopher slapped his face in his best Three Stooges imitation. "Now I know where I got my sense of humor. So, are we going to get down to business or continue discussing the merits of male height? I hereby call to order the meeting of the Three Amigos."

"Yes, Mr. Intensity," Nic chuckled, "let's get down to business. We are both wondering why you called us here so late."

"Guys, the Lord hasn't let me sleep most nights this week. Something big is brewing. When we started Church in the City, we aimed at developing a Kingdom movement that would reach L.A. and the world. Something beyond ourselves, beyond our own church. Something to bless other churches. Something to reach the unreached."

John and Renee Steward's move to L.A. with Christopher and Chara a few years earlier was no less costly than the Owens'. Nic and Stacy Fernandez, already doing business in L.A., joined them right at the start. The three couples fit like lock and key.

Christopher could see John shifting nervously in his seat.

"You guys know the status of our work better than anyone." Christopher sipped his coffee. "Frankly, I'm frustrated with our progress. Are we becoming a Kingdom movement? No! We need some major course corrections."

"I'm game for whatever changes you wanna make, buddy," Nic said. "In business, if we don't keep improving and adapting, we're history."

John cleared his throat. "Hold on, Nic. It doesn't take much encouragement for Christopher to jump at the next hare-brained idea. Christopher, I think we need a better grasp of the situation before we get the rest of the community stirred up."

"I agree with you, bro," Christopher said. "That's why I've asked you two to meet with me tonight. I need your gut-honest feedback. Your fingers are on the pulse of things as much as mine. Nic, you have the progress analysis?"

Nicolas, an entrepreneurial prodigy, located the appropriate spreadsheet on his tablet.

"The numbers arrived in record time from our IT whiz Timothy Wu. He confirms your hunch. We have started a large number of groups, but the members generally aren't reproducing. We have become a ministry that attracts people rather than a movement that builds disciple-makers."

Christopher signed deeply. "I knew it. I could feel it in my bones. We've settled into maintenance mode—marking time. That's not what we signed up for when we started this venture."

John, a professor of history at USC, objected. "It's not that bad, Christopher. We've made quite a difference in just a few years. And what we've got is authentic."

Christopher leaned back a bit and nodded, careful not to push too hard. "You're right, bro. If that weren't the case, nothing else would matter. It's just that I think we've focused inwardly so much we've forgotten our outward task. Los Angeles was supposed to be just the starting point. Remember? Nic, tell him what you learned a couple of weeks ago."

"About?"

"Three eras ..." prompted Christopher.

"Oh, right. Okay, so I'm taking the Perspectives class every Monday night. Dr. Ralph Winter summarized the modern missions movement into three distinct eras: the coastland era, the inland era, and the current era of unreached people groups. God's plan to bring His Kingdom to all the peoples of the earth is unfolding at an accelerating pace, and it may be nearly done. What Christopher has been teaching us is right. If we can get the gospel to all the remaining *unengaged*, unreached people groups, the task Jesus described in Matthew 24:14 could be finished! *Finished!*"

Christopher watched John stiffen. "Nic," the professor said, "do you have any idea how many unreached people groups there are? Probably tens of thousands. There's a reason it has taken 2000 years."

Christopher cleared his throat. "Uh, bro. Actually we're getting pretty close. According to databases manned by Joshua Project and the International Mission Board, the grand total of unreached groups is down to around 6,800. The number varies a bit depending on how you slice them and which database you use, but that's pretty close. The good news is that most of these have someone actively trying to reach them, leaving only 3,227 of these unengaged."

Nic glanced at his tablet. "I have a list here with all the names and locations. That's 3,227 unreached people groups that are still *not* engaged by anyone with a church-planting strategy aimed at multiplying disciples and churches."

John arched an eyebrow. "Well, count me wrong, O learned ones. *Only* 3,227 unengaged groups." He smiled and brushed a crumb off his tweed jacket. "Piece of cake."

Christopher leaned forward again. He spoke in a whisper, and the others had to lean in to hear his words. "Do you realize what you just said, Nic? We have names! Locations! No previous generation has been able to quantify what remains of the task. You guys, if we can quantify it, we can finish it!"

He tapped his fingertips together as his two friends waited.

Maybe it isn't a pipe dream after all. Maybe, just maybe ... Words came slowly to Christopher's thoughts. "Guys, don't you see? We need to embrace a sense of urgency about fulfilling Jesus' last command to His church. These are His marching orders for the body of Christ—the quest of quests. With God's help, we can do this! But I need you. I need the brainstorming power and the lock-step front of the Three Amigos."

John leaned back, took a long sip of his coffee, and said, "Okay, okay! Let's assume you're right for a minute. What has to be solved?"

Christopher's soul was a volcano ready to erupt. "What's to solve?! Everything! Like, how can we finish the task? How can it happen in our generation? That is, how can we become the last generation in history?"

John pulled at his disheveled beard. "I don't know, but I do know this. Renee's in the same class with Nic. She told me there have been over a thousand reach-the-world plans in history, and all have failed. What makes us think we'll succeed?"

"Because we must!" Christopher clapped his mug down on the table harder than he intended. Eyes turned his direction, but he was oblivious. "We must! Someone must finish this thing. Not finishing is unacceptable. There *must* be a way. The question is: How will we know when we are done?"

Nic said, "You mean metrics? How will we measure completion of the task?"

Christopher nodded. "Exactly. Paul the apostle faced this question in the eastern Roman Empire. In Romans 15 he announced his mission completed. After proclaiming Christ from Jerusalem to Illyricum, Paul said, 'There is no more place for me to work in these regions.' His work there was done; there was no place left where people did not have access to the gospel We must assault the gates of hell until there is *no place left*!"

Nic looked up. "No place left? That's a tall order."

Christopher said, "Even so, that is our mission objective."

Nic and John stared into their cups while they digested this.

Christopher leaned forward and whispered, "No place left! Come on, guys. This is the type of thing we signed on for!" He extended both hands for fist bumps. "Don't leave me hanging."

Nic smiled broadly and pounded his fist. John shook his head and did the same. "Okay, okay. I'm along for the ride with you two headstrong bucks, if for no other reason than to keep your feet on the ground."

Christopher smirked. "Now that's what I'm talking about. Three intrepid heroes marching toward Mount NoPlaceLeft."

"Or Mount Doom." John raised an eyebrow and tugged at his beard. "Well, you are hobbit sized. Maybe you won't be noticed."

Nic slapped John on the back. "Don't be so gloomy, buddy. 'No place left.' I like it. It forces us to start with the end result and find a path that'll get there. Hey, what if we set a date by which we aim for 'no place left,' a date that forces us to operate differently or fail trying? It has to be a date that forces us into a paradigm perhaps never before envisioned."

Christopher stirred in his seat. His heart began racing.

"You may have something there, bro. What's a reasonable date that would force us into approaching this in a new way?"

Nic scratched his head. "I don't know. 2050? 2040?"

Christopher said, "No way. Dates that far off still allow us to relax—business as usual."

They looked silently into their mugs for a minute.

"What about 2025?" said the tweed-clad teddy bear. "That's ten years from now. A lot can happen in ten years, but only if we radically alter course."

Christopher's eyes widened. "Professor Steward. You, the skeptic, proposing the most ambitious date?"

"Ahem." The academic dabbed some foam from his beard. "As a student of history, unlike you two ne'er-do-wells, I have the advantage of hindsight. I've rarely seen the type of course corrections you're describing without drastic, almost draconian, measures. I'm not advocating this date, but offering it as perhaps the only option to accomplish what you are describing— academically-speaking, that is!"

Christopher grinned. John talked tough but was with them heart and soul.

Christopher placed a napkin on the table and wrote: *2025 AD, 3,227 groups*, and *No Place Left*.

"Okay, guys, 3,227 groups to reach in just ten years. Progress is being made, but current momentum won't get us there that soon. A goal of the year 2025 forces a radical shift forward in momentum. What will it take for us to finish by then? How do we find the answers?"

"Well, I'm no academic," Nic said, shooting a glance at John, "but as an entrepreneur, I look for models and case studies that demonstrate the breakthrough I need. What if I contact several missions agencies to find out what good models are out there for this type of venture? *Mission Frontiers* has also had some good articles recently on models of multiplying churches."

Christopher wrote *case studies* and *Mission Frontiers* on the napkin. The tension in the pit of his stomach began to uncoil. "Okay, bro, you start checking that out. What else?"

"We'd be foolhardy not to examine history to extrapolate out momentum shifts of this endeavor over the last two millennia,"

John said. "That should reveal some clues about necessary course corrections."

Christopher laughed. "Uh, John, you know, you really need a pipe in your hand. You go ahead and work that angle." Christopher added *lessons from history* to his napkin.

"Timothy and I will contact the agencies that provided the databases for the 3,227 groups. I imagine their leaders have already wrestled with this problem. I will also send out feelers to friends who might have other leads. Listen, guys, think outside the box. Ask radical questions. Perhaps the fact that we work in different fields will lead us to innovative solutions. Follow every credible lead. Remember, we're the Three Amigos!"

John coughed. "Or perhaps the Three Stooges."

Christopher smiled. "I'll ignore that. Let's meet again in a week to compare notes. No more business as usual."

Nic pounded the table. "You got it, buddy. Let's get to work. We're burning daylight!"

John droned, "Uh, Nic. You do realize it's 11 p.m., right?"

"Never too early to start!"

John said, "Seriously, though, gentlemen. Do you realize where this could lead?" He shifted uneasily. "Questions like this can stir up a hornet's nest. The Christian establishment is pretty comfortable. And when professors challenge the status quo, we can get marginalized and branded as quacks."

Nic slapped him on the back again. "Come on, John. That's a risk we have to take. The payoff is too big."

Christopher paused and admired his fellow adventurers. No reason to worry. These two guys knew how to course correct each other, and him, too. He waited for a moment, then said, "If we pull this off, we could be the last generation—the one Jesus described in Matthew 24!"

Nic drained his coffee and stood. "All right, buddies. Much as I enjoy dreaming with you, I've got to go. Power breakfast downtown in the morning."

"And an eight o'clock class here. I'll walk out with you. Right honorable colleagues, I salute thee." John raised his cup, finished his drink, and wiped his beard.

Christopher laughed and saluted them with his mug.

"I'm gonna stay and do a bit more praying and journaling. Let's bathe this in prayer over the next few days." He smiled as the door closed behind them. They were in.

* * *

Out in the cool night air, Nic threw his arm around John's shoulder and nodded toward Common Grounds.

"That guy's crazy, you know."

"I know."

"I don't know how he keeps the pace he does. Seems like he can accomplish more in a week than most of us can in a month."

"Yeah," John said. He buttoned his coat to combat the chill wind. "Sometimes he scares me. But I've known him since our freshman year in college. Trust me, we're entering a new phase. The ride will be exhilarating—and exhausting!"

Nic slapped him on the back once more.

"Buddy, I've launched and sold businesses since I was about seventeen. I've negotiated deals worth millions. But nothing I've done compares to what our friend is proposing. I didn't want to discourage him. But, just between us, do you think it's possible to finish by 2025?"

John stopped in his tracks and arched an eyebrow at his friend. "I thought you possessed a visage of bronze, impervious to risk, drinking from an endless well of optimism, my friend."

Nic looked down at his toes. "Not impervious, John. No one is. I know when risk is perilous. The upside of this venture is limitless, but the downside is—well—fatal."

John now wrapped his arm across Nic's shoulders. "Humph. Maybe I'm not the best one to ask. I give Christopher a hard time, always have. But look at how far we've come since we started Church in the City, even spawning two other churches and multiplying many disciples and groups.

"It's nothing short of amazing, but Christopher doesn't see it—the progress, that is. He doesn't hear the accolades from others or give attention to the many requests to join the speaking circuit. He only sees what remains of the task—the gap. It drives him. It always has. Have you ever seen the quote Christopher has taped to the back of his desk?"

Nic shook his head.

"He doesn't like to parade it. It's worn and tattered now, and he keeps putting Scotch tape on it to keep it from tearing more.

"It's from the man who preached Christopher's ordination message. That old saint planted dozens of churches along the bayous of French Louisiana and, as an eighty-year-old, taught Christopher in Sunday School.

"As he spoke that night, he pointed a finger at Christopher and said, 'I just love young preacher-boys, because they don't know what God can't do.'

"*That's* what's taped to Christopher's desk. Limitless, Bible-based faith. It's something he has vowed to never outgrow. Naive sometimes, but always full of faith. I try to keep him grounded in reality and guard him however I can. But heaven forbid if I douse his faith."

John pulled out his keys and unlocked his car door. He turned and stared Nic in the eyes. "Is it possible? With other men, I'm not sure. But Christopher Owen might just pull it off. He sees no reason God can't do it." He sat down and strapped himself in. "Fasten your seatbelt. I don't think we're stopping till there is no place left."

John started his engine and drove off. Nic jumped and fist-pumped the air. "Yes! I knew it!"

FOUR

Senator Wroth might have been there all night. All Marlene knew was that he was still at the office when she finally left around midnight, and he was there when she returned early the next morning to finish her report.

Doesn't he ever sleep? Marlene finished her report, then waited until seven before gently knocking on his door. He looked as if he had rested, showered, shaved, and dressed in a fresh suit.

"Good morning, Marlene. Tell me what we've got."

"Good morning, sir. Jake Simmons said it was simple to get the numbers of all the calls. There was only one number that matched, besides, of course, our own calls to the senators. But the calls came from a public phone in Italy. I'm afraid we're at a dead end."

"We're never at a dead end. If the caller made an international call, he had to pay for it somehow. Check the Italian phone company's record to see how it was billed. Use Jake again. He owes me a lot of favors. Track the records as far as they will go. I know we're bending the rules a little, but we can't tolerate some outside force, perhaps an international one, having such strong influence on American policy making. And if we try to pursue traditional legal avenues, we will probably get nowhere."

Another aide burst into the office and thrust the morning's Washington Post into Senator Wroth's hands. Pasted across the front were pictures of two senators with a blaring headline: "TWO SENATORS KILLED OVERNIGHT, SIX DEAD."

Senator Wroth suppressed a gasp as he scanned the first article. Senator Hansen had been found knifed to death with his senior administrative assistant, Anita Burdette. They had stopped by a well-respected bar after a long day on Capitol Hill. After leaving the establishment, the two were apparently victims of a random mugging. Their money and credit cards had been taken, along with other valuables. Police speculated that the two may have resisted the muggers. There were no eyewitnesses, so the investigators had little to go on.

A second article said that Senator Spears and three aides were on a private Learjet en route to his constituency in California when the plane lost altitude over Colorado. All four, along with the pilot and co-pilot, were killed instantly. The NTSB had no clues yet regarding the cause of the crash, but all possibilities were being investigated, including foul play. Colorado officials were cooperating fully, but heavy snowfall was hampering access to the wreckage site near Castle Peak.

Senator Wroth was silent, his face pale.

This was no coincidence.

Marlene felt the need to sit.

"This is a sad day for America," Senator Wroth said, escorting the junior aide to the door. "See that the rest of the staff know."

"Marty Spears was a good friend," he said to Marlene after the door closed. "We passed the bar together in California and began our political careers about the same time. He told me yesterday that this was too big for me. Well, we're going to find out how big. There's a link all right, and we're going to find it. Call a press conference for eleven o'clock. In the meantime, get the chief of police over to meet with me. Then patch me through to whoever is heading up the investigation into the plane crash. Get them on the line after I talk to the chief."

"Yes, Senator."

Marlene gathered her notes. It was going to be a long day.

* * *

Chief Willie Merrill arrived at Senator Wroth's office around 8:30. Marlene ushered him in and left them alone. Senator Wroth stepped forward, hand extended.

"Thank you for coming, Chief. Your office must be a madhouse right now."

"Yes, sir. We are swamped with the investigation into Senator Hansen's death. I would be happy to drop by another time to visit, but today I can't spare much time. However, my wife did ask me to thank you for the bottle of champagne you sent for our twenty-fifth anniversary. She couldn't believe you remembered."

"It was nothing. Please have a seat, Willie. This will only take a minute, and I hope it can help your investigation. Are we off the record?"

"Absolutely, Senator. Do you know something?"

Senator Wroth poured the chief some coffee and escorted him to a sofa.

"Senator Hansen and I were fairly close. In many ways he was my mentor. Senator Spears and I were also quite good friends going all the way back to law school. And, of course, we were both senators from California. Honestly, it's hard to believe their deaths were just coincidental."

"I beg your pardon, sir, but just because you knew them both well doesn't exactly link them together."

"Oh, you're quite right," Senator Wroth replied with good-natured surprise. "I haven't given you the connecting details. Actually, something happened just yesterday that makes me think this wasn't a coincidence."

Senator Wroth hesitated as if searching for what to say. "The three of us were all set to vote yesterday morning against the Free Trade bill. According to our count it would lose, but it would be close—fifty-one against, forty-nine for. But when the vote was taken, both Senator Hansen and Senator Spears reversed their position, and the bill won fifty-one to forty-nine.

"I have to admit I was angry. We had all fought hard to block the loss of American jobs through this bill. I got a little fiery and confronted each of the senators privately. They both told me in no uncertain terms that someone they feared had pressured them to reverse their votes, but they wouldn't tell me who it was. Frankly, Chief, this was out of character for both men."

"They wouldn't say who it was, sir?"

Wroth said, "Not a word. But it sounded as if someone had really scared them. We're both off the record, right?"

The chief nodded.

"These men were my friends, and I smell a rat. I'm going to hold a press conference in a couple of hours to express my condolences and assure the American public that I will do all I can to see that these deaths are investigated thoroughly.

"I won't disclose any evidence you have, Chief, but I would appreciate knowing as much as possible so that I can speak intelligently to the situation. The death of two out of one hundred senators in one evening is a grave blow to America, let alone their staffs! Have you discovered anything that could indicate the deaths were premeditated?"

The chief was visibly encouraged. In a world full of reluctant witnesses, he was pleased that the senator, and perhaps even the entire Senate, was going to cooperate.

"Well, sir, I can't say anything regarding Senator Spears's death—that's out of my jurisdiction. And, of course, any information about Senator Hansen is strictly confidential. But there was something very curious in Senator Hansen's death. Wadded up in his closed fist was a note, 'Never betray a code ten!' But we have no idea what a 'code ten' is.

"None of the reporters saw the note in Senator Hansen's fist, so to them this is just another mugging. Did Senator Hansen mention anything to you about a 'code ten,' sir?"

Senator Wroth took another sip of coffee before responding, his brow furrowed slightly. "No, not that I can recall. What do you think it means?"

"We haven't the foggiest. The note could be pointing to a premeditated assault, but with nothing more to go on, it's going to be difficult to treat this as anything more than a mugging."

"It may be just as well that the public thinks it was random for now. I hope this was helpful. And thank you for coming over here discreetly; I didn't want to create the wrong impression by going down to the police station and all."

"No, Senator, it was better for me to come here. Don't worry about this conversation. If we need to follow up, I'll call you privately, or you can call me."

The senator walked the chief to the door.

"I won't say anything about the note in my press conference. Good luck in your investigation."

* * *

The conversation with the chief investigator assigned to Senator Spears's plane crash wasn't much different.

"We didn't see it at first, sir. It snowed lightly after the crash, obscuring the site. Wreckage from the plane was strewn over several hundred yards. After an hour of walking Castle Peak, one of my investigators noticed that someone had written 'CODE TEN' in three-foot block letters in the snow. We found the body of one of the pilots near the writing, so he may have been trying to signal for help, but if so he was apparently delirious. Whoever heard of a 'code ten'?"

The senator thanked the investigator and told him the same things he had told Chief Merrill about both senators being pressured by someone they feared into changing their votes. He also recommended that the investigator talk to Chief Merrill.

* * *

Senator Wroth's eleven o'clock press conference was perfectly timed. The news had spread, and all of America was in shock. Senator Wroth was the first senator to speak publicly on the two deaths. And eight o'clock Pacific Time suited his California constituency perfectly. Senator Wroth had a gift for connecting with his audience emotionally while communicating wise tenacity in pursuing justice. He kept his comments brief. First, he expressed his deepest sorrow at the deaths of his two friends. Then he promised that his office and hopefully the U.S. Senate would ensure the deaths were investigated thoroughly. Finally, he assured those listening that any wrongdoing would be dealt with swiftly.

Questions followed.

"Senator Wroth, do you have any idea if the crash or the mugging was premeditated?"

"Well, honestly, it's too early to tell. I have no evidence one way or the other, and, as you can imagine, I am not privy to the confidential investigations."

"But do you have any evidence on this case or know of any developments at this point?" another reporter asked.

"Nancy, as I mentioned, I'm just a senator, and I don't have any evidence. That's the job of the investigators. My offers of assistance have reassured me that both investigations are being pursued thoroughly."

"So, you have talked to the investigators?"

"These two senators were close friends of mine. I was deeply moved when I received the news of their deaths this morning. I have talked to the investigators in Washington and Colorado, not to interfere but to offer any assistance I can."

"Sir, what kind of assistance could a senator offer the police and NTSB investigations?"

"That remains to be seen. I have to run. I am meeting with the governor of California today to discuss the appointment of a new senator. Tough as it will be to replace Senator Spears, it must be done. The people of California need another voice to join me in guiding America. Thank you."

Senator Wroth and his entourage exited the podium confident the public felt reassured that matters were in good hands.

Back at his office, Marlene awaited Senator Wroth.

"Great press conference, Senator!" She looked up from some documents. "By the way, both those calls were billed to the same Italian credit card, but the account was then closed with no trace of a name, address, or other identifying information."

Senator Wroth seemed almost pleased, as if he were expecting such news.

"This guy is good, and he's still a step ahead of us. But we're going to nail him. No one is going to take out two U.S. Senators without consequences."

"Sir, don't you think we should notify the CIA?"

"Not just yet. There's no telling who's involved in this. We have the resources to carry out a swift investigation of our own and possibly get more critical, time-sensitive information than the normal bureaucracy. We can't afford to let this lag. We need to operate quickly and quietly.

"Marlene, we politicians think we're powerful because we shake our sticks at people and they run. But this guy is smarter. Somehow he's been working behind the scenes for decades with great restraint. Hansen said he had encountered a 'code ten' only four times, and he served over forty years. Spears got a similar call fourteen years ago—one call! This guy doesn't intervene often, just at critical points."

Senator Wroth continued as if teaching Marlene deep and important truths. "This guy may have already been strategizing while we were in diapers. His strength is his patience and his willingness to work covertly. There's a kind of power that people see and snap to. But this guy's power is much deeper. He influences people without being seen—that's real power. To nab him we'll need to remain behind the scenes ourselves and try to catch him unawares."

The two sat in silence for a moment before Senator Wroth returned to the task at hand.

"Have Simmons fly to Rome where he can handle the investigation directly. Have him use the special projects account to flash a lot of money around quietly at the Italian credit card company. Someone's bound to talk over there. Then work through your network with the other AAs on Capitol Hill to see if they've ever had a 'code ten' call. But be inconspicuous and offhand about it. They mustn't suspect anything."

"How much cash do I have to work with?" Marlene inquired.

The senator paused for a moment.

"Offer Simmons as much as he needs—no cap. And, Marlene, I want you to accompany me to San Francisco to meet with the governor this evening about appointing someone to fill Spears's position. We'll leave here at three."

"San Francisco? Not Sacramento?"

"The governor wants to meet quietly, off-the-record, at Dr. Larson Sayers's office," he explained.

"Dr. Larson Sayers? *The* Dr. Larson Sayers?"

Senator Wroth was visibly pleased at Marlene's response.

As Marlene was closing the door behind her, Senator Wroth called her back in. "One more thing, Marlene," he said, with just a hint of concern. "Ask Simmons to have one of his experts check our jet over thoroughly."

* * *

Jake Simmons arrived at the airport with his technical expert around 1 p.m. to scour the Bombardier Challenger 850 for any tampering. Bryce was good; if something were amiss, he would find it.

"Holy cow!"

Simmons ran to the nose of the 850, where Bryce was examining the front landing gear.

"Look at that!" Bryce exclaimed.

"What is it?"

Bryce handed Simmons a flashlight. "Shine that up into the landing gear assembly. The metal bolt has been replaced with a plastic replica. It looks fine but won't hold up under pressure."

"So, what does that do? Does it prevent the landing gear from deploying?" asked Jake.

"No way! That would flash a warning signal to the pilot, who could then retract the gear and try a belly landing. Nope, whoever set this up is a lot smarter than that. This bolt normally locks the gear down during landing. But without a metal bolt the landing gear wouldn't hold up during impact. The wheels would deploy, the pilot would land, and the front gear would buckle."

Moments later Bryce continued, "And look here. The same bolt was replaced on the back right gear, but not on the left. So the front and right wheel supports would collapse while the left gear would stay extended. The plane would swerve out of control and spin on the runway like a drunk—with a high probability of loss of life."

"Can you fix it?"

"Give me half an hour."

Bryce twisted the fake bolts loose.

"Hmm, it's hard to see under the grease stain, but this looks like the manufacturer's name: C-O-D-E T-E-N. 'Code ten'? Huh, never heard of it." He tossed the bolts to Simmons. "Souvenir for the senator."

* * *

Marlene was thrilled to accompany Senator Wroth to the meeting with Dr. Sayers at his suite atop the Bay Mist Tower.

Although the reception area sported magnificent views of San Francisco, Marlene was more interested in the interior decor. *Well decorated, but not ostentatious. Surprisingly modest for a man of his stature.* While the receptionist prepared their coffees, Marlene walked around admiring Sayers's photos—a private audience with the Pope; at the negotiating table with Arab and Israeli leaders; bottle feeding a famished infant in Somalia; relaxing at Camp David with the president; a private meeting with the Dalai Lama and the premier of China; and weeping with victims of war in the Balkans. *No wonder people love Dr. Sayers.*

The senator and Marlene were escorted to a comfortable sitting area where they greeted the governor and his aides. Marlene noted Senator Wroth's subdued excitement as he spotted a short, balding man sitting inconspicuously in the background.

Dr. Sayers rose swiftly. "Hello, Michael, it's been too long."

Senator Wroth walked quickly to Dr. Sayers, shook his hand, and then hugged him as if he were family.

Marlene was floored, as was the governor.

"I see you know each other," the governor said.

"I've known Michael's family all his life, Governor."

"Known us? Uncle Lars, er ... Dr. Sayers and my mother were childhood friends. He frequently joined us on family vacations. He's like an uncle to me."

"It has been a long time though, hasn't it?" Senator Wroth added, turning to Dr. Sayers.

"Yes, Michael, the last twenty-five years have been rather busy for both of us. You have become quite influential. Your father would be proud of you."

"You're being modest," the senator responded warmly. "You're the one who has been busy. Everywhere I turn, you are inspiring decision-makers toward peace. I've never understood how you do it. How do you see past disagreements to help guide opposing parties to agreeable solutions?"

"That's why I requested this meeting, Michael," the governor said. "We need Dr. Sayers's wisdom in this moment of crisis. But we only have a sixty-minute window, so if you don't mind, let's get started."

The three men and their aides sat at the mahogany table to discuss who should succeed Senator Spears for the remainder of his term. Many options were considered, with the governor and the senator generally in disagreement. Differences in ideology were reviewed. Prospects for re-election after Senator Spears's term ended were examined. One by one, leading contenders were eliminated as too divisive, too conservative, too ambitious. As the meeting progressed, one name rose to the top—Representative Philip Bowen. Neither the governor nor the senator would have chosen him, but as Dr. Sayers guided their considerations,

Bowen became the preferred choice for both.

"Well then, Bowen it is," the governor said, tired but satisfied. "We'll run a brief background check, and I'll talk with him personally to see if he'll accept the position."

"He'll accept, Governor," Senator Wroth said. "Philip is eager to serve in a larger capacity. He's itching to get into the senate."

Dr. Sayers stood, signaling that the meeting was over. "Gentlemen, I think you've made a wise decision," he said. "Now if you will excuse me, I must prepare for my trip to Benghazi tomorrow. Stay as long as you like. My assistant will wait and lock up behind you."

Dr. Sayers shook everyone's hand and gave Senator Wroth another quick hug before departing.

FIVE

I can't shake the feeling that I was destined
for something extraordinary, something history-changing.
The shouts of the ordinary—
the mundane, the self-focused, the trivial—
try to drown out the gentle call of the upward quest.
Oh, retune my ears to hear!

—Ruth Grant

"Thanks for staying up for me," Christopher said as he got into bed, where Chara was fighting to keep her eyes open.

"I couldn't wait to hear how your meeting with Nic and John went. So many of our hopes and dreams seem to hang in the balance." She yawned. "So they gave you helpful feedback?"

"More than you could imagine. In the abundance of counselors there is victory, and those guys are good counselors. They help me think in fresh ways. I mean, Nic's idea of simply setting a deadline was pivotal. And when John proposed 2025, I nearly fell out of my seat."

Chara snuggled up to him and pulled the blanket tighter.

"Honey, I forgot to tell you one more interesting tidbit from our Perspectives class," she said. "Get this—last year one major evangelical denomination spent 215 million dollars in *interest alone* on church debt. It makes me so mad. There are so many better things to do with that money!"

Her breathing soon indicated that she was falling asleep, even though she continued to mumble, "... so mad. Makes me so mad."

Christopher stared at the ceiling, replaying the evening's conversation in his mind. Sweat formed on his brow despite the chill in the room. He shuddered. *God, what am I getting us into?*

He slipped out of bed and tiptoed down the stairs of their deteriorating hundred-year-old Tudor home. Guided by the moonlight streaming through the living room window, he reached his study, carefully navigating lines of dominoes the kids had meticulously set up.

The night sounds clamored louder than usual. Christopher cocked his head in thought. *First I dragged my family to the inner city—well, not dragged. They came eagerly, but I'm still responsible. Now I'm dragging them into the final generation—the Revelation generation. What idiocy! I can just hear my kids in a few years, "Gee, Dad, thanks for letting us walk through fire and tribulation."*

Christopher shivered again, flung the quilt away, and dropped to the floor. *Crank out thirty diamond push-ups. That should do it.*

Twenty-one was all he could manage. *When did that happen? Exhaustion must be robbing my energy.* Slowly he pulled himself up and collapsed on the love seat.

He pulled out his Bible and journal and began writing: *Is it really possible to fulfill Matthew 24:14? Is it possible to get to the point of "no place left"? Or I'm just delusional? Surely this time I'm in over my head. The guys see the faith-filled Christopher. But they can't peer into my soul to see that my every faith venture is plagued by self-incriminating doubts.*

Christopher paused and waited on the Lord. He sensed the Holy Spirit guiding him once more to the familiar passage: "Since all these things are to be destroyed in this way, what sort of people ought you to be in holy conduct and godliness, looking for and hastening the coming of the day of God?"

"Oh, Lord," Christopher whispered, "what would it take for our generation to hasten the day? Can we really do it? Am I ready to pay the price?"

He put his pen down and began pacing, running his fingers through his hair.

Yes. You've guided me deliberately down this path. Father, give us a clear plan toward the end-vision of every nation, every tribe, every people and language knowing and worshipping You. Why has it taken us two thousand years?

Christopher picked up his phone and tweeted:

1000 finish-the-task plans in 2000 yrs all fell short of no place left (Rm 15:23). What can we do to finish by 2025? #NoPlaceLeft2025

As he sent the tweet into cyberspace, he shot a desperate prayer into heaven. Gunshots rang out nearby. He lay on the love seat in a fetal position. *Gunshots? Drive-by shootings? It's gonna get a lot worse than this.*

He couldn't sleep on the love seat again. The crick in his neck from previous nights of insomnia still screamed its objection. He tiptoed back into the living room. A police car shot down his street, lights flashing, siren silent.

Christopher carefully dodged the lines of dominoes, though several floorboards announced his steps. He crept back upstairs and into bed, where Chara snuggled next to him again. He stared into the darkness, praying for responses to his tweet that would unravel the mystery and perhaps set the quest in motion. He prayed he would have the strength to complete their new quest.

Downstairs he heard a rhythmic clickety-clack invading the silence. Christopher sat upright. Chara stirred beside him.

"What was that?"

"Oh, nothing. The dominoes have just started falling."

SIX

The data analyst printed a report and called to his supervisor.

"Yes, Greely?" Number Eight strutted over.

"Sir, we intercepted an email reply to a tweet from Los Angeles. It references two Priority E items and one Priority A item."

"Priority A, is it?"

"Yes, sir. I would not have disturbed you otherwise, sir." Greely shifted nervously.

"You ran a background check on the referenced items?" Number Eight took the report and studied it.

"Yes, sir," said Greely. "I have never encountered a Priority A item before, sir, but I think I handled it correctly."

"Relax, Greely. You have done good work." Number Eight glanced again at the report. "Just as I expected. The items have been quietly suppressed. I doubt anyone will care about either of the Priority E items, but it wouldn't matter much if they do. And all records of the Priority A item have been thoroughly erased. Excellent—carry on!"

"B-b-but, sir?" Greely hesitantly objected.

Number Eight eyed him with disdain.

"What is it, Greely?"

"Sir, don't you think we should inform Number Three?"

Number Eight coughed.

"How long have you been with us, Greely?"

"Five years, sir."

"Quite right. You are still green. And didn't your father work with us before you?"

"Yes, sir."

"I am surprised your father did not educate you better. A good man he was. Quiet. Diligent. Punctual. If he were here, he would tell you we do not inform Number Three of such trivial matters. We are quite capable of handling them."

"But sir, this is a Priority A item. It should ..."

Something in Number Eight's eyes told Greely to stop.

"Exactly my point, Greely. Being a Priority A item, it received Priority A attention from Number Three ..." he consulted the report in his hand, "exactly seventeen years ago. You see, Greely, when we act, we act thoroughly and unobtrusively. Number Three is the best there is. No loose ends. Period. Carry on."

Greely returned to his workstation and tried to put the affair out of his mind. He felt unsettled that the email was somehow missing any indication of who sent it. Theoretically this couldn't happen, but somehow it had. No matter. If Number Eight said it was taken care of, it must be. He turned toward the monitor and continued scanning reports.

SEVEN

Some generation will be the last generation,
the one that sees Your glorious return.
It will be a generation of your people
willing to lay down their lives without reservation.
Let my life be a catalyst for such a generation!
—Ruth Grant

Christopher's feet returned to the ground as John released him from another bear hug. "Hail, O fearless captain!"

Nic grabbed their coffee mugs and laughed. He led John and Christopher to a warm corner of Common Grounds.

As they followed, John slung an arm across Christopher's shoulders. "Hey, I found another five-foot-five compadre for you—Harry Houdini. Only you're not escaping our questions tonight. We've got more than a few knots for you to untie."

"Is that right? Houdini? Good company."

"You're dodging my meaning."

"Exactly!" Christopher winked. "By the way, guys, Lawrence of Arabia was only five-foot-six, and look at what he achieved!"

"That's it, hand it over," John said. "I'm ready to burn that list of yours!"

"Come on, buddy" urged Nic. "I want to hear more about what you've been texting us. It's driving me crazy. And the email you forwarded is especially intriguing. Why would someone send it anonymously, and how could they even do that?"

The three settled into plush armchairs.

"Now let me get this straight, Christopher," said John. "You got an anonymous response to your inquiry, and there's no way to track down who sent it?"

"Tweet, John, not inquiry. Inquiry sounds so academic."

John squared his shoulders. "Tweet, twit, email, whatever. I don't care how it was sent."

Nic pulled out his device. "Back to the email. No way to track it down?"

Christopher shook his head. "Timothy says it is impossible to send an untraceable email, but he sees no way to track this one to the source. If he can't track down the sender, I know I can't."

Once more Nic read the email's three short phrases:

Roland Allen: Various works

A.T. Pierson: Turn-of-the-twentieth-century missions mobilizer

M.J. Livermore: Dissertation, Franklin College, Ely, UK

He looked up from his tablet. "Buddy, this could just be some wild goose chase. Sounds pretty cryptic."

"Yeah, I thought about that, but the first item turned out to be a gold mine. Roland Allen was way ahead of his time. His books go in and out of print and can be hard to find and expensive, but the Kindle version of *Missionary Methods: St. Paul's or Ours?* was just one dollar!"

"What did he have to say?" Nic asked.

"Allen made some radical proposals that turned conventional missions thinking on its head and infuriated the Christian establishment at home and abroad. Kinda like what you said, John, about professors who challenge the status quo. He was sidelined and branded a quack."

John tugged at his ear and cleared his throat. "Hmm, so of course you're attracted to him."

Christopher toasted him. "Touché."

John took a swig of his coffee. "If he's been branded a quack, why listen to him?"

"That was a hundred years ago," Christopher said. "He even wrote that it would be fifty years before his views would be widely accepted, but he was optimistic. It took seventy years. But as his ideas have been taking root, the result has been nothing less than multiple church-planting movements."

"Wait a minute," John said. "You've been texting about this all week. Remind me again what a church-planting *movement* is."

Christopher shifted in his seat and began gesturing with his hands. "Well, reproducible simple communities of believers are launched in a region. Then these new disciples are given the vision, equipping, and encouragement to grow in their faith and simultaneously take the gospel to other places. When they do, they use the methods they were taught to start new groups every few weeks or months. These churches meet in homes, under trees, in storefronts, wherever. In time the gospel saturates the area. The King assumes His rightful reign. Since these movements produce successive generations of new churches, they are called *church-planting movements*, or *CPMs*."

Nic leaned forward in his chair. "John, it seems that over the last fifteen years CPMs have been really growing in number. Many of them originated in Asia—places like China and India. This is the best model I've found yet for completing our quest."

Christopher sipped his triple, tall, decaf Americano. "Amigos, we have a lot of learning ahead of us. I'm going to start reading all I can on this."

Nic gave John a knowing look but spoke to Christopher. "From what I've read, this isn't something you can learn just by reading a book. You need to taste and feel it, and learn from CPM practitioners."

"And Nic's got the perfect place to do that, or that's what he is telling me," said John.

"What would you and Chara think about going to Singapore with Stacy and me for a two-week training?" Nic asked.

"What?!"

"Listen, buddy," Nic said. "I've asked around about where to be trained in CPM methods, and the best course seems to be hosted in Singapore. Stacy and I have discussed it with John and Renee. I have more frequent flier miles on my company credit card than I can use before they expire. Unless I use them to fly us all to Singapore, they'll go to waste."

"Guys, I don't know..."

"You really should do it," John urged. "There are plenty of church growth conferences in America, but we aren't seeing the kind of movements here that you and Nic are talking about. We all know about the explosion of believers in places like China. I think it's time for the Western world to learn from Asia."

"You have a good point, and who wouldn't love to go to Singapore? But what about the kids? What about the church? Chara would never go for it."

"O ye of little faith. Chara has already started packing. Renee and I can hold things together at church for a few weeks," John announced with finality.

"You're not that indispensable, buddy," Nic added with a grin, "and we're taking the kids to Singapore, too."

Christopher shook his head and wrote *Singapore—Owens & Fernandezes* on a napkin.

"Well, it appears I have no choice. I have been outvoted by you *and* our wives. One nice thing about substitute teaching is that I can always take time off."

He took a sip of coffee, trying to hide his Cheshire-cat grin in the mug. *I've never had a poker face!* He screwed on his serious face again. "John, what have you learned from looking into the history?"

"I've done an initial search for factors that have increased or decreased momentum toward bringing the gospel to the entire world. I'm just in the preliminary stages, but I think I can help with item number two in the cryptic message: A.T. Pierson: Turn-of-the-twentieth-century missions mobilizer. And, by the way, I used real books from a real, musty library. You know, those things with leather on the outside and leaves of paper on the inside."

Christopher threw a napkin at him. "Okay, wise-guy."

"I discovered some exciting yet disturbing things about the response to Pierson's initiative. He endeavored in the waning years of the nineteenth century to build collaboration to finish evangelizing the world by 1900. This led to global conferences and a lot of new initiatives."

"Wow! That's fascinating!" Christopher was on the edge of his seat. "Someone before us had the same idea of proposing a specific date for reaching the world! What happened?"

John hesitated. He stroked his beard several times.

"The glamour waned," he said solemnly. "There was a lot of talk, but less activity. Prosperity had set in. When it came right down to it, not enough people wanted to make the sacrifices necessary to make it happen. The year 1900 came and went. Pierson kept trying to rally others, and the increased momentum continued well into the next century, but this 'Student Volunteer Movement' eventually died out."

Christopher leaned back and threw up his hands. "So the whole thing was a bust?"

"Oh no! A hundred thousand young people offered themselves for service to the nations. Twenty thousand went while the others supported them."

Nic asked, "So it worked, but then the effort dissipated?"

John nodded and continued. "A similar effort developed in the lead-up to 2000 AD, and this effort got us even farther down the path. But still it has not resulted in mobilizing the whole Church to finish the whole task. And more than three thousand unreached people groups are still unengaged—waiting for those in our *comfortable* churches to take the good news to the *uncomfortable* places."

Christopher stood up, paced a few times, and then plopped back down. Heads turned. "Wow! Two previous pushes have carried us many times around the track in this 2000 year long race. The finish line is in sight! The final lap is ready to be run."

"That's true, Christopher," John said. "But listen to what I said. The groups left to reach are also the *hardest* to reach, and much of the Church is asleep. We let the possibility of finishing by 2000 pass us by because we enjoyed our creature comforts more than the Creator's call. Will 2025 be any different?"

Christopher whipped out his phone and tapped out a tweet:

3000+ unengaged unreached people groups. The finish line is in sight! Who will run the LAST LAP with us? #NoPlaceLeft2025

"That settles it, Chris," Nic said. "We *have* to go to Singapore."

Christopher picked up the email printout. "What about this last item? M.J. Livermore. Any leads, bro?"

Nic swallowed. "That's been a tough one. It took me a while to track down a number for Franklin College. It's near London, just a shadow of its former self.

"I finally managed to reach the library to request a copy of the dissertation, but apparently the college still lives in the nineteenth century. I fancy myself a pretty good negotiator, but I may have met my match in this old British librarian. Mrs. Goodenough told me that they don't do loans, they don't make copies, and they don't disclose their dissertation titles. I even got our charming professor here to call as a distinguished academic, but she shut him down as well."

John winced. "Yeah, that one wounded my ego a bit! The bottom line is, if you want to read that dissertation you're going to have to read it in her library, under her watchful eye. And she probably walks around with a ruler in her hand! I knew a few of those kind at Cambridge."

"So that got us thinking," John said, with a knowing glance at Nic. "You already have me standing in for you at church. And Nic and Stacy will be with you in Singapore and can bring your kids back, so ..."

He and Nic both leaned forward and said, "Wait for it . . .!" John made a drum roll on the table with his coffee stirrers.

Nic beamed. "We think you and Chara should continue around the world for a little honeymoon in England. We've already checked with Chara, and she likes the idea."

Christopher sat back in his chair, a bemused smile on his face.

"Man, how much conspiring goes on behind my back? Guess I can't say no?"

They both shook their heads. "Why would you?" John added.

Christopher laughed. "Well, if that dissertation at Franklin is as significant as the other two items in the email, the trip will be well worth it! And of course it would be great to enjoy a stop in England with Chara."

He pulled out his phone and texted Chara, "Second honeymoon, here we come!"

Nic shifted in his seat. "Uh, guys, I've been thinking about this whole endeavor. Ephesians 4:11–13 makes it clear that the role of the pastors and teachers is to equip God's people for works of serving God's purposes. But it seems like the current model of church is for the pastors to do the works of service while believers just sit in the pew.

"This has got to hinder any lasting missions impact," Nic

mused. "I mean, if I focused on serving the personal needs of my employees rather than equipping them, we'd never get out and make deals. That would kill any business!"

John nodded. "Apart from Church in the City, that sounds like most churches I've been in. It's a challenge for pastors to send their members out to the nations, and it's hard for church members to develop the confidence and skills to actually go.

"Last week I was in Ephesians 1:9–10," John continued. "God has had a mysterious plan from the beginning of time to bring everything—every people group, every nation—under the authority of Jesus. This *must* be the central mission of the *whole* body of Christ—every member. If we don't take this on as our mission, then we're missing out on God's plans."

"Something's gotta give, guys!" Christopher said, more loudly than he intended, once again prompting looks his direction.

He lowered his voice. "I only wish we had started out more missionally at Church in the City. If we had been serious from the beginning about finishing the task by a specific date, we would have done a lot of things very differently."

John leaned forward and gripped Christopher's shoulder. Christopher, feeling the firmness, knew this was a rare moment. "Look at me! We've been faithful with what we've known. *You've* been faithful with what you knew. Now we must be faithful with the new things God is showing us. He is sovereign. No second-guessing. And our loving faith community is a great foundation to work from."

John continued, but his voice softened. "The six years since Church in the City started have been amazing, but you're just a pastor, and a bivocational one at that—substitute teaching and leading us in your free time. What more could you do?"

"No, bro," Christopher pulled back from John's grasp. "I'm not *just* a pastor. It's that type of thinking that has locked me into the ruts of maintenance ministry. I've got to think differently. *We've* got to think differently. Don't you see? I've got to think of myself not as a pastor of people but a pastor of pastors—like I do with our church plants. A pastor of sent-out ones."

Christopher's eyes watered as he looked back and forth at his friends.

"And our church, small as we are, must not be just a church any longer. We must be a training and sending base to the nations. A church spawning and shepherding new churches—a catalyst for movements."

His two friends nodded slowly, deliberately.

Without warning, Christopher bowed his head. His friends knew the familiar cue. They joined him in prayer.

"Let's pray for as long as it takes to clarify what God is saying to us. We must change our thinking, our faith, our expectations, our actions. Only in this way can we hasten the return of Christ!"

EIGHT

Nine men sat at a triangular table, three per side. The early morning light diffused through the pointed gothic windows, barely illuminating the outlines of the figures bent over the table. The small room was void of all markings except a few ancient tapestries that graced the walls. In the hearth, a dying fire awaited fresh fuel.

Near the head of the table, if one could call it the head, a particularly grizzled old man spoke with a raspy voice.

"Number Three, how is our man coming?"

"Splendidly," replied a man who was younger only by comparison. "He sees and thinks well. He has much potential."

"Will he find us?" Number One continued.

"Yes, Prime Director—if we don't destroy him first. Hopefully he will get past our traps."

"Very good," replied Number One. He brushed a fallen gray lock from his eyes, rose slowly from his seat, and hobbled out of the room.

In the hearth, the fire gave one last pop. A few glowing coals amidst the ashes were all that remained of its former glory.

NINE

As she had been instructed, Marlene appeared at Senator Wroth's suite in San Francisco's Clift Hotel at 7 a.m. The senator was finishing his breakfast with his tablet open to his five daily online newspapers.

Marlene sat down across the table. "I got word from Simmons just an hour ago. It didn't take long for him to find a data entry clerk willing to talk. She had been told to delete the account. But for the right sum she provided Simmons with the location of the paper file containing the original application."

"Paper file? This is the twenty-first century, right?"

"Yes, sir, but evidently not in this Italian credit card company. The file is in a warehouse, and Jake's on his way to get it. I told him to use the satellite number to reach us on the Challenger 850 when he has more news."

"Great work, Marlene. And what have you learned from the AAs on Capitol Hill?"

"Before we left yesterday, I sent them a discreet message. They'll go through their phone logs this morning, and I should have their results by the time we arrive back in Washington."

* * *

Three hours later, as the senator and Marlene were cruising home at forty-one thousand feet, Senator Wroth began reflecting aloud on the previous evening.

"Marlene, I've known Dr. Sayers all my life. There's a subtle magic in his ways. Think about it. How did the governor and I reach agreement on Bowen? Neither of us would have chosen him. He's a virtual non-entity."

Marlene kept her mouth shut as Wroth allowed her a rare glimpse into his private musings.

"The governor and I rarely see eye to eye, and I really expected a fight over Spears's succession. I was ready to lobby hard for Mairs to finish Spears's term. Bowen wasn't even on my radar, but he's the perfect choice. Why didn't we see it before Dr. Sayers suggested it?

"And then for the governor to agree—no, to advocate for— Bowen. It was a masterstroke. How did Dr. Sayers do it?"

A relaxed Senator Wroth returned from the bar with another drink and swiveled his plush chair to look Marlene in the eye.

"Marly, Uncle Lars always called this his 'gift'—this ability to look into someone's mind and almost read it, then influence their thoughts so the other person accepted Lars's conclusions as their own. I need to develop this gift. Find a time when I can meet with Dr. Sayers. I need his mentoring in this area."

Marlene's gaze was transfixed by her tall, Hollywood-handsome boss.

"Now, what briefs do I need to review?" Like a flipped switch, Senator Wroth was all business again. The precious window into his personal thoughts had closed.

Marlene blinked to attention. Before she could pull out the briefs, the satellite phone rang. Marlene answered and listened, her face looking first puzzled, then sober, then pale. After ending the call she stared at the senator, clearly shaken.

"That was Jake Simmons," she said, attempting to regain her composure. "He found the file with the original credit application. It was a personal account with the name..." She hesitated. "Your name. Michael Wroth. It listed your private Bel Air address, unlisted phone number, and checking account."

"That's impossible! No one has that information—no one!"

"Senator, Simmons ran a trace. There was a transfer from your account in Beverly Hills to the credit card account in Rome equal to the cost of both phone calls."

To Marlene's astonishment, Senator Wroth roared with laughter. "This guy's superb! How I have underestimated him! This makes it more imperative than ever that I find this serpent. Not only must I bring him to justice, there's much I need to learn from him."

Senator Wroth continued to chuckle in admiration. "Tell Simmons to guard that file! We wouldn't want the police to get their hands on it. They might not find the situation humorous, nor see so readily that I've been framed."

Marlene breathed a sigh of relief.

"Marlene, we're going to have to outfox this guy ever so quietly. There's a crucial vote in two days on a defense reduction package. It looks to be just as close as the trade bill was. Our caller just might want to influence that as well."

* * *

That evening at the conference table in Senator Wroth's office, Marlene reported more of her findings.

"So far seven senators' AAs have reported receiving 'code ten' phone calls—four Republicans and three Democrats."

"With the two dead senators, that's five Democrats," Senator Wroth observed, studying the list.

"Interesting," he continued. "All seven are fairly moderate. If we examine their voting records, I think we will find they've given swing votes in major decisions. Where's the list of senate bills they received calls on?"

Marlene handed him an impressive list. Not only had she identified the senators who received calls, she had also pinpointed the dates, pulled records of the legislation then under debate, and listed the votes and outcomes.

Wroth scanned it. "Extremely complex, but the direction is clear. The caller is influencing global policy toward greater worldwide cooperation. I think the vote in two days is too crucial for him to pass up. My bet is he'll want this defense reduction to pass—a weaker America will have less divisive power in the world he is trying to create. Give me the probable vote count as it stands today on the defense bill."

Marlene looked through her papers. "Most of the senators have expressed their intentions, and it looks close, sir. As it stands, the bill will lose forty-eight to fifty-two."

"How convenient," Senator Wroth said. "Four of our colleagues on the 'code ten' list have indicated they'll vote against the bill. If my guess is right, our caller will contact three of them, if not all four, to swing their vote for the bill. Call a meeting of these four senators in my office at 8 a.m. tomorrow."

"But sir, that will require calling them at home and ..."

One look from Senator Wroth stopped her objections. She

would find some way to gather these senators.

* * *

Once alone with Marlene and the other senators, Senator Wroth greeted them in his most congenial and disarming manner.

"Gentlemen and madam, I cannot thank you enough for being here on such short notice."

Several shifted uneasily in their seats.

"I won't take much of your time, but this is a matter of grave importance. I will be blunt and expect you to hold my words in the strictest confidence, as I will yours.

"You four have something in common. You have all received at least one 'code ten' phone call prior to a crucial senate vote."

The room became deathly silent. "I am not here to ask you about those previous calls. I don't want to know if or how those calls influenced you. But I have reason to believe the 'code ten' caller may have been responsible for the deaths of Senators Spears and Hansen."

The senators shifted nervously, but no one said a word.

Finally, one of them cleared his throat. "Michael, what you're suggesting is very serious. Why exactly have you called us here?"

Senator Wroth uncrossed his legs and leaned forward, lowering his voice. "This is far more than blackmail—this is outright manipulation of U.S. policy under force of threat. The 'code ten' caller has become bolder and recently found two of his 'pawns' expendable. Such a fate may await the rest of you.

"For this reason we must act swiftly, and I have asked you here privately to propose a confidential plan without the risks of involving others."

The room remained silent. Each knew a leak could well cost his or her office, or worse.

"There are no guarantees," Senator Wroth continued, "and our options are limited. But if we work together, I think we stand a good chance of beating this guy. Here is what I propose.

"You have all indicated that you will vote against the defense reduction bill tomorrow. From studying the 'code ten' caller's record, I have a strong suspicion he will call three or four of you to swing your votes in favor of the bill.

"I'm not here to suggest how you respond. I am only asking that when he contacts you, you have your AA immediately call my private number while you stall as long as you can before you take his call. I'll have a private force observing the phone booths this caller has used in the past. As soon as you report to us, we'll trace the call and move in to catch him."

"*Who* will move in on him?" the New England Democrat asked uneasily.

"I have arranged for a sufficient force to take this guy out of action—men who will not leak information."

"And if there are more than one?"

"We will have the caller under surveillance before taking action. If others are involved, we will know."

Senator Wroth stood and opened the door. "If you have no further questions, I think we all have work to do. Ms. Hayes will give you the number to call."

When all had departed, Marlene turned to Senator Wroth, "Do you think they'll do it?"

"Yes. They're scared, but they'll do it. They can't go on living the way they have. I just gave them their only way out."

Wroth paused and looked at the ceiling. He scratched his chin, then spoke. "Call the colonel. We've got just one more job for him."

TEN

"**Win, you've done it again!** Blast you! No matter the odds, you always beat me! I can't recall the last time I won."

Harry Evans sat on one side of the six-by-eight foot table, shaking his head in frustration.

"Ready to call it, Harry? If not, we can play it out." Even at sixty-five and graying, six-foot-four Win Dunbar was an imposing figure. He stood and surveyed the table of inch-high war-game figures spread over a valley bisected by a ridge. A large force of Germanic hordes lay scattered around the table, each unit fleeing a much smaller Roman cavalry as Roman infantry watched from the hilltop. Even someone unfamiliar with the hobby of ancient military war games could easily predict the conclusion.

"Play it out? Shoot, Win! With what? I outnumbered you three to one, and yet this is my worst defeat ever! I'm ready for you to retire the distinguished Julius Caesar. Don't you think he's won enough battles?"

Yet Harry knew it wasn't the miniature figure of Caesar on a black horse that won battles. It was Win Dunbar who won the battles—Colonel Winthrop Dunbar, to be exact. No one called him Winthrop and got away with it—except his feisty wife Jeanie. Others just called him "Win" or, more often, "Colonel."

Several years earlier he had retired from commanding Special Forces in the Marines. He had been passed over for promotion to general, and his rank and age had meant he could no longer command forces in the field. But paperwork and the political maneuvering of administrative duty didn't sit well with this highly-decorated, in-the-trenches commander. So he and Jeanie, his wife of forty-two years, had retired to the outskirts of Phoenix. There he had used part of their savings to open the small hobby shop specializing in miniature war games where he and Harry were now competing.

With his pension and Jeanie's substitute teaching, they didn't need the extra income, but military strategy was his passion.

"What did I do wrong, Win? How did you beat me?"

"Harry, you could have won this battle easily. You just made a few critical misjudgments. First, since you knew your Germans outnumbered my Romans three to one, you should have kept your line more balanced, bringing all your forces to bear equally on my small army, with maneuverable reserves ready to pounce on any weaknesses in my line. Instead, you let me lure you out of a good battle plan. Remember, strategy—your overarching plan for how to win—must guide your actions. Stick to your strategy, your battle plan, even if the moment-by-moment tactics change.

"Second, you lost the battle because you lost control of your troops and fought on my terms. You let your troops charge out of control, thinking they would overwhelm me. But when the real battle developed, on ground of my choosing, you could no longer control their movements—something every general must be able to do. Many a general had a great strategy but was unable to apply it because of poor troop control in the battle. My only chance with a much smaller force was to attack with a highly disciplined strike force when and where you least expected. I knew my elite units wouldn't turn back, even in the face of overwhelming odds.

"Finally, you were overconfident. After all, who can lose a battle when he outnumbers his foe three to one? An overconfident general, that's who! Why back in Desert Storm..."

The colonel's analysis after a battle could last as long as the battle itself. But seeing that Harry was in no mood to hear more, the colonel stopped mercifully short.

And so whether as Caesar or Charlemagne, Alexander or Attila, the colonel frequently found himself beating unsuspecting foes at the wargaming table. And if from time to time his sales managed to pay his modest rent, so much the better.

He was retired and satisfied, or so he told himself.

* * *

The shrill ring of the mobile phone startled them both. Jeanie picked it up and carried it across the room to her husband. Win eyed the caller ID. Unknown. That couldn't be good.

He pressed the speaker button. "Dunbar."

Marlene Hayes was at the other end. "Colonel Dunbar, we have one more mission for you—one of utmost secrecy."

Win wanted to toss the phone into the trashcan. He sneered, "Aren't they all?"

Marlene ignored the remark. "The senator would be very grateful for your services."

"I've fought his wars one too many times. I'm done with the turncoat."

"But this one requires your unique abilities."

Win breathed deeply and let out a long exhale. "After what he has done to me, you expect me to wag my tail like a lapdog?"

Marlene paused at the other end. "The senator wanted me to impress upon you how *very* much he needs this, and that he will continue to guard certain secrets, should you agree."

Jeanie shook her head vigorously and mouthed the word "no."

The colonel leaned forward. Beads of perspiration formed on his shaven head. His chest began heaving rapidly.

Jeanie grabbed the phone from his limp hand. "Ms. Hayes, your boss is a vile serpent in sheep's clothing. I advise you to distance yourself as far from him as you can. My husband no longer answers to the manipulative requests from Wroth's forked tongue. He has destroyed my husband's career. Never call again!" Then she ended the call.

Win looked up at her in disbelief. "Three years of silence. I thought we had escaped that life."

"We have."

"Do you know what you have done? The things he could reveal about me?"

Jeanie wrapped her arms around his bear-like shoulders. "And risk incriminating himself? I think this is a gamble worth taking. We are no longer selling our souls to the devil."

ELEVEN

Miracles?
You, Jesus, are the same yesterday, today, and always.
Why should I expect You to act differently today
than You did in the book of Acts?
The enemy doesn't stand a chance!
—Ruth Grant

Christopher chuckled inside as he and Chara relaxed in their business-class recliners on their way from Singapore to London. How had Nic swung this upgrade? "It's for your second honeymoon, bro," was all he would say. *God, sometimes You're just too good! I feel spoiled. We couldn't even afford our own tickets, much less business-class tickets!*

But for the steady hum of jet engines and the occasional snore of other passengers, the dark cabin was quiet. Just two spotlights shone on the journals the couple had opened on their tray tables. They conversed in hushed voices, unable to sleep.

"I'm telling you, Chara, I've been reading the book of Acts over and over each week for a couple of months now. I knew they could happen again—CPMs, I mean. But when Brother Ying shared about the movement in East Asia, I began jumping up and down inside. Now I am hearing with my own ears of Acts being repeated in modern times! It puts flesh on my ideas. Now I can see the way forward."

"I know what you mean," agreed Chara. "One point seven million new believers in just ten years! And Brother Ying is such a humble, unassuming man. But I have to say his example makes me a bit ashamed," she admitted sheepishly. "You heard him say that he and his wife pray for one or two hours each day before leaving their house, didn't you? Their commitment to reaching the lost is much deeper than mine."

Chara pulled the blanket tighter around her legs. "I get the feeling there's nothing Brother Ying and his wife wouldn't give up to see God reach the lost. What was that question he said drove him? 'How many of my people will hear the gospel today?' I was really convicted listening to him. It was also eye opening to hear about new disciples immediately making disciples who then make disciples. It's the Great Commission all over again!"

Christopher took another sip of tea and leaned close again. "Honey, you know there's nothing I want more than to be a man of the Word who obeys it without reservation. Too often these days I hear methods advocated simply because 'they work.' What encouraged me most in Brother Ying's story is that the methods and principles he teaches are straight from the Bible.

"Don't get me wrong. We do need to evaluate periodically whether what we're doing is 'working.' But if that becomes our final benchmark, it's like saying 'the end justifies the means.'"

Chara nodded, squeezed her husband's hand, and laid her head on his shoulder.

"No," Christopher continued, "what we learned these last two weeks starts with eternal principles set out in Scripture and then uses case studies to help illustrate those principles in various contexts. The methods these people are using seem to invite the Spirit of God to act. Does that make sense?"

Chara lifted her head and looked into Christopher's eyes. "I was thinking the same thing! That's what I love about you. You're such a man—a real man, a biblical man. This 'Training for Trainers' approach is just a vehicle for returning to very ancient biblical principles. We don't need something new, but something very old!"

"Shh!" Christopher whispered gently.

Chara suddenly realized how loud her remark had been. A flight attendant, aware they were the only passengers awake in the cabin, carried a tray down the aisle.

"Madam, would you like a tea also?"

Chara accepted the cup and carefully sipped the hot beverage.

Christopher quietly continued Chara's line of thought. "You're exactly right. Not new, but old. I think this is a process we could adapt in L.A. without losing the biblical principles.

"But you know, as I think about our two weeks in Singapore,

the thing that stands out most is how that time built my faith. Day by day, the clouds obscuring God's true nature were stripped away. And the more I was exposed to how our Father is working in this world, the more faith I felt in my spirit. This can happen again. Acts can happen again in new ways and places!"

* * *

Daylight stirred Christopher and Chara from their fitful slumber. They were now two hours from Heathrow, and the Singapore Airlines flight attendants were serving breakfast.

"Sorry to disturb you, Mrs. Ch-ch-chara?"

Chara rubbed the sleep from her eyes. "Uh, that's *Chara*—like the word *car* with an *uh* on the end," she said with a smile. "That's what I get for having a Greek professor for a father. He could have named me Joy, but gave me the Greek name instead."

"Okay, Mrs. Chara, would you care for a prawn omelet or mee goreng noodles to go with your croissants, fruit, and yogurt?"

"Oh, mee goreng, please. I fell in love with it in Singapore."

"And Mr. Christopher?"

"Prawns in an omelet? Gotta have it!"

Across the aisle from Christopher sat a pair of U.S. Marines, facing them.

"Business class is a rare treat for us," said Christopher. "Do you get this kind of luxury often?"

"No," one replied. "But sometimes when the economy section is overbooked an airline will honor us this way."

"Where are you men headed?"

"Back to a North Africa peacekeeping mission. This London stop is out of the way, but the flights through Dubai and Istanbul were full."

"How do you like North Africa?" Christopher asked.

The men hesitated.

"It has its moments, sir," answered the bigger man finally.

Chara probed further. "Not like home, right?"

"No, ma'am," the other Marine said. "No place is like the good ol' U.S. of A. But that's not what Private Harris means."

Private Harris glanced sharply at his companion.

"What I mean, ma'am," said Private Harris, "is that it has its moments. It's our post, ma'am. Doesn't matter what we think."

The Marines were young enough to engage Chara's mothering instinct. "I understand," she said. "I'm really sorry it's hard. We surely do appreciate you serving our country this way. What do you find so difficult there? Isn't a peacekeeping mission easier than some other assignments?"

"Well, ma'am, it's like this," said Private Lopez, glancing at his companion. "We're Marines, see? Marines. We're not trained for babysitting. I'm not saying that troops shouldn't be engaged in peacekeeping. Don't get me wrong. If the Commander in Chief wants troops, he knows best—"

"You're digging yourself into a hole, Gus," interrupted Harris.

"Ma'am, what Gus means is that we're not being utilized to the best of our training. We're Marines. We're at our finest when we're inserted into hostile situations as the initial shock troops. We establish beachheads—safe zones for the insertion of regular troops. Once we're done, we move on to other hostile situations. We're modern-day trailblazers in enemy territory. We're no good at the mopping up."

"What do you mean, mopping up?" asked Chara.

"That's jargon we use for everything that happens after our initial strike," Lopez answered. "Ma'am, we Marines feel that what we do is the most urgent part of combat—overcoming the primary defense or at least making a way for the army to come in and overpower the enemy. The mopping up is the part after that first wave; it's when communication and logistics are set up and the regular troops who are not trained for shock fighting scour the surrounding area, root out the enemy, and secure a strong base of operations. Mopping up is important. But we like to think the battle is won or lost with the Marines.

"Of course, the Army Rangers and Navy SEALs feel the same way," he acknowledged with a grin.

"Sort of like commandos?" Christopher asked.

"Yes, sir. We're not all like Rambo," Harris chuckled, "but that's the idea. The armed forces need the commandos or shock troops to go into the areas they're uniquely trained for. If they don't go first, no one goes in. We're not trained to sit around and keep peace."

Chara sympathized as best she could. "I see what you mean. But it sounds tough—the commando work."

"Tough isn't a strong enough word," Lopez said. "But we do it because we think it's the most important thing to do, ma'am."

Christopher was impressed with the deep confidence—almost arrogance—of these young men. No doubt they were good at what they did. And what a contrast these two serious, zealous young soldiers were from the relaxed Owens on their pleasure trip to England. These young men didn't fit the peacetime culture of their homeland. They belonged in dangerous, strategic areas—Iwo Jima, Afghanistan, or Somalia.

* * *

Unlike the twentieth century steel and glass universities of America, Franklin oozed stateliness and history. The simple archway inscription read: Franklin College, Founded 1659.

Chara felt the need to whisper in this hallowed place. "Do we have any colleges this old?"

"Barely. Harvard was the first college in the United States, and it's only two decades older than Franklin. As far as the Brits are concerned, we're spring chickens."

"Franklin looks like it's seen better days," whispered Chara. "And Christopher, I know you like to get right to the point. But when we meet the librarian, let me talk with her, okay?"

Eventually Christopher and Chara found the library where they met the very Mrs. Goodenough whom Nic had found so unhelpful—a large woman in her seventies, with creases worn into her forehead by a permanent scowl.

Before Christopher could speak, Chara began disarming the woman with genuine compliments about the school grounds and its extensive library. Soon the two were chatting easily about the classics. At an appropriate moment in the conversation, Chara explained their hopes of reading the Livermore dissertation.

"We've heard it's a landmark work, and we've traveled all the way from America to see it. But I'm afraid all we have is the author's name."

The librarian took her by the hand. "Don't worry yourself, dearie. It is a landmark work. Of that I have no doubt. Most of our dissertations are, of course. They are the crowning achievements of the Empire's finest scholars. Now you just come with me. This dissertation deserves your attention, and if anyone can locate it, I can."

After perusing the ancient card catalog for several minutes, the matron whispered, "Aha, you cannot hide from me!"

She put on her glasses and read, "A Dissertation Submitted Toward Completion of the Doctor of Philosophy Degree. M. J. Livermore. 1898. Title: 'The Collapse of the Military Metaphor in the Mission of the Early Church and the Resulting Stalemate in the Advance of the Gospel.'

"Ah, yes. Quite a significant work. Referenced often, I would imagine, by scholars in this century. Yes, yes. Quite significant. It will be among the dissertation stacks. Right this way."

The three walked down a flight of stairs and maneuvered their way through a seemingly endless maze of bookshelves.

"Hmm..."

Mrs. Goodenough looked at the card and examined the shelf again until she found a dissertation-sized gap.

"Well, this is rather odd. The book is missing! I patrol these stacks hourly. It must have been pinched this very morning."

Chara stared at the cobwebs in the gap. "What was that, Mrs. Goodenough?"

"Pinched, I say! I shall report this to the authorities. I assure you we shall apprehend the hoodlums swiftly."

"Perhaps you're right," responded Chara. "Unfortunately, we have to return to the States soon. Surely you keep a copy of these works on microfiche."

"Bite your tongue, dearie! We do not resort to such new-fangled contraptions. The library of Franklin College is as safe as the Tower of London!"

"Are you sure it's gone? Is there any other place we might find a copy?" Chara begged.

"Well, it has always been standard practice for doctoral students to make their own copy of the original manuscript. Such a volume might still be in existence as a family heirloom. Let me ring the alumni office and see if they can help us locate the family of M.J. Livermore."

The Owens followed Mrs. Goodenough to her office and waited. Finally she hung up the phone.

"Alumni records show one surviving family member, a Mrs. Gladys Somerset of Norwich—Dr. Livermore's granddaughter. That record has not been updated for a few years, so its current accuracy is suspect, I fear. Are you two dearies sure you don't want to wait for the bobbies to nab the burglar?"

* * *

The unkempt cottage was nestled snugly among similar bungalows on a narrow back street. Christopher knocked soundly on the door, waited, and then knocked again. Perhaps he and Chara had arrived a few decades too late. Discouraged, they returned to the car.

As Christopher started the engine, Chara touched his arm.

"Someone's at the door!" she said, jumping out of the car and bounding back to the doorstep.

An elderly woman peered past the chained door. "Yes?"

"Hi. We are looking for a Mrs. Somerset. I'm Chara Owen, and this is my husband, Christopher. We've come from America in search of a Ph.D. dissertation by a Dr. M.J. Livermore, Mrs. Somerset's grandfather. Is this the right place?"

"Do tell? Yes. I am Mrs. Somerset," the old woman laughed.

In no time she had the door unchained and was escorting them to the parlor. Though she must have been ninety, Mrs. Somerset moved buoyantly, as if she hadn't had a visitor in years.

The walls of the parlor were filled with shelves of neatly ordered volumes. On the windowsill, a fat gray cat vied with a Boston fern for the sun's warmth.

The woman pointed a finger and spoke to the cat. "Thucydides, you keep these young people company while I get them some tea and cake."

She hummed her way to the kitchen and returned bearing tea and white cake on a silver tea service. As Mrs. Somerset chatted gaily about the weather, Chara discreetly wiped dust from the rim of her cup and did her best to nibble at the stale cake.

As the conversation waned, Christopher asked again, "Mrs. Somerset, do you know anything about your grandfather's dissertation?"

"I'm sorry. I don't know where you got your information, but M.J. Livermore was not my grandfather."

Christopher's face fell.

"She was my grandmother—Mary Jane Livermore! She was Franklin College's first female doctoral candidate and hoped using the initials might gain her more respect. But it didn't help. Her research was rejected by her professors and her peers, and her degree was never conferred.

"The unpublished, unapproved dissertation did find its way to the library stacks, and she tried valiantly over the years to get someone to accept her thesis. But no one wanted to listen to a woman, especially one who had not completed her doctorate.

"As far as I know, you are the first people in at least fifty years who cared to look at her dissertation. Yes, I have a copy."

She pulled out an ancient, dust-covered tome and gently dropped it on the table. A thud reverberated through the room.

TWELVE

I have an odd sense that my death is imminent.
Could the death of a twenty-three-year-old be the
seed falling into the ground that will produce much fruit?
Oh, let not my death be in vain.
May it inspire others to realize it is a mere passing
into the next, more glorious stage, of eternal life.
What a simple sacrifice to serve the King!
                                                —Ruth Grant

Christopher and Chara sat in their living room, a precious photocopy of the Livermore dissertation on the table before them. With them were their closest friends—John, Renee, Nic, and Stacy.

"Enough with the suspense, Christopher," John said. "This isn't the last scene of a Sherlock Holmes mystery. Tell us about the dissertation!"

"In due time, Watson. Let's pray first."

Together they rejoiced in all God had done since their last meeting and sought His power to be faithful in all He was asking them to do.

Then Christopher began eagerly summarizing Livermore's insight.

"The early Church advanced rapidly—supernaturally fast— through most of the first century. At that rate, the known world would have been evangelized within a few centuries!"

"But then a major shift occurred," Chara added. "And world evangelization slowed to a crawl. Even though the pace picked up in the 1800s, according to Livermore it lagged far behind that first century. Now it was mission by the few rather then mission by the whole church."

"Livermore's analysis is brilliant," Christopher continued. "Her Salvation Army upbringing helped her see the wartime mindset the New Testament Church lived with, in which each Christ-follower lived as a soldier charged with advancing God's Kingdom."

"This is crazy!" Nic interrupted. "I've been reading ahead for our Perspectives class, and Dr. Winter has an article on this. Hold on..." Nic leafed through his book. "Yeah, here it is. *Reconsecration to a Wartime, Not a Peacetime, Lifestyle.* He shares this awesome example of how, when outfitted for war, the *Queen Mary* housed fifteen thousand soldiers even though it only had room for *three* thousand passengers as a peacetime luxury liner. Winter said that believers today are living with a peacetime mindset."

"Exactly," Christopher said. "The Allies were invested in World War II like the first-century believers were invested in advancing God's Kingdom. They had the end in sight. My grandmother used to tell us how everyone took part in the war effort and everything was rationed. Every able-bodied man joined the fight, and those who didn't felt ashamed. Women worked in the factories because the men were all at war. School kids saved their money to buy war bonds. Nothing was wasted. Everything was recycled. Everyone was mobilized. This is the kind of 'all in' mindset the early Church had."

Christopher stood and began pacing. "The early believers set their hearts on heaven rather than earthly comforts, and they embraced simplicity to focus on the spiritual battle. Their sense of urgency was fueled by an expectation of winning the war and welcoming the return of their Commander in Chief during their generation. Then," Christopher paused and looked down, "it all slowed down."

"So," Renee asked, "what changed?"

Christopher stopped pacing and bowed his head. "The loss of wartime urgency was the central factor in the church's declining zeal for Kingdom advance. Jesus didn't return in that generation. And without a finish line in sight, it became increasingly difficult for believers to live sacrificially with a wartime mindset. Later communities of faith matured more slowly, evangelized less aggressively, multiplied less frequently, and became entangled in lesser issues. The quest lost its urgency.

"The Church shifted to a peacetime mentality, and the end of widespread persecution gave rise to huge theological debates. Eventually the central mission of the Church became just one of its activities rather than its rallying battle cry."

"So how do we change that?" Nic asked.

"Livermore's thesis was that the only way to complete the mission was full-scale 'military' mobilization of the whole global Church, fueled again by an expectation of the imminent return of Jesus Christ.

"And here's the kicker. Livermore contended that around 90 AD God gave the book of Revelation to John—the last surviving apostle—to encourage the Church that He had not forgotten the mission. Revelation is God's promise to succeeding generations that He is in control and His Kingdom will prevail. Revelation is Christ's marching orders for His body, to inspire the Church to ever-greater exploits beyond the first century. Unfortunately, most believers throughout history have missed this central point amidst the symbolism of Revelation."

Nic could barely contain himself. "Okay, so the first believers expected Jesus to return soon, and they lived and labored toward that end. But later believers lost that expectation, and with it they lost the momentum to bring it about. So what can we do to recover this expectation and regain that lost momentum?"

The room was silent for a couple of minutes.

John voiced what they were all thinking. "So, … Christopher, what do you propose we do with this understanding?"

Christopher and Chara grinned at each other. "As Chara and I see it, we are closer to finishing the task than ever in history. Non-Christians outnumbered those first century believers three hundred sixty to one, while today there are only about seven non-Christians for every Christian. An awakened Church could move swiftly to 'no place left' without the gospel. We have to inspire and guide a new generation to live with a wartime mentality in anticipation of Christ's return. By His strength, it is so doable!"

"We must raise up laborers like those Marines we flew to London with," Chara said. "Christian commandos—missionary shock troops whose sole aim is to establish vibrant, multiplying communities of believers as 'beachheads' that will turn into movements in every remaining unreached people group."

"Our first step," Christopher said, "is for the six of us and then all of Church in the City to recognize and grapple with the fact that Jesus really could return at any time! And as we take the gospel to unreached people groups, we need to impart that same conviction to the new believers. Then, like the apostle Paul, we must charge them with responsibility for expanding the Kingdom among their own people and beyond in the power of the Holy Spirit while we move on.

"Like Paul, we may return periodically to follow up, but we can't babysit them. We must provide these new believers with initial discipleship and teach them how to feed themselves and others from God's Word under the tutelage of the Holy Spirit in submission to one another. We must trust the Holy Spirit in them. Then we must take some of them with us as we move on to other groups that have yet to hear."

Chara added. "Christopher's not implying that we don't also need long-term missionaries; just the opposite. The kind of shock troops we are discussing go in for a couple of years and establish new communities of believers. But after that, just as in military operations, others are needed to build up the resulting local church."

John rose from the couch and approached their makeshift whiteboard. Christopher winked at Chara. John was in, and he was about to do what he did best. "History tells us there's another reason the world may need something fresh like we are discussing. All types of movements tend to calcify over time."

He drew a line rising and then plateauing.

"For instance, our established organizations began as missions-sending *movements*. But over time, every movement develops institutionalism. This adds long-term stability while restricting innovation and risk-taking."

Nic added, "And these structures tend to resist risk-taking because too much is at stake. Happens in business all the time."

"Exactly!" John continued, "This calcification can take a few years or a few decades, but eventually what starts as a movement stalls out, and new initiatives are needed to continue forward progress."

With that, John drew a new line rising above the others. "A fresh initiative is needed if we are going to reach the remaining unreached people groups."

Christopher looked warmly at his normally skeptical friend.

"Exactly, bro. We need thousands of shorter-term, high-risk pushes to complement what is already going on. We can call and equip some believers as commandos—trained for initial entry and ready to give up all for the King's war effort in anticipation of His return. We can inspire others to pursue similar initiatives. We can call those unable to go to the front lines to live just as sacrificially in order to free up resources for the task.

"Our rallying cry must be Jesus' own words in Matthew 24:14 that the gospel be proclaimed to every remaining people group before His return. We cannot cause Christ's return, but we can fulfill the conditions!"

Christopher stood and joined John at the white board. John nodded, handed him the marker, and gave him a quick wink. Christopher wrote *2025—No Place Left* across it.

"We must embrace a target date by which we aim to finish this quest, no matter what it costs. Our mission objective must be nothing less than *no place left!*"

The two men sat down again, and silence reigned for several minutes.

Finally John spoke. "Renee, dear, I think it's time for you to show the group what you've got."

"Christopher wants a real-time tracking tool so we have a countdown showing what remains to be done. So I worked with Timothy on a system that can be available through a simple app to show the count of unengaged unreached people groups."

Renee turned her tablet to the group. *3,227 UUPGs* glowed in giant red text against a black background. "This way we can keep the urgency of the task always before us. I'll send you each a link to download the app and help us with the beta testing.

"Christopher says, 'If we can quantify it, we can complete it.' As an attorney, I'd say it this way, 'If we quantify it, we can tell when it is completed.'"

"It's doable!" Nic said exuberantly. "Stacy and I did some

initial market projections—battle assessments, Chris, in your wartime terminology. Using the most conservative figures, for every UUPG there are at least eighty Protestant churches in America alone! And today the Church outside the U.S. is far bigger than it is here. The resources are in place.

"Don't tell me we can't muster enough missionaries to engage these people groups and finish the task. It can be done! And maybe God will pour out His revival Spirit and empower us to finish!"

"It makes me so mad!" Stacy said. "The devil has been lying to us for centuries, and we've believed him. I grew up thinking the job of missions was so big that it probably wouldn't ever be finished. The lost world was just this big, nebulous ... oh, I don't know ... blob. Something we could never really tackle. We've been believing the devil and missing out on God's abundant blessing.

"Don't you see? I used to run marathons. There is a point where you feel totally spent, but when the end is in sight, you find new reserves and give it your all—no holding back. It hurts, but you know it will soon be over. You hasten to the finish line.

"Satan has kept the end out of our sight. As a result we've just been jogging, maybe just marking time. We haven't realized how near the finish line is. If we did, we would be sprinting now—no holding back."

Everyone fell silent again. Finally Christopher spoke.

"Only one generation witnessed the first coming of Jesus on earth. Only one generation will see the second coming of Jesus. We missed the first one. I don't want to miss the second. When He returns, I want to be able to say, 'I faithfully prepared for you.' I want to live to hasten the day of His return!

"Are we willing to live sacrificially in an all-out war effort to get to No Place Left without the gospel by 2025?"

"We would be a Kingdom preparation force," said Nic, "a humble group of Christian commandos preparing the way for the coming of Christ's Kingdom. A small strike force assaulting the gates of hell in each people group, escorting the nations into the Kingdom of God. The Kingdom Preparation Force!"

Stacy looked at Nic and nodded. "That's right! No more

peacetime living for us!"

"The name sounds a little corny," John said, "but I like the concept." He returned to the board and wrote *KPF* next to the ascending line he had drawn rising above the others.

"I like the name." Renee shot a glance at John. "It's descriptive. Descriptive is good. We're in too."

"So does this mean we're all in?" Christopher asked.

"I don't imagine that the evil one will take this final pursuit of God's Kingdom lying down," Chara said. "He'll throw everything he's got at us. And we'll need thousands of people to go—young, old, and everything in between. We *must* call people to this, but let's not forget," she looked at the group intently, "many of us will suffer persecution—and some of us may die.

"Let's remember the generation in Revelation 12:11: 'They overcame him by the blood of the Lamb and by the word of their testimony, and they did not love their life even when faced with death.'"

Christopher looked again at their dear brothers and sisters. "Are we willing to pay the price?"

Everyone nodded.

The six joined hands and prayed for strength to match their resolve. Christopher's heart swelled with the pride a father has in seeing his child excel.

* * *

Before heading to bed, Christopher tweeted:

#NoPlaceLeft2025 is impossible without a wartime mindset. Will you mobilize with us for the final effort? A Kingdom Preparation Force!

THIRTEEN

Greely looked up from his triple monitor array, genuinely worried. "Sir, could you come here please?" he called.

"What is it this time, Greely?"

Greely silently handed his report to Number Eight, who read the report—twice—and then turned it over to see if there was more. "How could they have gotten this item? That threat was removed seventeen years ago!"

"I-I-I don't know, sir. Somehow the American got a copy. Eight hours ago he uploaded a complete PDF onto the Internet—free of charge."

Greely saw Number Eight fidget nervously.

"Sir, if we act quickly, someone could snatch the American's hard copy, ascertain where the file has spread, and erase it."

"Are you insane, Greely?" The supervisor swore. "That would violate our essential posture of unobtrusiveness!"

"But sir. This is Priority A. Shouldn't *something* be done?"

Number Eight's glare dared Greely to raise his voice again.

"The Priority A item is not your concern. I shall report it to Number Three and notify the Timeline Room of a Level Six Possible Movement Insertion. Carry on with your work and keep alert for any further activity by this American."

He straightened his tie. "Carry on."

FOURTEEN

Jake Simmons had a small army at his disposal. The well-built man in his early forties had years of connections in the CIA and the military's special forces. The result was that dozens of men with specialized training and experience were loyal to Simmons and willing to keep their mouths shut. He hadn't agreed with Senator Wroth's order to take a major strike force to Rome. But Senator Wroth was paying, and he paid well.

Jake's twenty-four men were positioned in small squads around the six different public phones that the caller had used. How old school this seemed—their target using public phones when everyone and his cousin carried a cell phone. Yet there was no denying that public phones, however antiquated, were still an anonymous way to place a call.

Once each of the teams had radioed in, Simmons settled back to await Senator Wroth's phone call. It came on the satellite phone around 8 p.m. local time.

"Jake, this is Marlene. We've traced a call to checkpoint three. Stay on the line, and let me know if you get visual on the caller."

Simmons radioed Team Three, who confirmed that they were observing an elderly man in the phone booth in question.

"We've got him, Ms. Hayes."

"Okay, as we discussed, just tail him. I repeat, just tail him. I want secondary confirmation through other calls he may make. And keep me posted."

Two of Jake's men followed the caller a couple blocks to the booth under surveillance by Team Four. They radioed Simmons.

"Sir, we have visual on the old man. He's entered the Team Four checkpoint."

"Roger that, Team Three. Team Four, do you have visual?"

"That's affirmative, sir. Elderly man in a gray overcoat just entered our checkpoint."

"Team Four, assume surveillance," Jake responded. "If he leaves, two of you follow him. Team Three, return to your checkpoint."

"Roger, chief. We're heading back."

Several minutes later, Jake returned Marlene's call.

"Ms. Hayes, the suspect made several calls from two different phone booths. With two members of Team Four following, he went into a large, isolated building in an older section of town."

"Jake, put all your men around that building!" Senator Wroth broke in on the line. "I don't want anyone coming in or out of a door, window, or chimney without your men knowing where each of them goes! Stick on this guy like glue, but keep out of sight. I'll be there by morning. Tell your men if our man is still under surveillance when I arrive and we tag this guy, there's a five-thousand-dollar bonus for every man in your unit. And you'll get twenty-five."

"Yes, sir!"

* * *

Senator Wroth sat with Simmons in a dark sedan across the street from the ancient building.

"We watched all night, sir," Simmons said. "No one has come or gone."

This back street in the Eternal City seemed to have died. Traffic was sparse, and few pedestrians passed. The few who did walked hurriedly. The building itself sported a fifteenth century facade, rising sheer, dark, and imposing.

"Every exit is covered, sir," Jake continued. "I don't think a mouse could have snuck in or out. Our man's in there. You can't see it, but toward the back a chimney is venting smoke from a wood-burning fireplace. Someone is keeping it fueled."

"We don't move until dark tonight," said Senator Wroth. "Have your men rest in shifts so everyone stays alert. I'll be back at 9 p.m."

The car pulled around the corner and let Simmons out, then Senator Wroth returned to his suite. He needed to look his best for this evening's confrontation.

* * *

The six-foot-plus Senator Wroth looked imposing in his tailored suit and cashmere overcoat. The small bulge from the Beretta near his left breast was unnoticeable. As they drove toward the building that evening, Simmons wondered at how relaxed Wroth seemed, as if this sort of thing were a daily occurrence for him.

"Listen, Jake. I go in alone. I want you to personally monitor my wire. Have your guys burst in when I say 'Now, Jake!' but not a moment sooner."

Simmons was clearly uneasy with this plan.

"Sir, this just doesn't make sense. The proper course of action is for us to disarm the opposition while you wait for the dust to settle. We don't need *three* dead senators on our hands."

"Jake, we've been over this. What I'm about to encounter is top secret. I need to face this guy alone, and I don't want anyone but you listening. If I'm in danger, you'll have plenty of time to get there."

Senator Wroth got out of the sedan and strode confidently toward the steps, sensing that this ancient building held far greater importance than the Capitol building with which he was so familiar. He approached the tall front door and, seeing no doorbell or knocker, tried the knob. The door opened readily and, slipping off his shoes, Senator Wroth stepped silently onto marble tiles leading down a long corridor.

A single flickering light pierced the darkness from the end of the corridor. Stealthily, Senator Wroth proceeded down the hallway. He tried to reassure himself with the thought of his twenty-five-man army outside. *Why don't I feel safe?*

No sound came from the open doorway at the end—only a light dancing on the corridor walls in a senseless struggle against the darkness.

Senator Wroth mustered his courage and walked boldly through the doorway.

The room was dark, with a vaulted ceiling, fading tapestries on the walls, and a hearth at his left. There sputtered the fire casting the light in the corridor. To the right, the silhouettes of nine men loomed on the wall, as if illustrating the awe and timelessness Senator Wroth felt in the room.

Rising from the triangular mahogany table, an ancient man lifted his hand and pointed a trembling, long-nailed finger at Senator Wroth. His raspy voice filled the room with a strange European accent.

"We have been waiting for you, Mr. Wroth. We are glad you survived to make it here. You have shown much ingenuity and resourcefulness."

Senator Wroth was bewildered. He had figured that "code ten" knew about his search, but only he, Marlene, and Jake's army knew he was in Rome. How could these men be waiting for him? He was glad to have Simmons listening in.

"I am here to shut down your manipulation of the United States government. I expect full cooperation from each of you in unearthing the full extent and influence of 'code ten.' And should you think of trying to harm me or escape, know that surrounding this building and listening to our conversation are twenty-five of the world's finest commandos. You would not make it out of this building alive."

Spontaneous laughter from the others told Senator Wroth he had badly misjudged the situation. A graying man to the first speaker's left stood and spoke in a rich, English baritone.

"Mr. Wroth, I see that you do not yet realize the extent of your folly and impudence."

He motioned to the only empty chair at the table—a black velvet wingback.

"Please have a seat.

"Your mercenaries will not arrive," the Englishman said. "The moment you stepped into our domain, your twenty-four hirelings were eliminated and Mr. Simmons was immobilized. The whole affair took sixteen seconds. It all happened very quietly, I might add. No one out there is listening to you right now."

Senator Wroth paused to process this news.

"You are in for many more surprises, Mr. Wroth," said the Englishman. "Please put your gun in that rubbish bin, then come and make yourself comfortable. Here's your tea now—Darjeeling with a touch of caramelized sugar. Am I correct?"

A butler appeared out of the unseen recesses.

"Yes, of course," Senator Wroth whispered as surprise and bewilderment overwhelmed him briefly—emotions the senator rarely experienced. Regaining his composure, Senator Wroth tossed his gun in the wastebasket and sat with the nine men.

"Yes, this is exactly how I like my tea," Senator Wroth said. "Thank you. Please continue. You clearly know my name. May I know yours?"

"Yes, I think that is appropriate. I am Number Three, in charge of Religion and Education," the Englishman continued. "My esteemed colleague who first spoke to you is Number One, our Prime Director, also in charge of Politics. Seated around this table according to our specialization are ..."

"Yes, I can guess—Numbers Two through Nine."

The middle-aged to elderly men around the table all nodded.

A thin Chinese man rose slowly. In a quiet, somewhat-British accent he said, "I am Number Two, in charge of Economics and Science."

None of the other six introduced themselves, but Senator Wroth thought he could identify an Indian, an African, a Latino, an Arab, a Russian or Eastern European, and a Korean. All men. All old or moving in that direction. All confident.

"In time you will come to know all of us. That is, if you agree to join us," continued Number Three. "We do not use names any longer—our old selves have vanished. We have become something new and altogether greater. We are—"

"Code Ten," interrupted Senator Wroth.

"Incorrect, sir. We are simply *The Ten*. 'Code Ten' is the term we use when we visibly influence someone—a trifling toward which we are ill-disposed, but which is sometimes necessary. Now, Mr. Wroth, I will ask you to remain silent while I tell you a story. Be careful of jumping to conclusions. Currently you feel taken aback and are trying to regain an equal footing. Well, you are not on an equal footing—yet. Please simply listen.

"History tells us that in 476 AD a giant empire exhaled its last breath. The Roman ascendancy—which had dominated the Mediterranean world for seven hundred years—collapsed. The collapse was caused more by internal factors than external ones. Astute leaders of the late fourth century detected the decline in the empire and foresaw its demise a century in advance. The *Pax Romana*—the great Roman peace, held together by the strength of its laws and their enforcement by its army—eventually ended and was replaced by feudalistic strife.

"Before the collapse, a few clarion voices sought to forestall the inevitable. Some were heeded, but most were ignored.

"Over time, these aforementioned leaders—all men of great influence—began meeting secretly. We do not even know their names, but one was a bishop of influence in the church, another a senator frustrated by the impotence of the Roman senate, and the third a wealthy trader wanting more than wealth. Each was troubled by Rome's steady decline. Each peered nervously at the chaos on the horizon.

"That their empire would inevitably collapse was a foregone conclusion, one which they knew they were too late to alter. Yet as they met, a vision for a much grander world began to take shape. In their own realms these three had each seen how, more often than not, their greatest influence lay in working behind the scenes, unobserved.

"Gradually they realized that the strongest power is not in the emperor's scepter, but in the whisper of his trusted advisor; not in the dictums of a pope, but in the maneuvering to elect the right pope; not in controlling a trading market, but in inciting the public to desire certain goods. Together these three removed themselves from the public arena in order to influence the world quietly and unobtrusively.

"As Rome collapsed, the balance of power shifted unpredictably as men rose to carve out their fiefdoms. Yet as lawlessness loomed on the horizon, these three envisioned something greater and far nobler. They envisioned a coming Rebirth of this world into a single united government, far surpassing Rome's achievements, ensuring peace, stability, and abundance for all.

"These three were selfless, forward thinkers. They realized that a new peace governed by a new global empire was centuries or millennia away. The world must first be quietly readied for the idea. So even while the central authority was being squeezed out of the dying empire, they set into motion a mechanism—a force—to guide the world toward this goal; an invisible influence slowly centralizing power so that one day their successors could publicly usher in a new day.

"The three established their headquarters here in Rome—the Eternal City. Each enlisted two colleagues also of quiet influence, and together they laid out a strategy for the consolidation of power—three would influence politics; three, economics and science; and three, religion and education. One more was recruited as an apprentice in preparation for when the next of the nine would die, so there would never be a gap in their influence.

"Together they became The Ten—sacrificially dedicated to the Rebirth; not the vague, corrupt shadow they had seen in the dying Roman Empire or even in the imperfect peace of the Pax Romana at its zenith, but a fully united global peace to carry mankind into its greatest achievements. Together they made a covenant—not just to each other, but also to the world—vowing confidentiality and pledging lifelong allegiance to the vision of The Ten to their death.

"Their motto was *Movere potentiam sine notitia*—or, loosely translated, 'Influence without being known to influence.'

"Here, in this sacred spot, they began their work based on their shared experience that the greatest influence is the one that is not seen. Overt power invites resistance. But what of a group that influences the world without being seen or known? Who will whisper into that group's ears? Who will threaten excommunication or order a naval blockade against it?

"Mr. Wroth, the ultimate power in this world is the one that is free from outside coercion, either because it is secret or because it is so powerful outside influences irritate it only as a feather might irritate a diamond. Unable to become the latter until the Rebirth, The Ten became the former. Here from these quiet chambers in Rome, their work has continued undetected to this day. We are The Ten. The mantle of the original Ten rests upon us. And it is time for us to choose a tenth man. You, Mr. Wroth, are that man, should you accept."

"Yet I detected you. I traced you here. You are not quite as powerful as you thought," Senator Wroth responded.

Number Three chuckled.

"Mr. Wroth, had we not laid such a clear trail for you, you

would never have known about us. We would not have chosen to use a 'code ten' with senators who would reveal us unless we had a purpose. And then we removed them, as you know.

"You also sealed the fate of four additional senators when you met with them in your office. They will be removed shortly, along with all their secretaries who know anything. It will be seen as a terrorist act, but it will serve our purposes."

Senator Wroth stood abruptly, his chair scraping the floor.

"Sit down, Mr. Wroth, and stop feigning anger," Number Three said. "We have watched you for several years, since before you were a senator. We have watched and aided your rise through the circles of power in Washington. You have seen that covert power is greater than overt power, and you yourself desire more power. Yet how does a U.S. Senator become as powerful as you want to be? That is impossible, so what is next for you? Surely not governor. That would be a step down for you, Mr. Wroth. A run for the White House, perhaps? Yes, but then you realize that American presidents are mostly puppets controlled by popularity polls and hamstrung by Congress. Mr. Wroth, that is not the life for you. Your ambitions are higher. You will never let yourself be controlled by any outside group. Am I correct?"

Senator Wroth sat again, but now fully engaged—listening, processing, and synthesizing. "I could become president," he heard himself answer, "but I would never be re-elected because I wouldn't bow to popular opinion or special interest groups."

With his customary swiftness, he had assessed the situation and was developing his own plan.

"Please continue, Number Three," he said, no longer feeling off balance.

"We invite you to join us. Having recently suffered the loss of one of our community, we are inviting you to become our next apprentice. And lest the term 'apprentice' seem beneath you, let me assure you that our apprentices are more influential than any president, premier, pope, or tycoon.

"As an apprentice you will exert more power than you've ever had before. Today we operate almost omnipotently in line with our prime directive—to engineer world events to bring about the Rebirth as soon as possible.

"Each year, because of our influence, the Rebirth draws closer. Every means we use to hasten the Rebirth saves lives in the end. To kill a man is recognized by all as evil, but in the course of a just war, to kill when necessary is sanctioned by all. We wage holy war, using every available means to bring the ideal into the present. A tenuous thread keeps this world in balance, and we, Mr. Wroth, are that thread. Without us the world would drift back toward chaos as surely as a tide leaves the bay. Our actions will ultimately save the lives of millions of people."

The Nine remained silent as Senator Wroth rose from his chair and walked around the table—twice.

"By this encounter it seems you have given me only one choice. I doubt you will allow me to return to my old life now."

"You are correct, Mr. Wroth," Number One said, rising. "You can never go back to the life you knew or had dreamed of. That option was eliminated when we revealed ourselves to you.

"But would you?" He smiled at the senator knowingly.

"We are actually offering you three choices. I urge you to join us. I am the eldest of The Ten, and barring some unforeseen event, I shall be the next to pass. You will be my apprentice and specialize in influencing politics, although you will also train in the other two arenas in case you should be needed to replace someone else. Politics and control are your love. Join me, and you will discover how to influence world events in ways you have never dreamed of."

The not-yet-dead soul in Number One grew more animated.

"You will continue in your political circles, but with a new agenda. You may even keep one or two trusted advisors—bound to the same code of secrecy. And you will spend increasing amounts of time with us here, where the real nerve center is. You will be a free man, bound only by your covenant with the other nine.

"But we do offer two other choices. Through the centuries some have chosen not to accept our offer. Yet since we have taken their old lives from them, we feel responsible to provide an alternative. You may choose, then, to live a life of obscurity in the surroundings of your choosing, under constant audio-visual surveillance and subject to instant death through an implanted device should you attempt to expose us. This would be a life of ease, free from all worry, in which you would have anything you want. And you may take anyone with you into exile as our gift to you. We do not want you to be forced into choosing us."

"And my third choice?"

"Death. Strange as it may seem, a few souls have chosen this path, citing preservation of honor or some other archaic value.

"You have twenty-four hours to decide." The old man grabbed a cane and began hobbling out of the room. "We will discuss your decision over dinner tomorrow night at eight o'clock," he said as he departed.

One by one the others left, Senator Wroth guessed by degree of importance. Number Three stood but did not leave.

"I will show you to your room," he said. "You will find it quite well-equipped." He led Senator Wroth to another long corridor and up a flight of stairs.

"There's a tuxedo in your closet for tomorrow's dinner. It should fit you. There is also a phone on which you may call Ms. Hayes to inform her you will not be returning to your hotel. We know she is expecting your call."

"Aren't you afraid she might have the call traced to here?"

"My dear chap, what do you think we are? Bumbling idiots? All our phone lines are untraceable—our technology is more advanced than that of your National Security Agency."

"But Number One—he used different phone booths to place calls to our senators over the years."

The Englishman chuckled. "Number One is an old-fashioned, daring fellow. He still enjoys direct involvement in planting clues. Our technical staff told him he could call from here and have the line encoded with the phone booths' numbers, but he likes doing it the old-fashioned way when he can, and this is how he led you to us."

"He's been planting these calls or clues for me to follow all these years?" Senator Wroth asked, incredulous.

"Number One is a patient man. We all are. You have to be when you do what we do. We plan in decades and centuries. That was the only mark against you in your file—too rash. But you will learn to be patient by keeping the goal in sight.

"I must inform you that we will monitor you constantly while you are here. Do not try to escape. This neighborhood breathes the very air of The Ten. You would not make it out of the building, but if you did, you would be eliminated in seconds."

As they arrived at Senator Wroth's spacious room, Number Three suddenly warmed and extended his hand to Senator Wroth, who received the sincere welcome.

"My dear man, I like you a lot, and I hope you make the right decision. I know this is all a little startling—it was for each of us when we were chosen. Please do consider joining us. We all like you. I was the one who recommended you.

"There have been fewer than seven hundred members of The Ten since 383 AD. You stand on the verge of becoming one of the most influential men in the last sixteen hundred years and one of the ten most influential in your generation.

"Good night," he said, leaving the senator to his thoughts.

Senator Michael Wroth stood another moment, formulating plans within plans.

One in seven hundred isn't good enough. And I didn't come here to be one in ten, either—but it may be a place to start.

He picked up the phone to call Marlene.

FIFTEEN

The most demanding stage of a quest is starting.
From that point on, at least you have momentum.

—Ruth Grant

At the April joint meeting of campus fellowships, Christopher preached with deep conviction to the packed audience in USC's Taper Hall.

John and Nic stood at the back of the auditorium, watching.

"And he thinks there's no basis for me calling him Napoleon," said John. "Look at the little guy stir their hearts!"

"Not the little guy," Nic whispered back, "but the Spirit of the Almighty within him! I love it when he's like this."

Passion for Christ's cause flowed through Christopher in the Spirit-filled ecstasy of preaching God's Word. He was beyond himself—speaking with God's anointing. And God used his words to pierce the souls of those listening, stirring them to heart-felt obedience. The students sat transfixed in the tiered seats of the auditorium.

"... If you had been on that mountain in Galilee two thousand years ago, sitting at the feet of Jesus when He said, 'Go, disciple all nations,' would you have had any doubt regarding God's will for your life? College seniors, do you really wonder what God wants to do with that degree you are about to receive? Freshmen, sophomores, juniors—do you still have any question about why you're in school right now?

"Don't rest this week without settling the question of your obedience to the Great Commission. The unreached peoples of this world beckon to you with unparalleled urgency. Get in on what God is doing in this generation. Join a missions agency that will help you apply your skills, degree, and experience to enter limited access countries with the gospel and launch movements of God. There are many good organizations out there.

"If the Lord so leads you, consider joining our fledgling Kingdom Preparation Force. Give us a year, starting this summer. We will help you raise financial support for this venture. And while I can't offer you any guarantees, I do hold out to you the experience of a lifetime—an honest, whole-hearted quest to finish world evangelization. It will be tough—we're going to the edge of darkness!"

Christopher wiped a tear from his eye, sat on the front of the stage, and leaned toward the crowd. His hoarse voice was reduced almost to a whisper.

"The bottom line of the Great Commission is this: if you are not obeying the call to be a part of God's mission to the nations, you are living a disobedient life! We must all go or sacrificially help those who do. This is a war for which everyone must be mobilized. The enemy is fighting *to the death*. Are we willing to *lay down our lives*? Going *without reservation* must be *normal* for us! We must press forward until there is *no place left*! Will you consecrate yourselves for one last push?"

Across the back of the stage a large banner proclaimed: #NoPlaceLeft2025. Soon the dim auditorium was awash with the glow of mobile phones. Students around the room grinned at one other as they tweeted #NoPlaceLeft2025, urging their friends to join them in this new effort for no place left without the gospel.

As the crowd filtered out, some left in silence. Others took the information Professor Steward had at the back door. Several worked their way through the crowd to ask questions or seek prayer from Christopher or other members of the Kingdom Preparation Force. Long lines grew in front of both Christopher and John, whom many knew from his classes. People left changed—broken, convicted, inspired, encouraged, resolved, some even angry—but definitely not the same.

As the praying and sharing continued, a nondescript girl made her way from the back of the room and shyly waited to speak with Chara. She struck Chara as someone who would be easy to miss in the crowd, but something drew Chara to her.

"Hi. I'm Chara."

The girl's eyes met Chara's only for an instant before she looked down again.

"I'm Ruth. Ruth Grant," she said as she stretched out her hand. Her voice was so quiet Chara could barely hear her.

"What did you think of tonight, Ruth?"

"Wow, it was awesome," she muttered timidly. "God has already been working in me, speaking to me about these things, but I haven't heard anyone express it so clearly until tonight. God really speaks through that man. I feel, well ..."

The girl looked around uncomfortably. Chara could tell this was difficult for her.

"Hey, would you like to pop over to Common Grounds to talk privately? I think I can get a little time off now." Chara grinned.

"That sounds ... great. I'm a little shy around large groups."

Chara texted Christopher that she was heading to a quieter spot to talk with one of the students. Slipping into the nippy southern California evening, the two women talked more freely.

"So you came to know Jesus three years ago, huh?"

"Yeah. You could say my burden to share the gospel is stronger than my bashfulness. It's been a kind of quiet evangelism—joining the math club, getting to know non-Christians, and trying to share my faith with them one by one," replied Ruth.

The two women ordered cappuccinos and found the same warm corner that had witnessed so many late night discussions among Christopher, John, and Nic.

"What has God been telling you?" Chara asked.

"Well, several of my friends have followed Jesus through my witness, but I find myself longing for more." Ruth struggled to put her thoughts into words. "The last several weeks I haven't been able to get my mind off the world's needs, especially the needs of frontier missions—cutting-edge missions. What your husband described tonight is exactly what God has been putting on my heart. These 3,227 UUPGs! But ..."

She paused, summoning her courage for full transparency.

"But something's holding you back?"

Ruth looked straight into Chara's eyes as if she had known her for years. Her eyes brimmed with tears.

"I'm petrified! Have you ever known what God wanted you to do but were terrified of actually doing it?"

Chara smiled sympathetically. "When we moved here to L.A.,

we had no job prospects, no guarantee of our new church plant surviving, a kid on the way—you name it. I knew this was what God wanted, but I went through some times of real panic."

"That's how I feel. What if I join the KPF? How will I support myself? What will I do? How will I adapt to a new culture? How will I learn the language? What will my parents think? Will I ever get married?"

"Wait a minute, Ruth. I told you I have felt like this before too. The most important thing I've done in these situations is go back to the basic question: 'What does God want of me?' If I know what God wants, then all those other questions will work themselves out. But when I have made my obedience contingent on God answering my personal questions first, it has never worked out."

"But you don't know my parents! My mom—she already thinks I'm a religious fanatic."

"You're right. I don't know your earthly parents."

Chara reached across the table and took Ruth's hand.

"But I do know your heavenly Father. Just listen to His voice—whether it's to get a job, join the KPF, or some other step. Let's pray right now."

"Chara," Ruth said after they finished praying, "I'm graduating in May—wow, that's only a month and a half away. I want to join your group and help you get it off the ground. I know that's what God is saying. But I have one big fear."

"Which is?"

"My parents! Would you pray for me as I break the news to them? There's no telling what my mom will say. And my church back home? They will never understand me."

* * *

It was midnight before the six reconvened at the Owens' home. Christopher could tell the group was jubilant. The seeds of a movement had been planted that evening.

Excitement had been palpable in Taper Hall. Conversations with students had gone better than expected. The few who had made solid commitments were an encouragement, along with the many others who had said they would pray seriously over the next few weeks about joining the KPF.

"Uh, esteemed collaborators, I don't want to douse our fire," John said hesitantly, "but how are we going to storm the gates of hell with just six students?"

John's question shattered the excitement.

"I may be rather naive," Stacy said quietly, "but Gideon had only three hundred with him, and he conquered an army he couldn't number. Jesus started with twelve, and one of them was a dud. The six of us plus these six students gives us more than Jesus left behind. If God wants to storm the world with just twelve individuals, I think He's strong enough to do so!"

The other five knew Stacy wasn't talking from naivete. She had a deep, simple trust in God's Word and understood from personal experience that God is fully faithful and trustworthy.

"I apologize," John said. "Sometimes my rationalism overrules my faith. I don't want to quench what the Spirit is doing. You're right, Stacy. Six is enough if that is all God gives us. The Lord is able to save, whether by many or by few."

"Oh! That reminds me," Renee said. "I was talking to Timothy and Grace about our vision, and they are eager to set up a system to organize our little troop if we will get the right software and hardware. They really want to be a part, especially by using their programming skills."

"Great!" Christopher said. "Two more. Let's meet together next week to begin laying the foundation. Nic, we'll really need your planning skills. Otherwise, we are going to have people committed to us but nothing for them to do yet. Learn all you can about how various missions organizations are organized.

"And John, find out how enduring movements in history have structured themselves. Let's learn from others. When people say 'yes,' we need a structure that will train and support them in practical, biblical ways that lead to church-planting movements. It's only through movements that the remaining people groups will be reached.

"Let's pray earnestly for God to raise up people who have the skills to get us mobilized for action. Timothy and Grace Wu are a great start. If God has been merciful to raise up laborers, then He will also provide the equipping and organization we need."

"Chris, buddy," Nic interrupted, "I've heard that other leaders set a daily alarm for 10:02 to pray Luke 10:2 like this: 'Lord of the harvest, we beg You earnestly to send laborers out into Your harvest, starting with me as you did with your first disciples.' Is this something we could do?"

"This could make a huge difference for our goals!" agreed Christopher. "What do the rest of you think?"

"I'm in!" Renee said as she pulled out her phone and set the alarm. Everyone agreed and followed suit.

* * *

Before heading to bed that night, Christopher tweeted:

Today, a Kingdom Preparation Force was born to assault hell's gates. Set a daily alarm at 10:02 & pray Lk 10:2 for workers. #NoPlaceLeft2025

He breathed deeply and shot a quick prayer heavenward. *Father, my team will charge the gates of hell with me. But how far will we get without someone experienced? We need outside eyes to give us strategic counsel beyond our collective years and experience. Help us!*

SIXTEEN

Perhaps the most difficult step in any quest is the second one.
The first step is in the light, but the second in the dark.
We need help to walk untrodden paths.

—Ruth Grant

"Now tell me again who it is we are going to hear?" Win Dunbar said gruffly as he and Jeanie drove through the cool, dry Arizona night. "I had to cancel a battle with Sam Murchison that took me weeks to schedule! He's got a Hunnic army that's hard to beat."

"Honestly, Winthrop, your memory is like a sieve unless it has to do with battles and strategy. Tonight we're going to hear Nicolas Fernandez talk about the new mission work his church in L.A. is starting. He's Helen's son, grew up in the church here, and everyone is real proud of him."

"But Jeanie ..."

"Winthrop, we need to be there. For three years I've been wanting to get more involved at Grace, and Helen has become a special friend. She's so excited about Nicolas being here, and asked especially that we come. She thinks you'll like Nicolas."

"Jeanie, you know me. I can stare down the toughest sergeant and stand up under the most abrasive general. But when it comes to these"—he searched for the right word—"*spiritual* types, I feel helpless. Geez, honey, a *missionary*? I'll be completely out of my element!"

Jeanie looked at her husband fondly, knowing him better than he did himself.

"Don't worry, dear. Others may not see it beneath your crusty exterior, but you have a deep love for God. You don't need to feel intimidated. Just give Nicolas a chance.

"By the way, I told Helen the four of us could go out for coffee afterwards."

The colonel didn't respond. He would rather be speared on the wargaming table.

* * *

If Nic Fernandez possessed one thing, it was entrepreneurial zeal. Everyone remained attentive during the thirty minutes he had paced the stage.

"And so we now have twenty people committed to planting strategic beachheads to become church-planting movements, and that number is growing every week as word spreads. Pray that God will lead us in how to organize and prepare as Christian commandos in harsh lands. Satan has thrown up a big smokescreen for years to make us think he's too big to conquer in some of these places.

"Yet we know that a handful of wise and discerning people dedicated to God and empowered by the Spirit of God Himself can shatter the gates of hell—even in countries like these. We're small, but we're determined not to turn back even in the face of overwhelming odds. This is the final assault. We will see it through. This is the beginning of a movement that won't end until there is no place left without the gospel!"

Win had been doodling on an offering envelope but suddenly sat erect.

"We need some of you to give to support these missionaries. Maybe you heard your parents or grandparents talk about the sacrifice their family made to support the war effort of their generation. This is the greatest war effort. Let's make whatever sacrifices are necessary for those yet to hear the good news."

As Nic closed in prayer, Colonel Dunbar didn't bow his head. At that moment he was simply Winthrop Dunbar, child of God—clay in the Potter's hand.

Afterward at the coffee shop, the colonel kept reflecting on what Nicolas had said that evening.

"Nicolas, I know how excited you can get," he heard Helen say. "Are you sure you know what you're doing? It sounds to me a little like a cult. I mean twenty people can barely impact one city, much less reach the whole world. Maybe you should set your sights a little lower."

"It can be done," Win blurted suddenly.

The others looked at him in surprise.

"What do you mean, Win?" asked Helen.

"Just a minute, Helen. Nicolas?"

"Yes, sir?"

"You mentioned Christian commandos. What did you mean?"

Nic paused, thinking.

"Well, I guess we've concluded that the key to completing the Great Commission is to penetrate every unreached people group with small, highly committed teams that will start multiplying disciples and churches as beachheads and then move on. We see our role as blazing a trail for others to follow—sort of like special forces in the military."

"These people you are recruiting," the colonel said, studying Nic, "what's their commitment like? What do they expect to do?"

"None of us knows what we will do. We're just starting. We just know we want to penetrate people groups with the gospel by any and every means God gives us. We're trying to find folks who can guide us into what to do. As far as commitment, well ..."

Nic turned and spoke gently to Helen. He hoped she would understand, but he knew these would be difficult words for any mother to hear.

"I don't want to upset you, Mom, but we've agreed that we're willing to lay down our lives. I know it's not common but it is ... uh ... appropriate. An uncommon but appropriate sacrifice for the cause of Christ—that's what it is. We serve an unstoppable God, and no one can take our lives from us unless He allows it."

Nic turned his attention back to the colonel.

"Commitment, sir? We are unconditionally committed to the greatest cause and the most worthy Master the world has ever seen! Some of us may even die. We are willing for even that if it means the salvation of the nations!"

Excitement burned in the colonel's eyes.

"Then I say it again. It can be done. For years I have trained and led small, elite teams of commandos into difficult missions I am not allowed to discuss. Some seemed impossible. But we always succeeded. Why? Because we were Americans or had great weapons? Spare me."

He gently pounded his fist on the table.

"We succeeded because we were trained to succeed even to the point of death. We had a single focus—to beat the enemy no matter the odds. We entered hostile situations more determined to win than our enemy. Sometimes we achieved our goals only at great loss of life, make no mistake about that. But everyone in these missions knew the risks and was prepared to lay down his life for the team and the cause.

"Now you tell me you want to do the same thing in spiritual missions. I say it can be done! If I took young men and turned them into an invincible fighting force for a secular cause, why can't it happen for a greater spiritual cause?

"I haven't felt drawn to most churches. My faith has always been more personal, partly because most churches are made up of people half-heartedly pursuing goals not worth giving their lives for.

"But when Christians come to grips with the God we serve, and we dedicate ourselves to Him as the King of kings, our churches will begin to look like my special forces units, with greater intensity and truer sacrifice—tempered by love."

Jeanie nudged her husband. "Winthrop, don't be so hard."

Win ignored her. "Now you tell me you have a group ready to take on the world? To lay down their lives? To risk everything for the King of kings? As a military man, I have been willing to lay down my life to follow my commanding officer, a mere man. How repulsed do you think someone like me is by Christians who aren't willing to lay down their lives for the Commander in Chief of the universe?

"Instead, we argue over whether we have to tithe pre- or post-tax income. We complain if we are called on to go to too many meetings. We're not called to anything glorious, and so we make no glorious sacrifices. We have robbed our faith of our call to sacrificial commitment! We're not real community, we're not real people, and we're not real significant in this world!"

Colonel Win Dunbar poked a large finger into Nic's chest.

"Get this straight, young man. People are willing to lay down their lives if there is something worth laying them down for. I should know. I've trained them for years."

Nic grabbed the colonel's hand and shook it with both of his. "Christopher Owen says the same thing, in just so many words! He's the one leading this endeavor."

"Sounds like the man I need to meet. This is the way missions ought to be done, the way church ought to be done. Son, don't let anyone discourage you. By God's help, you can do it. If I could do it with earthly authority, you can surely do it with heavenly authority. We fought against other human beings—our equals in some respects. But the forces you fight in God's power are just a creation of the God we serve. There's no contest there."

"That's right, Colonel. But we have a very real problem. When our country's commander in chief wants to accomplish a mission, we have people like you to train the special forces for military missions. But when my commander in chief orders me or our other teammates to complete a mission, look what He has to work with! None of us knows the first thing about developing this type of force. My friend Christopher has a grand strategy and is an inspiring leader, but he's never been down this path before. He'll keep us on course, but we don't know how to even set sail!"

Win paused and looked at Jeanie long and hard.

"I know that, son," he said. "That's why we're moving to L.A. To help you—if you'll have us."

"What?" Jeanie gasped, choking on her coffee. "Do you know what you're saying, Winthrop? You have never been comfortable around church people."

"I know what I'm doing, Jeanie. We've made a lot of moves in our lives, but none as significant as this one. I'm in my element with these folks. They're my kind of Christians. I've not found such before."

He turned back to Nic.

"Nicolas, I know strategy and tactics. I know how to train for a task. I know how to lead men into battle. If you give me your priorities for the missions, I will train your folks and lead them. If your teams are willing to pay the price, I can train them. We'll find the best missions tactics out there and implement them.

"But let me warn you," he looked at Nic sternly. "I won't be any easier on KPF members than I was in the military. If anything, I might be tougher—the stakes are higher."

Colonel Win Dunbar stood to his feet, giving full respect to the young man seated before him.

"The U.S. military may have no more use for a sixty-five-year-old has-been colonel. But I am at your service, sir, if you will have me."

Nicolas stood and shook the colonel's again.

"Don't call me 'sir,' please. You'll meet the real 'sir' in L.A. When can you start?"

The colonel made a quick calculation. "June first."

"A month and a half!" Jeanie exclaimed. "I guess it's time to start packing again! A soldier's family must be always ready to move, again and again!"

* * *

Jeanie lay next to her husband in bed. Neither could sleep.

"Winthrop, are you sure you know what you are doing? Don't you remember what happened the last time you deployed? And the time before that?"

She snuggled closer. "It's why we moved out West, to forget the past. Remember, he can bring you down in a moment."

Win shook his head in the darkness. "I know ... I know. But my training has prepared me for this moment—we can't escape that. This wounded soldier must take up service in one last cause, even though it may cost us everything."

SEVENTEEN

Senator Wroth was flying over the Atlantic when the news he was anticipating arrived. Marlene and Jake watched the live CNN broadcast with him.

"My goodness!" Marlene cried. "How could they do this?"

"*We*, Marlene," corrected Senator Wroth, glancing down at the ancient diamond now on his finger. It had been passed down from the member of The Ten he replaced, but the new band was inscribed with his successive number in that elite group. "We are now one with those who did this, and you and Jake have agreed to join me in this new venture. There's no turning back."

"But—but—Senator! Killing four senators and their AAs? Plus all those innocent bystanders?"

"Quiet! Let's listen!"

Behind a somber CNN reporter, smoke was rising from one wing of the Capitol building and from the Russell Senate Office Building across Constitution Avenue. Lights from dozens of emergency vehicles flashed around the perimeters of both the structures.

"It's sheer pandemonium here at the Capitol. Details are still sketchy, but it appears four bombs exploded simultaneously at seven twenty-three this morning. One large blast hit the senate wing of the Capitol while three others rocked the senate offices in the Russell Building next door. The majority of employees had not yet arrived. We are still waiting to learn whether anyone was killed or injured. Firefighters are battling the blazes, and appear to have the upper hand.

"The sight of our white Capitol with blackened exterior and the senate office building in flames is overwhelming. No one knows yet if this is another terrorist attack like that on 9/11. This, just on the heels of the recent deaths of two senators ... hold on a moment ..."

The reporter's face darkened as he listened to his earpiece. "We have unconfirmed reports that four senators and some of their staff may have been near the blasts. No names have been disclosed. Again, these are unconfirmed reports."

Senator Wroth turned to Marlene.

"Get me a phone connection to report that I am safe and sound at home. Make sure the call is routed through my unlisted home line."

In minutes Senator Wroth was reassuring an officer that he was at home and okay, and that he could be reached there until further notice.

"Technology is wonderful," said Senator Wroth as he finished the call.

"Marlene, we'll be on the ground around noon. I want a news conference set up for three this afternoon. Jake, did your men get everything set up in my office?"

"Yes, sir. They checked the other senators' offices last night and determined what type of explosives The Ten were using. We set up an identical bomb with a faulty detonating device in your office. If the D.C. bomb squad is any good, they should have it sniffed out before your news conference."

"I hope so, Jake," Senator Wroth replied, "for your sake. We can't afford any mistakes. You don't know what it took for me to persuade The Ten to let you live as part of my team. I'm sorry about your twenty-four friends. Both of you need to understand we are playing hardball now. If we stay ahead of everyone else, we can beat these guys at their own game. But one mistake, and we're all history. Don't assume anything. Check, double-check, and triple-check everything. Build three or four alternate plans into every action so that no matter what happens, we'll always come out on top.

* * *

Late that afternoon Senator Wroth stood silhouetted against the crippled Capitol and Russell Building. With cameras rolling, he spoke briefly to an audience hungry for leadership.

"Today we witnessed the most appalling event in America since 9/11—a deliberate attack upon the senate of the American people. Rescue workers are still sifting through rubble looking for survivors while investigators search both buildings for more bombs. Approximately two and a half hours ago, I was informed that dogs had sniffed out a bomb that failed to detonate in my own office.

"Just last week two senators and some of their staff died, and I pledged to the American public that, if there were foul play, those responsible would be brought to swift justice. I imagine this bomb in my office was to deter me from that pursuit. It will have exactly the opposite effect. We *will* get to the bottom of all of these deaths.

"These latest attacks on our public servants strongly suggest terrorist involvement. Whoever you may be, if you are listening to my voice right now and think you can scare us off your trail, know that we will track you down and you will be brought to justice!

"Amidst our shock and our mourning, I urge our president to immediately establish an anti-terrorism task force with sweeping executive powers to coordinate not only the investigation of these murders but also the preparedness of America to deal with such atrocities. Apparently the measures taken since 9/11 are still inadequate. This task force must be empowered to cut through red tape and implement rapid changes so that you—the American people—can sleep securely at night without fear of terrorist activity. This task force must be empowered to eradicate terrorism no matter where it is—at home or abroad.

"You, Mr. President, are the commanding officer of our armed forces. When a military emergency arises, we have vested you with authority to mobilize and commit U.S. troops even before notifying Congress. Mr. President, we are at war again.

"Fellow Americans, this assault has shaken our country to its core. I, for one, support whatever action our president may feel necessary in response to this crisis. And I call on you to join me.

"From my own family estate I now pledge twenty-five million dollars for this task force. Let others who want to contribute send their donations, in care of the White House, designated for an anti-terrorism task force.

"Commit the forces of our government, Mr. President, until there is no rock under which terrorists can hide from the long arm of the most powerful nation on earth. We stand with you!

Let terrorists not soil this pure land of liberty! Though the nations fall into chaos and upheaval, we will stand tall as a haven of peace! Let us awake from our lethargy! God bless America!"

By day's end, Senator Michael Wroth was a household name, and the common enemy to which the senator pointed galvanized the American people to solidarity and action. Americans were so stirred by Senator Wroth's challenge that the president's speech later that day was anticlimactic. Thousands called the White House to support the president in implementing Senator Wroth's proposal, and tens of millions of dollars were pledged to track down the terrorists.

It was thus no surprise that the following day the president announced Senator Wroth's appointment as head of the newly formed Anti-Terrorism Task Force, with broad executive powers unparalleled by any other cabinet member. Senator Wroth was catapulted into the spotlight as a national hero.

* * *

Number Ten spent much time traveling abroad—ostensibly to investigate terrorist activity in foreign countries. This allowed him time in Rome. Within weeks he was reviewing changes in the worldwide political scene and observing developing trends with Number One. And when he wasn't in Rome, he found that many of his duties and studies as a member of The Ten could be carried out in Washington.

Soon after Number Ten began studying under Number One, the elderly man reprimanded him in his thin, raspy voice.

"Number Ten, I am concerned about your public involvement in America, especially your recent actions to become more prominent in the eyes of the American people. I thought you understood the value of influencing without being seen or heard. This new development disturbs me greatly."

"Yes, Number One, I see that I acted a little rashly. I should have consulted you. But I was so new and unacquainted with The Ten's procedures. However, I think my rising popularity can help carry us toward the Rebirth. The founding Three envisioned a day when The Ten would rule visibly. At some point we must move into the public arena. I have set up a scenario in which we may do so."

Number One picked up a heavy, bound sheaf of reports, shuffled to Number Ten's side, and plopped the packet on the desk next to him. A crooked old finger pointed to the pile of reports.

"These are last month's reports from every major political sector in the world. Your name figures prominently in many of them. Young man, you are making the same mistake the rest of us did in our early days. You must realize that we—The Ten—do not yet have enough consolidated power to go public. When we do go public, it must be with an invincible hold on the world. And that will be a decision we all make together."

The crooked finger jabbed Michael in the chest. "No one of The Ten has a right to bring us public before our time. Do you understand?"

Number Ten gathered his thoughts and responded with that swift agility that confounded his enemies. "I understand that clearly, and I intend nothing of the sort," he said reassuringly.

"It is only I who have gained prominence. I have not hinted in any way at the existence of The Ten. I would not be so foolish as to make that blunder, Prime Director. All I have done is lay some groundwork through which we may consolidate our power for the future. This is the goal of every decision we make. Of course I know who masterminded the deaths of the six senators, and of course I am not going to expose us.

"In the scenario I am pursuing, we will frame a terrorist group that acts contrary to our purpose. Not only will this bring more power to us, it will also eliminate one of our obstacles."

Number One sat at a large mahogany desk, fingertips together in contemplation.

"Yes, this will serve our purposes. Your error has been in not consulting me first, but we can use this move to our advantage."

He looked at Number Ten intently.

"But *not* to go public. We will not be ready for that for a long time—surely not in my lifetime and probably not in yours."

Number One leafed through several reports, then handed one to Number Ten. "Here. This is the terrorist cell to frame. Our people will assist you in tying the evidence to them." He finished by spelling out a detailed plan.

Number Ten hesitated before leaving.

"Number One, it has been sixteen hundred years since The Ten was formed. Is it possible that, over the centuries, lethargy has set in? Perhaps even a self-fulfilling expectation that the Rebirth must take place in some later generation—with the result that no generation of The Ten really attempts to usher it in?"

Number One rose, walked around the desk, and once more jabbed his crooked finger into the younger man's chest.

"Young man, such thoughts are what almost disqualified you from being chosen. When it is time for the Rebirth, we shall know it. It will be apparent in our diagramming of world events. The lines from the past will point to its time. Do not mistake our patience for lethargy. There is nothing every member of The Ten would like more than to share in ruling after the Rebirth! Now go! Do as I have instructed you!"

Though outwardly composed, Number Ten steamed inside.

* * *

Three weeks later, Senator Michael Wroth strode down a hall of the Pentagon, past Secret Service agents, and into the office where the president was waiting.

"It's time, Mr. President."

The two men proceeded back down the hall to a dark room filled with video monitors, computers, and a large illuminated map of a Middle Eastern country.

A voice came through the speakerphone. "Roger, Desert Sheik. Roadrunner One heading to pluck Wile E. Coyote's prize."

"Roadrunner?" asked the president.

"A little humor, sir," answered Senator Wroth. "You know how no one could catch the roadrunner in those cartoons."

All eyes were on a ninety-inch, wall-mounted display showing the movement of four teams in a desert area.

* * *

At 2 a.m. local time two Apache helicopters crested a ridge, swooping across the desert floor. Overhead, AWACs jammed all radar and radio transmissions. The helicopters flew swiftly over the rugged terrain for half an hour before setting down behind a low ridge of rocks and sand dunes where low clouds and fog had cooperated by plunging the area into total darkness.

Twelve black figures slipped from the choppers to the sand and then the top of the ridge. Eyes bulging with night-vision goggles, the twelve ran silently down the other side of the hill, like huge black insects. Before them lay a small village—a perfect hiding place for a splinter group of international terrorists.

Within seconds, the commandos reached the village and slipped swiftly through the quiet streets, sure of their route and destination. Moments later, they rushed through a doorway, quickly and silently subduing everyone in the house. Most of the occupants were simply gagged and bound, while two men and a woman were gagged, bound, blindfolded, and drugged.

Again the band stole into the streets, this time carrying with them their drugged objectives. They were halfway through the village when an alarm sounded over the mosque speaker.

Lights began to dot the dark village as suddenly-alert men emerged from houses, guns in hand.

Carrying the three figures slowed the team considerably as shots rang out, whizzing past them. Ahead lay the moonless desert which held their hope for a safe escape, while behind a quickly growing posse of villagers was gaining on them.

Suddenly a villager's bullet found its mark in one of the commandos. The leader halted his team behind a vegetable cart, while two soldiers crawled on their bellies toward their fallen friend. From behind the cart, two other soldiers unslung heavy weapons and squeezed their triggers. Rockets blazed a fiery trail before exploding into the crowd. Instantly the two rescuers lifted their fallen companion and ran back to the team.

The remaining eleven carried their four burdens from the village into the black desert. A few villagers attempted to follow, but were foiled by the darkness. The team boarded the waiting helicopters, and half an hour later landed across the border to deliver their three "guests."

* * *

"That's it, Mr. President!" Senator Wroth said, after the hour and a half drama.

"All four teams successfully apprehended the terrorists. Only one team was observed. They suffered one injury, and it appears that soldier will pull through. All eleven terrorists are now in the custody of the Anti-Terrorism Task Force. We expect to have them all in the United States within twenty-four hours."

The president stood in elation. "Excellent! Wonderful work, Senator Wroth! And General, let me congratulate you also."

"Thank you, Mr. President. But our success is due in large part to the intelligence Senator Wroth somehow obtained on the whereabouts of these bad guys. He made our job simple."

"So he did, so he did. Michael, how did you get to the source of the senators' murders so quickly?"

"We just had a few lucky breaks, that's all."

"Senator Wroth, I know you better than that. I don't think anything you do involves luck, but I'll leave it at that. As soon as these murderers are safely on U.S. soil, I want the two of you to join me for a press conference in the Rose Garden to announce the swift resolution to this crisis."

Shaking their hands, the president exited with flair, flanked by his cavalcade of Secret Service agents.

* * *

The next day the president declared victory to a listening nation.

"Yesterday, about 2 a.m. local time in a small Middle Eastern country, four groups of America's finest commandos launched strikes into four remote villages under the direction of the Anti-Terrorism Task Force. Their targets? Eleven ruthless terrorists we believe to have masterminded the recent deaths of our six U.S. senators. All four teams apprehended their suspects and emerged with only one injury. And that brave soldier is in stable condition.

"Just a few hours ago, ATTF representatives arrived on U.S. soil with these eleven terrorists, now confined in a maximum security facility. Under a recent provision of Congress, the ATTF has special authority to prosecute these criminals in expedited hearings. And should they be convicted, they will be executed immediately as a warning to all terrorists around the world. We, the people of the United States, will not tolerate such attacks on the freedom we have fought so hard to preserve.

"Guiding this investigation and operation is ATTF director Senator Michael Wroth. In two short months, he has done what many thought humanly impossible. He has more than fulfilled his promises to you, the American people. I would like him to share a few words with you now."

Senator Wroth unfolded a paper as he stepped to the podium, then wadded it up and stuffed it into his pocket.

"That speech wouldn't communicate what I want to say."

Members of the press chuckled appreciatively.

"Over the last two months, I have missed a lot of days in the senate, devoting my attention instead to tracking down those responsible for the death of my colleagues. I have been consumed with finding the perpetrators of these heinous crimes. I want first to apologize to the people of California for this lapse in my senatorial duties.

"Apprehending these terrorists has been bittersweet. I hope that the deaths of my six friends ..." He wiped his eyes with a handkerchief, "... will not be in vain. May their deaths become a rallying cry for our nation—the greatest protector of freedom in the history of the world. Let us rid the world once and for all of any group that threatens the peace and freedom of mankind. Thank you!"

Senator Wroth left the platform amidst applause from the press corps and appreciation from the American public on TV.

"How did you manage to cry during your speech?" Marlene asked quietly as they walked up the Capitol steps toward the mostly repaired senate offices.

Wroth looked at her reproachfully. "Marlene, I'm disappointed in you. Don't you believe I was moved to tears by this whole affair?"

The pair rushed past reporters into the reopened Senate Chamber. And for the first time in months, Senator Wroth was genuinely shocked. As he walked the aisle toward his seat the whole Senate—both Democrats and Republicans—stood in his honor, applauding thunderously.

Over the next forty-six days, eleven terrorists—all of them guilty of other crimes but innocent of the deaths of the six U.S.

senators—were tried, convicted, and executed for crimes against the American state. The planted evidence appeared rock solid, and the jury was unsympathetic. The last minute appeal to the Supreme Court for a stay of execution was denied. The Eleven terrorists were executed by lethal injection. And the American public felt avenged.

Freedom had a new champion.

EIGHTEEN

A man digging in a field discovered a treasure
and joyfully sold all he had to buy that field.
What a no-brainer decision!
My heart bursts with joy at the prospect
of gaining more of You and less of me.
My joy is as endless as my treasure—You, Jesus, and Your Kingdom.
I gladly sell all to know You and make You known!
—Ruth Grant

George Yang spotted his friend Lance Chu chatting with Kellie Davies and other friends near the USC Tommy Trojan statue.

"Hey, Lance! Talk to your folks about the KPF yet?"

Lance's smile almost jumped off his face. "Dude! They gave the okay!"

"Woo hoo!"

"Hey, guys. What's up?" asked Lance's friend Phil Young.

"Dude, haven't you heard what's happening?" Lance asked. "Christopher Owen has been speaking at all the campus fellowships, sending seven point shock waves throughout. He's launched a high-powered missions group called the Kingdom Preparation Force. They're saying we can help prepare for Jesus' return. They're talking 2025 as a target date. It's kinda radical, but a lot of us are praying seriously about joining. A gap year for some, or for George and me ...," he grinned broadly, "after graduation in a few weeks!"

Phil's eyes widened. "What? You guys are going to skip out on getting a job to join up with some new missions group? What will your parents think?"

"My parents are good with it!" Lance smiled broadly. "It's only for a year," he added. "And, ya know, the job market is kinda soft right now anyway. But I've also been thinking. I've been vainly pursuing the American dream. But 2025? Dude, that's just ten years from now. I can do *anything* for Jesus for ten years!"

"It's not just us, Phil," George said. "A lot of folks are signing up. Of course, it will take more than a year to finish the whole task, but we're starting with a one-year commitment. This is the real thing, man. It fits with what we know in our hearts and minds to be *right*. Christopher Owen has been around here longer than any of us. Even Professor Steward, from the history department, is part of this."

"Professor Steward? Really?" Phil shook his head. "If what you're saying is true, this may be it—just what I have been searching for!"

"Uh, probably not," George said, glancing worriedly at Lance. "This isn't for everybody. We'll be going places missionaries aren't welcome. There's a lot of risk involved."

But Phil wasn't to be dissuaded. "Okay. Maybe I'll give this Christopher guy a call."

Lance grabbed Phil's arm, perhaps a bit too firmly. "Dude, you'll need to move fast. Our first meeting is May 24th, a week after graduation. Make sure this is what you really want to do. It's going to be a tough year."

George said, "And if that's not enough, Church in the City has been calling all of its members to make disciples who make more disciples who make more disciples. Just like the Great Commission says."

Lance nodded. "Like it's the pattern all Jesus-followers are supposed to have. You know, follow Jesus and fish for men."

Kellie motioned for the three guys to come closer. "Do you guys know Ruth Grant?"

Phil raised an eyebrow. "That bashful nerd from math class?"

Kellie smiled. "Well, she's raising havoc on campus. I've never heard anyone share the gospel so much. In fact, I hadn't heard her say more than ten words until recently. But she led two sorority gals to the Lord just a few weeks ago. She's been discipling them in the study center. And those two gals have now led so many of their sorority sisters to the Lord that they've formed a discipleship group in their sorority house living room."

Lance laughed and looked around. "So that's what happened! Now it makes sense. One of my ATO buddies was led to faith last week by a girl in their house. He's now started a new group with several of the guys in our frat house at 6 a.m. on Tuesdays! Dude, nobody gets up at six!"

"All I'm saying," said George, "is that this call Christopher Owen is making is not just to finish the missions task. It's a call to return to biblical discipleship. They're trying to start a discipleship movement here in L.A. before they leave for the nations."

Kellie smirked as she spoke. "Ahem, my sister is Christopher Owen's wife, Chara."

George raised his hand to his mouth. "Oh my gosh! I hope I didn't say anything embarrassing!"

Kellie playfully punched him in the arm. "Yeah, I'm keeping track of all you guys say! Seriously, though, Chara is telling me that just through Ruth's touch, we have *six* new generations of disciples and groups! Greeks, athletes, math students, landscape workers on campus! It's crazy!

"When I think about how shy and introverted Ruth is, if the Holy Spirit can do that through her, there is hope for me—for all of us. God wants to launch a discipleship revolution through us that will touch the nations. We are going to do *there* what we are doing *here*. Ruth is proof that it can work."

She paused and nodded her head slowly. "I'm with you, Lance. I can do anything for Jesus for ten years! And my brother-in-law who's leading the charge? He's the real deal!"

* * *

Sunday, May 24th, arrived. The Owens' adjoining living/dining areas were crowded with thirty-six people on chairs, couches, windowsills, and pillows on the hardwood floor. This former brainstorming center for the six original conspirators had now become the launching pad for a movement.

Professor Steward, familiar to most of the students, stood first to introduce Christopher.

"Our fearless leader and organizer is the esteemed Christopher Owen. Don't let his short stature mislead you. Beethoven was only five-foot-three, and look what he accomplished. And he was deaf, so Christopher not only has three inches on him, but also good—though maybe selective—hearing."

He winked at Christopher.

"Or consider James Madison—founding father of our country and fourth president of the United States, standing just five-foot-four," he continued. "We believe that Christopher is founding something far more significant here, not unlike ..."

Christopher jumped out of his seat and shoved John aside. "Enough already! Welcome to the first meeting of the Kingdom Preparation Force, the most hastily-organized missions force in history!"

The room erupted in cheers, applause, and laughter, releasing a bit of the nervousness many felt. Christopher's heart rate began to come down.

"Your presence here so shortly after the KPF's conception is very significant. In less than two months, God has stirred many to volunteer. We have interviewed and accepted only those we feel can live up to the high-but-difficult calling of sacrificial service at the ends of the earth. You are the fruit of this!

"The KPF has just one purpose—no place left without the gospel by 2025. Our calling is to prepare for the return of King Jesus by taking the good news of His Kingdom to every last UUPG on this planet."

Christopher turned to survey the room; his eyes settling briefly on Ruth Grant before he continued.

"You will have to endure not only harsh field conditions, but our own inexperience. Think of yourselves as our guinea pigs."

Several laughed nervously.

"But you may also receive more direct support from us than later recruits will as this effort grows. Let me introduce you briefly to the staff that will be serving you this year. Our original conspirators, to whom God gave the founding vision for the KPF, are with me here at the front. First my wife Chara and myself. Then many of you know Professor John Steward from school, and some of you have met his wife, Renee, a practicing lawyer. Finally, Nic Fernandez, entrepreneur, and his wife, Stacy."

"In the back are Timothy and Grace Wu." The couple smiled as Christopher motioned in their direction. "The Wus are our IT and communications specialists. They will help us stay on top of communications and monitor our efforts among the unreached.

Everyone I've mentioned so far also plays an important part in the church I was pastoring—Church in the City. With our church's support, Chara and I are taking a sabbatical this year as part of launching this endeavor.

"Next to the Wus are Frank and Clarisse Howard." The pair next to the Wus waved. "They have prior overseas experience and will be leading one of our field teams.

"In addition to our staff," Christopher said, pointing toward a slender girl in a back corner, "Julie Konami is a recruit and, like several of you, just graduated from USC. But she has also shown a servant heart as my assistant at Church on the City over several years. I will be relying on her as a liaison in communicating with the rest of you. If she comes asking you for something or delivers a message, it will be on behalf of our staff.

"Our staff of twelve is committed to training, developing, and leading you. That's one of us for every two of you. Think of us as your tactical and logistical command team. We are committed to the KPF for the long term. We are only asking you to commit for one year, but in this year we are asking you to give yourself one hundred percent under our direction to seeking God's Kingdom among the remaining UUPGs.

"If you were counting, you noticed I only introduced ten of our twelve staff. Let me now introduce the final couple, Jeanie Dunbar"—Jeanie, seated next to Clarisse, waved—"and Colonel Win Dunbar.

"Colonel Dunbar has spent forty plus years serving in the military—training elite forces, directing special operations, and doing things too secret for any of us to know about. More important, the colonel loves God with all his heart and desires nothing more than to advance His Kingdom. God has graciously brought the colonel to help us prepare for spiritual battle in a way that may never have been done before. He will be in charge of your training over the next few months, and an integral part of our field operations through the rest of the year."

The imposing figure stood next to his wife.

"Colonel, why don't you share a little with the group, since they're going to get to know you *real* well?"

Colonel Dunbar stepped to the front as silently as a cat, and gazes that met his were quickly averted. Christopher shook his hand, then the diminutive figure attempted to give the towering Marine a bear hug. He was swallowed up in the return embrace. A few chuckled before the colonel turned to face the group, commanding everyone's full attention.

"As the commander shared, my name is Colonel Win Dunbar. You may call me Colonel, or simply Win.

"Battle isn't as glamorous as it sounds from a distance. I know. I've been shot eight times and stabbed six. I've stormed more beaches than I can remember. I've dropped behind enemy lines, burrowed through tunnels in Vietnam, and disarmed countless booby-traps. I have turned thousands of raw recruits into the world's best fighting units. I've had to make countless split-second decisions about people's lives with bullets racing by me, mortar shells dropping around me, and jets strafing me. I have carried many wounded soldiers to safety even when I was badly injured. I have helped depose dictators, rescue hostages, establish beachheads for troops, and remove daunting military obstacles.

"But nothing in my life compares with what we are about to attempt together."

Win stopped to gaze around the room and let this thought sink in. Jeanie winked at him from the back, knowing how much he was enjoying this. Christopher watched him, admiring how quickly he had gained command of the group.

"No quest is so worthy as the one we are embarking upon. The eternal destinies of more than three hundred fifty-four *million* people in these UUPGs are at stake. And no other enemy is as diabolical, powerful, and entrenched as the one we face.

"Despite such opposition, I have utter confidence we will prevail. That is why many call me Win. And I do not expect to fail now.

"No goal is more worthy than No Place Left. No time frame is more compelling than 2025, and no outcome more ultimately certain. Our omnipotent heavenly Commander has declared that this gospel of the Kingdom *will* be preached in the whole world to every nation. If the Lord of Hosts is with us, who can be against us?

"In the military I always answered to a commander, and my service with the KPF will be no different. In this operation, Christopher Owen is my commander, and that is how I will refer to him. I am honored to follow his lead, and I will expect you to respect him as you respect me. We can only be effective if we have clear lines of authority. This is a military organization. I repeat—*military*. If you can't handle strong leadership with clear authority, now's the time to back out. Otherwise, when we say jump, you need to do it. Your very life, or someone else's, may depend on it. On the field there will be circumstances where orders need to be followed without questioning, lest you heighten the danger to yourself and others."

The colonel began threading his way among the listeners, whose heads swiveled to follow him.

"We pursue an objective some consider impossible. Since learning about the KPF, I have done little else besides study the practicality of NoPlaceLeft2025.

"If God is with us, and we are truly ready to lay down our lives, it can be done! I aim to be in the final generation—the one that finally buckles down to complete the conditions He gave for His return. I'll turn seventy-six in 2025."

The colonel grinned broadly.

"I'm not asking you now for ten years. I am just asking for your undivided, focused effort for one year. However, at the end of that year, you—the battle-hardened spiritual assault troops with field experience—will be equipped to lead new recruits for many more years to come. You are the seeds of this movement."

The colonel continued his circuitous meandering among the recruits, forcing them to twist their necks and bodies to follow his movements.

"In preparation for harsh field conditions, your training must be rigorous. In one week we'll officially begin the three-month KPF Boot Camp. And believe me, I know how to run a boot camp! Within a few long weeks, some of you will hate the sight of me."

The colonel picked up a worn Bible and held it up.

"Battles are only won by those who believe they will win. Our faith must be grounded in God's Word, so you will read through

Acts and Revelation every two weeks to give you unshakeable confidence that God will back you up in His unstoppable plan to redeem this world. Our objective will be accomplished. You need to believe that. No Marine ever wins who lacks confidence in his own abilities or in his team's. If you doubt, you will fail, so I want you immersed in God's victorious Word.

"For tactical training, you will be reading classics by Roland Allen and modern texts on church-planting and disciple-making movements. For sacrificial devotion, you'll read *Foxe's Book of Martyrs* and selected missionary biographies. You stand on the shoulders of giants. We will be finishing what they started.

"Here in the L.A. basin are pockets of the very peoples whose homelands we will be entering. This summer you will begin learning your target language, and how to reach these folks. In this boot camp, you will master just enough language to continue learning in your assigned field. Language is essential for your mission.

"After boot camp you will be divided into four teams to be inserted among four different people groups. There you will find people whom God has prepared to receive our King and His Kingdom. You will help them start churches in their own homes, which will then multiply among that people group.

"You're gonna work your tails off to have enough language to get started, and pray like crazy for bilingual national partners to help. Like the Green Berets, you will train locals to carry the mission forward after you leave. Like Paul's missionary band, you may move from place to place seeking to catalyze the kind of multiplication we see in Acts! And, like Paul, you will find ways to return to strengthen the work you have started."

A young woman in the front raised her hand.

"Yes?"

"Sir, I don't want to question your confidence, but something doesn't make sense to me."

"What is that, young lady?"

"Sir, there are already lots of missionaries out there, and they don't start churches as quickly as you're talking about. Some have been there for years without these results. So how can we expect to see results so quickly?"

"That's a great question. You are thinking critically, and I like that," replied the colonel.

"Some long-term workers *are* seeing churches planted much more quickly than can sometimes be reported. We are already tracking several *dozen* church-planting movements in very unreached areas. And we are learning a lot from them.

"Your role is to be missionary shock troops. We do expect you to plant multiplying churches soon after your arrival. How? By virtue of who you will have become. You will be high-risk, short-term, spiritual combat troops. You will quickly comb through hundreds, even thousands, of people to find those through whom God has prepared to launch movements. You will take risks that might get you thrown into prison, thrown out of the country, or even killed. Yet by taking greater risks, you will see greater results more quickly.

"You are going to plant reproducing churches. And you are going to cooperate with God to start movements because you *must*—not because you are better than any other worker out there. Your role is simply different.

"If we can inspire others by our humble and sacrificial example, so much the better. Yet the evil one can accomplish immeasurable damage through any KPF recruits who become proud, cocky, or unteachable.

"I have said enough. At the end of one year you will return here, Lord willing. As God leads, you will then be able to renew your enlistment or choose another course.

"At this very moment, you have friends who are accepting positions with Fortune 500 companies, starting their own businesses, or getting ready for their first day of law school."

Win planted both feet squarely and put his hands on his hips.

"Recruits, your friends don't know what they're missing! With God's help, we will hasten the fulfillment of His unchanging purpose. We will join Paul in saying, 'There is no place left.' And I, Win Dunbar, will stand with you to the end!"

Cheers erupted around the room.

Lance stood up.

"Yes?" said the Colonel.

Lance looked around with a bashful grin.

"Well, sir, some of the dudes here ... we were wondering ... well ... if we would get to wear green berets or something?"

Everyone laughed, including the colonel.

"No. No green berets. However, I might be able to arrange a ten-thousand-foot jump for you," said the colonel, "... without a parachute!"

"Okay, that's enough." Christopher smiled and dismissed the twenty-four recruits with prayer. He and the staff had a mountain of logistical details to climb before boot camp started.

NINETEEN

You tell me, like the man in Luke 9,
not to even say farewell to my parents.
You know me all too well.
I would look back too often, constrained by their fears,
shaped by their hopes.
Therefore, my hand is to the plow.
I go to the field at Your command
with only a reluctant blessing from my parents.
I am incapable of saving them, Jesus!
I entrust them to Your care.

—Ruth Grant

Christopher basked in discussing with the colonel how to fit the KPF command center into the Owens' home. Finally, he had someone to talk with who shared his love for strategy and could think a step or two ahead of him—most of the time. Timothy and Grace trailed behind, tablets in hand, to record their decisions.

Chara offered a voice of reason—limiting the headquarters to just two back rooms and the basement. "And absolutely no dorms on site!" she called out as they went into the next room. "Are you listening?"

"Okay, boss, what's our technology budget?" asked Timothy.

"Uh, I'm not sure—it'll need to be cheap," Christopher replied. "See what we can do on a shoestring, okay?"

Timothy's eyes betrayed disappointment, but he said nothing.

"No worries there, Timothy," the colonel said. "I've still got connections in the private defense industry and do a good bit of pro bono consulting. Make a list of what we need, and I'll find a way to get it donated."

"In that case," Christopher said, unable to contain himself, "there are just a few things I absolutely want. First, we must have real-time countdown displays everywhere—in every office, the entryway, and the KPF dorm. They need to show the number of days to January 1st, 2025 and how many unreached people groups remain unengaged so that we don't become complacent with a few early advances.

"Second, I want a big monitor in the basement—our securest location—displaying where the UUPGs are and where our teams are. Of course, we'll need a good world map for the wall.

"Finally, and this might sound a bit silly, but I want one of those lighted transparent military planning boards you always see in the movies. This will help us remember that this really is war. Oh, and whiteboards everywhere—big ones!"

Chara could stand it no longer. "Honestly!" she said, "Boys and their toys!"

Christopher looked at the colonel. "Overkill?"

Win looked at Chara and winked. "Perhaps, Commander. But I get the idea. The Wus and I will fix you up."

* * *

Three days later an unmarked panel truck backed down the driveway onto the lawn and swung wide its loading doors to form a virtual tunnel from the truck to the front door of the house as a screen against snoopy neighbors. The four Owen kids watched eagerly as a burly private security squad unloaded crates from the truck, through the living room, and into the new KPF command center. The colonel was directing traffic, and the men nodded in respect as they entered and saluted after delivering their first load. In less than an hour, the equipment was set up and the truck gone.

No sooner had the truck left than the Owen preschoolers darted around the living room chanting, "We've got the best house! We've got the greatest parents!"

Grace and Timothy spent the next few days rewiring the house for the new equipment. Christopher and the colonel used the whiteboards, wall map, and planning board to discuss potential scenarios and refine their strategy for this first year. The colonel was pleasantly surprised at Christopher's aptitude for strategy.

"Don't suppose I could lure you onto a wargaming table,

could I? You'd be a worthy opponent!"

Soon the command center was online. And each evening the Fernandezes and Stewards stopped by to review plans on the whiteboards and add their own suggestions. And when the fresh recruits moved into the KPF dorm near campus, everything was ready for boot camp.

* * *

"Lance, wake up!" George shook Lance for the third time.

Lance pulled the corner of his sheet down just far enough to peek at the red glow of the alarm clock then quickly pulled the sheet back over his head.

"Go away, dude. It's only five-thirty! I'm not ready to face the day yet." He rolled over, wondering how he could be so totally exhausted after just three weeks.

George was out of patience. He ripped the sheet off the bed and flipped on the bright overhead lights.

"Oh, dude! Okay, okay. I'll get up—just turn off that light—please!" Lance rolled out of bed and onto the floor, then stood looking around for his sweats. "I know you're our exalted team leader and all, but tell me again why I need to go meet this guy instead of you or Phil?"

"Come on, Lance. Your Mandarin is a lot better than ours, and we don't know how much English this guy speaks. You're our best potential link to him."

"Me? Our best link? That's not very encouraging!"

George began to leave the room.

"Bro, where are you going so early?" Lance asked.

"I've got a lot to do," said George nonchalantly. "And I need to finish our weekly team report and get it to Julie before I meet with Nic at eight."

Lance's eyes lit up mischievously. "Julie, huh? Remember our no-dating policy this year."

"Lance, chill."

George stepped onto the second-story landing that doubled as a hallway for the new KPF dorm—a run-down, eleven-bedroom Victorian mansion near campus. With the monthly rent only seventy-five dollars per person, it was easy to overlook some flaking paint, dripping faucets, and an occasional rat. And they all understood that these quarters were better than what they would likely have on the field. Thirteen men lived upstairs and eleven women downstairs.

George grabbed a cup of coffee and found a quiet place to finish his team report. It wouldn't be all positive. Everyone was making a determined effort and good progress, but most were also feeling overwhelmed and discouraged.

By the time he was finished, the dorm was shaking off its slumber. In another corner of the common area Ruth, Kellie, and Phil were playing Mandarin MP3s, trying to comprehend the words and phrases. Others were just emerging from their rooms in search of coffee. George grabbed his bag and headed out the door for the KPF headquarters.

* * *

Julie looked up from her small, military-surplus desk.

"You're late," she said playfully. "That report was supposed to be here last night. You're lucky I'm behind on processing them."

George plopped onto a chair between her desk and the printer-fax-copier wedged in the corner of the tiny room.

"Yeah, I *feel* lucky," he said sarcastically. "I don't think you want this report anyway. I just emailed it to you, by the way."

Julie squeezed around the desk and sat on it to be closer.

"That bad, huh?"

"Bad? I've never seen Lance so discouraged; he's usually Mr. Gung Ho. Phil is failing Mandarin 101 and even Miss Sunshine Kellie is getting moody. It's hard to tell about Ruth. She keeps to herself a lot, journaling mostly. Me? I've never led a missions team before, much less started a church."

"At least we'll have Christopher to advise us," Julie said. "He says we'll be following a much simpler pattern for starting churches than we're used to in America. His training in Singapore gave him a lot of practical ideas for helping us."

"Yeah, you're right," George said, "but even Christopher has never done this before. I mean, I know he planted Church in the City, but that's a lot different from planting a church in a foreign culture. And our team is lucky. We'll have Christopher leading our team. What about the others? If I hadn't made a one-year commitment, I'd be tempted to throw in the towel."

Just then a cheery voice interrupted their conversation.

"Excuse me, you two. I thought you might enjoy a morning snack." Chara walked in balancing two coffee mugs and a bowl of fresh strawberries. "Can't say that it's fancy, but at least the strawberries are clean."

She sat on the desk next to Julie, putting her arm around her gently. "I've seen you guys looking better. What's up?"

George knew Chara already had a lot on her plate and was hesitant about adding to her burden, but he was grateful for her concern.

"Oh, I guess everyone is a bit discouraged," he said as lightly as he could, "and pretty tired."

Chara herself was worried about the training schedule. The colonel seemed to have things booked twenty-six hours a day, and she wondered how long these raw recruits could keep it up.

"Mm-hm. And how much sleep is everyone getting?"

"Realistically? Four or five hours a night. Or else someone sleeps in by accident and misses assignments. Either way, people are feeling down."

"Have you talked to Christopher or the colonel about this?"

"We haven't had a chance," Julie said. "They're busier than we are. Besides, it's all in the reports."

"You need to talk to Christopher," Chara said gently. "Emailed reports aren't the same as face-to-face communication."

"I don't have an appointment, and my day is full as it is," George said. "He'll read the report."

Chara stood and looked George square in the eye.

"George Yang! You now lead five other people, and you are responsible for their well-being. If they have an urgent problem, go talk to Christopher. My husband appears busy because he's so focused. But when something is pressing, he wants you to let him know. He'll make time for you. You're his priority.

"And you, Julie. You virtually control Christopher's schedule now, don't you?"

Julie looked at her sheepishly, "Yeah, I guess so."

"Of course you do. So clear time in his calendar for urgent

appointments like this," Chara said, lovingly but firmly. "He won't know any difference."

* * *

"Have a seat, bro."

Christopher directed George to the lone couch in the room instead of the chairs at his desk. George handed him his team report, which Christopher skimmed briefly.

"Julie emailed this to me a couple of hours ago. It looks a lot like the other team reports."

"Christopher," George said, "I—I'm concerned about the teams. I've been talking to the other team leaders. We all agree that—well—that everyone is exhausted and discouraged. I'm concerned that we may lose the war before we even get into it."

Win Dunbar poked his head in the doorway behind George. He began to retreat when he saw that Christopher was occupied, but Christopher waved him in.

"George, repeat for the colonel what you just said, please."

"Well, I don't mean to be critical or complaining."

"You're not complaining. You're raising real issues."

"Well, I just thought you should know the state of your troops. Everyone is exhausted and discouraged. I'm concerned that we may lose the war before we even get into it."

Christopher and Win exchanged knowing glances.

"We're already in it, George," said Christopher.

"What do you mean?"

Win placed his hand gently on George's shoulder. "Son, the war begins the moment a soldier begins training. This isn't some artificial environment. You are learning to persevere now. If you fall down now, where's it's safe and controlled, how will you stand when the actual operations begin?"

George looked up with pleading eyes. "Colonel, I appreciate your realism, but this isn't actually a real war. These are college kids. They have other options that seem a lot more attractive right now."

The colonel remained silent while Christopher paced for a few seconds before speaking. "George, do you really believe that? That this isn't an actual war?"

George threw his hands in the air. "No. I guess not."

Win sat down again next to the George. "Son, what you young people are going through is normal. I'm surprised none of you have dropped out yet.

"This is hardening every one of you for what is to come," the colonel continued. "We mustn't short-circuit the lessons because everyone feels bad. It hurts a lot worse to become a casualty of war. The teams must suffer now in preparation for what they'll face later.

Christopher glanced at Win, then spoke to George. "The level of spiritual opposition we'll face scares me more than anything else. And those spiritual adversaries will use human instruments against us."

* * *

After his meeting with George and Christopher, the colonel sought out a quiet spot downstairs in the command center. He lowered the lights and his knees gave way as he huddled on the floor in the corner. The quiet whir of computers masked the chatter of his teeth. His trembling hand found and extracted his phone from its pocket. Through the haze clouding his vision, he found the number he sought.

"Jeanie, it's happening again," Win managed amidst his rapid breathing. "Please, sweetie, get over here quick."

He dropped the phone and curled up to wait.

Fifteen minutes later Jeanie scurried in the front door and down the basement stairs. Christopher heard her and followed.

On the basement floor Jeanie cradled the colonel's head in her lap. She pulled out a towel and mopped perspiration from his brow, then forced a pill between his lips.

"Chew this, big guy. You'll be okay in a few minutes."

Hearing the wooden stairs creak, Jeanie looked up as Christopher rushed to her side.

She gripped Christopher's arm firmly. "He'll be all right. This has happened before, and it's not life threatening. But no one must know about this or it will undermine his leadership. Do you understand?"

Christopher nodded. His face said he understood, but his

heart sank at the prospect that this old soldier might have already fought one battle too many.

* * *

Successive weeks proved less taxing as the recruits adjusted to their new pace of life and gained increasing fluency in their new languages. The colonel moved among his trainees with increasing frequency, mustering their morale as a general would his troops. And Christopher brought in someone he and Chara had met in Singapore to answer the recruits' practical questions about what to do on the field.

True to his pledge, the colonel's boot camp turned these raw recruits into confident combat units. Confidence and faith now characterized them, as well as servant-hearted humility. These KPF recruits found their spiritual vitality deepened by their sense of fulfilling their Father's mission.

Their main limitation was the need for secrecy. Lest they be deported prematurely, each of the four teams needed to maintain a cloak of security regarding the countries to which they were going. Most of their prayer and financial supporters knew only the general area, as the KPF was doing all it could to insert the teams quietly. The colonel made a special point of this, as he had experienced premature information leaks before—sometimes with disastrous consequences.

The commissioning service was held mid-August on a Sunday and was attended by about two hundred and fifty relatives and friends. Afterward, the staff offered tours of the facilities and operations. Team members guided groups of ten through the main office, where Owen's ordination credentials were on the wall. They descended into the communications center where Timothy and Grace explained how they could maintain contact with each team on an almost continual basis. And they met Colonel Dunbar, decked out in his dress uniform. Several were visibly impressed to see that the operation was directed by such an experienced and decorated officer.

The highest priority for KPF leadership was being available to relatives of the recruits to establish a good communication base for going forward. When the leadership team compared notes afterward, it was clear that this objective was achieved. Most of the relatives were obviously pleased and impressed, and some doubters had become active supporters.

After the long day, a weary Christopher crawled into bed next to his also-weary wife. They snuggled close.

"Honey," said Chara, "I think the day went great! Don't you?"

"Better than I dared dream. I met quite a few parents who had called or sent emails expressing concern. Their tone today was a lot different. Several thanked me for the private number we gave them to call. That was a great idea."

Chara snuggled closer. "I just tried to think of what I would want if it were my college grad getting ready to go overseas.

"And you know what was the real kicker?" she asked.

"What?"

"Colonel Winthrop Dunbar with all those medals and ribbons on display."

Christopher chuckled. "Tell me about it! Every time I passed by, he had a small crowd listening to his military escapades. I saw moms and dads nodding like, 'If he can pull our troops safely out of hostile territory, he can take care of my child.' Several of them had seen him on news reports."

The two laughed, then Chara yawned.

She said, "Honey, I have to admit I have had times of doubt over the last few months. I have a curious feeling though. I feel both amazed and strangely not amazed when I think about all that God has brought together in what began as a 'harebrained' venture."

"Yep, I have the same feeling. Just think about the people Father has led into this enterprise. I can't believe how quickly He has brought this together."

Chara hugged him. "Sometimes I'm amazed at your faith."

Christopher paused. "Faith? Honey, I can't tell you how many times I have awakened in the middle of the night in a cold sweat, asking myself what I've gotten us all into."

* * *

The next evening, KPF staff and team leaders gathered together for a final briefing. Christopher sat before the group, flanked by John and Nic.

"This is the last time we'll all be together before we return next summer. I have asked the colonel to brief us, confidentially, about where the four teams will deploy. Colonel?"

"Since this is our first year, all four teams will be in the same general region of the world—Southeast Asia—so we can interact frequently and share personnel and resources."

The colonel pointed to various locations on a wall map.

"Laos, in former Indochina, is the black hole of the UUPG world. There are more than seventy-five UUPGs there, and there are dozens more nearby. The Fernandezes will lead an exploratory team inside the country to feel things out so that we can increase our footprint there in years to come. The Owens will lead another team in southwest China, across the border from Laos. Their people group, the Tuxiang, spills over into both Laos and northern Vietnam, but they'll approach it from the China side. The other two teams will be based in Vietnam—with the Howards and Jeanie and me."

Christopher noticed the slight pause in the colonel's speech as he mentioned Vietnam, and saw the beads of perspiration forming on his brow. His eyes moved from the colonel to Jeanie, who smiled at her husband and winked. There was more to this than the basement episode. He made a mental note to ask Jeanie about this some time.

The colonel glanced at Jeanie and continued.

"Each team will have a staff member on the ground with them—Christopher, Nic, Frank, and myself—as well as a team leader who will never leave the group. One reason we are all in Southeast Asia is so our staff can travel to serve the other teams as necessary.

"Each team has a communications specialist. He or she will set up secure communications to keep us in contact. I've even managed to acquire some used military grade satellite phones for use when regular phone lines are down or a team is in an area without mobile access.

"These are to be used only in an emergency," he emphasized, "as they will attract attention if spotted by local authorities.

"The Wus will remain here and monitor communications. The Stewards will also be here to oversee the headquarters and continue recruiting for next summer. John has cut his teaching load so he can preach for Christopher and oversee the church.

"Watch out, O silver-tongued one!" John teased. "After they hear my preaching, they may not want you back!"

"I'm shaking in my boots!" Christopher shot back.

"Commander," Colonel Dunbar said, "now that we've made known the confidential deployment areas to this small nucleus, I think we can call in the rest of the team members."

They filed in noisily, a buzz of anticipation filling the air. The colonel raised his hands to get the group's attention.

"Well, look at yourselves. Go ahead. Turn around and look at each other. What do you see?"

The group looked around, not sure what they were supposed to be looking for.

"I see a room of confident, prepared Christian commandos!" declared the colonel.

"At the beginning of the summer you were raw and nervous. You stumbled over your own shoestrings. By about the third week, some of you were ready to quit. I should know—I've had your rooms bugged!"

"Really?" Phil asked.

Everyone laughed.

"But you worked hard, gained confidence, and finished your training. Now you're ready! You're green and unseasoned, but so is every commando on his or her first mission. All I can tell you is to remember your training, rely on the Lord, and stay alert.

"Paul told the Ephesians in chapter six to use their armor and weapons with prayer. Pray every chance you get, then pray every chance you don't get. And if I were the devil, I'd be nervous. The army of God is coming!"

A chorus of cheers went up.

As Colonel Dunbar took his seat, Christopher took over.

The room grew completely quiet. Christopher opened his

well-worn Bible. Others pulled out Bibles or smartphones.

"In Luke 10, when Jesus sent out his seventy disciples on their short-term mission, he told them to go to new regions, look for people of peace who would accept them, and share the gospel through their lines of relationship. Jesus knew the Holy Spirit would go ahead of them to prepare those people in advance. In the same way, the Holy Spirit is convicting people right now, preparing these 'houses of peace' for your message.

"The disciples were to tell the people, 'The kingdom of God has come near to you.' In other words, Jesus is coming. God is about to usher in His Kingdom. Be ready. He's coming—for some as Deliverer, for others as Judge. We all need to be prepared. That was the clear message. There was an urgency, and there were remarkable results. Satan's kingdom was falling.

"Brothers and sisters, if we are to succeed in seeing Matthew 24:14 fulfilled in the coming decade—the gospel going to all people groups in preparation for Christ's return—then this same message must be on our lips. What is there to keep Jesus from coming back in ten or fifteen years? That's not much time, is it?

"If Jesus is coming back soon, do you have time for a relaxed witness? Share the expectancy of Jesus' imminent return with your people groups. Don't just tell them 'Jesus loves you.' Tell them 'Jesus is coming soon, and we have to go tell others!' When they realize the time is short, they will be eager to spread the word among family and friends.

"You *are* a Kingdom Preparation Force. Don't settle for less. Millions of eternities are at stake. Let's *hasten* the day! Don't stop until there is *no place left!*"

TWENTY

Marlene Hayes rushed into Senator Wroth's office.

"He has redeployed, sir!"

Wroth looked up unperturbed. "Who are you talking about?"

"Colonel Dunbar! Not only did he spurn your request for him to take the Rome job, but now he has deployed again. He has come out of retirement."

Wroth slammed a hand on the mahogany desk. "What? Who got him? You get me that general on the line this instant! Dunbar belongs to *me!*"

Marlene's face almost matched her red hair. "None in the armed forces, sir. He's gone to work f-f-for the Christians! He's redeploying to Southeast Asia, and is wrapped up with some pseudo-commando Christian organization—something called the Kingdom Preparation Force."

Marlene watched Wroth's face. For once it registered true bewilderment. In a moment, however, his visage grew stony.

Wroth leaned back in his chair and tapped the ends of his fingers together. "Christians, huh? He's slyer than I thought. What a great cover!" He laughed. "Get Jake in here immediately, and make sure we are not disturbed."

* * *

Marlene ushered Simmons in. He stood at full attention.

Wroth cleared his throat. "At ease, Jake. We've got a situation that calls for the utmost discretion. I need you to tail Colonel Win Dunbar to Southeast Asia. He's using a Christian organization as his cover, yet I find it hard to believe he has no political motive in this. He is no doubt attempting to undermine me in some way—perhaps through the Chinese."

Simmons shifted his feet uneasily. "Uh, sir. The colonel was my mentor. He'll recognize me immediately. Besides that, he taught me everything I know. He's forgotten more strategy than I've ever learned."

Wroth leaned forward and spoke in a whisper, forcing Simmons to cock his head forward. "Jake, I don't mean *you*. I mean your forces. He must be observed discreetly, and if necessary, thwarted without him realizing it is us."

Marlene edged closer to catch every word.

Jake's voice grew hoarse. "Uh, yes, sir. I understand. But . . ."

Wroth slapped a hand on the desk. Marlene jumped. *This is clearly getting under his skin. What is it about this Dunbar?*

"Spit it out, man! What's the problem?"

Jake diverted his eyes from Wroth's gaze. "Well, sir. It's like this. Colonel Dunbar is a legend. Soldiers worship him. I don't know of an American soldier or private mercenary that would lift a finger against him. Besides, no one can outfox him. Surely you've heard . . .?"

Wroth rose and shoved his chair against the wall. Simmons stood at full attention. "And what about you, Simmons?"

Simmons looked straight ahead. He spoke woodenly. "My allegiance is to *you*, sir."

Marlene blinked twice but said nothing.

"Get this straight, soldier. I hired you because you have been trained by Dunbar. It is time for you to rise above your mentor. Think beyond our mere U.S. assets. It is time to bring the full force of The Ten against him."

Wroth looked around the room, then glanced at Marlene. "Are we completely secure here?"

Marlene nodded.

"Then, Jake, you will use our connections through The Ten to activate foreign assets. But that circle of conspirators must know nothing of this. Do you understand?"

Simmons cleared his throat. "Absolutely, sir. Neither Dunbar nor The Ten will have any idea of our movements."

Wroth straightened his tie and sat down again. "You better be absolutely sure of this, soldier. One misstep on either side, and Dunbar or The Ten could bring us down in a moment. Do not underestimate either of them.

"Remember: influence without being known to influence."

TWENTY ONE

On the field, priorities suddenly become crystal clear.
Lostness stares me in the face, hems me in all about.
Issues are black and white, life and death.
How many of our church squabbles, debates of theology,
and worries about politics could be set aside
by getting our eyes back on the lost masses?
The priority of their eternal destiny trumps all these lesser things.
—Ruth Grant

As they waited for their flight to Guangzhou, China, the KPF team assigned to Tuxiang tried to get comfortable in the crowded rows of fixed chairs at Gate 123. It was 1 a.m., and there was still no indication when the flight—originally scheduled for 11:42— might depart. Christopher read while Chara rested with her head on his shoulder. Their children dozed fitfully in various awkward positions, with the exception of David who managed to curl into a tiny ball on the seat of his chair.

On the next aisle, Ruth and Kellie tried to catch a few winks while Phil and Lance played their fourth game of chess and George and Julie talked together quietly. Opposite them sat a short, middle-aged Chinese man dressed in a dark suit. No one sat on either side of him, which was a little unusual given how crowded the gate was. Perhaps it was because he was so restless: standing up, sitting down, going to the counter and fussing at the attendants, then doing it all over again. Occasionally he would go to the nearby security checkpoint to protest loudly in Mandarin, but none of the security personnel could understand him. Julie eventually ventured to speak to him.

"Excuse me, sir. Can we help you with something?"

The man looked up without much hope.

"Sorry. Not speak much English," he said.

Julie looked at George for help.

"I'm not sure my Mandarin is ready for this yet." George said. He struggled to put the right words together. "Excuse me, sir. I speak some Mandarin. Is there a problem I can help you with?"

"You're an American. But you speak Mandarin?"

"My dad and all of my grandparents came from Taiwan. My name is George Yang. What is upsetting you?"

"Thank you, Yang. I am Ching Fei. Yes, I have a problem. I just arrived from San Francisco on American Airlines, but the flight was delayed. There will not be another flight with China National Airlines for three more days, so I rushed to get to this. But in my hurry I left my briefcase on the other plane. When I got here I realized my error, but the staff and security people tell me I cannot leave here. I *must* get that briefcase. It contains all the work from my trip here."

George looked at the relaxed gate attendants and said, "It doesn't look like we're going anywhere for a while. If we hurry, we should be able to get there and back in time."

The pair walked quickly to the security checkpoint, but the young female TSA agent stopped them. "If you're here for the China National flight, you can't leave."

George said, "This gentleman left an important briefcase on his flight from San Francisco. We need to go get it before that plane leaves."

"I'm sorry, but if you want to travel on this flight, you'll need to stay put. It could board at any time."

"Surely you can make an exception in this case."

"No exceptions. If the gentleman has lost a bag, he can fill out a form at the baggage counter and have his briefcase forwarded on another flight."

George interpreted this for the man, who became even more dejected. Then George turned back to the agent.

"Ma'am, you don't understand. That briefcase contains all of his work from this business trip—work he will need to refer to when he returns to the office."

"Sir, rules are rules. If I let you go out, all of the people sitting here are going to want to go eat at the restaurant or shop or whatever, and we'll never get them boarded. This is the last flight out for the evening. Go back to your seats."

George felt stymied.

"Are you sure you can't make an exception?" Christopher asked from behind Ching Fei. Hearing the commotion, he had come to the aid of his teammate.

"No, sir."

"This poor man has been pleading with you for over an hour and a half. He could very well have gotten there and back long before now. What kind of impression does this make on visiting dignitaries and business people?"

The agent hesitated.

"C'mon,"—Christopher glanced at her nametag—"...Carla. I'll bet you could solve this problem. You could send a TSA agent to escort him to Terminal Four and back in no time. Think about what this would do for United States-China relations! You've got that latitude. What better way to make a difference today!"

Christopher could see the wheels turning in Carla's head.

"You're right," she said at last. The young woman motioned a coworker over and spoke to him privately. He hurriedly loaded George and Ching Fei onto a security cart and whisked them out through the checkpoint with lights flashing and horn beeping.

The TSA driver flashed them a huge smile. "Hi! I'm Stan. This sure beats handing people little plastic trays with their valuables as they pass through the checkpoint. Now hold on!"

The cart rushed down the walkway, around construction detours, and through a service area, eventually arriving at the tarmac leading to Terminal Four.

As they drove, Ching Fei described the bag and his seating location. George translated, and Stan relayed the details through his walkie-talkie.

Fifteen minutes later, an airport police officer rushed out from a Terminal 4 side door, briefcase in hand.

"I'm awful sorry about this mix-up, Mr. Ambassador," he shouted over the din of nearby jet engines. "It took us a while to track your bag down as the plane had already been cleaned. I hope you and your assistant make your flight!"

"Ambassador?" George whispered to Stan.

"Shh!"

"Thank you, officer!" Stan shouted. "We've got to hustle back;

their plane is boarding."

Without waiting for a reply, Stan set the cart in motion while using his walkie-talkie to let Carla know they were on their way. He bypassed the terminal entrance and pulled the cart alongside the exterior steps to the Gate 123 jet bridge.

"The plane's already boarded," he shouted to George. "But don't worry, I've taken care of everything."

Stan bounded up the steps two at a time with George and Ching Fei right behind. Carla stood at the top, making sure the attendants didn't close the aircraft door.

"Mr. Fei, we hope you had a wonderful stay in America," she said. "It was our pleasure to help you find your bag and help with the success of your trip. If there is anything Stan or I can do to be of service to you on your next trip, you only have to ask."

She handed him a business card.

Ching Fei eyed George with amazement.

"Who are you and your friend Christopher?" he asked as the two men walked into the aircraft.

"Oh, we're followers of Jesus Christ who try to treat others the way we would want to be treated."

Now back in *his* element, Ching Fei spoke to the flight attendants in rapid Mandarin. They escorted him to his first class seat, while George searched out his companions in coach. All eyes were on George as he sat down next to Lance.

"Dude!" whispered Lance. "I thought we were supposed to keep a low profile!"

As the airplane taxied from the gate, a flight attendant approached the Tuxiang team.

"Officer Ching would be pleased if the twelve of you would join him in first class, compliments of the Chinese government."

The team gathered their carry-ons and made their way up the aisle of the taxiing plane, through the curtain, and into the seats of their choice—for aside from Ching Fei, the first class section was empty.

George sat down across the aisle from Ching Fei and tried his Mandarin again.

"*Officer* Ching? You didn't tell me you are an officer!"

"You never asked. I have just a small government position.

But your escort and my government ID make the flight crew think I am more important than I am."

He looked directly into George's eyes.

"Besides, this is the least I can do for all the help you and your Christian friends have given me."

"Thank you!"

George leaned back uneasily, a little concerned about the way Ching Fei had emphasized the word *Christian*.

* * *

"Thank you again for help in Los Angeles," said Ching Fei. "Without your help I not sure your friend get us through security. But I still not understand why you want teach in southern Yunnan."

Despite his limited English, Ching Fei's conversation with Christopher lasted for hours. Sometimes they switched over to Mandarin, which Christopher struggled with despite studying several semesters for his work with Chinese international students. Frequently they settled into a sort of "Chinglish."

"We love getting to know Chinese people, especially those who have had little exposure to the West. Since I'm a Christian, I love to tell others about God's love for them. This opportunity arose for me to teach, improve my Mandarin, and get to know Chinese people, as well as the minority nationalities, better."

"Ah! Chinese minority nationalities are an important part of China history! Very good, very good!"

"I think so, too. Most good English teachers don't want to go to a remote college like this one, so I think we'll be real assets there. I'm still young and able to do this sort of thing."

Christopher sensed that Ching Fei was more important than he let on and hoped he would perceive their intentions as good, even though they were Christians. This whole encounter seemed like a "divine appointment," which Christopher thought might open the door for the team in some unexpected way.

A voice over the loudspeaker interrupted their conversation, first in rapid Mandarin and Cantonese, then in something meant to pass for English. Unable to decipher it, Christopher asked Ching Fei.

"Did you understand what the flight attendant said?"

"Yes. We are preparing to land. Fasten seat belt."

"Thanks. You have made this flight so much more enjoyable."

"You have been kind to me. I have only begun to repay you."

* * *

Looking at the long lines at immigration, the KPF team resigned themselves to a long wait.

Suddenly, a commotion erupted near one of the immigration stations. Following a brief, loud objection, the crowds parted like the Red Sea to make way for a short Chinese man accompanied by six uniformed officers. Ching Fei and his cadre were heading directly for the KPF team.

"A Communist country," Phil muttered to Lance, "totalitarian government. This doesn't look good. I figured that they might discover us, but not so quickly."

George did his best to interpret for the team as Ching Fei spoke rapidly in Mandarin. "He wants our passports—now. Then we are to follow these officers to identify our luggage."

The team handed passports and immigration forms to George, who surrendered them to Ching Fei.

Ching Fei gave the whole stack to an officer who turned sharply and left.

"Quickly. Follow me!" barked Ching Fei.

The whole group, surrounded by the officers, walked past the immigration officer who kept his eyes down as they passed.

"What do you think they'll do to us?" Chara whispered to Christopher.

"I've no idea. We haven't broken any laws yet. Of course, if they're hoping to find something against us in our luggage, the Bibles we brought might be an issue."

The officers herded the group to the baggage claim area.

"You identify luggages to officer who put them in special area. After identify luggages, go to waiting area next to me."

In a daze of jet lag and disbelief, the Tuxiang team members scoured the assortment of suitcases and boxes to identify their bags. These were then tagged by an officer with orange tape and moved to a cordoned area.

While the Owen boys thought the whole ordeal was "cool," Elizabeth began crying. "Mommy, why are they doing this? Are they going to take us to jail?"

Chara wrapped the five-year-old in her arms, brushing away her long tresses. "Don't worry, princess. Jesus is taking care of us. His angels are here with us," she whispered.

"But Mommy, I'm scared!"

"Don't be scared, sweetheart. What's the worst thing that can happen?"

"They'll put us in jail?"

"Is that the worst thing you can think of?" questioned Chara.

"They could kill us." Tears streaming down Elizabeth's face.

"I think you're right. That's the worst they could do to us, and I don't think anything like that will happen. But even if it does, then what? What happens if they kill us?"

Elizabeth hesitated, then a grin spread across her face. "We'll go to heaven!" she whispered excitedly.

"Exactly, honey. So don't worry, they can't really hurt us."

Elizabeth's eyes lit up, full of confidence and faith. "So Jesus' angels are here to guard us, right, Mommy? They'll either guard us from getting hurt here, or they'll guard us so we get to heaven safely."

Chara's throat tightened so that she couldn't reply. She just wrapped her treasure in a hug of affection.

"Okay, let's go. Leave bags here. Hurry!" Ching Fei motioned for the group to follow him and the other officers, while another officer stayed to watch the team's bags. Christopher had hoped Ching Fei meant well, but when they were separated from their luggage, he began to expect the worst.

Okay, Lord, we were honest and loving with him. I'm scared to death. It's up to You to turn what he means for evil into good.

Glancing at his watch, Ching Fei spoke to several officers and quickened his pace. One of the officers ran ahead, disappearing around a corner. Three other officers picked up the smallest three Owen children so that the group could move faster.

"Christopher, walk with me," called Ching Fei.

Christopher hurried ahead to keep pace with Ching Fei.

"You missed plane to Kunming. You fly with me to Kunming

on new plane. No waiting in lines. No time."

"So that's what's happening?" Christopher said incredulously. "You're helping us get to Kunming?"

"Yes, of course. I told you. I just begin to help," Ching Fei said, as if surprised there would be any question. "All is taken care of. Just follow me."

Ching Fei led them to a domestic gate where an officer stood holding the plane for them. Ching Fei explained that their bags were also being whisked to this plane so that they would arrive with them.

* * *

In Kunming the team travelled with Ching Fei in government SUVs from the airport to the Kunming South Bus Station.

Outside the station, Ruth and Kellie stared in shock.

"I've never seen so many people in all my life!" exclaimed Ruth to Kellie. "They're everywhere. Most of them are lost and without much opportunity to hear the gospel. How many do you think die in this city each day without Jesus? And this is a small city for China—just six million people!"

Masses of humanity pressed around them. As people passed people they showed no recognition of being fellow human beings; they treated one another as obstacles between them and their destination. Individuals by the hundreds pushed past each other, around carts, through oncoming bicycles and motorbikes, and between the ubiquitous, blue compact taxis. Pedal powered carts piled mile-high with goods for the market streamed by, while alien aromas filled the air.

Sounds battled for supremacy in the surrounding cacophony: the ceaseless honking of horns, the clinging of bicycle bells, the hawking shouts of street vendors, the loud haggling over the price of goods, and the shrill whistle of a policeman attempting to influence the torrent of traffic. Everywhere—people!

On top of their jet lag, Kellie began feeling her first waves of culture shock. "Ruth, surely God can't stand the tragedy of them filling up hell. I know He must be ready to do something major. If we sense the horror of so many going to hell, what does *He* feel who hears the scream of every soul that misses heaven?"

"Yes, you're right," Ruth said sadly. "Thousands of people groups. And we Americans don't know the name of more than a handful. How could so many hundreds of millions have gone so unnoticed by the Christian world for so long? I've never seen anything like this, even in New York City."

As the team watched the crowd, Ching Fei arrived with a young Chinese man.

"This is Zhi Liang. He help you go Nancheng by bus and to Yunnan Southern University. He work for me and is good man. His English much better than mine."

"Welcome to China," said Zhi Liang.

Christopher protested that it wasn't necessary to send Zhi Liang with them, but Ching Fei insisted repeatedly, giving Christopher his business card and making him promise to call if there were any problems.

Exhausted, the team members grabbed their luggage, grateful now that they had been limited to one easy-to-carry suitcase plus a personal backpack. Zhi Liang led the group in weaving through the crowd to the right gate. The trip was hardest on the youngest children, who could no longer tell morning from evening. But the ten-hour bus ride seemed mercifully short because everyone except Ruth slept the whole way.

Ruth, however, seemed energized. She opened her journal to record all that had happened so far. Every change in the passing scenery prompted a new entry: a man plowing in a water-logged rice paddy behind a trudging water buffalo; a busy scene of fruit, vegetable, and meat stands in a small town market; the endless terraced mountainsides; and cascading waterfalls around each bend in the road.

The team found Nancheng—set amidst the rich, green mountains of southern Yunnan province—far less oppressive than the teeming masses of Kunming. By the time they reached Yunnan Southern University, it was late Friday night. Zhi Liang had phoned ahead so that a small welcome party was waiting to take them to their rooms in an old administration building segregated from the rest of the students, a small wing of which had been cordoned off and converted into a semi-Westernized set of apartments.

Two units, each with one tiny bedroom and one bathroom, housed the six singles. The Owens were provided their own two-bedroom unit with a bathroom. All three units shared a common kitchen and dining/living area. Although the local staff couldn't imagine why Americans prefer such an arrangement, in an act of abundant hospitality the university had even converted all three toilets from standard squat-pots to Western toilets. By southern Yunnan standards, the group would be living in luxury.

Christopher called the group together for a short prayer of thanks and ordered everyone to sleep in as long as possible. The team members gladly obeyed—they only had until Monday to get rested for their classes.

Christopher—the last one to bed—wasn't sure why Zhi Liang stayed in their common living area until after they had all gone to bed. When they awoke the next day, he was gone, presumably back to Kunming.

TWENTY TWO

Somewhere in this mass of non-responders
is a person prepared by the Holy Spirit.
I will give myself no rest till I find her.
She is the key to a movement of God.

—Ruth Grant

Christopher began teaching English immediately and quickly established a rapport with his students. He sensitively introduced the topics of God, Christ, and eternity into the classroom. Occasionally students came to his office or stayed after class to talk with him, but they always seemed leery of being too open with their questions.

Chara spent much of her time homeschooling, although the kids also attended a half-day Chinese school to accelerate their language acquisition. Chara divided the rest of her time between her own informal language learning—strategically arranged with Tuxiang students—and making a home for the team with meals, medicine, and mothering.

The six young singles—George, Lance, Phil, Julie, Kellie, and Ruth—were very purposeful with their time outside of their Mandarin classes. Several times a week they held "conversation corners" in which students could gather together in a quiet spot on campus to talk with them in English. These were always well attended, as the students were naturally inquisitive and eager for the opportunity to practice their book-learned English with the native English speakers—something none of the students had ever encountered.

Altogether the team was only interacting with a fraction of the thousands of students, but this fit their strategic objective of starting something that could take root and grow rapidly before it was noticed by the officials.

Whenever the team debriefed indoors, they took special care

to speak cryptically, using terms they had practiced during boot camp, and not to refer to any student by name. Then, as the weather permitted, they would take a walk after dinner to find a quiet place in the countryside where they could talk and pray more openly. One nice November evening, Ruth broached a growing concern.

"I've become increasingly frustrated over the past two months, and I don't think it's just culture shock, though we've all felt a bit of that."

Everyone nodded.

"I'm sure feeling culture shock," Lance said. "Kids pooping on the sidewalk, people spitting on the floor in restaurants, old men shooting snot-rockets on the ground."

"What bothers me most," chimed in seven-year-old Joshua, the Owens' oldest, "is the way everyone stares at me and wants to touch my hair or skin!"

"I know we have to adjust to that kind of stuff," Ruth said, "but that's not what is bothering me.

"I didn't, by any stretch of the imagination, expect to see a fellowship planted yet, but I feel like we're not getting anywhere with our witness. We're bold and purposeful in our witnessing, but no one is responding. And they are so lost. One student asked me, '*What* is a Jesus?' Not *who*! *What*? Can you imagine?"

Several nodded in agreement. The lack of any understanding about God among the students shocked each of them deeply.

"They are so lost. And they don't even seem interested," Ruth continued. "At this rate, I don't see that we'll bring anyone to Christ this year, let alone start a church."

"Yeah," Phil agreed, "we might as well go home for all the good we're doing!"

Others murmured in agreement.

Christopher broke in.

"Okay, let's talk about this. Ruth has raised an important issue which can lead either to despair and defeat or ... to a deeper trust in God and victory."

Chara said, "What you mean is 'Let's wrestle through this honestly,' right?"

Christopher looked at her and nodded appreciatively. She had a way of clarifying his words so others understood them better.

"I agree with Ruth," Kellie said. "I've been feeling this too, and I don't think it's because of a lack of prayer. Every day we are crying out to God in our early morning prayer times and throughout the day. But unless God does something, nothing will happen. I feel a need to dedicate more time to prayer … and to fast, too."

"Perhaps," said Christopher, "we need to spend some time *now* praying and hearing what God has to say regarding our situation. Let's skip our regular after-dinner debriefings and each spend extra time alone over the next three days—praying, fasting as we feel led, reading our Bibles, and asking God for guidance. The Lord didn't bring us here to fail. As we wait upon Him, He will reveal His plans—He always does."

* * *

The three days passed quickly, and the group reassembled to see if there were any new insights.

"Bros and sisses," Lance said hesitantly in his own unique vernacular. "I think the Lord showed me something."

The group was quite visibly surprised. Lance was always solid and dependable, but he was known more as a jokester than someone who offered critical insight.

"Like, you know, we've been basing our ministry and stuff a lot on Luke 10, right? So I go back to it to figure out what we're doing wrong. I mean, if it worked for Jesus' disciples, why not for us, right?

"When I went back and read it, I got this radical thought, like I was in the disciple dudes' own shoes. We read it today from a modern perspective, but this stuff's ancient history. So I read it thinking, 'Okay, think of yourself as Lance, the disciple.'"

Lance's teammates chuckled.

"Hey, go ahead and laugh. But I say if a smelly fisherman could be a disciple, so could I. So, anyway," Lance continued, "I think of myself as a disciple following this Jesus guy around some hot, dry countryside for a year or two. Every day I see Him doing some amazing miracle, things only God could do, telling me to believe that I can do it also.

"Then one day, He sends me and disciple George out. He tells us to go into some new villages where He hasn't been yet, where He's going to come in a few weeks. But in the meantime, we're supposed to get these towns ready for His coming. So we leave, a little scared at being all alone—lambs among wolves and all that stuff—but we go and do the same thing all of us have been doing. We start looking for these people of peace.

"Why? Because there's no motel, dudes! We're starving and cold at night, so we need to find someone hospitable. Some dude walks by us, sees we're strangers who are hungry, and feels sorry for us. Shazzam! We're staying in the Bethel Bed and Breakfast with Mom and Pop Methuselah."

Lance ignored the snickers in the group.

"Bear with me! After a warm meal and hot bath, they ask us, 'What are you boys doing here?'

"We say, 'Oh, we're here telling everybody about the Messiah. He's arrived in Israel.'

"What's their response? They chuckle and humor us, but then Pop says, 'Now, boys. I can see your excitement, but we've had our share of messiahs, and none have turned out to be legit. But, seeing as how you're nice boys, you can stay anyway as long as you need to.'

"We begin thinking, dude, these people are nice and even listen a little, but they don't believe, much less want to make a commitment to Jesus. Then it dawns on us what Jesus said. The light in our attic flickers on, and we get to thinking, 'We were once like that. What changed us? We saw Jesus do what only God could do!' Then we recall Jesus' final words to us before we left Him. See, it's right here in Luke 10:9: 'Heal those ... who are sick, and tell them, 'The kingdom of God has come near to you.'

"Now, we've never done this before, but we realize we need to show some convincing proof that Jesus is different, that things are about to change. So the next time Pop Methuselah's daughter, Methuselina, is sick in bed with a fever, we gather the whole family and pray for her in the name of Jesus and command her to get up. And Shazzam again! She gets up. Miracle! And then Pop Methuselah says, 'What did you say the name of this messiah was again?'

"From that point on we begin to tell them that the Kingdom has come to their village, and the King is on His way to see them. Everything's going to be different now because this new King has awesome power. We start praying and doing things that can only be explained as coming from God. And any day we expect to see Jesus walking down the street to see if we've been getting the town ready for Him. *Now* people are listening and repenting. Why? Because we prayed fervently in our daily team meeting? No, that was just the foundation. People start listening because they see us doing something that's never been done there before. It validates what we've been telling them, and now they believe. We're bold and take risks, trusting God openly for God-sized stuff. That's the difference!"

No one spoke, and Lance began to fidget, wondering if he had been wrong to get so serious.

"Don't get me wrong. I don't mean to imply we have to work miracles, but somehow we've got to show that knowing Christ and His Kingdom affects things supernaturally. A miracle or two might shake things up a little."

Christopher was carefully watching everyone's faces.

"Wow!" Kellie finally said. "This is going to seem really strange, but I read Matthew 10 and had just the same impression. Jesus is even clearer there about telling the disciples to work miracles. We are missing this element of bold expectation. We aren't putting ourselves and God's Kingdom on the line the way those disciples did. I've had several students tell me that what I believe might be right, but that there are many paths to God—if He even exists.

"Sounds like in Luke 10 and Matthew 10 the issue was settled pretty quickly when the Kingdom of God broke out in a clear way. We've focused on telling people about Jesus. But we've thought very little about pursuing His practical, supernatural intervention in people's lives. In fact, one of my classmates that I've been witnessing to is sick. If I tell her that I am going to pray for her to be healed and God does heal her, I think she's going to believe. That's something years of simply witnessing may not accomplish."

"Yeah? But what if God doesn't heal her? What then?" asked

George. "We live in a world full of sickness where people die. Hospital rooms are full of believers praying faithfully, and people still die. What are the implications if God chooses not to heal?"

Kellie started to defend her idea but was interrupted by soft-spoken Ruth. "That's why we never do stuff like this. We're afraid that God isn't going to come through. George, I know your dad's a doctor with a deep faith in God and has struggled with this. But we are in a critical spot, seeking the Lord's direction in this time, in this place. God is speaking to *this* group.

"He doesn't always choose to act in this manner, but if He is now, we should be brave enough to move forward. It seems to me that if we ignore His leading on this, we're letting people go to hell. George, most Christians I know—including myself—use your question as a convenient excuse not to take a risk like this."

Ruth's eyes glistened with fervor.

"Well, I'm ready to take a risk!" she continued. "After all, God is big enough to take care of His own reputation! And as far as I can see, everyone around us is already stampeding toward hell. I don't think anything we try can drive them there any faster, even if we fail!"

"I guess you're right. It's time to expect God to do God-sized works!" conceded George. "We're commandos in the Kingdom Preparation Force. We'll never see the miraculous until we step out in faith. I don't know that I've ever seen a real miracle, but I'm ready to trust God to do something new. And—knowing this group—I'm not too concerned that we'll go off the deep end theologically."

Christopher sensed that he had let the conversation go on long enough.

"I'm glad the Lord is speaking to several of you this way, because I've been drawn to the same conclusion over the past few weeks," he said. "This is a time-defined mission, and we have to accomplish our objective before we leave.

"Mark 16:20 reads, 'Then the disciples went out and preached everywhere, and the Lord worked with them and confirmed his word by the signs that accompanied it.'

"And listen to Acts 4:29–30. 'Now, Lord, consider their threats and enable your servants to speak your word with great boldness. Stretch out your hand to heal and perform signs and wonders through the name of your holy servant Jesus.'

"I've waited to suggest this because it involves increased risk. You do all understand that there may be consequences we haven't yet considered, right? I've been meditating on this a lot. We ourselves need to obey *all* of Jesus' commands in Luke 10. We also need to consider the fact that *only* when we lay down our lives and bear the consequences will we see fruit. Listen to Jesus' words in John 12:24: 'Very truly I tell you, unless a kernel of wheat falls to the ground and dies, it remains only a single seed. But if it dies, it produces many seeds.'"

Christopher closed his Bible and watched his team's faces.

"As team commander I could make a unilateral decision. But since taking greater risks will affect all of us, I want us all in agreement that this is what God is leading us to do. Does anyone have an objection to where this is going?"

No one spoke. Phil started to say something but held his tongue. Christopher waited several minutes.

"This is the kind of commitment and expectation we had when we signed up," Ruth finally said. "I think we've all agreed that we need to go for it. Besides, you're our commander. We're following your lead."

When Christopher checked in with the leaders of the other KPF teams that night, he shared the process and conclusions of the Tuxiang team and encouraged the others to seek the Lord about how to implement this strategy in their own contexts.

The next day, the Tuxiang team members began actively seeking opportunities to demonstrate the power of God's Kingdom to their classmates. Although expectant, they were also nervous.

Days passed, and embarrassment settled over team meetings. Their initial enthusiasm faded into wondering whether God had really spoken or if they had simply indulged in wishful thinking.

* * *

As two girls joined Ruth at their regular conversation corner, she noticed that their roommate was missing again.

"Is everything okay with Yijing?"

The girls looked down, not wanting to bring shame on their friend by telling a foreigner about her situation. Yet the nice American seemed to really care about them.

"Teacher," one of the girls answered, "Yijing have high fever. This happen to her often. Problem since she little child. Yijing stay in bed one, two weeks. Doctors no can do anything. Yijing just rest and get behind in school—sometimes fail class. She not want you to know; you maybe worry. She very sorry have to miss conversation corner."

Ruth felt concern for Yijing, then remembered Luke 10 and prayed silently in her spirit. Scanning the small group of regular attenders, she made a critical decision.

"I'm afraid I have to cancel today's conversation," she said to the group. "Most of you know I'm a follower of Jesus. I think that if Jesus were here, He would leave all of you who are well to go take care of Yijing who is sick."

She turned to Yijing's roommates. "Please take me to her."

At the dorm entrance, the girls were intercepted by the gruff Communist dorm mother who spoke sharply in Tuxiang. Yijing's friends translated.

"No foreigners allowed in Chinese student dormitory."

Ruth felt emboldened in her spirit.

"Tell her that God sent me here to pray for Yijing to get well," she said.

The two girls were shocked by Ruth's message, but the clear resolve of their American friend and the intense look in her eyes prompted them to translate what she had said. It took the dorm mother a moment to process this, but she finally pushed the sign-in sheet toward Ruth, obtained her name and ID number, and waved her through the entry.

The two girls led Ruth by the hand through dark, windowless corridors to a small room with one set of bunk beds, another small cot, and not much room for anything else. On the cot lay Yijing, sleeping fitfully. Beads of sweat rolled down her face. Her drenched hair plastered her head.

One of the girls gently shook her awake. Yijing smiled weakly when she saw Ruth. She attempted to speak but began coughing instead and then drifted back to sleep.

Her roommate began crying. "I worry about her. It never so bad before. Yijing not want us to tell anyone."

"Why haven't you taken her to the hospital?"

Both girls fell silent.

"We have no money," one finally said quietly, "and thought the hospital would cost too much."

Kneeling next to the cot, Ruth took Yijing's fiery-hot hand in her own.

"I will help pay the doctor's fee. Let me text my friend to see if he can get a doctor at this hour. But while we wait, there is something more I must do."

She paused.

I've never done this before, but I can't stand to see Yijing so sick.

"The God I serve is here, and He is powerful. He loves each of us, and He loves Yijing dearly. You remember me telling you He loves us so much that He sent His Son Jesus to die for our sins? Well, that same Jesus is here, even though you can't see Him."

The girls looked around the small room nervously.

"The Bible tells us that one time Jesus healed a woman with a fever similar to this. He wants to heal Yijing because He loves her and so that all of you will believe in Him. I'm going to pray for Yijing in the name of Jesus."

"Teacher Ruth, the doctors no can do anything for Yijing. They try in past, but no can do anything! If God can do something, please try. We afraid for Yijing."

Ruth, seeing the pleading in their eyes, bent over the still form of Yijing. She felt compelled to lay her body across the seemingly lifeless girl. For a few minutes, she prayed silently, groaning softly. Then she began to pray aloud, as much for the girls' benefit as for Yijing's. A growing compulsion rose within her as she cried out, asking God to shower His mercy on Yijing.

"Oh, Father, glorify Your Name in this place!"

Almost a half hour passed as Yijing continued to lie deathly still, occasionally muttering in delirium, yet Ruth never wavered in the faith that had overtaken her. She wiped her brow with a wet cloth.

The two roommates watched with keen interest, careful not to make a sound. They were filled with superstitious awe, sensing that something spiritual was happening.

Yijing's coughs broke the silence. Spasms ran through her body. She cried out two or three times, and her roommates feared that she might be dying.

But Ruth's faith remained firm as she continued praying, lying prostrate on Yijing's body until she was quiet.

Then Ruth felt the fever break like a cool wave flowing across the still form. She stood up, and Yijing opened her eyes. Where Yijing's eyes had been swollen and bloodshot during her fever, now they were clear and lucid.

"Teacher! I am well!"

Yijing looked up and down her body, felt her forehead, and probed her former aches.

Ruth grabbed a glass of cool water and forced Yijing to drink all of it.

"I am well!" Yijing said again. "Teacher ... your Jesus! As you were praying, I had dream ... *real* dream, not imagination."

The eyes of both roommates widened.

"The spirit of one of my ancestors called to me, telling me I must not fight fever. It part of family curse. I must let it punish my family fully. If not, will pass on to my children. I recognize this spirit. It speak to me often during my fevers.

"But before he finish, a man in white stand before him. He tell me His name Jesus ... your Jesus, Teacher! He tell me that my ancestor spirit lies. Jesus speak to me in my Tuxiang language!

"'Yijing,' He say, 'this spirit not your ancestor. This evil spirit!' Then He rip mask off, and I see horrible evil spirit!

"I cry out in my dream, but Jesus say not be afraid. He tell me no more fevers. He tell me listen to you. Then He touch my head, and I am well. I open my eyes and you are here. Teacher, your Jesus heal me!"

The other two roommates stared in shock as Yijing quickly repeated this to them in Tuxiang.

"No, Yijing," Ruth answered, "not *my* Jesus. He is now *your* Jesus. Do you believe now that He is God, and that He is alive today?"

Yijing looked at her two friends, then nervously at the door.

"Yes," the girl said. "Yes! I not know much about Jesus, but I know He is alive. And He has done what doctors no can do. And I know He do this because He ..." she choked back her tears. "He love *me*! I not know why else He would come to me, but He did!

"Yes, I believe Jesus!" she cried with excitement.

Yijing's two roommates were ready to trust in Jesus also. All four girls cried and shared with joy their first day as sisters, as Ruth took her time to fully explain the gospel to them.

"As far as I know, you are the first Tuxiang people to follow Jesus. He may return to earth soon in judgment. We may not have much time. You must take this good news to your people. If they don't follow Jesus, they will suffer in hell."

This last thought sobered the girls, since relationships are of highest priority in Tuxiang culture. To know that every man, woman, and child of their families and villages was lost and on his or her way to hell drove a knife of grief to the core of their beings. Yet to realize that they were the first bearers of hope among their own people brought a sense of responsibility well beyond anything these girls had ever experienced.

The girls felt as if they alone possessed the antidote for the venom of a serpent that had bitten their people. Whether or not anyone else believed or joined them in proclaiming this good news, these nineteen-year-old women knew they would carry forever the burden of letting their people know about the great salvation they had just received. They were so grateful that God had found them; now they must find others that were lost.

Ruth began reading to them about Pentecost and the early Church. "We need be baptized, too!" Yijing interrupted.

Ruth paused, knowing the value of baptizing new believers, yet also recognizing the gravity of the request.

"Yes," she said hesitantly, "you can and should be baptized. But do you understand that when you are baptized, you may not turn back? Do you realize that when others find out you are followers of Jesus, they may try to harm you?"

Yijing and her friends conversed for a few moments in the Tuxiang dialect, then turned back to Ruth.

"What is there to go back to? We have gone from nothing to everything. We never have joy like this before. We were poor before, but now we have a treasure. We never know God before.

We never have eternal life before. What we have no one can take from us. Please baptize us. We will not turn back."

The two roommates nodded their affirmation.

"Okay," Ruth said. "Let's practice the three questions we will ask at your baptism. First, have you decided to follow Jesus?"

"Yes, we have decided to follow Jesus!"

"Do you know that Jesus has forgiven you of all of your sins?"

"Yes, we know that Jesus has forgiven all of our sins!"

"And are you telling all these witnesses that you will follow Jesus and never turn back?"

"Yes, we are telling these witness that we will follow Jesus and never turn back!"

"Then I think you are ready to be baptized!"

Ruth hugged each of her new sisters.

* * *

Ruth and the three Tuxiang girls stood in the park outside the foreigners' apartments and shared with the rest of the team what had just transpired.

"Teacher Christopher, there is a river just one hour walk from here. It is very red ... how do you say, muddy? But we don't mind. If hurry, can be back before dark."

Chara quickly grabbed towels and blankets. As they walked to the river, Ruth pulled Christopher and Chara aside. "I'm a bit nervous about this. After all, it is my first baptism."

"You'll do fine," Chara said reassuringly. "Christopher will be in the water to guide you. You've practiced this. You can do it."

Soon the group stood on the banks of a lazily flowing river as Ruth and Christopher eased themselves into the cool, autumn water. One by one, the three Tuxiang women joined Ruth and Christopher and declared their allegiance to Christ before being submerged under the flowing waters. They emerged with smiles of great joy to the applause of those watching from the bank. Ruth and Christopher finally exited the water and joined the others in wrapping themselves in towels and blankets.

The three new believers quietly sang a chorus of resolve they had recently learned, but now in their own Tuxiang dialect. Standing on the riverbank, their clothes were permanently stained crimson but their hearts were forever cleansed white.

Those quiet waters—disturbed only momentarily by these intruders—flowed silently through lazy bends before joining the larger Lancang River, merging with the mighty Mekong, and then emptying into the South China Sea hundreds of miles away.

That small body of baptismal water bore silent witness to the first Tuxiang believers in history, but it was not the only witness. As the group returned home another witness trailed them, being careful to make as little noise as possible among the fallen bamboo leaves.

TWENTY THREE

Greely chewed his well-worn fingernails. Should he say something or not? How many times had he brought such news to the attention of Number Eight only to be chided as impetuous and premature in his assessments? The ever-present Indian paced the room watching those under his charge, glancing not infrequently over at the young clerk.

Greely's look of uncertainty sparked a reaction in the prim Indian. "Spit it out, Greely. Something is bothering you. What is it? More predictions of revolutionary doomsday cults?"

"Sir, it is this new Christian missions troop. They have sent at least one team into Southeast Asia. Our contact there is sending weekly reports. Until now, there has not been much cause for concern, but recently they have seen a few locals convert to their religion. Our contact reports that there are rumors of miracles occurring. I think that if ..."

"Greely! A *few* proselytes? *Rumors* of miracles? My word, man, if we ran this organization on rumors and in search of every little group garnering meager results, we would require a staff of tens of thousands. And even then we would never see the forest for the trees! Listen, young man, we are after *trends*, not individual incidents. Did your father not teach you anything?"

"Uh, sir, ... what if this is the beginning of a trend? Do you not think we should perhaps begin tracking it?"

"Of course I do, Greely," Number Eight sighed deeply. "That is why you are at that fine desk of yours! You are supposed to track these incidents and inform me when they merge into a trend. Not before!" He turned away.

"B-b-but, sir," Greely persisted, knowing he would regret it. "You remember that Priority A item you had to report to Number Three? This is the same group. They are growing very—"

Number Eight did not appreciate being reminded of his prior misjudgment. Nor did he like the threat—implied or not—that this underling might inform Number Three.

"I remember everything. That is why I am one of The Ten and you are a monitoring clerk. You will not be a clerk for long, however, if you cannot learn to distinguish between trends and individual, unrelated events."

The other clerks gazed at their screens like robots, hoping not to be noticed.

"In case you do not remember," Number Eight continued, "there is only one way out of this organization for a clerk that cannot function properly."

"Yes, Number Eight."

Greely returned to his computer. Obviously he couldn't go over Number Eight's head for something trivial, but his informant was like a rabid dog on a leash—each of his messages grew more alarming. Somewhere, sometime, something would give.

TWENTY FOUR

Senator Michael Wroth strode into the Oval Office and took his customary position across from the president. Henry Merrit, the National Security Advisor, was already sitting to one side. Outside the window, the last leaves of autumn drifted to the ground.

"Michael, I want to talk to you about an important matter," the president began in his down-home manner.

"As you know, I'm finishing my second term, and the vultures have descended, vying for the right to sit in this office for the next four years. Every day someone asks the question, 'Whom will the president throw his weight behind?' It's an important question because my job approval rating is the highest it's been since I took office. That is due, in no small part, to you and your anti-terrorism efforts."

"*Peace* efforts, Mr. President. I want to focus on preserving world peace, not just nabbing terrorists."

"Yes, of course," the president said, "but the fact is that in the last several months you have managed to shut down several major terrorism networks, thwart a fistful of terrorist attacks on U.S. soil, and strike fear in countries harboring these cowards. America sleeps more peacefully each night because of you."

"Now, Mr. President, I think that's going a bit far."

"Not at all. You're a household name ... a positive one. Even the *press* likes you! Trust me, if you can get them on your side, you can do anything. And not only do you have the backing of the American public, you also actually accomplish things. People like that. I like that. Heck, even Congress has taken a shine to you. It's nice to have them no longer deadlocked. Somehow, you know how to get things done and win people to your way of thinking. That's what a *president* needs."

"Whoa! Hold on, Mr. President!" Senator Wroth sat upright. "I see where you're going with this and you can forget it. I ..."

"Shut up and listen, Michael. Maybe someone needs to knock

you over the head to help you see straight. You're the man the people want. I know it's late to get into the fight, but you could still win hands down. Doesn't matter which of those debaters wins the primaries, they couldn't beat you in an election. You're the one everyone wants. You're the one *I* want. And with my support, you're a shoo-in. Michael, you would be the most powerful man on earth. I know you. You like power. Shoot, even *I* am sometimes putty in your hands."

Senator Wroth stood and paced the floor for a moment before sitting down again.

"Mr. President, your suggestion is very tempting, and it's not the first time I have thought about this. My staff is constantly urging me to run for this office. And you're right, I'd love the power. But there's something more important than that, Mr. President. It has to do with values and ideals. I want to continue in my role of preserving peace."

"That's what I'm talking about, Michael." The president leaned forward earnestly. "From this room, you have the power to check any aggression in the world."

"With all due respect, Mr. President, I have to disagree."

The president raised his eyebrows. "Do you know of a more powerful position than mine?"

"No, sir. Not yet."

Merrit was intrigued. "What exactly do you mean, Senator Wroth?"

Senator Wroth looked at him, then back at the president.

"Mr. President?"

"It's okay," the president said reassuringly. "Whatever you tell me, I would tell him anyway. But nothing confidential will leave this room."

Senator Wroth looked directly at the president.

"Since taking this assignment as the ATTF Director, I have become more interested than ever in achieving and maintaining world peace. Do you realize how close we are? No nation on earth can compete with us as a superpower. And we have used our military might for the good of U.S. citizens and the world.

"Other nations are now looking to us for training in how to thwart terrorism. But they lack the military power and the ground-level intel to actually stop it, especially across borders. The United States can send a commando team into Columbia and who's going to object? But if Costa Rica wants to do the same thing? No dice!"

Senator Wroth stood again. "Gentlemen, for the first time in decades, we are in a position to use our influence to rid the planet of all the violent and intolerant groups that threaten the well-being and tranquility of our world. I'm not just talking about terrorists ... I'm thinking on a grander scale.

"Soon the world won't stand for the United States sending its Special Forces wherever it pleases, even if it is for the good of all. No one likes a bully, even if he is well intentioned. I could win the presidency and continue trying to exert our influence, but the international political climate could swing against us in my first term."

Merrit tried to interrupt, but Senator Wroth ignored him as he resumed his seat.

"What's needed is a new plan. The ATTF was a good idea, but only as a temporary measure. One country can never achieve world peace. We can't even maintain our own internal peace for long. We must establish an *international* body working toward peace—the International Coalition for the Preservation of World Peace. Such an entity would operate essentially like our task force, but with the backing of most of the world's nations."

"Michael, we've been through all this before," the president objected. "No U.N. peacekeeping force has the authority to do anything really, except to sit in their observation posts with their baby-blue helmets on. They can't even shoot unless their lives are threatened!"

Merrit nodded in agreement.

"But Mr. President, I'm not talking about the United Nations. What I am proposing is to bypass them and set up a whole new structure. You have NATO and numerous other international organizations with clout. Why not a new coalition? With your leading and the support of our allies, we can make this thing work—put some real teeth in it. The world is clamoring for someone to step in and eradicate radical terrorists!

"Ordinarily, this might take some time to set up, but I have to be frank for a moment. You were right about my popularity level. It's high not only here, but also around the world. For the first time, nations previously plagued by terrorism and unrest have some hope for peace. At the risk of sounding vain, I think if you propose my name as the first director of this coalition, there might be consensus rather quickly.

"If I were president, I wouldn't be able to pursue this avenue. But as Michael Wroth—an ordinary man from California—I'm much more palatable to the world community."

Now it was the president's turn to pace the floor. Finally he turned to Senator Wroth. "If we give this coalition power, what keeps it from turning against us?"

Wroth said, "That's simple! We supply the troops and foot the bill. We give ourselves the lion's share of the voting ability with first shot at nominating a director. We keep a director allied with the presidency and threaten to pull our troops if it goes in a direction we don't like."

"It might work, Mr. President," Merrit interjected.

"There's only one problem," mused the president. "We still haven't solved the issue of the presidency. Suppose I pull this coalition together in the next few months. What's to keep an opposing president from scrapping the whole thing. Without our support, this International, uh ..."

"International Coalition for the Preservation of World Peace."

"Right, this International Coalition will never work without presidential support. We need someone we can count on in this Oval Office." He paused. "Michael, which of the presidential candidates do you most agree with?"

"I don't know. Springer, I guess."

The president smiled. "Can you control him?"

"Pardon me?" Senator Wroth sputtered.

"You know what I mean; I want to know if you can bend Springer to your way of thinking."

"Well, sir, I believe I can. Yes, I think I can get Springer to see things my way when the need arises, especially if he were to choose Bowen as his running mate."

"All right, it's settled. You and I will both throw our support to Springer. With a little coaching, he will win. In the meantime,

I'll quietly call a few key world leaders to build a consensus for this coalition."

The president leaned forward, signaling the end of the conversation.

"Thank you, Mr. President," Senator Wroth said as he headed for the door. Then he stopped short.

"Mr. President, I will need executive power for this coalition to work, like I have now. Almost absolute power, accountable to the president alone. Without that, it won't happen. None of this will, sir."

* * *

"How did it go?" Marlene asked, back inside the limo.

"Putty. He was putty in my hands."

TWENTY FIVE

Water not running some days. Electricity out other days.
No American food. Missing family and friends.
Unable to communicate well.
They call this culture shock, I guess.
But all this "shock" has become wonderfully bearable
in the joy of reaping our first fruit!
—Ruth Grant

Christopher wondered whether the miracles ever became commonplace for the apostles. *When Peter walked down the street for the umpteenth time with the lame and sick being healed by the touch of his shadow, did it become so routine that he just expected it? As people took handkerchiefs from Paul to bring healing to a loved one, did he ever cease to be amazed?*

Christopher daily lived in amazement as the spectacular things that transpired in southern Yunnan province became so frequent that they were almost commonplace—almost. In this season scores of new sons and daughters entered the wide-open door of God's Kingdom. And—as in Acts—many believed without personally witnessing miraculous signs, simply under the conviction of the Holy Spirit that the gospel preached was the power of God for *their* salvation.

Christopher's nights grew shorter as he sought God urgently for discernment in guiding the budding movement while hiding it from the eyes of officials. As the numbers increased, he felt he and his team were barely holding on by their fingernails. They resolved to focus on helping the believers grow in the Word.

The three Tuxiang girls devoured their Chinese New Testaments, living each new chapter by faith. Within two weeks, many of the girls in the dorm had made commitments to Christ and been baptized by their fellow Tuxiang, disturbing again the muddy waters of the little Lancang River tributary.

Over the next few weeks, testimonies of these events spread among the Tuxiang students. Little groups of three and four women began to meet to read their new Bibles. Knowing that the return of Jesus might be near, they prayed fervently for salvation for their families, friends, and the Tuxiang tribe. Only women had believed so far. Although only a sophomore, Yijing rose to prominence among the new believers. And as she led the other girls in prayer, they sought God for the salvation of the young men on campus.

* * *

Christopher finished class and stepped into the busy hallway. A faintly familiar face ducked around the corner—a face from the past that didn't want to be seen. Christopher sensed whoever it was must have been watching him. A little concerned, he went to his apartment for a team lunch, trying to recall where he had seen that face before.

"Guess who I saw this morning?" Phil said during lunch. "Zhi Liang—the guy who helped us get to Nancheng after we left Kunming. I yelled to say hi, but he didn't seem to notice. Instead, he ducked into the first building he came to. That wouldn't seem strange to me except it was the gym. What would he be doing in the gym?"

"That's strange. The same thing happened to me a week or so ago," Kellie said. "I saw him watching me from down the hall of our classroom building. When I got to where he was standing, he had gone. You would think he would recognize me, since I am one of only three Caucasian women on campus. I wonder why he didn't say hello?"

"That's because he doesn't want to be seen," Christopher said suddenly.

The group looked at him questioningly.

"I saw Zhi Liang today also, but I didn't realize who it was until just now," Christopher continued. "I suspect he is watching us. I'm still not convinced that all the help we got from Ching Fei was free from ulterior motives.

"Like it or not, he works for the Chinese government and has a duty to fulfill that probably includes reporting on questionable foreign activities. Now that God is working openly here, we had better be prepared for repercussions."

Christopher stopped himself short, walked across the room, and turned on the music rather loud. When he sat back down, he spoke softly so that everyone had to bend close to listen.

"But God *is* at work, and we are about to start our first church!"

* * *

Over the next two weeks, when the KPF team gathered for early morning prayer the Tuxiang girls also gathered in pairs to pray for the conversion of the guys on campus, asking that the Lord would raise up one or more as pastors. Each Sunday, eight to ten girls stole away in pairs for the hour-long trek to the river. There, one of the KPF team members would teach the Word to them, answer questions, cast vision, teach them a few songs of worship, pray with them, and rejoice in any new baptisms. Occasionally on the way to or from the river, Tuxiang believers and KPF members reported hearing someone following them, but they never actually saw anyone. And so the number of new believers continued to swell.

One day Yijing brought three young men with her to their Sunday worship meeting at the river. "Teacher Christopher," she said excitedly, "we have found our pastor! These three boys want to become Christians, and Li Tao wants to be the first pastor."

Christopher barely kept himself from laughing.

"Yijing, maybe I should explain a little. You don't just make a person a pastor because he wants to be one, especially when he's not even a Christian yet! There are critical qualifications from Titus that must be developed in him."

She bounced up and down. "Please, just listen to their stories. Please!"

The troop sat down by the river in the fallen brown leaves. Christopher saw the earnestness in their faces.

"Okay, Li Tao," said Christopher, "since you're the one that wants to be the pastor, why don't you tell your story first?"

Li Tao sat very straight, his face twisted in earnest emotion.

"For five weeks I have been making fun of Yijing," the young man said. "All my life, I know only science, not God. I think she crazy girl, even though I like her for one year. But she suddenly different. Every time we see each other, she tell me about God, especially Jesus Christ. I always laugh at her.

"Then last night I go to bed early, tired from studying for exams. And I have dream. Not normal dream. I see man in white, shining in front of me. He tell me His name Jesus. Why I make fun of His followers? He tell me to come see Yijing to find out how to have my sins washed and have new life. He tell me also that I will be great leader of Christians for Tuxiangs but also much p-p-persecuted. I should talk to you. Then dream over.

"I wake up breathing hard, sweating even though cold in room. This morning I tell Yijing. Same thing happen to my two friends here, though they not hear part about leading Tuxiangs. Yijing say we should talk you. Teacher Christopher, we believe God. We want to be baptized in river."

The other two shared similar stories—almost exactly the same dream, each one being instructed to see Yijing the next morning. The Owens listened, amazed once again by God. Chara couldn't help crying.

Christopher grilled the young men, as though trying to deter them from being baptized, to make sure their experiences were genuine.

"Boys, it's December and the river is cold," he finally said. "Are you sure you want to get into that water?"

Li Tao stood up and put his hands on his hips resolutely. "Mr. Christopher, it not nearly as hard as dying on cross. Baptize us!"

Before they could make their way to the water, Yijing timidly stopped them. "Teacher Christopher, you know we ask three questions when we baptize people. The sisters and I have been talking. If it is okay, we like to add a fourth question."

"This is the Tuxiang way of baptizing," Christopher said. "What question would you like to ask?"

"We would like to ask, 'When they come into your house, drag you away, throw you into prison, and threaten to kill you, will you still follow Jesus?'"

Christopher asked her to repeat her question, to make sure that he had understood her correctly.

Yijing stood erect and repeated the question slowly and purposefully.

Christopher wiped his eye. "If you want to add that question, I think it would please Jesus very much."

Li Tao hurried into the water, eager for Christopher to ask him the four questions. Once baptized, he rose to leave the water, but Christopher stopped him.

"No, Li Tao, you will stay here with me, and I will help you baptize your two brothers."

"Me? No, you are teacher."

"Yes, Li Tao. You must begin to take responsibility for others now. That's what servant leaders do."

Immediately Christopher helped Li Tao ask the other two new brothers the four questions and baptize them. None felt the cold until the ceremony was over. Then, as quickly as possible, they rushed to the riverbank.

* * *

Li Tao shivered in his towel. "Teacher Christopher," he declared. "I must tell my people about Jesus. Teach me to be strong leader and good shepherd."

Christopher and Chara looked at each other, elated that their dreams were finally becoming reality.

"Yes, my brother, I will," Christopher said. "By the way, you have a great name to fit the role you will have!"

"What do you mean?"

"Well, doesn't 'tao' mean mighty wave? God is building a mighty wave to sweep across the Tuxiang people and beyond!"

* * *

Christopher scanned the email before sending it to the colonel through an encrypted network.

LT and his two companions have worked hard to grow in their faith. They meet with me or one of the other men every day—eagerly learning how to feed themselves spiritually. And Chara or one of the other KPF women meet daily with YJ and a few other female leaders.

As we disciple the new T leaders, they do the same with other newer believers, with amazing resolution. It's hard to believe, but they have covenanted to become ch*rches based on Acts 2!

Win, it's finally happening!

I'm a bit worried now that the believers number around seventy-five. It is increasingly difficult to hide the new ch* from the eyes of the authorities. To keep a low profile, the three ch* pastored by LT and his friends have decided to stay small and give birth to four more second-generation ch*.

* * *

Li Tao sat next to Christopher with his Bible open.

Christopher hesitated, closed his Bible, and looked into Li Tao's eyes. "Next semester our team could be detained or even deported by the authorities for sharing Christ with you all. And you yourselves may face interrogation or persecution.

"Li Tao, you must tell the students to get the gospel out to their villages during the winter break before that happens. As they visit their families, they should tell them all that they have seen and heard. They should do with them exactly as we have done with all of you. Teach them to disciple others as we have discipled you. Remember, Jesus may return soon!"

Li Tao nodded his head solemnly. "We will lose no opportunity."

Christopher said, "Our team will divide up to accompany you all and support you in any way can. But first, my family must make a trip to Kunming."

* * *

"Oh, Christopher, what pleasant surprise! It so kind you visit me. Last I hear, you in Nancheng. What brings you Kunming?"

Ching Fei seemed cordial. In the corner, the young Zhi Liang shifted uneasily.

"We've just finished our first semester," Christopher said, "and came to Kunming for a few days of rest and to pick up some supplies before returning to Nancheng. Our highest priority, however, was to visit you and to bring you a few gifts."

Ching Fei, though remaining composed, seemed shocked by the last statement.

"To visit me? Why?"

"Every year, Christians celebrate Christmas to remember the time God gave us the gift of Himself—when He was born into this world in the person of Jesus Christ," Christopher said. "To celebrate, we give gifts to family and friends. Ching Fei, you were our first friend in China, so out of love we bring you these gifts."

"You have been very kind to us, Mr. Ching," Chara added. "Were it not for your help, we might not have made it to our university on time. As a mother of four kids, I was especially touched by your hospitality. Our friends wanted to come, but they are taking final exams this week. They asked us to bear their gifts to you. We all thank you."

Chara brought out a box containing a number of wrapped presents. Ching Fei promptly set them behind his desk.

"Aren't you going to open them?" three-year-old David asked eagerly.

"What? Oh, in China, little friend, we not open presents in front of giver. But since these are American presents, we open *your* way, okay?" Ching Fei laughed sincerely. "But Uncle Ching not so strong any more. Will you help Uncle Ching open them?"

As one, the four Owen children rushed to his side, and David hopped onto his lap, pulling out the presents to be opened.

"*Aiya*, little ones! Let us open one at time, okay?"

First the children ripped open the presents from the various team members. A personal note of appreciation accompanied each gift.

After those six, the children exclaimed, "Now open mine!" "No, mine!" Ching Fei was visibly moved that even the children had gifts for him.

Joshua's gift was a drawing: "This is a picture of us with you at the airport. I drew you having wings because you were like an angel to us."

Next were the gifts from the twins.

With Chara's help, Elizabeth had recorded an audio file and

put it on a flash drive. "I like to sing, so I thought you would like to hear some Jesus songs I sing. I also sang 'Happy Birthday' on there so you could play it on your birthday."

Caleb had carefully wrapped a Chinese dollar. "This was my first renminbi. I wanted you to have it because I know a lot of people in China don't have much money."

David awaited his turn with great patience. His gift box held rubber bugs, snakes, and scorpions in an assortment of colors.

"Little David, what are these for?"

"Use them to scare off bad guys!" David said matter-of-factly.

"And now, our present to you," Chara said.

The painting Ching Fei unwrapped employed tiny, colored fingerprints as paint daubs to form a shepherd caring for his sheep in mountains like those in southern Yunnan.

"The Bible tells us that God cares for us like a shepherd," Chara explained. "Sometimes He cares for us through individuals like you. The picture is formed from the fingerprints of our whole team because we are the sheep who have felt your care."

For several moments Ching Fei simply hugged little David and said nothing. "You must stay with me and be my guest for winter holidays," Ching Fei finally said.

"Ching Fei, there is nothing we would rather do," Christopher said politely. "But we have promised our students to visit some of their villages to meet their families. We cannot break our word, especially since some of these families are expecting us."

"Yes, you are right," Ching Fei said. "If you not go you cause families to lose face. But stay with me as guest until you leave for Nancheng."

Over the next four days, the Owens saw many of Kunming's finest attractions and enjoyed most-favored status. Then Ching Fei arranged two government SUVs to carry them home. As they waited outside, he excused himself to make final preparations.

"Mommy, why did we bring so many presents to Uncle Ching if he has been spying on us?" Caleb asked.

"Because we really do appreciate what he has done for us. More important, Jesus told us to love our enemies and to do good to those who hate us. Maybe as we show our love for him, God will change his heart."

* * *

In his office Ching Fei gave final instructions to Zhi Liang.

"As before, you will accompany our friends to Nancheng and see that they arrive safely."

"Yes, Officer Ching. My informants tell me these Americans plan to visit the villages for the winter break. I believe they want to spread their propaganda there as well. I will have several men follow to observe them and report back to me."

"Yes, but you yourself are not to go. Wait in Nancheng for reports from the informants. Do you understand?"

"Of course, Officer Ching," he said. "Some of them also may try to go into border areas near Vietnam and Laos. Should I have them arrested if they do?"

"No, you fool! Don't have anyone arrested before talking to me! In fact, none of your surveillance or the identity of the Americans or Tuxiang students is to be reported to anyone but me. Is that clear?"

"But Officer Ching! What if this propaganda spreads farther? Shouldn't we put a stop to it now before it gets out of control?"

"Do not question my orders, or you will soon be enjoying the long winters of Tibet!"

* * *

The evening after the Owens returned from Kunming, George knocked on their door. "Hey, Christopher, wanna take a walk?"

George's voice sounded nonchalant, but his face and hand motions conveyed urgency. Rather than turn up the music to hide their conversation, they went outside.

"So, what's up?" Christopher inquired as they walked out the campus gate.

"I'm convinced we're being watched closely. Several of the more recent converts are asking us which villages we're going to. Fortunately, we honestly don't know.

"So far, only Yijing knows where we are going. But since Lance, Julie, and I have Asian features and can travel to restricted border areas less conspicuously, she has asked us to accompany her, first to her village and then to several surrounding villages that some of her friends are from. And she hasn't even told them yet. Both Yijing and Li Tao think there are some informants among the new disciples, though they're not sure which ones."

"So, what are you thinking, bro?" asked Christopher.

"Well, most of the students know we're leaving tomorrow, so it would be easy for someone to follow us. Then it'll be nothing for them to have us arrested when we go into the border areas.

"Instead, we'd like to sneak out tonight around midnight with Yijing and two friends she trusts. Yijing says we can take an ox cart along a little-used mountain road to a nearby town and catch one of the first minibuses out in the morning. Then no one will be able to follow us."

Christopher thought as they walked. He felt uneasy, but could think of no alternative. "Okay, I guess that is the best plan."

He turned to face George.

"But the three of you must stay together the whole time—no exceptions! Take one of the field radios the colonel gave us so we can stay in contact. You may not have electricity in some places, but it's got a hand crank. I'll take the other with me. I want you to report every evening by cell phone—or by radio if you don't have mobile service, okay?"

The two men sauntered slowly back across campus, praying for the endeavor. As they approached their apartments, Christopher paused.

"George," he said, "this is our first foray into the Tuxiang mountains. You're Christian commandos. Bring God's Kingdom to those villages!"

A face peered through binoculars from a nearby window.

"Comrade, the two leaders are returning to their building."

"Very well," responded Zhi Liang, "bring in another student you trust. The two of you must watch the door to their building until they emerge tomorrow. Inform me as soon as you see any movement from them."

* * *

"Commander, you understand the risk you are embracing in this excursion—especially given your reports of the last few weeks?"

Christopher readjusted his ear buds for the encrypted conference call with the colonel in Vietnam and Nic in Laos.

"Yes, Win, I understand it all too well. That's why I wanted to alert your teams and get your advice on how to plan for various contingencies. And ... well ... if anything happens to us, for you or Nic to be ready to fly here and step in as needed."

"Listen, buddy," said Nic, "you'll all be fine. We're planning a few excursions of our own here across the border. However, we'll be ready to cover your back."

"Commander," said the colonel, "you still believe you're being watched?"

"No doubt about it, guys. The stakes are high, but this is what we came for. Now, what advice do you have for us?"

TWENTY SIX

The burden of all of the believers
lies heavy upon my teammates and me.
We are deprived of sleep. In the villages we get sick.
Hunger pangs ravage our bodies
as they refuse to keep strange foods down.
Weariness plagues us at each step.
Our mortal bodies waste away, yet what else can we do?
We must offer ourselves morning, afternoon, evening, and night
to give life to these precious brothers and sisters.
Death works in us, but life works in them.
They are our joy and our crown. Their life is our victory.
—Ruth Grant

"Lance," George whispered, "wake up. It's time to go."

"Dude, what?" Lance opened his eyes with a look of *"Whoever came up with this crazy idea of leaving in the middle of the night?"* Then his adrenaline kicked in.

Julie was waiting for them in the common room, looking very Tuxiang in clothes borrowed from Yijing. Lance walked toward the main door that led outside, but George grabbed his arm, shaking his head. Lance nodded, remembering the plan.

Silently they walked to the back of the common room where a vent opened at the top of the wall. Earlier that evening—with music blaring—they had removed the cover grille, assembled a makeshift ladder against the wall, and sent Lance exploring for an appropriate escape route. Now Lance ascended the ladder into the vent, lifting a small backpack behind him. He inched along, pulling his bag behind him.

Julie lifted her backpack into the crawlspace and scooted in after him. George then inserted his bag and crawled into the vent, knocking their improvised ladder to the floor with a crash.

A light came on in the girls' apartment, and both Kellie and

Ruth rushed out.

"What was that noise?" asked Ruth loudly.

"Oh, nothing," replied Kellie just as loudly. "Perhaps one of the rats knocked something over. Let's go back to sleep."

Quick thinking, girls! George thought appreciatively as he caught up with the others.

Lance, in the front, came to the grille he had loosened earlier that evening, tied a piece of twine to it, and carefully lowered it to the floor of a dark hallway. Then he quietly dropped to the floor. Julie tossed him the bags and dropped into his arms. George joined them, then they carefully replaced the grille on the air duct and scanned their surroundings.

"What was that noise?" whispered Julie, no longer concerned about listening devices.

"Our 'ladder' fell over," George said. "Fortunately, Kellie and Ruth covered our escape, I hope. Now let's find an exit on the *back* side of this building. No one should be watching there. And remember, from this point on we speak only Mandarin. We can't risk anyone suspecting us of being foreigners."

They soon found an appropriate exit, but it was chained and padlocked shut from the outside, as were all the others.

"What will we do?" Julie said, beginning to panic. "We can't get out, and we can't go back to our apartments! What will they do when they find us here?"

"Windows," said George. "Check the windows."

Hurriedly they searched the first floor, but found that all the windows lay behind locked doors. The second floor held mainly unlocked classrooms, but the drop from those windows was a good fifteen feet—too far to jump.

Lance fidgeted nervously. How would they explain their presence there in the morning? *Oh, God, help!*

A sound caught his attention—a large, leafless branch was scraping the building in the wind. "Dudes! We can do it. We can climb down that tree!"

Julie eyed the branch skeptically.

"I'm not sure about getting to the trunk," said George, after studying the branch. "But we can grab hold of the branch and hang by our hands. Then the drop is only seven or eight feet."

Leaning out and grasping the branch with both hands, Lance pulled his body through the window. After he stopped swinging, he dropped safely to the leaf-covered ground below. George and Julie dropped the bags to him before following.

Safely on the ground, the three slipped away unobtrusively. In their borrowed clothes, anyone seeing them would likely take them for Chinese students. Avoiding the campus gates, they hopped the fence and headed for the prearranged meeting spot. Three beaming but nervous Tuxiang girls emerged from behind some bushes to meet them.

"Hello," Yijing said in Mandarin. "We walk to farmhouse where we take ox cart to next town. We already late. Hurry!"

The six walked in rapid silence, watching their steps intently and shivering in the crisp, starlit darkness. Presently they came to a small hut where a young man waited with a large cart drawn by a single ox. The six piled on board and rode toward the next town. When they arrived at the bus station, they looked every bit the part of worn-out, overworked, rural students. Here Yijing and the KPF team parted ways with the other two girls.

As they waited to board a 6:45 minibus, an officer approached Julie and asked her where she was going.

"We are from Yunnan Southern University," Yijing answered quickly, "and are going to our villages for winter recess."

"Why are you here? Why not catch the bus from Nancheng?"

"We are very eager to get home after a long semester. As you know, the bus leaves here much earlier than from Nancheng. A friend brought us here early this morning to catch it."

The guard muttered something about crazy Tuxiangs and sauntered away.

* * *

The bus ride was a harrowing four hours, winding around deep gorges at breakneck speed on partly washed-out roads. Finally the group reached their next destination, a pull-off alongside the road. Despite their exhaustion, they proceeded immediately on the long hike through narrow switchbacks, arriving in Yijing's village as evening fell.

The four walked through dirt alleys to a small, tile-roofed hut where many women were gathered, weeping loudly. Yijing's father stumbled out the door white with shock, oblivious to his newly arrived daughter.

Yijing rushed to him and they spoke briefly in Tuxiang. Then she turned to the three Americans and screamed, "My mother is dead!" Anger toward the Americans filled her eyes.

"This is what God does with my horrible sickness! Instead of destroying the spirit that afflicted me, He sends it to my mother. I wish I had never met you or your God! I would rather have stayed sick than for my mother to die. She is going to hell and I to heaven, forever. I would rather go to hell with her than to be separated from her forever!"

The three pushed into the hut, where Lance rushed to the mother's side. He felt for a pulse. Nothing. He spoke urgently in Mandarin, "A mirror! Does anyone have a mirror?"

Yijing's father brought a shard of broken mirror to Lance. Carefully, Lance placed it under the nostrils of the still form. The temperature in the small hut was almost as chilly as that outside. Ever so faintly, a small patch of fog materialized on the mirror.

Lance breathed deeply and looked around the room. "There is still life in her. We must get her to a doctor immediately!"

Yijing began sobbing. "There...there is no doctor within hours of here. Her life is still in her, but there is nothing we can do!"

A strange resolve began to materialize in Julie. She walked over to Yijing, took her by the arm, and looked deep into her eyes. "It's not too late."

George and Lance looked at one another nervously.

"Jesus was raised from the dead," Julie continued. "He even raised others from the dead! If God wills, He will raise up your mother from this coma so that you and all your people may know that there is one true God."

Even Julie was surprised by the words coming out of her mouth, but it was too late now.

"Are we really doing this?" Lance whispered to George.

The still body of Yijing's mother lay on a wooden pallet, surrounded by candles. Smoke from the incense rose to merge with the soot-covered rafters. The incense had been burning for a while, and the air was thick and pungent. Julie's eyes burned.

The stark reality of hopelessness engulfed them all. What kind of spiritual battle had they landed in?

"Pray!" Julie whispered to her companions in English. "Pray with all your might that God may have mercy and claim this as a victory for Himself!"

George and Lance stood on either side of the body and lifted their arms heavenward, wrestling aloud with God in prayer.

"Don't stop believing, Yijing! For your mother's sake, believe. Based on what God has already done in your life, believe. For the sake of all the Tuxiang, believe!" Julie pleaded. "Pray with us that God would restore health to your mother and grant her salvation with you."

Yijing looked at her father. Sensing his approval, she seated herself by her mother's head, stretched out her arms, and began praying aloud. George, Lance, and Julie joined her.

The four prayed for hours—sometimes audibly, sometimes silently. Yijing's father dozed repeatedly. The last onlookers left, and it became silent outside. The four labored on, despite not having slept for over twenty-four hours. Yijing pleaded with God, vowing to serve Him faithfully if only He would give her back her mother.

"Perhaps God has chosen not to give life to my mother," Yijing finally conceded. "Perhaps ..."

She was interrupted by a cough. Not from anyone in the group, but from the stirring form of her mother.

Another cough, and the woman's eyes began to flutter. She inhaled slowly. Ever so slightly she turned toward Yijing. Seeing her daughter, she spoke weakly to her in Tuxiang. "Yijing! Your God has come at last!"

* * *

"Quick! Bring water and something to eat!" George spoke more loudly than he had intended.

This woke Yijing's father. Seeing his wife well again, he began jumping up and down, shouting excitedly.

Yijing quickly fetched some hot green tea for her mother. Then she propped her head up gently.

"Ah, Mother. Jesus has visited you too, hasn't He? Now we

can join each other in heaven when we die, if only you believe."

The woman sipped her tea slowly, regaining her strength. "My daughter, how can I not believe?" she finally whispered. "Who in China has ever heard of a God like this?"

"A God not only for China, but also for the Tuxiang, Mama. God loves the Tuxiang. That is why my friends are here!"

Yijing's father was soon running through the village shouting that his wife was alive again. Sleepy villagers peered out of dingy windows and slipped out of mud-brick huts to see this marvel. They crowded the doorstep of Yijing's parents' home, hoping for a glimpse of the healed woman.

With great difficulty, Yijing quieted the crowd. "Please, my mother needs to rest, as do my friends. I promise you that after they have rested we will explain what has happened."

One by one, the group dispersed down the dirt lanes and the murmurs faded into the night.

* * *

By the time Yijing and the KPF team emerged the next morning, the whole village had gathered. George began speaking about the Kingdom of God, with Yijing translating into Tuxiang. Starting with Creation, George explained the good news.

"Friends, we have come to tell you a story that is changing the lives of people all over the world."

He then recounted how the Almighty—the Most High God— had created a man and a woman and in love for them put them in a garden to be in relationship with Him. But for their sin—for their disobeying Him—God punished them with death and with separation from Him.

"All of us are like that first man and woman," George shouted to the listeners. "All of us have sinned and, without God's help, will spend eternity punished in hell, away from His presence."

George then explained how God had established a righteous standard for mankind in the Ten Commandments, and provided for them to make animal sacrifices and confess their sins.

"For without the shedding of blood, there is no forgiveness of sins. But over time, people's hearts grew cold toward God, and their sacrifices became just empty rituals. God had had enough!

What could be done?"

Murmuring spread throughout the crowd as the Holy Spirit convicted the villagers of their own empty rituals.

"At just the right time, God sent His only Son Jesus to earth."

George then described how Jesus brought people back to God with His wonderful teaching and many miracles.

"Jesus has the power to meet our needs!" he declared after recounting the feeding of the five thousand.

"Jesus has power over nature!" he shouted after describing how Jesus calmed the storm.

"Jesus has power over the evil spirits!" he yelled after telling how Jesus cast out the legion of demons.

"Jesus has power over death!" he concluded after sharing how Jesus raised Lazarus from the grave.

George continued, "Though sinless, Jesus was put on trial and nailed to a cross to pay for our sins, cover our shame, and bring us back to God. Jesus took our place of punishment."

The villagers stood in rapt attention, giving no thought to the time. Never had they imagined that God could have such great love for them. They had made many sacrifices to their gods but had never heard of a God who would sacrifice for them. As George described the crucifixion, the crowd grieved as if each one present had just personally witnessed a loved one die for them. And when they learned that Jesus rose again from the grave in victory over death, such joy erupted that Lance and Julie wondered whether the shouting could be heard in neighboring villages!

George ended by sharing the story of the prodigal son who had left his father but then repented and returned home where his father ran to him and received him with open arms.

"God is eager to welcome every one of you into His family, to cleanse you from your guilt and shame as you turn from your sins and put your faith in Jesus alone. You must turn from your worship of spirits and make this Jesus your only King before He returns to judge forever all those who have rejected Him and to welcome into His eternal paradise all who have trusted Him.

"The time is short, friends. It may not be long before Jesus returns. I urge you to begin following Jesus this very day by trusting in Him and obeying His command to be baptized. Then you must take this message to all of the Tuxiang and the other people groups who have not heard."

As George uttered these words, the Spirit fell upon the group. As one, they repented of their sins and placed their faith in Christ. Immediately Yijing's father, Yi Jie, the village headman, led the eager throng to a mountain stream for baptism. George and Lance baptized Yi Jie and a few other men. These in turn baptized all the villagers who believed, three hundred sixty-two.

* * *

The second night after the group had left campus, Christopher finally received a radio call from George. "Where have you been? You were supposed to call us last night!"

George explained in coded language all that had happened, from Yijing's mother being healed to the whole village believing.

"We saw three hundred sixty-two 'dipped.' It was amazing!"

"Three hundred and sixty-two?" Christopher paused to take it all in. *A whole village believing? This is more than I ever expected!* "Well, we've seen no response so far, though we feel things are about to break loose here. Frankly, we've been distracted by worrying about you."

"Don't worry about us any more, Christopher," the staticky voice responded. "We're pretty esteemed in these parts. Starting tomorrow we'll train leaders from this village to train others and then take some of them with us to other valleys. Word is already spreading about us, and we think it's best to stay ahead of the rumors. We'll try to call again tomorrow night."

* * *

Over the next two days, the trio and Yijing trained her father Yi Jie and a few other key village leaders in the discipleship process. These in turn trained others what they had just been taught, and these trained still others until all those recently baptized were being trained to obey everything Jesus commanded.

The team gave the villagers a handful of Bibles and designated Yi Jie and five other men as elders in the newly formed churches in this village.

Taking Yi Jie and five other leaders with them, the three then began going to other valleys while the first villagers went to neighboring villages.

George, Lance, and Julie lived in a state of exhaustion. Every night they were whisked to a new town or village—on which side of the China-Laos border they didn't know. On these winding mountain paths there were no official border crossing stations. They slept whenever they could—riding on bumpy oxcarts or on smoke-belching mountain tractors.

Only Yi Jie knew their itinerary, which prevented word from leaking out to the Chinese or Lao officials ahead of time. In each new village, Yi Jie would call on one of the leaders, announcing that the "three preachers" were there. Within an hour, the public dirt square would be filled with people looking for healing, or simply coming to hear the stories of what God had done.

It was a season of reaping. Often the trio preached the gospel and ministered for hours, although just as often Yi Jie exhorted the crowds himself. Out of their limited supply, the KPF team could leave only one Bible in each village. One of their Tuxiang companions would remain in this village a few extra days to train a small group of men to assume leadership responsibilities. Meanwhile, as suddenly as they had arrived, the trio and the rest of their companions from Yi Jie's village would disappear in the middle of the night, when no one was watching.

After a few days, Yi Jie and the other Tuxiang men began to do most of the preaching, while the "three preachers" attracted the audience. As they did, the harvest grew even more abundant.

* * *

Yi Jie jumped off the oxcart and gestured quietly for Lance, George, and Julie to do the same.

"Pardon me, dear friends. This is the last town where we must preach before we begin our return journey. My runners tell me the police have been following close behind in every village. We do not have much time.

"It is past midnight. We will only stay here two hours. Please preach with all of His might, and then we will take you home. This village in particular has been a center of demon worship.

This spiritual stronghold must be broken!"

Yi Jie and the three preachers mounted a small platform in the square as townspeople emerged from adjoining lanes. Lance stood with George and Julie. Their legs shook with exhaustion.

A spiritual heaviness hung over the square like a dense fog.

Julie sat on a squat stool. "Guys, I can't stand up for this one. I'll sit here and pray while you preach."

George pulled up another stool. "I can feel the darkness. I'll pray with Julie. Lance, you have to preach along with Yi Jie."

A few torches lit the gathering crowd. Lance surveyed the inquiring faces and summoned his remaining strength. *When I am weak, then I am strong. Lord, help me to be faithful.*

An unknown fear gripped his heart as he saw a shaman on the edge of the gathering, chanting and gesturing in his direction. *God, help! I'm in the presence of a demon-possessed man!* He hesitated before speaking.

Wait! What am I thinking? He should be the one in fear, for the presence of the Almighty God has entered this place! Lance stood erect and shared the Creation to Christ gospel message while Yi Jie interrupted, at times adding testimonies of what God had been doing already. Heads shook in amazement, and tears streamed down several wrinkled faces.

Lance glanced at the shaman. As the name of Jesus was lifted up, the shaman stood still, unable to chant any longer.

Lance spoke in a loud voice. "Be saved from this wicked and perverted generation. Leave behind your worship of demons and turn to the one true God!"

A number of people fell on their knees and began uttering pleas for salvation. Yi Jie's traveling companions wended their way through the group, gathering families and helping them call upon the name of the Lord.

A disturbance began at the far edge of the crowd. Lance looked up. George and Julie stood and came to his side.

Non-Tuxiang officials—tipped off by a local villager—were trying to push through the crowd. Whistles pierced the cries of repentance as soldiers shoved the villagers aside.

The shaman began chanting again. He waved frantically for the attention of the soldiers and pointed to the crude platform.

The soldiers made eye contact with the three preachers and redoubled their effort to push through the crowd.

George, Julie, and Lance stood paralyzed with uncertainty.

Yi Jie pushed them aside and began shouting. "These Chinese officials are here to arrest the three preachers who bring hope to the Tuxiang people!"

He repeated this several times. The crowd began to push back to impede the soldiers' progress. The whistles grew more shrill, and batons made contact with several villagers.

Yi Jie jumped off the platform, pulling the three preachers with him. Quickly he hid them on a cart, under a load of sugar cane stalks and ordered one of his companions to lead the cart away down a back lane.

Laying the last stalks over them he whispered, "Stay there. I will do my best to come to rejoin you. Regardless, my friend here will drive you to safety."

Before the cart could depart, Lance overheard Yi Jie talking in a loud voice to a village elder.

"Oh, my dear friend, I am so glad to see you!" Yi Jie said. "The Chinese officials have found us! That crowd will not be able to hold them back for long. We need your help. Quick, be a good Tuxiang! Run back and tell the soldiers we have headed back to my home village. They will pursue us that way. But we can choose another."

The elder ran back toward the commotion in the town square.

No sooner had the man left than Yi Jie transferred the trio to another cart, hid them behind some crates, hitched the new cart to a horse and led it down the road toward their home village. The three preachers were filled with confusion.

"No, brother! Do not choose this way!" objected one of their traveling companions. "This is the way you told them to pursue!"

"Yes, brother, you are right," Yi Jie smiled slyly, "but by now you should know that I never tell anyone where we will go each night. I can assure you that the officials will not follow this path.

"You see, the man I greeted is the only one in this village with a phone. He is the only one who could have notified the officials.

"Besides, I know him. He is a greedy man—always seeking bribes. He will tell the officials that we are pursuing another route than this. They do not have many men, but with the few they have they will pursue other routes. We will be home among our people before they know we have eluded them.

"For the next several days, rumors will undoubtedly circulate that the three preachers are in distant towns and, as usual, the officials will not catch them there either. By that time, the three preachers will be back in Nancheng."

TWENTY SEVEN

Senator Wroth's limousine waited at the ancient entrance of an English manor. The iron gates slowly swung outward, driven by a modern hydraulic motor, to reveal a long, winding drive that led past armed guards hidden behind stately trees. As the limo crested a small knoll, a massive manor appeared before them. Soon the car reached the front door, and Senator Wroth stepped out in his black overcoat.

"Ah, Number Ten!" said Number Three, descending a flight of steps to greet him. Senator Wroth cringed inwardly at the label. "I am glad to see you arrived safely. I am afraid we have quite a winter storm brewing. What a pity we have not yet learned to control the weather! Come, come. Let me show you around while one of the servants gets you a cup of Darjeeling with caramelized sugar."

Depositing his hat and coat with the butler, Senator Wroth followed Number Three into the headquarters of the Religion and Education Department.

"We have had this location for roughly eighty years. All our intelligence and command operations are headquartered here. My personal staff is one hundred seventy-eight persons, mostly local villagers. Number Eight—you remember him, the Indian gentleman—and Number Nine, the Korean gentleman, both work here with me to supervise our operations. During this portion of your training, I will orient you to our operations.

"I doubt you will actually be joining our department. Number One feels that he himself will be the next to pass from this life, so obviously you are being groomed for a position in his Politics Department."

The word *groomed* made Senator Wroth squirm. He couldn't stand being groomed any more than being tenth in importance.

"Ah, here we are. My office," continued Number Three.

The two entered a beautifully appointed corner room, large even for this manor, with fireplaces on either end and windows lining the walls. The morning daylight streamed in, creating a cozy ambience. Tea was served, and the two were left alone.

As they sat in two leather chairs near one hearth, Senator Wroth broke the silence. "Number Three, would you to honest with me?"

"Dear friend, we are comrades bound by an insoluble oath to each other. I cannot lie to you. Please, ask me anything."

"Is this room bugged? Is anyone able to listen in on our conversation or to observe it?"

"No. Not in this room," Number Three replied. "In this manor, I reign supreme. Even Number One would defer to my authority here. Other parts of the manor are bugged, though not the offices or quarters of Numbers Eight and Nine. *We* are bound by our word. Only the workers are watched and listened to."

"What about the room where I will stay?"

"Previously it was bugged, but out of respect for you and your new office I removed all surveillance equipment yesterday."

"Good. Thank you. First of all, I want to know your name. There's no way I am going to call you 'Number Three' the rest of my life. And I surely don't want you to call me 'Number Ten.'"

The English gentleman smirked. "You Americans. So averse to formality!"

Senator Wroth stood and walked to a fireplace, then stared into the Englishman's eyes. "Look. I walk in formal circles all the time, and I bow to protocol till my face turns blue. But if I am going to devote my life to The Ten, I need at least one comrade I can call by name and talk straight with. You, Number Three, are the only one I really trust. I'm asking you to open up to me, also. But we have to get some names out first. You know mine, but I don't know yours."

Number Three studied him a moment before speaking. "Very well. My name is no secret. When in public, I cannot go by Number Three. My name is Ethan Farnsworth.

"However," he continued, "when one becomes a part of The Ten, one is called by his number to prevent the development of favorites and unhealthy cliques. Using personal names tends to focus on us as persons with individual histories rather than us as a part of The Ten, so we don't use them with each other.

"Sometimes it *is* a lonely existence." He smiled wryly.

"I was asked to be part of The Ten twenty-six years ago. I was very young at the time—just thirty-one—but with considerable influence in the intellectual world. But I'll tell you that story another time.

"Michael, I sense something special in you. I liked you from the moment you strode into our Rome headquarters with your Beretta. That took some gumption!" He smiled at the memory.

"My, you were a sight when we told you we had removed your commandos! At that moment I felt a special affection for you. You may call me Ethan, as I would very much like a genuine friendship with someone on my level. I am tired of these cold, impersonal bonds among The Ten. Yes, call me Ethan, but only in private. Around others, you must call me by my title, and I will do the same for you."

Senator Wroth clapped his hands together. "Great! Now we can talk as men! But I have a far deeper question, Ethan. Please be frank with me. After all, you're training me.

"A few months ago, Number One reprimanded me for making myself too prominent politically. I pointed out that he himself has said that in time, we, The Ten, will emerge into the limelight to usher in the Rebirth. I told him that it seemed to me we have such a firm hold on the events of the world that if I could achieve a position of greater influence, we might usher in the Rebirth sooner. He reacted by saying, 'We've waited fifteen hundred years and can wait another fifteen hundred years for all I care. It's not time to go public, young man!'"

"Yes. I can hear the Prime Director now," the Brit chuckled. "Your accent is spot on. But there is a lot of truth in what he says. We must wait for the right time. A number of The Ten are quite disturbed that you are stepping forward into the public spotlight rather than stepping back."

"Blast it! I don't care what they think."

"But you have sworn an oath to them!"

"You're right, but I don't have to give in to their attitudes. Nor did I sign up in order to become a carbon copy of the others. Ethan, don't you see? I'm not concerned about the *timing* of the Rebirth, but the attitude. I want to see this Rebirth take place. I want to see us take control and bring peace and stability through it. The sooner, the better. But Number One's *attitude* is what bothers me. He's old and apathetic. He's not driven to usher in the Rebirth. He hasn't seen it in his lifetime, so he's content to let it be postponed another fifteen hundred years.

"So far, I haven't found any of you who actually expect it to occur within the near future. What are we here for anyway? Why can't we be that generation? Are *you* satisfied just to tinker with world affairs hoping that one day some group of The Ten will have the ability to usher in the Rebirth?"

Farnsworth stood to face him. "Are you certain you are not mistaking patience for apathy?"

Senator Wroth placed both hands on Farnsworth's shoulders, looking him in the eye. "Ethan, I know what it is to be patient. I can wait forever in pursuit of a definite plan. But from what I can see, The Ten are getting nowhere. This is not patience. This is just resignation and apathy. The Ten are marking time! But we are supposed to bring about the Rebirth, not simply wait for it."

Farnsworth continued to study Senator Wroth intently, then moved to close the draperies. Next he turned on something above the hearth that looked like a radio. Finally he pulled both chairs very near the hearth and sat down.

"I know this room to be free of surveillance," he said quietly, "but still such words are risky. They would get us both killed if Number One were to learn of them.

"We can never be too careful, so these drapes have a special coating to block any audio pick up aimed at the vibrations on our windows. I would not be surprised if Number One were trying to eavesdrop on us somehow. After all, you are the new kid on the block. The 'radio' on the hearth is a short-range scrambler. Our conversation will be scrambled when we are near it.

"Michael, your words stir me, not with anger but a mixture of excitement and some fear. Fear because we are never free from Number One's prying eyes and ears. He *is* the Prime Director. And with excitement because for decades I have longed to hear someone speak as you do.

"I will be frank with you. I agree that Number One has grown apathetic, but not all of us have. As younger men we all dreamed of being the group that ushered in the Rebirth, but the older members always cautioned us to be patient. Over the years, with the Rebirth outside their grasp, older members of The Ten grow apathetic and dampen the vision of new members. Because the younger ones have less power, they can only comply until they, too, eventually conclude the Rebirth is for another generation.

"However it's not as bad as you make out. Every generation of The Ten *has* grown more powerful in world influence. And not all of us have succumbed to Number One's attitude; there are a few of us who still hope to personally share in the Rebirth."

"Why are you telling me this?" Senator Wroth asked.

The Brit looked about nervously. "Because I think you are the one to lead us to the Rebirth!" he whispered.

"No one before you has had the public power, recognition, or potential to become a world leader like you. More importantly apart from Number One none of us has had the—how do you say it—killer instinct you do. Michael, you have the ability to get things done and make people follow you. That is what stirred some of our other younger comrades and me to attempt our most masterful coup yet."

"What do you mean?"

"We arranged for you to be selected as Number Ten while persuading Number One that it was his idea. We used the very principles of The Ten against him—swaying him without him realizing he was being influenced. You, Michael, are going to lead us to the Rebirth."

Senator Wroth's face registered surprise. "I had hoped to bring about the Rebirth, but I had no idea others of you were counting on me to do so."

"Michael, for the last twenty years I have followed your every move, waiting to see if you were the one. I studied several others, but none possess the unique combination of skills needed. You are the one. You must continue to grow politically, but you would never remain a world leader without The Ten's support. In just days we could undo you completely—through scandal or even outright assassination.

"We—the conspiratorial inner circle as it were—have a plan. It's very tentative right now, but a plan nonetheless. In ten to fifteen years we believe we can usher in the Rebirth with you at the helm."

"Ten to fifteen years? Ethan, the one thing I know about planning is to double whatever time frame you are anticipating. Unknown factors always delay things. Double fifteen years and we're at thirty. Do you expect to be in your prime when you're in your eighties? Ethan, ten or fifteen years is too long."

"If you have a better plan, Michael, I'd like to hear it."

"I don't have a plan yet, but I can assure you I will."

"Very well. Let's work on this over the next few days while you are here. In the meantime, a word of caution. You will soon be appointed the first director of the International Coalition for the Preservation of World Peace. We all see what unparalleled influence you will have through that position, and it is a concern to Number One and a few others among The Ten. It may be they will tolerate your new role for a while as the well-intentioned but misguided plans of the newest member, but not for long.

"But if Number One gets even a hint of your aspirations, he will bring you down in a second, and I will be unable to stop him. I probably won't even know about it until after the fact.

"So watch your step carefully, my friend. Only you can take care of Michael Wroth. And remember to always refer to me as Number Three outside this room."

* * *

Senator Wroth spent most of his time at the manor with the three members of The Ten. Frequently, they asked his opinion, then taught him principles for deciding how to influence various events and movements.

In one large room, all four walls were covered with a giant digital timeline detailing the various streams of religious and educational thought throughout history, illuminating how The Ten had exerted their influence and displaying the current state of the world. He had seen a similar display in Rome dealing with politics and imagined there must be another regarding science and economics at the third headquarters. Whenever he was not with other members of The Ten, Senator Wroth was examining this display intently.

"Magnificent, is it not?" Number Three said over his shoulder. Senator Wroth had been studying so hard he had forgotten the other man's presence.

"It shows our progress over the centuries. Especially note where lines converge, illustrating our success in creating one stream of thought compatible with the Rebirth. Notice how many of the world's religions are becoming more uniform in thought—usually with a New Age or animistic base. And see here, where many Christian denominations began succumbing to post-modern relativism," Number Three continued.

Senator Wroth surveyed a large section of the wall, observing the minute lines—each captioned with dates, names, places, and subjects. At any point on the touchscreen wall, he could zoom in or out to examine the details.

"Magnificent," he finally agreed. "But progress? I'm not sure you're winning the battle."

"Oh, we are quite aware of the cults and extremists out there," Number Three said. "Of course, many fit perfectly into our plans. We are still working to bring a few in line, but they are relatively minor. And the strident activity that plays out in the news obscures the eagerness of the masses for new, peaceful leadership. The time is right for us to take out the militants."

Senator Wroth traced one line that branched into multiple lines that branched into still more.

"I'm concerned about this line, Number Three, conservative Christian missions—evangelical, charismatic, what have you. These have shown increasing influence since around 1800."

"Oh, that. Yes, we are working on that one with, we think, some success, with the same strategy we used in the late 1800s."

Number Three stepped to Senator Wroth's left to follow the lines back a little.

"Notice here how abruptly—within a decade or so—many of the diverging lines of expansion suddenly ended after 1900."

"I was wondering about that," Wroth commented.

"We realized then how easily we could immobilize Christians through distraction. Increase affluence and toss pleasures their way. Most have become functional universalists anyway. They don't believe people who are not part of the Christian religion really go to hell. If affluence doesn't work, we highlight other legitimate compelling causes such as poverty and injustice to divert them from their world mission. And by allowing them success in other arenas, we had little difficulty getting most to abandon any focus on world proselytization.

"Success can take many forms—expensive programs, new institutions, magnificent buildings. And this strategy has worked. Back then we rerouted their ambition into less expansionary avenues, and we are doing the same today. Just this last week I received a fresh report that spending on new buildings and staff continues increasing while missions giving is in steady decline. In ten to twenty years, we should have this movement right where we want it again. Patience, Number Ten. It all comes down to patience."

Senator Wroth studied the wall with a puzzled expression.

"The way I see it, Number Three, this particular movement is expanding too fast for us to wait ten to twenty years to stem it. You may not have that much time."

Number Three took Senator Wroth's arm and turned him around gently. "Michael, if you are contemplating some form of persecution, you are wrong. Study this timeline in depth and you'll discover persecution invigorates Christian missions—like pouring petrol on a fire to extinguish it."

Now Senator Wroth took Number Three by the arm and led him around the room, pointing out various lines he had studied over the last several days.

"When done properly, Number Three, there are ways of squashing movements without fueling them. Some of history's more inept leaders have erred in thinking force alone could stop such a movement. But certain forms of persecution have been successful, along with various other means of swaying public attitudes. See here for example."

Senator Wroth enlarged a portion of the screen. "If we act now and twist things just a bit, I think we can turn the hearts of many more our direction.

"I know I am training primarily in politics, but I believe you, Number Three, are dealing with the area of greatest influence. When you can control a person's beliefs, you can command his allegiance—politically, economically, and so on. As a matter of record, some of history's greatest leaders became successful by incorporating religion into their agenda."

Suddenly the door opened, and a woman entered carrying a single sheet of paper.

"Excuse me, sir. This just arrived from China. We thought you might want to act on it."

Number Three skimmed the report, handed it to Senator Wroth, and strode quickly to one of the command rooms.

Senator Wroth quickly followed.

"Stuart, before I talk with Number Eight, brief me on what is happening in China," said Number Three as he entered the command room.

A balding man answered from his computer console.

"Sir, it is bloody strange. For several months we have had a tiny group of Americans in China under observation. They call themselves the ..."

"Kingdom Preparation Force," interrupted Number Three. "Yes, yes, how presumptuous! If I am not mistaken, there are actually four teams operating in Southeast Asia right now. All based out of California."

"Yes, sir, that is correct."

"One team is near the Laos border in a city called Nancheng. In their first few months, they had little success at converting Chinese students."

"Chinese?" Number Three asked skeptically.

Stuart reddened. "Not exactly, sir."

"Then be exact, man!"

"Yes, sir," Stuart said quickly. "They have focused on students in the Tuxiang minority group. Our source tells us not many students have been converted, maybe no more than a hundred."

Senator Wroth's raised his head abruptly.

"A hundred? That doesn't sound like a small number!"

Stuart glanced nervously at Senator Wroth.

"Unfortunately, 'only a hundred' was the good news," Stuart said. "Over the last several weeks—winter recess for them—the team has traveled all over the Tuxiang countryside converting whole villages. And everywhere they have gone, there have been reports of miracles."

"Miracles?" asked Senator Wroth.

"Yes, sir. You know—healing people. This has me worried. And it seems the three teams in Laos and Vietnam are starting to see similar things. The tribes in these areas, being uneducated and superstitious, are responding in droves."

"This has been going on for weeks? Why are we just now hearing about it?" Number Three demanded.

"That's the strange part, sir. When the team was in Nancheng, Number Eight's section followed their every move through his informants. But three of them suddenly disappeared one night, and our contacts were unable to catch up with them. Everything we got from then on was hearsay. The locals apparently covered for them so that even our contacts in Tuxiang began to wonder if these reports were merely rumors or even about ghosts.

"Technically this is in Number Eight's region, but a clerk named Greely forwarded the information to me, suggesting that we should be aware of it."

"Went over Number Eight's head, did he? Call in Number Eight and this Greely fellow—now!"

A few minutes later the dignified Indian entered with his nervous clerk.

Number Three turned to face them.

"I am a bit shocked to learn so belatedly about the magnitude of this KPF enterprise."

Number Eight stood ramrod stiff. "We notified you earlier of their discovery of a Priority A item, and sent a notification of a 'Level Six Possible Movement Insertion' to the Timeline Room."

"Yes, I remember. So you did."

Senator Wroth couldn't bear the cryptic language. "Excuse me. What exactly does it mean that you 'sent this notification to the Timeline Room'?"

Number Eight gave Senator Wroth an annoyed glance. "It means, Number *Ten*, that a note was sent to the supervisor of that room telling him to be prepared to add the group to the schematic should this develop into a significant movement."

"In other words, it means nothing. Am I right?" Wroth asked. "Some guy sitting in the Timeline Room added this paper to a stack a mile high while taking *zero* action. This is bureaucracy at its best! And what about you, Greely? Didn't you consider this situation to merit more attention than you gave it?"

"Number Ten, I—I—I tried to bring this to the attention of—"

"I am sure you did your job, Greely," Number Three said before the situation got out of hand. "You report to Number Eight. I would, however, like to know where the three are now."

"Back at the university," said Greely. "Our contact there tells us they are under full surveillance and will not be lost again."

"But the damage is done," Senator Wroth said loudly.

"Pardon me, sir?"

"You fool!" said Senator Wroth, slamming his fist on the desk. "Don't you see? The damage is done! Now the locals are infected and it's beyond our control. You had this bottled up, and now it's poured out. Who cares if we have the team under surveillance again? They've already accomplished their purpose!

"There's one thing I want to know," Wroth said, snatching up the report. "This KPF group—why aren't they on the schematic down the hall?"

Number Three stepped in to defend the others. "Number Ten, we do not add new groups to the timeline until we are sure they are going to significantly influence religious thought. I'm sure that in Number Eight's judgment this did not yet constitute a major trend. Now that it does, it will be added to the schematic. Until then, reports like this serve our purpose."

"But didn't any of you anticipate this?" said the implacable Senator Wroth.

Greely wanted to defend his original concerns, but Number Eight spoke first. "So-called miracles are an unpredictable factor that exaggerate the short-term influence of new movements. History has shown, however, that movements based on miracles rarely endure, so we don't generally pay them much attention."

"Miracles may be generally unpredictable," Senator Wroth said, "but the report that came to *your* section specifically says these 'miracles' occurred on campus earlier, to a lesser degree. They have moved beyond a short-term occurrence. And, you, Greely, the one monitoring the situation, should have anticipated this development when they went to the villages.

"But ..."

Senator Wroth composed himself. "This *was* a spectacular turn of events. You made a small mistake, Greely, and this has unfortunately been magnified by the success of the KPF group."

"Yes, sir," responded Greely.

"Well, Number Ten," Number Three said sarcastically, "you're here to learn. But if you have such a good grasp of the situation, what do you suggest we do? Perhaps you would like to suggest a way of solving this problem?"

Senator Wroth sat and thought for a moment while everyone in the room ceased working to watch. Seizing the opportunity, he stood confidently to address the room.

"Number Three, Number Eight, and other dear colleagues, forgive my outburst. The Ten may have chosen me for my ability to anticipate future events, but they certainly didn't choose me for my long-suffering!"

Everyone—including Greely—relaxed as Senator Wroth broke the tension.

"Sometimes I am too hard on others for not seeing what I see so readily. Number Eight and Greely have done the right thing in bringing this report to our attention. It was a mistake on everyone's part not to anticipate the potential for what happened here. But that is behind us now. If there is one thing we must do, it is learn from our mistakes. What has happened in China can work into our plans beautifully. We will turn this temporary setback into a resounding defeat for this group, and for all who stand in the way of the glorious Rebirth—something I hope we will all witness within our lifetimes."

The room lit up in hope.

"I will discuss the specifics of my proposal with Number Three. Once we are in agreement, you in this primary command room will implement them under his direction. We will all share in the coming victory, and Number Eight and Greely will lead the way.

"Now learn all you can about these four teams, and report to me as you obtain additional information. If you will give up sleep tonight, so will I. We must act swiftly."

Senator Wroth smiled and shook hands with Number Eight

and Greely. Number Eight left, indignant at having been publicly upbraided, while the others returned to their tasks inspired with more hope than they had felt in years.

* * *

Senator Wroth and Number Three said nothing until they were back in Farnsworth's office. Drapes drawn and scrambler on, Ethan congratulated Michael.

"Splendid! You were splendid! *That* is what you were chosen for. You did in there what I could never do—you inspired them. Just be careful of being too obvious about your aspirations. Number One has ears everywhere. And since Number Eight is one of the newer members of The Ten, I'm not sure you want to alienate him. Now, I suppose you have a plan?"

"Of course I have a plan. A grand plan. But, first, I had to wrest control of this situation from Number Eight. My plan, Ethan, is much greater than these four KPF teams. They merely provide an opportunity to crush certain obstacles to the Rebirth. This is coming along better than I could have anticipated."

"But back in the command room you were clearly upset by these recent events!" exclaimed Number Three.

"Upset? Did I convey that so effectively as to fool even you? No, my friend, it takes a lot to catch me off guard, and even more to upset me. Before we ever reached the command room, I had a plan in mind. Our friends there needed motivation, and I gave it to them.

"And now I want Marlene present when we discuss my plan."

"That's fine, if you trust her. But can you give me an overview in the meantime?"

"I trust no one like Marlene. She would die for me. I entrust to her all logistical issues so that I can focus on overall strategy. As for hearing my plan, you will have to wait. All I will tell you is that it is grander than you can imagine, and will take all night to map out in detail."

* * *

The fire in the hearth in Rome roared furiously. An elderly at-tendant entered and stood, waiting silently behind the grizzled old man slumped forward in a chair by the fire. Finally, the old man stirred.

"What word do you have?"

"Pardon me for disturbing you, Prime Director, but it is as you suspected. Number Ten was overheard in the British office promoting aspirations of ushering in the Rebirth."

"And a bastard Rebirth it would be. Premature. Improperly fathered. Temporary and short-lived. Number Ten is going well beyond his boundaries. And what of Number Three?"

His attendant hesitated nervously.

"Speak up, man. I said what of Number Three? Your loyalty is to me."

"Sir, Number Three stood by Number Ten and did nothing to correct him. Afterward they went together to Number Three's office. Perhaps there, Number Three corrected him in private."

"Nonsense! If he did not correct him in front of others, he did not do so in private."

His hand trembling with age, the old man took a pad of paper and scribbled several numbers on it. Then he tore off the top sheet and handed it to his attendant.

"Notify these members of The Ten to be here at the time I have indicated. You will notify only these, and you will instruct them to tell no one they are coming. Tell them to make it appear they have never left their offices. This meeting must be completely covert. Now go!"

TWENTY EIGHT

Finally I get to see the heartland
of the people group You have called me to.
How I have longed for this opportunity!
Oh, let me prove faithful with the stewardship
You have entrusted to me.
So many great men and women of God of the past
have prepared a heritage for me to walk in.
This cloud of witnesses surrounds me, watching.
Glorify Your Name!

—Ruth Grant

"I'm telling you, Win, that little troop of yours is sending shock waves through the Chinese intelligence community. Our sources have seen a sharp increase in references to them. What are you doing there? Is some late-life crisis prompting you to traipse around with religious fanatics? Over."

Colonel Dunbar huddled in a back room of his Vietnam apartment, using a device that scrambled his communication with the latest encryption technology—all thanks to his defense contractor contacts.

"Tal, you and I have been through a lot together and seen what the military can accomplish. Salvation isn't there. Never was. Now I'm part of the real thing. Remember all we've discussed? Please consider following Christ and joining us. Over."

Tal Gillam's cynical but friendly laugh crackled back. "Would you try to convince me so easily, my friend? But there's no time for that now. People pretty high up have serious concerns about your group in China and a remarkable awareness of their details and movements. Over."

The colonel took a moment to digest this. "You know I don't like to abort a mission while there is a chance of success. How clear is the communication among Chinese officials about what's going on? Over."

"Five by five, Colonel."

"How soon do you expect them to act?"

The radio sat silent for a few seconds, then the voice resumed with heightened urgency. "It's time to abort. I repeat, time to abort! Over."

"Roger that, old friend. Keep your ear to the ground for us. I'll do my best to get them out in time. Over and out."

"Win, act now! You don't want to get burned again!"

* * *

"Please, Christopher!" Ruth pleaded. "If I keep my scarf on, no one will notice that I'm a foreigner. I can travel unnoticed in the border region."

Christopher shook his head. This was going too far. "You know our team rule: no non-Asians in restricted areas. If a woman must go, we will send Julie. If you're caught it could jeopardize the whole movement, and there's no telling what might happen to you. What makes you so certain God wants *you* to go?"

"I told you, Christopher. My student Zhao Hong has a very sick aunt, and none of the new Tuxiang believers have been able to heal her. Since the Lord used me to heal Yijing that first day, Zhao Hong believes I can heal her aunt. For some reason she only trusts me, and this village is in an area that has no Christian presence yet."

Christopher said, "From what I hear, this area has been very resistant to what little witness it has received so far."

"Exactly! Christopher, you yourself said that God often uses miracles to break through in pioneer areas like this one. Zhao Hong's hometown hasn't seen anything miraculous yet. I know this is risky ..."

Her voice wavered as a tear coursed down her face. "But how can I go back to America in a few months knowing that I had an opportunity to share the gospel but didn't because I feared for my welfare? We're commandos, remember? We take risks."

Chara pulled Christopher aside. "Honey, listen to them. The more the pressure has mounted in the last few weeks, the more controlling you have become. You can't restrict a movement of God. At least pray about this!"

Christopher studied Ruth, Lance, and George's earnest faces and recalled his own willingness to risk all for the sake of Christ. To risk his own life was one thing, but to risk the lives of his teammates? This must be what real military commanders faced in battle.

Silently he prayed. Finally he broke the expectant silence. "Perhaps you are God's key to busting open this area for the Kingdom. Do you all understand the risk of being a foreigner caught in a restricted zone—perhaps on the wrong side of the border?"

"Yeah, boss," Lance nodded. "Like, I think we have a pretty good idea. We've done this before, you know."

"But not with a Caucasian."

"You're right," George said. "But we figure if we're caught, the worst that will happen is they might kick us out—maybe the whole team, if they connect us to you."

Christopher said, "No, they can also confiscate our computers and stuff. And if they connect us to the teams in Vietnam and Laos, they could bring pressure to bear on those governments to expel the other teams as well."

"We have discussed this before," Chara said. "We don't know what will actually happen, but we do need to seriously consider the possibility of imprisonment or physical harm."

"What's the *worst* that can happen?" Ruth interjected. "I heard you telling one of the kids this in the airport in Guangzhou. The worst is that we could die. And like Elizabeth said," she added with a shy grin, "that's not so bad when you think of where we'd be then."

Over the next few hours, the team prepared to send the trio on a second mission into the restricted zones. Except for Phil, the rest of the team was a little envious, as tales of the three preachers were continuing to circulate throughout Tuxiangland. Around 4 a.m. they sent the three on their way through the same air vent as before. Christopher ordered them to contact him every six hours, no matter what.

* * *

Zhao Hong met them at the same spot where Yijing had met the earlier team. Together the four walked to the next town, where they caught the noon bus. For the next several hours the bus twisted and turned on the mountain roads, venturing deep into the Tuxiang countryside. Ruth kept to the window seats, a scarf covering her head. Lance was diligent to text in progress reports by cell phone.

From their stop, the four trekked into a valley and reached the village at dusk. There Zhao Hong led them through dark, quiet paths to her home, where they were greeted warmly by her mother and father.

When Zhao Hong asked about her aunt, however, her parents launched into a heated discussion with her. George interpreted for Ruth what he could understand of their mixed Tuxiang-Mandarin.

"It seems the village leaders think Zhao Hong's aunt did something wrong, so they put a curse on her, and they believe this is causing her sickness. Zhao Hong's father doesn't think we should pray for her because it might cause the village leaders to lose face, especially if she is healed. He wants us to go back to Nancheng and forget the whole thing. Zhao Hong is pleading with him to reconsider for the sake of the aunt—his sister. She is telling him that we came all the way from America to bring the whole village a life-changing message of hope."

The argument continued for some time, until Zhao Hong's father finally agreed to take the team to the aunt's home and let them pray for her.

"We will pray for Zhao Hong's aunt tonight so as to attract less attention," George said.

"But that defeats the whole purpose of coming here to make the gospel known!" Ruth objected.

"Don't worry. If we're successful, the word will get out. This is a village. We need to go about this in a respectful manner. Remember, we're the guests."

It was past the appointed time to connect with Christopher, and there was no cell phone coverage, so Lance and Ruth asked to be excused to try a radio call. Static poured from the tiny speaker, broken only by an occasional word from Christopher.

"Must be interference from the mountains," said Lance.

"What do you think we should do?" Ruth asked.

"Hmm, we'll just send a one-way transmission. Like, apparently they're picking up some of our message. Maybe they're hearing more than we are. I'll make three identical transmissions explaining our plans. Then we'll listen for a response. Then I guess we'll go ahead with the plan."

Ruth nodded.

Briefly Lance explained that village leaders had cursed the aunt, but they were going to pray for her unless they received instructions to the contrary. After repeating this twice more, they waited tensely. No response came, and the static grew worse as lightning storms appeared on the horizon.

Zhao Hong and her parents led the three Americans through darkened alleys to her aunt's small home. There they found her lying in bed, attended by her only son. Zhao Hong explained that the aunt could no longer use her legs as a growing numbness consumed her body.

"Let's pray," George said. "Zhao Hong, I don't know whether to expect a sudden healing or not. God is in control, and it's His timing that's important. Ask your family to be patient."

The four believers knelt around the bed and began praying earnestly, waiting and hoping for a miracle. Thunder rumbled through the valley outside.

After about two hours, agitated voices yelling in Tuxiang could be heard outside, followed quickly by a banging at the door that reverberated through the one-room house.

The team glanced nervously at one another. There was no place to run or hide. As Zhao Hong's parents cracked the door open, four men pushed their way in, barking questions.

The eldest saw Ruth's unveiled Caucasian face.

"Foreign devil! Foreign devil!" he shouted in Tuxiang.

Lance raised his fists to defend Ruth, but her gentle hand on his shoulder stopped him.

"Brother, we didn't come here to fight. You can't accomplish God's purposes that way."

The men hauled the threesome outside, where flashes of lightning revealed a large angry mob.

The sight of Ruth's face stirred the crowd to a frenzy as they picked up the cry. "Foreign devils! Foreign devils!"

The ensuing journey through dingy back streets was a nightmare for the Americans, with the deafening shouts of the crowd aggravating their fears of what would happen next.

The horde grew as the Americans were paraded through the village. George glimpsed a distraught Zhao Hong and her parents following the procession. Occasional heavy raindrops splattered the crowd and sizzled on the burning torches.

The swelling mob brought their captives to the village square. The eldest captor ascended a crude platform of rough-hewn stone blocks, followed by the other three with their prisoners. The crowd continued chanting, "Foreign devils!"

"Brothers! Sisters! Uncles! Aunts!" the eldest captor began, quieting the assembly. "We found these foreigners in the house of Zhao Wu!"

Flashes of lightning cast ghoulish shadows as he spoke.

"You know that several months ago she refused to accompany us to pray for our ancestors at their graves. She had listened to lies of outsiders and violated our people's customs and religion. We invoked the names of our ancestors, asking them to strike her down if she was guilty. And so they did, beginning with deadness in her feet which has been progressing through the rest of her guilty body."

A murmur of agreement passed through the crowd.

"But now, these foreign devils have come here to upset our ancestors with their magic. We caught them in the act! Two tried to trick us by looking Chinese. But this one ...," he said, grabbing Ruth by the hair and pushing her forward, "is clearly a foreigner. We must judge them and punish them in accordance with our ancestral laws."

The Americans didn't need to understand much Tuxiang to know they were on trial. They smiled at each other weakly, quietly mouthing words of encouragement. Murmurs from the crowd grew louder, and villagers began shouting insults, but the old man restrained them from rioting. Raising his voice, he urged the crowd to remain calm while they tried the foreign devils.

As the roar subsided, a strike of lightning illumined the area, followed by shrieks of recognition. The Christian commandos watched the flickering torches part with the throng, starting from the back as the cries grew closer to the front of the crowd.

A lone figure walked boldly through the sea of people to the front of the mob. In the clearing stood Zhao Hong's aunt—healed. Those nearest her backed away in fear.

"Quick!" Ruth urged George in the confusion. "Speak to the crowd. This may be our only chance to tell them about Jesus."

While his guard was distracted, George sprang forward.

"Brothers and sisters, what you see today is God's goodness. The God of all the earth, who loves every one of you, has this day set Zhao Wu free from her bondage and longs to set all of you free from the bondage of shame, guilt, fear, and hopelessness. He offers you this new freedom and eternal life through His Son Jesus Christ."

The crowd returned their attention to the platform. A few nodded as if they had heard some of this before, and now it made sense. Lance and Ruth prayed fervently.

The three guards grabbed George and a hand was clamped over his mouth just as the storm unleashed a drenching rain.

The villagers' voices grew louder, unsure of just what was happening—who was right, and who was wrong. Some wanted to hear more. Others picked up rocks and glared at the stage.

Ruth glanced at Lance. "I must!" she mouthed.

Lance shook his head firmly. Then he saw her look into the heavens and smile. As her guard was distracted with George, she dashed forward and shouted above the din in simple Mandarin.

"Jesus loves you so much He was willing to die that you might have life with Him forever. Zhao Wu is proof! Ask Him today to forgive your sins. Trust in Him. Today is the day of your sal—"

Thud.

Crumple.

Everything went black.

Lance regained consciousness as the falling rain splashed on his upturned face. Pandemonium reigned. Inky darkness and lightning alternated as the crowd milled about. The guards fled.

Lance crawled around the platform, searching for his friends. "George! Ruth! Where are you?"

Lance found George and slapped his cheek. "George! Get up!"

"What? What happened? What's that screaming?"

"The crowd suddenly began throwing rocks, and we were both knocked out. Everyone's gone crazy!"

George quickly sat up. "Oh, no! God, please no! The last thing I saw was a huge rock hurtling at Ruth. Where is she?"

The pair searched frantically for their friend until Zhao Hong's father ran forward, torch in hand. On the ground near the platform they found Ruth's crumpled body lying in the mud. Blood mixed with the muddy rainwater around her head. A baseball-sized rock lay on the ground next to her, a silent participant in the drama.

George and Lance stared in horror, oblivious to the growing chaos. Zhao Hong shook them. "Come on! You must leave here before you are killed too. The mob is regrouping. Follow me!"

The two commandos lifted Ruth's fallen body, draped her arms over their shoulders, and raced after Zhao Hong and her father. Whistles sounded in the distance as soldiers arrived to disperse the crowd.

Sympathetic villagers helped the foreigners onto a horse cart. Lance stared at Ruth's body as the cart sloshed through the mud. George held Ruth's hand. "Call Christopher immediately!"

"I have no cell coverage!" Lance said. "And the radio's in the village!"

Zhao Hong's father hurried the cart down a muddy lane while the rough ride hindered George and Lance's efforts to search Ruth for signs of life. Gently Lance shook her by the shoulders.

"Ruth! Ruth! Wake up! Please wake up!"

The cart made it out of the village, but Zhao Hong's father didn't slow their pace. "There is a town on the other side of the mountain pass," he shouted over the din. "Maybe we get you to bus station before last bus departs. Medical clinic there as well."

"Wrap her scarf around the head wound," George yelled to Lance. "And make it tight!"

Just over the next hill, the cart stopped abruptly as a parked army truck barred their way. The truck's headlights flashed on, silhouetting armed soldiers and blinding the fleeing party. An officer strode forward through the rain and placed George and Lance under arrest.

"We have been expecting you. But don't be afraid. You are safer in our hands than with the mob back there. Quickly, into the truck."

"But our friend. She's hurt badly. She needs medical care!"

"Her health is not my concern!"

"But she needs—"

A soldier rammed George between the shoulder blades with his rifle. Zhao Hong screamed objections. Lance ran to help his friend up.

The two Americans picked up Ruth's limp body and climbed into the back of the truck. Zhao Hong cried out apologies as they departed.

The truck swerved down the mountain road, fighting with the thickening red mire. Guards in the canvas-covered back watched the three warily. Finally able to examine Ruth more carefully, Lance huddled over her body while George cradled her head in his lap.

"George!" Lance said. "George, I can't find a pulse."

George's already serious face grew ashen. "Father, help! We don't know what to do! Please save Ruth!"

* * *

The downpour gradually subsided, and the truck bounced along while the soldiers puzzled over their strange captives.

"We talked about this—that it could happen," Lance said.

"But that doesn't make it any easier." George put his face in his hands.

"Why didn't we listen more closely to Chara's warning?" Lance continued. "We all knew the risk before we came. I just don't think any of us expected it could really happen."

"No," George said slowly. "I think Ruth did. God often seemed to speak to her more clearly than to the rest of us. I think God showed her exactly what she was getting into."

Lance stared at Ruth's face. "George, just after the guards pulled you back, Ruth looked at me. It was a knowing look. I could see it in her eyes. I knew what she was about to do. I shook my head, but she said 'I must.' She had a premonition that she was going to pay a price for her next words."

Lance shook his head in grief. "Why did she do it? Why did she do it?"

"Because of her love."

As the truck rumbled on, the two brothers poured out their hearts in prayer for Ruth, just as they had for Yijing's mother.

* * *

The electrical storm disrupted communications throughout the region. In his bedroom Christopher huddled over the military radio. Amidst the thunderclaps, the contraption jumped to life.

"Come in, Commander. This is Win. Over."

Christopher jerked to attention and grabbed the mic. "This is Christopher. What's up, Win?"

"Sir, you need to abort current plans and evacuate your area ASAP. And do not send that smaller team into the mountains. I repeat, do not send out the team. My sources tell me there is a high risk of mission failure. Over."

"I'm afraid you're too late, Colonel. The team left very early yesterday, and we've lost contact with them. We can't evacuate without them."

Christopher listened for a moment to the blank static. Finally the voice replied.

"Sir, this is mission critical. The entire effort is at stake. Evacuate immediately once you have contact. Give the alternate rendezvous point we discussed. And if you don't make contact in the next few hours, I urge you to evacuate regardless. I myself will be on the next flight to the rendezvous city. Over."

TWENTY NINE

A brief lull in the prayer vigil for Zhao Hong's aunt.
A deep peace and a strangely expectant faith
has descended upon me despite the storm brewing outside
and the circumstances inside this mud hut.
You are about to bring breakthrough in one form or another.
The spiritual clouds are about to break.
This is why I left America.

—Ruth Grant

"Where are they?" Chara whispered aloud as she paced the living room at 3 a.m. "They should have checked in hours ago!"

Since piecing together Lance's three transmissions, the group had prayed on and off throughout the night. At first they simply prayed for healing for Zhao Hong's aunt. But after the check-in time passed, they began interceding for the team as well.

"Perhaps they're still transmitting but it just isn't getting through," suggested Kellie.

"That's possible," replied Christopher, "but I think we would have heard a word or two, or at least a break in the static. There's been nothing."

The military-style radio hummed quietly in the corner with static while Phil listened attentively. Music from the other end of the room helped mask their conversation.

As the team continued in prayer, they heard a break in the static. Everyone froze in anticipation.

"Hello? Can hear me? This Zhao Hong."

Phil snatched up the transmitter. "Zhao Hong! This is Phil. What's happening?"

"All is terrible!" filtered through the static. "George and Lance captured by soldiers."

"What about Ruth?" Phil asked.

Nothing.

"Zhao Hong, what about Ruth?"

The team heard sobs through the static, followed by garbled Mandarin. Phil urged Zhao Hong to repeat the message.

This time they heard clearly. "Ruth hurt. I don't know. No respond!"

The team members sat down, stunned.

Phil continued monitoring the transmission.

"I sorry! Somehow they knew foreigners coming ... waiting for us. You may be in ..."

The rest of the message was lost, but the meaning was clear.

* * *

Christopher took charge immediately. His arms waved as he gave orders. "You all have essentials in one small backpack, right?"

Everyone nodded.

"All right, we leave in twenty minutes. I'll alert the colonel and have him call the other teams. If the authorities know about us, they may notify the Lao and Vietnamese governments. We may all be in danger. Jesus taught the disciples to flee to the next town when persecution came. We are all getting out of this country immediately until we know more. Now, hurry!"

Team members made final preparations to flee as Chara woke the kids. Continuing storm interference kept Christopher from contacting the colonel, so he typed out a quick chat message on his keyboard:

Christopher: Bro, u there?

Nic: Hey, buddy! Give us the word. We've all been here talking to Father about the team since you last called.

Christopher: We're gonna try to get out thru GZ & prob into HK. Will keep u posted. Get ur team out to Thai ASAP. Relay this msg to the col & let him know what's happening. Then—

The door slammed open, and several policemen rushed in. Christopher jumped to his feet. "Hey, what are you doing?"

He lunged to quit the chat, but an officer whipped him across the head with a baton as another grabbed the computer.

The chat screen remained open.

Nic: Hey, buddy! You there?

Nic: Waiting for a response ...

Nic: Assuming the worst.

Phil stood to obscure the field radio in the corner as Chara ran into the living room. Sleepy children followed her. Joshua, seeing his daddy lying on the floor, rushed to his side. Hearing the commotion from next door, Julie and Kellie rushed in. As Chara comforted the younger kids, the two women helped Christopher up.

Ignoring the team, the police ransacked the apartment for evidence. Then two soldiers entered the apartment, carrying rifles. Behind them sauntered Zhi Liang. The police stopped their search and stood at attention. At Zhi Liang's signal, they resumed their search.

Christopher stood feebly with Kellie and Julie's assistance. Caleb and David hugged their daddy's legs while Joshua moved to protect Chara who was holding Elizabeth.

"Zhi Liang, what is going on?" Christopher demanded.

Zhi Liang held his hand up for silence while a policeman spoke in his ear. Then he looked squarely at Christopher.

"You are under arrest for espionage and inciting revolt against People's Republic of China. You were caught using computer traced to illegal activities. And you aided three Americans who infiltrated a restricted zone."

Just then an officer returned from the back corner carrying the military radio.

"Ah! This deeper than we thought," Zhi Liang said. "American military radio. Obvious link to CIA. Seize this man and place him in custody.

"Mr. Owen, you will be tried before Chinese officials who will decide fate of you and"—he glanced at a sheet of paper—"Yang George and Chu Lance. You Americans always have romantic ideas of your government rescuing you, but many have died for lesser crimes in our country."

Zhi Liang turned to Chara, and his features softened a bit.

"The rest of you have one hour to pack for deportation. Any resistance and you, too, will be tried for espionage."

Chara stepped forward to object.

"Stop!" Christopher shouted, fearing she might take the next blow of the baton. "All of you, do exactly as he says! You can't do anything for me here. Get back to the States and call Win ASAP. I love you all and am ready to give my life for the glory of God ..." His voice trailed off as the soldiers hurried him out the door.

Chara ran to the doorway. Her shout stopped the procession in the hallway. "Zhi Liang, what about Ruth? What's being done with her?"

Zhi Liang did a quick about-face and consulted the same sheet of paper.

"The girl is dead."

Chara collapsed in the doorway.

* * *

Christopher's wounded head swam. *Ruth dead? Is it really true? How is it possible? Oh, God! Protect the rest of the team! Please, God, let them get to safety, especially the children.*

The main door from the apartments opened. Dizzy with pain, Christopher carefully placed his foot on the top step. A soldier pushed him from behind, and down he tumbled. A deep gash opened over his brow, and blood seeped into his eyes. Cackles echoed from the landing.

Father, forgive them. They're so young. They have no idea what they're doing.

The soldiers pulled Christopher to his feet to manacle his wrists and ankles. Then as he shuffled toward the truck, they tripped him and—laughing—kicked him repeatedly.

Oh, Father, strengthen me. Let me not bring shame on You!

Christopher's left eye swelled shut, and his right eye grew blurry. Hurled into the truck like a sack of potatoes, his body was pummeled repeatedly by rifle butts. Lying on the bed of the truck, he was tossed by the lurching truck into the soldiers' legs. Each one he touched spit on him or kicked him with their hard-toed boots, and every jolt of the truck magnified his agony.

Oh, Lord, protect George and Lance. Please, protect them from experiencing this. Yet use my life—our lives—to save the nations!

Once, to find a less painful position, Christopher tried raising himself up and leaning against the bench, but the soldiers struck him with the butts of their rifles. He didn't try to get up again.

Yet somehow, Christopher didn't find the pain as terrible as he would have expected. He remembered reading accounts of martyrs who had endured excruciating pain by the grace of God and wondered if he himself was experiencing such grace.

An hour later he lost consciousness as his blood covered the bed of the truck.

* * *

Christopher awoke to daylight and a soldier tossing muddy water into his face. He didn't know how long he had been traveling. Pain seared every part of his body.

Two soldiers pulled him from the truck, but he couldn't find the strength to stand. The soldiers resorted to half carrying, half dragging him into the gray stone prison through hallway after hallway and turn after turn. Christopher faintly perceived a blur of fluorescent lights as he slipped in and out of consciousness.

The guards finally stopped before a metal door and dropped him on the cold floor. Another guard opened the door and shoved Christopher into the cell with his boot. Christopher heard familiar voices shouting from the dim interior, but couldn't place them. *Jesus, where am I? Help me!*

The door slammed shut, and Christopher passed out again.

* * *

When Christopher regained consciousness, he could make out the concerned face of George in the dim light.

"Well, Chief," said George, "I hate to admit it, but I'm glad you could join us!"

Christopher smiled weakly as George dabbed at his bleeding forehead with a blood-soaked strip torn from his own shirt.

"I'm glad you're okay. What about Lance?" he said weakly.

"You call this okay, dude?" asked Lance, as he leaned into Christopher's field of vision.

"Well, neither of you seems badly hurt. And the lodging

you've chosen is better than some dorms I've seen. I just hope the food's okay."

The two grinned at their leader. They were relieved, despite their circumstances, to be reunited. Then George became sober.

"Christopher, I have something difficult to tell you."

Christopher grimaced as he turned his head. "I already know about Ruth. Is she really gone?"

George nodded grimly. "I don't know what happened. I didn't think to stop her. The crowd went wild, and Ruth ran forward to preach the gospel. Rocks began to fly. Somehow a rock ... a big one ... I don't know how I could have ..."

"It's not your fault, George," interrupted Lance. "We've talked about this. They were holding you to keep you from preaching. If it's anybody's fault, it's mine. I should have stopped her."

George raised his voice. "Well, maybe I should have kept her from coming with us! I was supposed to be in charge!"

"Guys ..." Christopher's hoarse voice silenced the argument. "If it's anyone's fault, it's mine. I'm the commander. I authorized the mission," he ordered with finality. "Please, just tell me what happened ... if you can bear it."

He laid his head back on the cold stone floor, and the two men recounted their experience from the time they entered the vent. They laughed and cried together through the story.

Lance stared vacantly at the wall. "She had that look in her eyes, Christopher. She said 'I *must!*'"

"And then," added George, "her Mandarin was so bad ... but for that brief time she spoke like a native!"

Overwhelmed with their loss of Ruth, his injuries and fatigue, and concern for his family and the rest of the team, Christopher began crying again.

"The Lord's will be done," he said softly. "He is good, and His lovingkindness endures forever." Christopher opened his eyes again and spoke each syllable deliberately. "I'm so proud of Ruth. Her death will not be in vain; the death of a martyr never is."

"A martyr?" Lance said. "I never thought of Ruth as ..."

A key clattered in the lock. The door swung open, and Zhi Liang strode in with guards. "Thank you for that confession, gentlemen. Will be most helpful in prosecuting you fully!"

"Zhi Liang, I demand to speak with Ching Fei," Christopher said. "He will be most distraught over this."

Zhi Liang walked closer to the bloodied form of the KPF commander. "I so sorry to inform you, but Comrade Ching Fei relieved of duties. He turn back on your illegal activities. I now in charge."

Christopher wheezed and coughed up blood. George and Lance raised him up to sit against the wall. "Then I demand to speak with a member of the U.S. Embassy immediately. The U.S. government will not stand for such treatment of its citizens."

Zhi Liang smiled. "Again, am sorry to inform you that U.S. government has no jurisdiction here. They not know you are missing, nor can they help. You break important Chinese laws, and no government help you now. I assure you, however, trial and punishment be swift, so you not suffer long in prison."

"Please," George said, "at least give us something to bind Christopher's wounds. Some are bleeding uncontrollably. And look! He's coughing up blood. He needs a doctor."

"Maybe he should not resist People's Liberation Army so much. It not matter, for much worse happen to you soon." Zhi Liang turned and left as suddenly as he had come.

"Lance, tear the rest of my shirt into strips," George said, ripping off his shirt. "We've got to stop this bleeding. Meanwhile, Christopher, you rest."

But Christopher was already unconscious.

* * *

The brief consciousness of their commander—even to the point of playful banter—gave rise to hopes that were dashed bitterly the next day. Christopher took a turn for the worse. Between blood loss, internal injuries, and dehydration, he slipped in and out of a fitful delirium. Fever raged through his body.

Lance mopped Christopher's unconscious forehead with a wet cloth. "George, do you think we're going to die?"

"Maybe. Good possibility as long as Zhi Liang is in charge."

"Yeah, that's what I figure," said Lance. "I thought if it ever came to this I'd be scared stiff, but I don't think I am. You know, the fear of persecution seems worse than the persecution itself.

I've been thinking a lot about death—especially heaven. I figure we might be there pretty soon. What do you think it's like?"

"Hmm. Like nothing we've ever dreamed of," mused George. "Our deepest desires will finally be completely satisfied."

"You know what I'm looking forward to when we get there? No more temptation! Just life like it was meant to be."

George nodded. "I can't wait to see Jesus. I think He will meet my longings in ways I've never thought to expect."

"George," Lance hesitated, then asked meekly, "do you think Jesus will tell me, 'Well done, good and faithful servant'? I mean, even after all the sins I've committed as a Christ-follower?"

George put an arm around his friend. "I know He will, Lance. I know He will."

"That will make all this worthwhile," Lance said with finality.

"Yep, sure will," agreed George. "I just hope that someone will continue the KPF work. I'm worried about what will happen without Christopher. He should never have come to China with us. He's the leader of this movement!"

"Dude, as headstrong as he is?" said Lance. "How could anyone have stopped him?"

The men sat in silence, each deep in his own thoughts.

"Hey, George? Would you do one more thing with me, bro?"

"What's that?"

"I know I don't sing too well, but let's sing some praises, just like Paul and Silas did in prison. What more can they do to us?"

The two children of God sang for over an hour in Mandarin and English. The lyrics of their sweet, discordant tunes rang through nearby cells as other prisoners cocked their heads to listen.

When the duo saw Christopher resting more peacefully as they worshiped, they sang all the more jubilantly. And at times they heard other prisoners humming along.

* * *

The next morning Christopher was weak but conscious, and the three men were brought to a small room where an officer sat behind a lone desk. Zhi Liang stood to one side as the officer read the charges.

"Owen Christopher, Chu Lance, and Yang George," the officer said in flawless English. "You are charged with espionage and inciting revolt against the Chinese government, first by forming secret societies of Tuxiang students and then by provoking the villages of the Tuxiang countryside against the common beliefs and practices of China.

"Do you have anything to say to these charges?"

"I'm afraid anything we say will be meaningless in this court," Christopher said softly to George and Lance, who were helping him stand.

"We have nothing to say, except to demand that we see American counsel and be represented appropriately."

"You have no rights here!" the officer spit fiercely. "This is a military court. Here are confessions. Sign them and your charges may be reduced. You have five minutes to read them and decide."

Zhi Liang and the officer departed, leaving the three to themselves. Lance examined the confession bearing his name.

"Maybe we should sign them," he said.

"You two do as you think best," Christopher said. "I can't sign a pack of lies just to save my skin ... to avoid persecution."

"You're right," Lance said, ripping the page in two.

"We're in this together to the end," said George, following Lance's lead. The three shredded their confessions and began tossing the pieces in the air, laughing together.

When the officer saw the shredded paper, he was furious.

"I do not need your confessions anyway!" he bellowed. "I had hoped to sentence you to hard labor, but since you have been uncooperative, you will die before a firing squad tomorrow night at 1800 hours.

"Guards, take them back to their cell. Next case, please!"

Zhi Liang watched with satisfaction as the Americans left the room. The three condemned prisoners were surprised at how many others were awaiting their turn before the military court.

"Well, I guess that settles it," said Lance meekly. "I had been wondering how we would die—you know, Chinese water torture, bamboo up our fingernails, stoning, lice infestation. Actually, I think that ten bullets through my body is much better than the alternatives!"

"Lance! How can you joke about this?" George exclaimed, but when he saw Lance's face he started laughing, quietly at first, then hysterically.

While Christopher slept, the other two spent much of the day listing horrible ways to die, then expressing gratitude that they would die quickly. Somehow, the humor enabled them to take back some control and make the best of their hopeless situation.

Before nodding off to an uneasy sleep that night, their songs of thanksgiving again reverberated down the halls. And when they could sing no longer, they drifted off to sleep.

THIRTY

You always deliver us, whether in life or in death.
To die and be with You is better.
To remain on in the flesh, though, means more fruitful labor.
I am hard pressed which I prefer.
But regardless, You are our Deliverer—
whether escorting us to Your welcoming arms in heaven
or escorting us to safety on earth.

—Ruth Grant, martyr

The next morning George tore up Lance's shirt and dressed Christopher's wounds afresh. Despite George's best effort at binding the strips around Christopher's head and over one eye, the gash refused to stay closed.

"No worries," Christopher mumbled. "It won't matter soon."

Around midday, a young corporal with several folders came for the three prisoners.

"Why are you taking us so early?" George asked in Mandarin.

The corporal didn't seem to understanding the question and said that their punishment was to be administered elsewhere. This time they were treated more humanely—Christopher was carried on a stretcher and assisted by several guards into the canvas-covered back of a waiting military truck.

The truck rumbled along for several hours.

"Probably want to find a nice, secluded spot where no one can see 'em shoot us," Lance said, "to keep this thing quiet."

The men noticed that the truck stopped at least three times at military installations, where their files were checked. At each point, fresh guards and a new corporal took charge of the three Christian commandos. Evening rolled past, and the truck seemed no nearer a destination than when it had started.

Several hours later, Lance saw increasing signs of civilization showing through gaps in the canvas. Soon it was apparent the truck was entering Kunming. It passed through the city streets—now vacant—until it entered a dark way station.

A young corporal they hadn't seen before opened the back of the truck and had the guards unload the prisoners.

"Well, bro, I guess this is it," George said to Lance. "You've been the best friend ever."

Lance was too choked up to respond. He stepped out of the truck as the guards unloaded Christopher on the stretcher. "George? Why would they bring us here to execute us? Do they want to make an example of us?"

The guards stood George and Lance by a wall and placed Christopher next to them. With unexpected reserves, he stood and remained standing, supported by his two brothers in Christ.

"We stand together till the end!" he whispered.

Bang!

The three jumped as a truck door slammed closed.

"Why are they waiting?" Lance said.

"I don't know," Christopher grimaced, "but quick. Let's pray Stephen's prayer. *Father, do not hold this sin against them!*"

"We agree! Amen!" George and Lance whispered.

"Go ahead," George said in Mandarin as the corporal approached the threesome. "Finish it. Shoot us. We're at peace!"

"Shoot you? What do you mean?" the corporal replied. "My orders are to bring you here and release you."

"Release us?"

The young corporal sighed impatiently and opened a folder for George to view in the moonlight. Inside was a photo of a young Chinese man about George's age but definitely not George. And someone else's name was on the file.

"See here!" the corporal insisted, pointing with his finger at the first page. "My orders are to release you in Kunming, but no other instructions." He spun on his heel, climbed into the truck, and drove away.

The three men stared at the taillights, and Christopher slumped to the ground.

"Somehow they mixed up our files," George said to the others in disbelief. "That wasn't my name or photo in that file."

"But what about me?" Christopher asked. "It's obvious I'm an

American."

Both men laughed.

"Christopher, if you could see yourself you'd understand," Lance said. "You're eyes are swollen, so their shape is hidden. A bandage covers most of your head and face. And the guards haven't looked at you the whole time. To them, you're Chinese."

Christopher braced himself against the brick wall and stood again. "Then I suggest we get out of here while we can!"

"Where can we go?" George said. "We have no money, no identification, and no shirts!"

"Help me walk, brothers," Christopher said. "This stretcher will attract too much attention. I think I know a place we can go."

* * *

Shivering, George and Lance half carried Christopher through the deserted streets of Kunming. After two hours of hobbling and frequently resting, the trio stood before a metal door on the top floor of an apartment building.

George rang the doorbell.

"Wei?" they heard faintly from behind the door.

"We are three friends who met you in a foreign country," George said in Mandarin.

Immediately the door opened. The occupant ushered them inside and closed the door quickly behind them.

Ching Fei became ashen as he beheld Christopher, George, and Lance. "What you do here? I thought you in prison."

"My dear friend," Christopher said, "we'll explain everything if you will just let us rest a whi—"

George and Lance caught Christopher as he collapsed. Two other men rushed in from a back room.

"Nic? Colonel?" Lance wondered if he himself was dreaming.

"Shh! Quiet!" ordered the colonel, scooping Christopher in his arms and carrying him to a back bedroom.

After a few minutes, Christopher recovered from his swoon. He found the colonel administering first aid and dressing his wounds. "What are you doing here? What about the others?" Christopher asked.

"Don't worry about everyone else, buddy," Nic said. "They're safe by now. Your family and the rest of your team were escorted to the airport and flew home, and we have sent them a secure message that the three of you are now with us. The colonel and I left our teams in safe territory and got here as quickly as we could. We came to try to negotiate your release, but it looks like you've done a good job of that yourself!"

"You think this is a good job?" Christopher said, laughing weakly and then wincing. "I'd hate to see a bad job!" He wheezed, coughed up blood, and closed his eyes again.

Ching Fei dropped to his knees at Christopher's side. "Can he hear me?" he asked the colonel.

"I'm not sure. He's fading in and out, but you can try."

"Christopher, I don't know if you hear me. I have been in charge of observing you in China. At first I only do my duty to keep you from spreading religion. But you have been very kind ... more kinder than any person I meet.

"Then I begin protect your activities, for I see that God you teach is good for Chinese people, not bad. Zhi Liang work for me, and I try keep him in control. But he ambitious. He have me investigated and dismissed. He responsible for your problems in countryside and at university.

"I very sorry. Please forgive me. Please not judge Chinese people by actions of few individuals. China need more people like you and your friends."

Christopher opened his eyes and turned toward Ching Fei. "My friend, I don't judge you or any of the Chinese for what has happened. I love the Chinese people. I want them to know how much God loves them. All along we figured you might be spying on us, but it made no difference to us. We all forgave you long ago. I only hope you will one day decide to know God personally through his Son, Jesus Christ."

Ching Fei's lip trembled. "If there any way I can help you, I will!" he said resolutely.

George put his arm around the man's shoulders and explained to him the way of salvation while the colonel continued monitoring Christopher's condition.

Once Christopher was stabilized, Colonel Dunbar turned his attention to Lance and George. "Boys," the colonel said, "how did you manage to get away?"

George and Lance took turns telling their fantastic tale.

"If that's the case, we must get you to the American Embassy in Beijing immediately," the colonel said.

"Must act quickly," said Ching Fei. "File mix-up likely be found by morning. All roads watched after that. Must hurry on first flight."

"But we have no ID for airport security," George said.

"Leave that to me," said Ching Fei.

The colonel attended Christopher for the rest of the night, rehydrating him with sports drinks and administering antibiotics for infection.

Somehow Ching Fei secured airline tickets. Shortly after dawn he ushered the five Americans through security, with Christopher's wheelchair seeming to expedite the process. The plane's first-class cabin gave Christopher room to recline.

In Beijing, Ching Fei arranged a taxi van for the day while the colonel grabbed the first English newspaper he could find.

In the taxi the colonel reported, "You three are described as dangerous subversives—stirring up revolt in China's provinces. Speculation links you with the CIA, anarchists, radical terrorists, fascists, intolerant missionary proselytizers, and so on. They even got the name of the group right—KPF. Getting out may be harder than we thought. I'm going to place a call to my friend in the embassy right after I update Jeanie."

To avoid being traced, the colonel used his satellite phone.

"Hey, sweetie, I found them,"

"Thank God! Have you talked to Tal yet?"

"Just getting ready to call him. Gotta find a way to get out ... again." Suddenly the colonel's hands began to tremble. Soon his whole body shook. He could no longer talk.

After a moment of silence Jeanie urged, "Alright, soldier! Remember. You've done this dozens of times, and every time you've gotten your troops to safety. Do what you do best!"

"Not every time ..."

"Yes, you have. Now do it and come home! I believe in you!"

Win heard the line go dead. Taking a deep breath, he drew himself together and punched in a number he knew by heart.

"Tal! This is Win ... Yep, that's right ... You called it, only we aborted too late. We're doing damage control now and need an exit strategy."

They discussed the situation at length as the taxi wound through Beijing traffic toward the embassy with Christopher passed out in the back. When he hung up, Win looked grim.

"It doesn't sound good. The Chinese government has secured the entrance to the embassy, admitting only people with proper authorization.

"And that's only half of it. Tal says our government is letting China deal with this as an internal problem. In other words, the embassy offers no sanctuary for us."

These words fell like a bombshell ... to have come thirteen hundred miles only to discover their own government wouldn't intervene.

The colonel wasn't finished.

"I do see one possibility, but to investigate it I'm going to have to go to the embassy ... alone. My military radio and satellite phone aren't adequate for what I hope to do. I need to use the embassy's secure communications equipment. I doubt the police know of my connection to the KPF yet, so I may be able to get in.

"You men lie low, and wait for me near McDonald's. You'll find it just a few blocks from the embassy. Christopher's vital signs are very weak. Watch him."

"Wait," Nic said. "Let's pray for you to get in safely and to find a way out for us."

After a brief prayer, Win exited the taxi mid-street and wound his way to the embassy. It was only with much cajoling and prayer that the colonel gained admittance to the embassy.

* * *

Ching Fei and the team took turns monitoring Christopher as he lay in the back of the van. He was obviously in pain, and his condition was becoming more critical by the hour.

Parked outside McDonald's, the fugitives were inconspicuous amidst the many foreigners flocking to this Western oasis. George and Lance wolfed down Big Macs while Nic kept an eye on Christopher. He offered him a sip of soda any time he opened his eyes, but to no avail.

Early that afternoon the colonel rejoined the group and checked Christopher's vitals. "Ching Fei, we need a port where we can hire a small boat and put out to sea. Any ideas?"

"Just go one hundred fifty kilometers to port of Tianjin. Very close. Two hours."

Colonel Dunbar considered this then shook his head.

"No, then we'd have to travel too far by sea. Tianjin is at the western end of the Bohai Sea, and is too heavily watched. We need to get to the Yellow Sea."

"Perhaps Qingdao. Good-size port. Could take minivan and not arouse suspicion. Then try to find boat operator to take us. Wait! I have better idea. I have childhood friend who live in small port called Weihai. It is at point where Bohai Sea end and Yellow Sea begin. He own small fishing boat."

"Great!" said the colonel. "Let's hire our van to take us all the way there."

"That very expensive!" Ching Fei objected. "Weihai eight hundred kilometers away. Ten hours at least."

"We'll pay the money," the colonel said, unfazed. "But Ching Fei, the driver must keep our destination secret. Also, we need several bags of IV fluids. We've got to rehydrate Christopher."

The van driver agreed, and soon they were racing to Weihai.

* * *

The weathered, wrinkled old man didn't like being awakened so long before sunup. Even without hearing the words, those in the van could tell he was arguing heatedly with Ching Fei.

"What if he won't take us?" Lance asked.

"Trust Ching Fei. He's still got clout," answered the colonel as they watched the animated gestures of the two "old friends."

The door to the small home closed, and Ching Fei returned to the van. "He not happy, weather bad today, but will do it. Quickly! We must hurry to boat before he change mind."

The boat was the first to leave port that day. All morning they traveled due east, out into the open water of the Yellow Sea. The putrid smell of rotting fish and the growing swells combined to send Nic, George, and Lance repeatedly to the railing to vomit.

Christopher, down in the hold, continued slipping away.

Around ten, the captain saw a Chinese coast guard helicopter approaching. "Quick, get below! Stay out of sight," he ordered.

The chopper made several tight circles overhead, apparently wondering at the lone vessel braving the worsening seas while others stayed in port. The captain gave a friendly wave, and the helicopter flew off again.

Later that afternoon the colonel climbed the pilothouse roof to use a radio he had picked up at the embassy. Then, satisfied, he returned to the cabin. Throughout the day the team members took turns trying to keep Christopher cool, dipping moldy towels into the chilly sea and then laying them across his body.

Twice more that night the colonel made radio calls. After the last call, he left a small device on the roof of the pilothouse, where it emitted a faint beeping sound. Then, as only an old soldier can do, he dropped quickly into a deep sleep.

Around 4:30 a.m. the device on the pilothouse began to chirp loudly and flash a brilliant strobe light. The colonel sprang to his feet, smiling broadly. He ran onto the rocking deck and braced himself against the gunwale. The others followed, intermittently blinded by bright-as-day flashes punctuating the pitch-blackness.

"Hang on to a rail!" shouted the colonel above the roar of the diesel engine as the little box continued to flash its pulsing light.

Within a minute, two F-15s passed a few hundred feet above the boat, deafening those on deck with their engines.

"Good morning, Colonel," a voice squawked over the radio. "Glad to see you could make it. Over."

The colonel picked up the transmitter. "Good morning, boys. Not as glad as we are to see you. Over."

"Roger that. The whirlybird should be here in an hour, just at daybreak before the swells are forecast to get even worse. We'll form a perimeter to ensure you get no other visitors. Now that we have your location, it'd be best for you to shut her down and stay put. It's a privilege to serve you again, sir. Over."

"Roger that, son. Please advise the chopper crew to have a medic ready. The first man we will transport needs immediate attention. Over."

"Roger, Colonel. My wingman's already transmitting. Over

and out."

The team stared incredulously at the colonel's new radio. Ching Fei surveyed the colonel with new awe while the captain and his mate cowered in the pilothouse.

"How in the world ...?" Nic began. Then he stopped short, refusing to be surprised any longer at what the colonel could pull off. "Aren't you concerned that the Chinese authorities will pick up your transmissions, sir?"

"Naw. We're using a short-distance encoded transmission. These guys are flying so low that they won't be picked up on radar, and we should have entered international waters two or three hours ago. Of course," the colonel conceded, "China may not agree with that assessment.

"Nic, prepare everyone to depart. For the safety of Ching Fei and the captain, we have to remove any evidence that we have ever been on this boat."

For the next half hour, they scoured the boat for any evidence of their presence and bagged it to take with them.

"Colonel, this is wing commander," the radio crackled again. "Do you read me? Over."

"Go ahead, son. Over."

"Sir, our radar has picked up a Chinese naval cutter heading your way. If we've spotted them, we figure they've picked us up as well. You're still out of their range, but not for long. Head east at top speed. We will attempt to divert their attention without provoking an international incident. Over."

"Roger, wing commander. We'll head east. Over and out."

The captain hurried to the helm and strained the ancient motors as far as he dared to stay outside the naval cutter's radar. Suddenly a shout pierced the feverish activity. The captain's mate stood pointing at a black dot just above the horizon, skimming over the surface of the water toward them.

"It's the helicopter!" shouted Lance.

The radio sprang to life. "Good morning, Colonel. This is Mama Bird. Do you read me? Over."

"Copy. We've just spotted you on the horizon. What's the status with that Chinese naval cutter? Over."

"Sir, we have a window of about fifteen minutes to get you on board before they get us on their radar. We'll have to work fast. Let's transport the injured man first. Over."

In less than a minute, the helicopter was hovering above the boat, wind and water spraying those in the ship below. Two crewmen descended on a cable atop a litter. The rough seas made the landing difficult, but as soon as the litter hit the deck, the crewmen loaded Christopher.

With well-trained efficiency, one crewman rode up to the chopper with Christopher. Five times more, the harness was lowered and the remaining KPF members plucked from the ship, followed by the crewman. The whole operation took under twelve minutes, and then the helicopter raced to avoid detection. From the open doorway, George watched the fishing boat vanish, with Ching Fei smiling and waving.

In the cockpit, the colonel greeted men he had commanded in prior missions. "Frank! Been a long time," he said to the captain. "Everything arranged to get these guys back to the States without going through immigration?"

"Yes, sir. But it wasn't easy," the captain replied. "Kind of strange, actually. We had some trouble from up top that we didn't expect. You know, ever since the International Coalition has taken over our special ops, we've had a lot of autonomy and authorization to really kick butt.

"However, when we came up with this little scheme, we got a personal call from the director's office telling us to lay off. Really surprised me, sir.

"But you know the men, sir. We can't leave one of our own behind. We sort of ignored the director's orders to do this."

"Thanks, Captain. How many people know about this?"

"Oh, I'd say only about fifteen. Highest up is your friend, General Dixon."

"Dixon, huh? Great! He wouldn't crack under a congressional hearing. Okay, son, let's get these people home as fast as possible."

"Our ETA, sir?" the medic called out from the back. "This man needs more help than I can give, and his vitals are marginal. He needs surgery, and he needs it fast. There's only so much I can do in the air. It may already be too late."

Colonel Dunbar looked at the captain gravely. "He may not look like it, Captain, but this is a mighty important young man. I'd lay down my life for him. Christopher is my commander, if you can believe it. And a darn good one, too."

"Yes, sir," snapped the captain. He made a beeline for the nearest aircraft carrier equipped for emergency surgery, while Christopher's life hung in the balance.

THIRTY ONE

Wroth picked up a two-thousand-year-old Chinese vase and hurled it against the wall of his California home. Shards fell at Marlene's feet. She glanced over at Jake Simmons. He stood at attention, unflinching.

"You had them in your grasp, Simmons! One fell swoop by the Chinese military, and they're history. The colonel! This upstart Owen! You had them in a neat little net!"

Wroth circled Simmons like a shark closing in on its prey. "Do you have nothing to say for yourself?"

"Sir, thirty more minutes and we would have had them. No one anticipated the U.S. Navy intervening. We had them . . ."

Wroth shoved a chair across the room. Marlene jumped.

"I warned you about Dunbar. I told you he would be one step ahead of you. Could you not foresee that he would pull strings with the military? What did you think he was doing there in the embassy in Beijing? Having tea with old chums?"

"Sir, he will not escape again."

Wroth stood nose to nose with Simmons. "Oh, no? In well over forty years of military service, no trap has yet held him. How do I know you can do this, Jake?"

"Director, I have failed you. I tender my resignation."

Marlene looked up in surprise.

Wroth sat in a plump armchair and sighed. "I don't want your resignation, Jake. Sit down."

Simmons was incredulous. He stole a glance at Marlene, who nodded. Then he sat, facing Wroth. Marlene's pulse slowed.

Michael Wroth stared at Simmons for what seemed like an eternity. No one dared speak. Finally Wroth broke the silence. "No, you will do. You have it in you, Jake. You just don't realize it. Your mind is young and fresh. Dunbar's is old and set in its ways. He outfoxed you this time. But you can beat him.

"Think about him—about his stratagems. Tell me how you are going to bring him down. Tell me how you are going to supplant him as the greatest military strategist."

Jake turned and looked into Wroth's eyes for the first time. Marlene watched the exchange. The director was doing it again. Turning another soul to his purposes and inspiring him to draw upon unknown reserves.

"Sir, the colonel escaped because he chose the battlefield. It was terrain suited for his purposes. He had reserves in place we knew nothing about.

"The next skirmish will be on ground of our choosing. We will have reserves behind reserves. No matter where he turns, he will be hemmed in. We will find men with no connection to the colonel. They will have no qualms about crushing him.

"But for that we must plan meticulously. It may take some time, sir, but we will get him."

Wroth rose and poured two drinks. He handed one to Jake. "I know you mean that, Jake. Prove to me that you can take him down. When you do, you will rise to global prominence at my side. Nothing will stop us."

The glasses clinked as they toasted. Both men took a deep gulp. Wroth smashed his glass in the fireplace and grinned broadly. Jake followed suit.

Marlene jumped twice as glass slivers fell amidst the porcelain shards at her feet. And the fire in the hearth leapt as the brandy flamed.

THIRTY TWO

No place left?
Assaulting the gates of hell will cost the Church
unlike anything in history.
Paul told us, "Death works in me but life works in you."
Life in them—the lost?
No cost is too great for their salvation.
We endure all things for the sake of the elect
that they may obtain salvation (2 Timothy 2:10).
                                        —Ruth Grant, martyr

Christopher lay in an intensive care trauma unit in Seoul. Chara sat praying by his bedside, as she had since arriving three days earlier through another of the colonel's connections.

Christopher showed no sign of emerging from his coma. His injuries were worse than Win had feared, and Chara's heart was heavier than she thought humanly possible.

As much as she had tried to prepare herself for the possibility that one of her own family members might give his or her life for God's Kingdom, it was harder than she had ever imagined—first dear Ruth and now her beloved Christopher.

Without warning, the line on Christopher's heart monitor went flat, triggering an alarm. Before Chara had time to think, the code team burst into the room. Chara retreated to the corner and watched. A nurse stood ready to activate the defibrillator.

"Clear!"

Christopher's body jerked violently upon the bed, but the ECG continued flat.

"Clear!"

Again, the body jerked. Again, no heartbeat.

And on and on it went, a dizzying pace of IVs, medications, respiratory equipment, more defibrillations, and CPR. A quiet word from the lead physician brought a hush to the room. "We need to call it. There's nothing more we can do."

And just as suddenly as it had started, everything stopped.

Christopher Owen, brainchild and luminary of the Kingdom Preparation Force, was dead.

* * *

Renee burst into the room, awakening Chara from her nightmare. Christopher was still in a coma on the bed next to her.

"Oh, Chara! I came as soon as I could get a flight!"

Chara was drenched in a cold sweat, her hair plastered against her scalp, and there were dark circles under her eyes.

"Honey, you look terrible." Renee said, hugging her friend.

Chara didn't try to hold back the tears. "We all knew it was risky, but did we really expect this? Ruth killed. Christopher on the brink of death. He's lost so much blood and is injured so badly. The doctors ... don't know if they reached him in time. It's all so ... I don't know what we'll do if ... The children ... The movement ..."

She couldn't continue.

Renee stayed with Chara for the next couple of weeks while Stacy watched the Owen kids back in Los Angeles. A parade of visitors dropped off flowers and notes from people interceding around the world. Nic and the colonel came and went from Southeast Asia as they balanced directing KPF field operations and handling media attention with their concern for Christopher.

While his was not yet a "church-hold" name, Christopher and the KPF had received much attention. The martyrdom of Ruth Grant was gripping a new generation. Tales of a church-planting movement in Tuxiangland and rumors of the "three preachers" and the Acts-like miracles all rippled around the world.

Laying in his hospital bed, Christopher came to symbolize a new hope for fulfilling the Great Commission—a hope that great mission agencies and little churches alike found inspiring.

* * *

After three weeks in a coma, Christopher opened his eyes, trying through the fog to make sense of what had happened. Chara sat in a chair next to him, holding his hand. He blinked several times. Finally he choked out, "Water. I'm so thirsty!"

Chara jerked to attention. She looked at him, her eyes filled with tears. She leaned over and hugged him for an eternity. Christopher, arms limp, basked in her embrace, then whispered again, "Water, honey. I'm so thirsty!"

Chara jumped to her feet. "Oh! I'm so sorry! Wait a minute, my love!"

She ran into the hallway. Several nurses rushed into the room, checking his vital signs.

Moments later a doctor strode in. He checked Christopher's chart and consulted with the nurses. A smile spread across his face. "Welcome to the world of the living again, Mr. Owen! I believe you are *out of the woods*, as you Americans say. I'll be back to check on you later this evening."

The doctor left. One by one the nurses, many of whom had cared for Christopher for weeks, bowed with embarrassed grins and backed out of the room.

Christopher and Chara savored being re-united. As the hours passed, Christopher's wits slowly returned, as did his memories of the ordeal he and his fellow soldiers had endured.

He turned his eyes toward Chara. "Is Ruth really—dead?"

Chara nodded but said nothing. Her tears dropped upon the bed sheet as she held his hand, her words barely audible. "She is dead. And we thought you were dead."

She paused, then began sobbing uncontrollably. "And it's all my fault! I'm the one that pressured you to let her go!"

Christopher reached for her hand, then drew her into the bed with him. He held her trembling body for the longest time. "It's not your fault. If it's anyone's fault, it is mine."

Chara looked into his eyes. "No way! I told you to let her go."

"No, you told me to *pray* about it. I did. God seemed to be leading that direction, and I said 'Yes' to Him."

Christopher sank deep in thought. Chara lay beside him and said nothing.

"No," he continued. "God made it clear that it was His will. Somehow God designed all this to make His name more famous among the Tuxiang and to the ends of the earth. Ruth was a grain of wheat falling into the ground. Her death will bear much fruit. And her death will not be the last."

Chara hugged him again. "I'm so glad you're alive. I don't know what I would have done if you had died."

Christopher continued deep in thought. He broke the silence. "I feel guilty that she died and I lived. It should have been me! I started this venture!" Tears began streaming down his face.

Chara wiped the tears from his cheeks. "No, my love, Father makes His choices about which of His servants to take. He left you here for a reason."

She placed her hands on both sides of his face and kissed him. "That's right! He left you here for a reason. Let's live in a way that honors her sacrifice."

Christopher nodded weakly. The room became foggy again. Chara's words continued to ring in his ears as he slipped back into a deep slumber. Chara slept beside him, a smile on her face.

* * *

News of Christopher's recovery spread quickly through prayer networks around the world, stirring yet more prayer. His mind continued to grow clearer and his strength began returning.

When Nic visited he said, "It's a good thing you survived, buddy. Without you we wouldn't know what to do next."

Christopher sat up in bed. "Sure you would. Just do the same thing we've been doing among the Tuxiang."

"While you were sleeping we decided to refer to them from here on simply as the 'T'—for security reasons. And about our next steps, you don't understand. We, um ..."

Nic caught himself. His teasing betrayed something he wasn't quite ready to talk about. "Uh, look, forget it for now. Let's talk when you're stronger."

"Bro, something's bothering you. I can't do anything in this confounded bed except read, think, and pray. So at least let me listen to you."

Nic hung his head sheepishly and searched for the right words. Christopher trained his eyes on him, searching for a clue as to what was eating his friend.

"You're not going to like it," Nic said quietly.

"That's okay, bro. Iron sharpens iron."

"Touché," he said. Still he paused. "The last couple of weeks I have been really worried, and not just for you. I cry privately in my hotel room. And do you know how hard it is to hide such emotional displays from the colonel when he is staying in the same room?"

Christopher smiled. "He's probably doing the same thing and hiding it too. You macho types! What will we do with you?"

"It's not just for you that I'm worried," said Nic. "What would become of the KPF if something happens to you? John, Win, or I would take over, but we're clueless about what comes next.

"We've seen unbelievable success. Dozens of churches have already been started, most of them by the new believers themselves. But what's next?"

Nic looked hard at his friend. "Christopher, I'm going to tell you something you don't want to hear. You need to be at HQ. You need to get off the front line and oversee the budding KPF movement."

"I *am* overseeing the movement," Christopher responded just as firmly. "I'm leading our troops from the front."

"No, Chris, you've been leading *your* team. Now we need you to lead the whole movement. You got busted up pretty good, buddy, and we almost lost critical parts of the KPF's future."

Christopher bristled at the insinuation. "No way. No one is indispensable. You, Win, or John could lead the movement if something happened to me."

Nic leaned closer to the hospital bed. "Let me be straight with you," he said. "First, you've been so focused on getting the KPF off the ground that you haven't brought us up to speed on your long-range plans. John, Win, and I need to know what you're thinking.

"Second, you're wrong about not being indispensable. God put this vision in *your* heart. He gave you the ability to communicate it. He made you the strategist. That's God's gift to His body through you. None of us can do what you do. Go back to Los Angeles. Lead!"

"The colonel is every bit the strategist I am."

"Yes, regarding battle. But when it comes to shepherding a movement, you're the man God chose. John, Win, and I are your lieutenants. At this point in the movement, the facts are simple: knock out Christopher Owen, and you wipe out the KPF. The enemy came awfully close to accomplishing that."

Christopher lay back down and thought for several minutes about what Nic had said. The same familiar complaint—keeping his ideas and plans to himself until they were fully developed.

"You're right, bro," he finally said. "I needed to *start* by doing what I'm asking the troops to do—exposing myself to the same field risks and seeing the fruit firsthand.

"But the truth is, if I went back, it would be because *I* really want to be on the frontline. And that's not the right reason to be there. This is God's mission, not ours, and the important thing is for each one of us to fill the role He has for us—not the one we'd like to have. If I can be more useful to His purposes at home, I must be willing to *not* be on the field."

Christopher took a deep breath. "And it's true. I haven't brought you guys in on my long-range thinking the way I did at first. I'm really sorry, bro."

"No worries, buddy. We've all been busy," Nic said. "And it was right for you to lead us to the field. But now you *have* done what we're asking your troops to do. You have been counted worthy to suffer for His name, and you've got twenty-four stitches above your eye to show for it. Like Paul, you bear in your body the marks of Jesus. The troops listened to you before, but now that scar will remind them you've walked in their shoes!"

Christopher reached his hand to the bandages wrapped around his head.

"Hey," Nic said, "I do have some good news for you. Win was able to contact some of the T church leaders through Chara and meet with them across the border to set up continued mentoring for them as the movement grows.

"Also, Ching Fei was so distraught at how his guests were treated that he moved heaven and earth to get everything that the team left in Nancheng shipped to your home. He's got a friend with Fed-Ex in China, and the stuff's already in L.A. Go figure!

"Even better—while those things were being packed up, Zhao Hong showed up with everything Ruth, George, and Lance left in her village. Would you believe we've even got Ruth's journal?"

Christopher shook his head in amazement. "Nic, bro, I can guarantee you that journal is filled with spiritual gems from this movement's first martyr."

THIRTY THREE

The fire in the hearth in Rome once again cracked and popped. Moonlight streamed through the windows. The elderly attendant stood still as a statue behind the Prime Director.

Select members of The Ten sat around the ancient triangular table. Number One rasped, "Is everything set?"

Only his attendant's lips moved. "Exactly as you ordered, Prime Director."

The old man cackled. "Excellent! Excellent! Watch and wait, men. This is the fate that befalls traitors. Only thrice in our illustrious history has this been necessary. Let's hope it is the last."

* * *

Michael Wroth, director of the International Coalition for the Preservation of World Peace, strode down the steps outside his office. IC agents flanked him as he approached the armored SUV.

Jake Simmons scanned his surroundings, as did dozens of agents. Marlene marched by Wroth's side. The setting sun caused her to squint despite her sunglasses.

Suddenly two agents in front of her slumped to the ground.

Blood splattered her glasses, and the world turned crimson.

Shards of marble pricked her face as automatic gunfire churned up the pavement.

Three more agents fell to the ground as others returned fire.

Jake's shouts rose to take charge above the din of the battle.

Michael Wroth fell at Marlene's side.

Rough hands grabbed Marlene's arms and pulled her to the waiting SUV.

She was tossed in like a rag doll, and the door slammed shut.

"The director!" she cried out. "Where is he?"

Automatic rounds pinged off the bulletproof windows.

The door flew open and the director's body was hurled into the vehicle. Wroth's head lay on her lap.

Simmons jumped into the front passenger seat. "Go! Go! Go!

The glass won't hold much longer."

The driver's window exploded into thousands of fragments, and he slumped against the wheel of the idling vehicle.

Marlene screamed.

Simmons didn't hesitate. Sliding over he shifted the SUV into drive. Using the driver's body as a shield against the barrage of bullets, he gunned the engine.

A rocket propelled grenade exploded behind them and the rear window shattered.

The SUV jerked forward, swerved down the road and rounded a bend out of the range of gunfire, where it slammed into a dumpster.

Two more IC SUVs sped to its aid and flanked it.

Simmons turned to Marlene. "The director?"

She stared at the blood-soaked form in her lap. "I can't find a pulse!"

The side door flew open and agents manhandled the still form of Michael Wroth out of the wrecked vehicle. They loaded his body into one of the other SUVs.

Jake jumped in and the vehicle sped down the road.

Another agent quickly led Marlene to the back seat of the other SUV.

The closed door muffled the sounds of the waning battle.

Her chin fell to her chest and she wept.

* * *

His attendant whispered into the Prime Director's ear. His grey eyes sparkled. He rubbed his bony hands together and crowed, "It is done. The usurper is dead. Now, we must begin the search for his replacement."

THIRTY FOUR

I see the old Chinese grandmas constantly knitting.
Sometimes I imagine that my life is like a skein of yarn,
completely unwound and stretching beyond the limit of my sight.
It represents the timeline of my life.
Then I realize that this earthly portion
is just an inch or so long on that unending thread.
Whatever I do here in that short period—
just a few decades—
makes all the difference for the main event—
the rest of eternal life.
Let me live these few years to have the greatest impact on eternity.
                                             —Ruth Grant, martyr

Although the Grant family held their own private funeral, Ruth's parents drove to Los Angeles for the memorial service the KPF held on Easter Sunday.

The rented auditorium was packed. Droves of KPF supporters and well-wishers turned out, along with a variety of leaders from several mission organizations. Ruth's parents sat on the second row while reporters sat in the back, discreetly taking notes.

Christopher stood before the group, his face puffy and an eye still bandaged. John stood close by to assist him.

Christopher spoke into the mic. "From the outset, the Kingdom Preparation Force has understood that, like Christ's earliest followers, some of us would suffer—yes, and possibly die—if we were to seriously pursue no place left without the gospel by 2025. All of us, Ruth Grant included, embraced that risk knowingly. Yet as much as we tried to prepare ourselves, none of us really expected that Ruth Grant or anyone else would die in the service of our Lord.

"Ruth demonstrated a devotion to Christ for which all of us should strive. Two days before her death, Ruth told Chara, 'This is a risky venture, but I'm willing to risk everything so that others may find the same salvation I have.' This side of heaven we will never know how many will receive salvation because Ruth risked everything."

Christopher sat on a stool on the platform as George told about the team's trip into the village and how Ruth died. Many of those present wept silently, struck by the faith and passion of this young woman.

Chara spoke next. "Early on, Ruth asked me to disciple her, so we spent a lot of time together. And wherever we were, Ruth had a little journal to record insights God was teaching her and her prayers back to Him."

She held up a green spiral notebook. "This is Ruth's journal. I don't think she would mind me reading you a portion if she knew it would build you up. I—I—I ..."

Chara bit her lip and tried to hold back tears. Christopher hobbled forward and put a hand on her shoulder while the crowd waited patiently.

"I just want to read one excerpt from last fall, when Ruth was frustrated with our lack of progress and helped us move into deeper faith. She ... she said that ... I'll just read it ..."

Chara fumbled through the pages, then read aloud:

Philippians 2:17—But even if I am being poured out like a drink offering on the sacrifice and service coming from your faith, I am glad and rejoice with all of you.

Dear Father, Let me be poured out as a drink offering for the T. people. What is my life worth compared to their lost souls? I am secure—who can snatch me from Your hand? What risk is it for me to pour out my life on the altar? Truly as Paul wrote, to be absent from the body is to be at home with the Lord. Strangely, I have no fear of dying, yet even so I am a little nervous to write— no, I am not. I have made up my mind. Father, I have always said I want to live for You but have never thought that I might need to die for You. Yet, if You can receive more glory through my death than through my life, then

glorify Your Name. Pour me out like a drink offering for the sake of others.

Chara finished reading only with great difficulty. As Christopher escorted her from the platform she hid her face in his neck, sobbing once again.

Christopher returned to the stage. "For the security of the continuing field work we can't report certain details, but Ruth did not give her life in vain. Our first team, the one Ruth was on, believes there have been at least fifty churches planted and two thousand baptisms among their people group in the last eight months."

A murmur passed through the room.

"The most exciting thing is that these churches are not only thriving individually, but the majority of them are also starting other churches.

"The gospel has been spreading like wildfire. Another of our teams believes at least twenty reproducing churches have been planted as they've trained existing underground churches with a similar vision! Our other two teams are just now starting to see some breakthroughs."

"Praise the Lord!" erupted spontaneously around the room.

"Some of the individuals from these various church-planting movements are already going places outsiders can't go. In a few instances, whole villages have come to faith. And some of these new laborers are even crossing people group lines, taking the gospel cross-culturally from recently reached groups to even more remote unreached groups."

Christopher paused for a moment, half in awe of what God was doing and half in sudden dizziness.

"The Kingdom of God is more powerful than we can imagine. It's out of our control! Would you join with someone near you and pray together for the continuation of the work for which Ruth has given her life? We must vow to honor her sacrifice with our efforts. More than that, we must honor Jesus' sacrifice with our efforts!"

Murmurs in the audience grew in volume as God stirred the hearts of His people. The prayers became louder until suddenly a spontaneous song swept through the auditorium. The worship continued for another hour.

* * *

Christopher stood near the back, thanking those who had come and answering questions. As the crowd dwindled, two middle-aged men in conservative attire approached him. One spoke in a southern drawl as he extended his hand.

"Mr. Owen? My name is Stu Gage, and this here is Fred Stearns. We represent a couple mission boards you may know."

Christopher shook their hands warmly. "Nice to meet you. How can I serve you?"

Gage looked at Stearns and then back at Christopher. "We've come to California both to honor Ruth Grant's sacrifice and learn more about these mobile, church-based teams that are seeing such good results. Our churches have needed such a ministry model for a long time."

"Frankly, we know we need to change some paradigms," Stearns added, "take greater risks—advance the gospel more forcefully—respond to situations more rapidly. We'd like to hear more about your approach."

"Even knowing the costs that come with it?" Christopher grimaced, glancing toward the front of the auditorium.

Stearns hung his head reverently, then looked back at Christopher. "Especially knowing the costs," he said. "God's Kingdom grows through seeds willing to fall into the ground and die to bear lasting fruit. This generation needs to be reignited to count the cost to finish the mission of Jesus. Your military metaphor, your push toward the No Place Left end goal, and your sacrificial surrender—well, your ethos is compelling."

"It's gonna take radical participation from Christians all over the world to finish the task," Gage added. "Your little organization is stirring up a sleeping giant—the North American church establishment—with faith to finish the task. News is spreading quickly; just look at the media that was here today. We want to talk about how to leverage that for greater impact. Would y'all be able to meet with us over dinner tomorrow?"

"S-s-sure!" Christopher said, dumbfounded.

"Mr. Owen, we track church-planting movements all over the world," Stearns said. "And what you've done is unique. You are sending short-term teams out of a local church—mid-term teams, really—and launching church-planting movements! We need to learn from you so we can help others do the same. Shall we pick you up at your home at six tomorrow?"

"Six? Sure, that should work. Can I bring my wife and two of my leaders?"

"Of course. See y'all then."

As the men walked off, John wrapped his arm around Christopher and said, "I was your 'doubting Thomas' when we began talking about this at Common Grounds a year and a half ago. But I have to admit—it's really happening. And this is still just the beginning. I guess I've become a true believer."

* * *

Ruth Grant's parents were among the last to leave. For a long time they stood near the front of the auditorium where a frame held their daughter's picture.

Christopher limped toward them, then waited with enough distance to allow them privacy in their mourning.

He was glad they had decided to come. John, Stacy, and others from Church in the City had driven to Orange County to offer condolences, but this was the first time Christopher had seen them. He had been back in Los Angeles a couple of weeks, but each time he or Chara had contacted the Grants, they had made it clear they weren't yet ready to talk to the Owens.

When the Grants finally turned and began walking up the aisle, their eyes met Christopher's for the first time.

Mrs. Grant's face contorted.

"You! You're responsible for this! You and your band of play soldiers! What do you think this is? Some ... some ... *game*? Do you think you can just play around with the lives of impressionable college students? My Ruth had such a future until she met you Jesus freaks!"

She spit out the last words as if they were profanity.

"Mrs. Grant, I'm so sorry—"

"Sorry? What does 'sorry' do for me? What does it do for

Ruth?"

She lunged toward Christopher but was restrained by her husband. "You're a manipulator, Mr. Owen!" the angry woman shouted. "A charlatan! Parading around on the stage, working your audience into a frenzy during a memorial service for my daughter! You use your wounds to stir sympathy, but *you* didn't die. My Ruth did! You and this rabble are nothing more than a mind-control cult. You're the reason my Ruth is dead!"

"Mrs. Grant, I—"

"You'll be hearing from us, Mr. Owen," said Mr. Grant with exaggerated calm in his voice. "Something has to be done about people like you." He then gently led his grieving wife past a white-faced Christopher.

Halfway up the aisle, Mrs. Grant turned and shrieked. "And I want the rest of Ruth's personal items returned to us at once, including her diaries. How dare you allow your wife to read through Ruth's personal writings! You've not only killed my daughter, you have also publicly violated her private life. You have raped her soul in front of all these people and the media!"

Christopher plopped down on the front row of the auditorium. How could such a beautiful service have turned so quickly into a scene of personal attack?

John tried to encourage him, but the KPF leader remained unresponsive.

THIRTY FIVE

Michael Wroth's eyes fluttered open. "What happened?" he whispered.

Marlene gasped. "Michael, uh, sir, you're awake!"

Doctors and nurses rushed into the hospital room and began checking vital signs.

After a few minutes a senior physician said, "Welcome, back, Director Wroth. It was nip and tuck there for a while."

Jake burst, in flanked by two IC agents. "Sir, you're okay!"

Wroth looked around the room, then glanced at his IV.

Marlene realized she was holding his hand, released it and reddened.

Again he whispered, "What happened?"

Jake said, "You survived an assassination attempt. We thought we had lost you."

Marlene said, "Jake's team saved you, sir. It was a real battle zone, but they pulled you through."

Wroth stared at Simmons. "Thank you, Jake. I really owe you. Did we lose anyone?"

"Seven men, sir. We were ambushed by a group of highly trained professionals. There were ten of them, with automatic weapons, armor piercing rounds and RPGs. They're all dead."

* * *

Number One cursed in Italian while his fellow conspirators among The Ten sat wooden-like. Finally he switched to English. "The usurper is alive? How is that possible?! You told me we sent our best team."

The attendant said, "We did, Prime Director. And we saw him go down. Our marksmen dropped most of the men in his party. Number Ten was carried to his car unconscious, covered in blood. We assumed he was dead."

Number One waved his hand slightly, and his attendant

became silent. "Now we have revealed our hand to Number Ten. We have violated our cardinal rule of influencing without being known to influence."

The attendant spoke haltingly. "Prime Director, I believe we are still in the clear. All evidence will point to retribution at the hand of terrorists. Our assassination squad all had clear links to terrorist cells in the Middle East. Number Ten will assume it was payback for his work as IC director."

Number One waved his hand again. "Enough assumptions!"

He turned to his fellow conspirators. "Every one of you must act as if you knew nothing of this attack. You must express your sympathy to Number Ten and draw him into your confidence. He must believe he is gaining more influence over each of you. In fact, you must play as if you prefer his leadership to mine.

"We will bide our time as we have for fifteen hundred years. He will make a mistake. And when he does, we will crush him."

* * *

Wroth motioned for everyone to leave the room except for Marlene and Jake. IC Agents secured the door and stood guard. Marlene gazed at their semi-automatic weapons.

"Was it them?" Wroth's words startled her.

He looked around the room. "The Ten?"

Marlene glanced at Jake, who nodded. "We can't be sure," She said. "Everything points to a terrorist group that the IC recently took out."

"But this was better orchestrated than that group is capable of," Jake added. "It smells like The Ten. We really don't know."

As his brows knit in concentration, Wroth tried to tap his fingers together but the IV restricted his movement. A minute passed before he spoke. "If it is The Ten, such brazen audacity is unlike them. This is good. Number One may be backpedaling. I wish I could be a fly on the wall in Rome right now."

Wroth chuckled and closed his eyes. "I don't think they will try this again very soon. Even so, Jake, we have to increase our security."

Jake nodded.

"Jake, Marlene, we need to crush them, but we have to choose the proper time. If we act prematurely we lose everything. The game's afoot, as they say, and we must be at the top of ours. I'm tired of being played by them. Jake, you will work with me on a long-term strategy to destroy them. They will discover too late the full measure of Wroth's wrath!"

Marlene cringed inside, and even more so when she saw how eagerly Jake grinned and nodded.

Wroth turned toward her and spoke, "And this KPF group led by Owen and Dunbar—I will not be outwitted by them. Marlene, you will work with me to bring them down, especially Dunbar. He will not escape our trap. First we will destroy his little mission troop. Then we will wipe Dunbar from this earth."

Marlene shuddered again on the inside but nodded her head and made a few notes on her tablet.

Wroth removed the oxygen tube from his nose and began pulling at his IV. "Now get me out of this confounded hospital!"

THIRTY SIX

"'Don't be afraid,' the prophet answered.
'Those who are with us are more than those who are with them.'
And Elisha prayed, 'Open his eyes, Lord, so that he may see.'
Then the Lord opened the servant's eyes, and he looked
and saw the hills full of horses and chariots of fire
all around Elisha." (2 Kings 6:16-17)
On my better days, I remember this,
and it gives me the strength to prevail in the divine quest
until there is No Place Left!
—Ruth Grant, martyr

"Christopher, you need to come see this! Please!"

What now? More bad news? Christopher hadn't smiled much since the memorial service. Well, since Ruth's death really. The Grants' words had wounded him more than he let on. *What could I have done differently? How could I have prevented Ruth's death? Why wasn't I the one to go to the countryside instead of her?*

He saw the others struggling also. Chara—the deep-thinking exhorter, a little less patient, especially as her husband seemed so fragile; Renee—the brilliant legal mind, now seeing threats behind every bush; her husband John—the rational one, a tad more cynical than usual, challenging Christopher's ideas more often; Timothy—the overachieving techno-geek, more flustered than normal; and Grace—the ever-cheerful one, less buoyant.

Each dealt with Ruth's death in his or her own way. And watching their leader suffer nearly the same fate as Ruth had traumatized everyone. Encouragement was in short supply, and how the teams in Asia still carried on, Christopher didn't know.

Not only are they processing what happened to Ruth, they're also worried about me. At least the Tuxiang team is here with us, so we can continue to process this with them. Phil seems to be struggling, but the rest of them are coping remarkably well. It looks like they'll emerge from this baptism of fire as long-term leaders of KPF.

Christopher approached the stairs to the basement.

The staff meeting two nights earlier was a good step toward healing. Private concerns were brought to light and, more importantly, into the light of Scripture. Christopher reckoned it might take a while for full healing, but felt they were on the right path.

"Christopher, please!"

The words jolted Christopher from his reflections.

Timothy stood at the bottom of the stairs. His straggly, black hair hadn't been cut in ages, and wandered aimlessly about his face. "Grace is doing all she can to manage the incoming email, but it's piling up. Our website has more postings than you can imagine! And your blog is getting thousands of hits a week!"

Christopher joined him in the basement.

Grace smiled broadly for the first time in weeks. "Boss, this is so exciting!"

"Timothy tells me you're swamped," Christopher said.

"My husband exaggerates, but look at this. Three weeks ago— just after the memorial service—we posted a sanitized summary of team results, with an overview of the KPF and an invitation for others to get involved. We invited people to follow your blog and the KPF Twitter account."

"I remember. So? Any response yet?"

"Yes. As of two minutes ago, 18,394 page views."

"Eighteen *thousand*? That's a lot, right?"

"Almost *nineteen* thousand. And those are only the ones who have looked directly at our site," Grace explained patiently. "Those who are interested then email, Facebook, tweet, and everything else it to their friends. If on average they share with two friends, that's impacting nearly sixty thousand people. And if then they share it with their church, that's up to nineteen thousand churches—in only four weeks.

"More significantly, it's mushrooming. The first week only five hundred people accessed our report. The second week it was two thousand. The third we had six thousand views, and this week it's over ten thousand. And the week's not over yet."

Christopher tried to think, to grasp what she was saying.

"I think I get the picture. So are we getting any applications?"

Timothy stood up to face Christopher. "Are we getting any? In the last week and a half we've received 718!" Timothy ran his fingers through his mop of hair worriedly, while his ever-optimistic wife grinned excitedly.

Christopher felt ambivalent. *This is amazing, more than we dared hope for! But what will we do with all these applicants? We don't have that kind of capacity. Wait! What am I thinking? We'll make capacity!*

"Now let me get this straight," he said. "The 718 applications are to join the KPF and serve overseas? These aren't just requests for further information?"

"Right!" responded Grace. Her computer beeped, and she pressed a key. "Now it's seven hundred *nineteen*."

Now Christopher's fingers were running through his hair, his mind spinning. "And you have told them that they will have to raise their own support; that they will be living as if in wartime conditions; that one person has died, another been beaten, and three jailed; and that we are now asking for a minimum two-year commitment—all that?"

"Yes, Christopher. Grace and I have clearly communicated all that information. It's crazy. I just don't understand it."

"What's wrong with you two?" Grace said. "I understand it! Listen to this: 'Why I am applying: I want to be in the generation that completes the task so perhaps Jesus will return in my life-time. It sounds like God is stirring and may well accomplish that in the next few years. I want to take off at least a couple of years before getting my MBA to be a part of what God is doing. In a word, I want to render my spiritual military duty to my King.'

"All the others read like that too. Christopher, they're all join-ing for the same reason we did. They want to be the Kingdom *Preparation* Force. They don't want life to pass them by."

Christopher walked around the small room twice, then sat down. "After all we've been through," he said, half to himself. "You would have thought new prospects would be intimidated. But instead, they're inspired. They see what it might cost, and yet they're applying in even greater numbers. Amazing! While we've all been in an emotional fog, God has been stirring hearts."

His eyes rested on the glowing LED display above the wall

map—the number of remaining UUPGs. *3,176.* He blinked, trying to recall what the number had been when their quest began.

"That's the other thing, Boss," Grace smiled broadly from her workstation. "The number of unengaged, unreached groups has dropped by 50 in the last six months, mostly through efforts that started before ours. Without the 2025 vision, it could take another 35 years or more to finish the task. But as churches and organizations embrace the 2025 vision, momentum is building, and the number of UUPGs will drop faster and faster! God is starting a movement just like we hoped for. And He did it just when we were most discouraged. It's going to happen!"

Overhearing their voices, John descended the stairs.

"By the way, O wounded soldier, I've neglected to brief you on what's happened with Church in the City while you were gone. I guess we've been too busy with crisis management and Ruth's memorial service.

"We started applying the same CPM principles you've been using overseas, and guess what? You remember that first conversation at Common Grounds, when we recognized that the many groups we had started weren't reproducing?

"That's completely changed. Now many of our small groups are starting new churches! We've seen sixty-seven new churches start in the L.A. network alone, and many of those are fourth generation or beyond. In a couple of cases, this has already gone seven generations. The disciple-making is becoming viral!

"In fact, there is a growing No Place Left network applying these principles across North America and globally. CPMs are emerging even here—where everyone says it can't happen!"

"It's happening!" Grace hummed.

Christopher tilted his head upward and closed his eyes in prayer. "They meant evil against us," he said softly to himself, "but God meant it for good. They meant evil against us, but God meant it for good ..."

When he opened his eyes, Grace was grinning even harder. "This may be the last generation, just like you said!"

Then Christopher began smiling—really smiling—for the first time in weeks.

THIRTY SEVEN

I have a sudden realization that there will be
many more twists and turns in this quest
than any of us imagined.
Much of what happens will appear to be very evil.
Oh, let us respond in Christ-like ways
and always trust that what people mean for evil,
You mean for good,
to bring about the salvation of many (Gen. 50:20).
—Ruth Grant, martyr

"Read this." Renee shoved a sheaf of papers into Christopher's hands. She was more agitated than Christopher had ever seen her. He looked at the first sheet, then back to Renee.

"What is this, Renee? Plain English. What's the problem?"

"We're being taken to court—that's the problem! The Grants are suing us for forty-five million dollars!"

"What are you talking about?"

"We were served this morning, so I talked to their attorney. They couldn't convince the D.A.'s office to file criminal charges, but they have filed civil charges. In plain English, they are charging us with violating Ruth's civil rights to life, liberty, and the pursuit of happiness."

"Can they really do this?"

"Christopher, in our legal system they can attempt whatever they want. They may not win—that's for the jury to decide—but they can file charges and tie us up in court for months or even years. And I don't know if you've noticed, but they're fueling a media firestorm. They're doing all they can to drag our name through the mud."

Christopher looked up in surprise. He almost never checked the news. "So, what do we do?"

"Are you really responding to what I'm saying with just five-word sentences?" she asked in disbelief. She grabbed the sheaf of papers from Christopher and threw them on the coffee table. "What do we do? We fight this tooth and nail! We have to win this thing, Christopher, or it will wipe us out! We have to fight and fight hard. We've made progress launching a new initiative; we can't let this cut it short. When it comes to law, you've got to fight as determinedly as the world does."

"I'll tell you what we have to do," came a voice from the other room. A short, gray-haired woman walked in, her heels tapping rapidly on the wooden floor. Jeanie Dunbar lovingly pushed Renee onto a nearby couch and waved a finger.

"Listen, you two. I've spent forty plus years in the military hearing the colonel and his buddies talk about beating this, wiping out that, kicking these tails, busting those you-know-whats.

"I don't have any problem with the KPF being a military-type organization assaulting the gates of hell. I can see that spiritually. But we're still the people of God. And Jesus gave us some clear guidelines for dealing with this type of problem."

She pulled out her well-worn King James Bible.

"'But I say unto you which hear, Love your enemies, do good to them which hate you, Bless them that curse you, and pray for them which despitefully use you. And unto him that smiteth thee on the one cheek offer also the other; and him that taketh away thy cloak forbid not to take thy coat also. Give to every man that asketh of thee; and of him that taketh away thy goods ask them not again. And as ye would that men should do to you, do ye also to them likewise.'

"That sounds to me like marching orders!"

Renee stomped her foot on the old wooden floor. "Jeanie, surely you don't expect to apply that in this situation." She tried to rise from the couch, but Jeanie sat down and wrapped her arms around her.

"My dear, just when *are* we to apply it?" Jeanie asked.

"Well, ... I don't know. Maybe on an individual basis, but not when you have a whole organization to protect."

"Honey, we have to trust God to protect the organization. Jesus didn't put up a fight in the Garden of Gethsemane, even when His arrest scattered His disciples. He Himself lived by His own words."

Renee shook her head stubbornly and turned to Christopher for support. "This goes against all my legal training. Come on, Christopher. Tell her why this isn't appropriate in this situation. You're the theologian, not I."

Christopher took the sheaf of papers, thumbed through them for a full minute, and set them down. Then he sat down opposite Renee. "I can't see any reason this passage doesn't apply to us," he said. "We're not going to fight. Instead, we're going to love the Grants, bless the Grants, pray for the Grants, and give to them."

He paused to consider the implications.

"If they take everything we have, God has still more. We're going to show our true colors in this crisis, not revert to the world's ways. Jeanie's right. We're not here to fight anyone but the evil one. We can't use the weapons of this world to assault the gates of hell."

Renee, mouth agape, shifted her gaze to Jeanie and back again to Christopher. "You're serious, aren't you? You're just going to roll over and die. They're going to plow right over us. I don't know where they found the money, but they have a crack team of lawyers that makes the O.J. Simpson defense team look like amateurs. This is suicide!"

"Let's put it before the core leadership—bring in Win and Nic by video call. But I think we have the Lord's answer already. *He* is our Defender and Counselor. Maybe we should try to contact the Grants and let them know our position. Let's see if we can settle out of court, giving them as much as we can."

"I'll contact them, Christopher," Renee said. "But I tell you, if those attorneys get one whiff of this decision, they won't let us get within a hundred miles of the Grants. If they see a weakness, they'll go for the jugular."

* * *

A few minutes later John found Christopher resting in a quiet corner of his study and tossed a newspaper on his desk before sitting on the couch.

"Congratulations, my imperturbable accomplice," he said. "We made the *Washington Post*."

Christopher sighed as he scanned the headline: *L.A. Pastor Speeds Up the Return of Jesus.* "Really, bro, you shouldn't pay attention to these things."

"They're saying we think we can dictate when Jesus returns. They're saying we're taking Matthew 24:14 and 2 Peter 3:12 too far, as if the moment the last unreached people group is reached, Jesus *has* to return," John said.

Christopher studied his longtime friend. "There's more to it, though, isn't there, bro?"

"Well," John admitted, "I've had similar questions, lingering questions. We're gaining a lot of momentum, so I haven't wanted to rock the boat—especially since I often appear critical.

"I'm not! I support you and this mission unreservedly! But, Christopher, what if they're right? Are we trying to dictate when Jesus will return? How can we actually hasten Jesus' return? This is the question that plagues me. Isn't God sovereign? Hasn't He set the date for Jesus' return? How can we speed up the coming of that day?"

"Bro, I wish you had said something sooner," Christopher commented. "Actually, I wish that *I* had said something. We're getting a lot of kickback on this, so I've been studying it more deeply—making sure we're not off base. And here's the thing. Of course God is sovereign. And at the same time, we play a role in bringing about His sovereign plans. Think about it this way. Remember when you came to faith?"

"I was quite the rabid dog, wasn't I?" John said, smiling. "Couldn't shut up about my new life."

"Well, not exactly. You were also really, really nervous about talking to your dad about it, remember?"

"Well, who wouldn't be?" John said. "He was a Rhodes scholar. Tenured faculty. Twice the intellectual—and cynic—I am. And always finding fault with born-again Christians."

Christopher nodded. "You kept praying, 'Lord, send someone to witness to my dad, someone with the intellectual faculties to back him into a corner.' Remember?"

John winced. "Yes, until that fateful day when I realized my dad was *my* responsibility. It was up to me to share the gospel with him."

Christopher leaned back in his chair. "Now, think about it, bro. How long did you wait to open your mouth? Six months?"

"Yeah, but I finally got convicted to do something about it. Otherwise I probably would have waited six *years*, or perhaps even *sixteen*."

John paused. "One of the hardest things I've ever done was buying that plane ticket to Boston. But you know, after we had spent a little time together and I shared my story, he just melted. I was speechless."

"Bro, the testimony of your changed life and your love for him was more powerful than any apologetics someone else might have debated with him," Christopher said, smiling.

"I—I guess so. I'm still amazed my dad's a Jesus-follower. The cynic now an evangelist!"

Christopher leaned forward. "Now think about this, bro. You were the instrument God used to lead your dad to faith. You wanted to wait years and very well might have if God hadn't convicted you to speed up the process.

"You and I know the date of your dad's salvation was set in heaven before the earth was formed. But, in a way, you hastened that day by buying that plane ticket and witnessing to your dad. Perhaps if you had waited six years, he would have believed later, but you didn't wait. You hastened the day, though from heaven's viewpoint that had been God's plan all along. Your motivation fit within God's plans."

"God destined my father's day of salvation, but I became His instrument," John repeated to himself. "From my vantage point, I speeded up that day by acting in faith sooner rather than later. Someone was going to win him. Why not me, and why not then? How was I to know it wasn't to be his day of salvation?"

"It was the same when Church in the City sent our first short-term team to China," Christopher said. "Remember the medical clinics we did in the villages? There were people there who might not have heard the gospel for many more years if we had not come. God knew when He created them when they would believe, but from our perspective, we hastened the day of their salvation.

"Look, bro. Fatalism drove those who opposed William Carey.

They told him, 'Sit down, young man. ... When God pleases to convert the heathen, He'll do it without your help or ours.'"

John chuckled. "Uh, yeah, I could have been one of them."

Christopher continued, "All I know is that someday God will raise up a generation with the motivation, the wherewithal, and the perseverance to finish the task—the *last* generation. From earth's vantage point—whether or not we become *that* generation—we *are* hastening that day by focusing on finishing the task. From God's vantage point, He has chosen *someone* to finish the task and appointed the times and seasons of their final work. If we are the ones He has chosen, we're not speeding God up; God is speeding us up to usher in the day He prepared long ago.

"Bro, we're on solid biblical ground. Solid not just according to me but also respected theologians. Listen to Marvin Vincent's hundred-year-old comments on 2 Peter 3:12."

Christopher picked up an ancient tome, gently leafed to the appropriate page, and read:

> **I am inclined to adopt, with Alford, Huther, Salmond, and Trench, the transitive meaning, hastening on; i.e., "causing the day of the Lord to come more quickly by helping to fulfil those conditions without which it cannot come; that day being no day inexorably fixed, but one the arrival of which it is free to the church to hasten on by faith and by prayer."**

John contemplated these words.

"Will Jesus come back the moment the last UPG is reached?" Christopher asked. He glanced once more at the headline as he grabbed the paper again. "I don't know. I just know that this is the mission He left us with, and that He said we would finish before His return. I want to finish the task He has given us.

He tossed it back down again and said, "He's not waiting for permission from us to come back. Rather He is patiently waiting for us to do what He commanded, and He'll come back when the time is right."

"I am embarrassed to ask this, Christopher, after all we've been through already. But why would we want to hasten the day? I mean, our lives are pretty good. You know personally the cost of this 'hastening.' We lost Ruth, dear friend, and we almost lost you. I guess I'm just not sure it's worth it."

Christopher gingerly touched the tender scar over his eye and limped across the room to sit next to his friend.

"Why?" he said. "Why not? It's the last and greatest mission Jesus gave His followers. How could we not devote ourselves to it, despite the cost? Can you imagine the glory of seeing our Lord return and knowing we were a part of this amazing quest?

"And bro, you're the history professor—the one who taught me that this relatively peaceful life Christians enjoy today in America is quite an anomaly in world history. Persecution has been the historic norm for Jesus-followers. In many parts of the world our brothers and sisters are already experiencing it, and it seems inevitable that it will come to us here, too."

"It's already coming," John said. "It's been coming for a while; the Church has just been slow to recognize it. Things are getting much more difficult for the Church in this country. And you know, it seems like we should be afraid, but since Jesus warned us in advance ... I don't know, somehow that takes some of the dread out of it."

Christopher closed his eyes. His mind wandered back to the Chinese prison. "Yep. And from personal experience I think the fear of persecution is generally worse than the real thing. God's grace comes when it's needed, but not necessarily before.

"There *will* be a last generation. Why not us? Carey suggested his generation speed up the Great Commission by going. I ask why we can't hasten *finishing* this task. By God's grace I will lay down my life to see it completed. Perhaps God's plan all along has been to raise up *this* generation as His *vehicle* for finishing the task before He sends Jesus on the day appointed from the foundation of this world."

He stood, then swayed with dizziness. John jumped up and put an arm around him.

Christopher waited for the swirling to stop, then turned to John. "Come on, dear friend. We've walked this road together since college. Let's walk it all the way to the end!"

"Or at least limp!" John winked.

"John, let's pull Nic in on a video pow-wow. We've got to get some good counsel to address two issues. First, how to sustain the growth developing overseas, especially in the T. movement. And second, how to structure the KPF movement to maintain our values and focus amidst a rapid influx of new recruits and media attention. We also need Nic praying with us about a new legal threat Renee just told me about."

"Roger that, O bearer of dizzying intellect," said John. He picked up the paper, eyed it one last time, and tossed it in the trash. Then he lifted his friend off the ground in a giant bear hug.

Christopher winced.

"You know, my little friend, that Yuri Gagarin, the Soviet cosmonaut, was only five-foot-two," John said in his best Russian accent. "He was the first man in space—previously unexplored territory. He inspired a generation to that frontier and ushered in a race to the moon.

"My brother, you've been to the brink of death and back—now let's see if we can inspire our generation to run the last lap of the most important race!

"One more bear hug?"

"Stay away, bro. My ribs still hurt!"

* * *

Colonel Dunbar huddled over a laptop in his rented bungalow in the mountains outside Chiang Mai, Thailand. Here he could talk, free of monitoring devices and governments trying to hack his video call. The grainy image on the screen froze frequently, but the audio was clear, as were the piercing eyes of the thin, unshaven face on the screen.

"I'm telling you, Win, the reaction to what you guys are doing is disproportionate to your impact. I've polled all my sources—discreetly, of course—and it's unanimous. The KPF is not just on China's radar. It's being discussed at very high levels in the United States and internationally."

"For crying out loud, Tal, it—we're—a religious group, not some terrorist organization."

"You know it. I know it," Tal replied, "but that's not what the chatter indicates. The 'powers that be' are strangely nervous about the KPF. It's like there's a much larger story going on, but we're only seeing the edge of it."

Win sat back and pulled his laptop closer.

"Like 'Nam in '72?" he asked soberly.

Tal looked both ways and moved so close to the webcam only his eyes showed. "No, brother, much, much bigger. That time you and your team were innocent pawns in a much larger drama. What I'm hearing now dwarfs that beyond compare. And some of my regular sources are suddenly clamming up. It's baffling. I don't know what's going on, but I'd keep both eyes wide open if I were you."

Win gazed out the window at the tropical paradise so similar to the jungles of Vietnam. "Bigger than 'Nam in '72. My heart died there, though my body fought on for decades. And I'm still battling my illness.

"Innocent pawns in a much larger drama? Naive is probably a better word. But I am naive no longer. I worry though, Tal, for my idealistic comrades in the KPF. They've been bloodied, but they're so full of optimism and faith, and so naive still. Perhaps that's all right."

"Win, greater forces are at work here than they are aware of, perhaps than we're aware of. They're in way over their heads."

The colonel continued staring out the window.

"They're innocent babes carried along in a great drama—a story more complex than they've imagined," Win said softly. He turned again to the grainy video image.

"As I think about it, Christopher Owen may have a clearer idea than we do of the forces involved. He may be the only one in the KPF with a grasp of the ultimate implications of this drama. I think that's what weighs on him so. He's not the same since China.

"Innocent babes? Yes. Naive? Most likely. But they're more shrewd now and have an all-powerful God watching out for them. And that makes all the difference."

Recalling a phrase learned in childhood, Tal asked, "shrewd as serpents and innocent as doves?"

"Something like that," Win said.

The colonel disconnected the link and moved to the rattan chair on the porch. There he stared at his cell phone. Finally he dialed the number.

"Sweetie, it's me. I'm afraid our worst fears are materializing."

"Is *he* involved?"

"I think so."

The phone was silent for a few seconds.

"God help us, Win!"

THIRTY EIGHT

Jesus, You said that if anyone loves father or mother more than You,
he or she is not worthy of You.
I have obeyed Your voice to believe in You.
I have followed Your voice to go to the nations.
I have loved, respected, and pleaded with my parents
to know You and Your ways.
I don't know how You will do it,
but I believe that when Your children obey Your voice,
You take care of everything else.
So once more I plead with You to
save my parents and use them for Your purposes.
—Ruth Grant, martyr

"Mrs. Grant, you have the opportunity to help us shut down mind-control cult leaders like Christopher Owen. The growing intolerance of such groups—be they terrorists, fascists, or religious fanatics—serves to shackle the freedom of all those created in the divine image. We're going to stamp out such intolerance.

"It sounds like Ruth was a fine Christian girl inadvertently lured into an extremist group."

"Yes, sir, she was a good Christian girl."

"My point, exactly, Mrs. Grant. Seventy-eight percent of Americans are good Christians, affiliated with regular local churches, trying to live out fine Judeo-Christian values. Other Americans are similarly good Jews or good Muslims, all living together peacefully.

"But there is an insidious minority of staunchly evangelistic Christian extremists who want everyone to believe their way, to sacrifice all they have to their cause, and to obey them blindly. I liken them, ma'am, to the radical fundamentalists of the Muslim world who appall most good Muslims.

"These cult-like groups give our tolerant religious groups a bad name. You're in a perfect position to make a difference. And we can help you with that."

"Thank you, sir. We appreciate all the support from your office." Patricia Grant hung up the phone.

* * *

The Grants sat in their living room amidst lights, cameras, and a news crew. From the shadows, a capable redhead was quietly orchestrating the interview.

"Now, remember, Mr. and Mrs. Grant," the interviewer said, "this will be edited and aired on prime time later, so relax. We can do as many takes as we need."

* * *

"Honey?" Chara called. "Get in here quick. You need to see this!"

She grabbed Christopher's hand as he joined her. The TV showed a close-up of Patricia Grant with mascara running down her cheeks.

"... She was a good Christian girl. Our whole family has been churchgoers for generations. We've contributed our money to help the needy ..."

The camera panned to Mr. Grant.

"The vast majority of Americans are good people," he said, "affiliated with local churches and synagogues. We try to live by good standards. But there is an insidious minority of Christian extremists who want everyone to believe their way, to sacrifice all they have to their cause, and to obey them blindly. They're no different than the radical fundamentalists of the Muslim world, who appall most good Muslims."

Mrs. Grant spoke again, her voice cracking with emotion.

"Christopher Owen is a charlatan, and the KPF is nothing more than a mind-control cult. They're the reason my Ruth is dead. She was a good Christian until she met them. They changed her. They subverted her. How is this Christopher Owen different from any other murderer? He belongs in jail.

"Parents and teachers, guard your children from him!" she pleaded before breaking down in silent sobs.

The camera panned out to include a sympathetic news anchor

waiting patiently.

Mr. Grant spoke again in a controlled monotone.

"Christopher Owen and the KPF need to be stopped like any other subversive paramilitary group. We didn't sue them for their money—in fact, we're going to donate it all to help the families of other victims like Ruth. We're suing the KPF to shut them down."

The interviewer nodded and waited.

Patricia Grant lifted her bloodshot eyes and glared once again into the camera. "We won't be stopped until you are, Christopher Owen. We will hound you as long as it takes. Someone has to protect our children from groups like yours."

The news anchor appeared again on the screen.

"And there you have it. The Ruth Grant Foundation has been formed to help families and individuals victimized by cults and paramilitary groups. To donate, visit the website shown below."

Christopher squeezed Chara's hand softly and asked, "How could the Grants have moved so quickly ... and so effectively? This isn't the same couple I heard a few weeks ago. They have a bigger agenda that I didn't hear then. I can't put my finger on it, but something's not right."

Chara hugged him and whispered in his ear.

"Remember what you keep saying, honey. 'Unhindered'—the very last word in Acts. All that Kingdom advance in Acts came with *much* persecution. Paul was still preaching, but from prison. Even so, the last verse in Acts says Paul continued proclaiming the Kingdom unhindered. We're living the same story."

"You're right. You're right," Christopher said, pulling her tight. "Regardless of what happens to the KPF, nothing will stop His Kingdom from spreading—not lawsuits or media, not persecution—nothing. There will be no end to the increase of His Kingdom and of peace. Not just *no end to His kingdom*, but no end to the *increase* of His kingdom."

Chara rested her head on Christopher's shoulder. "May we be found faithful. Let's hasten the day, mighty man of God!"

"Thanks, honey. Now, let's pray for the Grants."

* * *

The interview had taken its toll. Patricia Grant found a quiet corner of the house and began sobbing uncontrollably.

Marlene found her and put an arm around her shoulder.

"You did great, Patricia," she said reassuringly. "Don't worry. The director—our whole office—will be with you through this. Things are going exactly according to plan."

* * *

The Rose Garden at Exposition Park was just what Christopher needed to clear his head. There he enjoyed wandering aimlessly, poring over his Bible, listening, journaling, and processing. Somehow alone amidst other visitors, he found there a world unto himself.

This day he felt a deep need to renew his understanding of God's perspective. His shoulders slumped, and he wandered aimlessly. *How many times have I entered such a day of prayer ready to quit, only to depart ready to take on the world?*

Somehow, this day felt heavier than other Rose Garden days. The weight of the movement slowed his meandering. He couldn't keep walking.

Chara had warned everyone not to disturb him. For the Church's sake, for the movement's sake, and for her sake. They needed this man to hear from God—to return to normal.

Christopher found his mind replaying each stage of their quest. *Why do You keep taking my mind back to the very beginning, to that initial stirring You put in my soul? Am I still missing something in our push toward No Place Left?*

He sat on a bench and felt drawn strongly to Revelation. He devoured it for hours.

That's it! I've not truly thought through the implications of being the last generation. In my eager pursuit of "hastening the day," I had forgotten what the days leading up to that day would be like. Perhaps "ignored" is more accurate. Matthew 24:14 can't be isolated from Revelation, or from what Jesus described in Matthew 24 as the birth pangs that would precede the end. These are part and parcel of the same generation.

Christopher vaguely recalled the discussions he and the team had in the early days about the "Revelation generation." He wrote feverishly in his journal.

If we are a part of the glorious last generation, then we are part of a much larger storyline than our own small catalytic role. This is the storyline of history. This is the culmination of Your plans for this world. The Revelation Generation. You're orchestrating all the movements into a climactic ending—summing them all up under the Lordship of Jesus. I can see it now. I can taste the end.

There will be no victory without a final "at all costs" assault on the gates of hell. And it will cost everything. They are a part of the same grand storyline.

I accept both.

The sun was just setting when he finished writing.

Peace.

Amidst the turmoil—the lawsuit, the responsibilities, and the persecution—peace flooded his heart and mind. He relaxed on the bench and basked in the rays of peace that pierced his heart as the rays of the noonday sun might pierce his eyes.

Leaping from his bench he raised his hands and, to the astonishment of other park visitors, shouted, "No Place Left!"

Christopher's cell phone interrupted his celebration.

"Commander, this is Win, calling from Chiang Mai. Sir, I've just gotten off a call with my intelligence contact. I hate to say this, but I'm afraid we may be pawns in a much larger plot than any of us imagined. International forces are manipulating events around us to fit a larger agenda.

"Commander? Are you there? Commander!"

"I know, Win, I know," Christopher finally replied, joy now back in his voice. "Isn't it great? It's actually happening! Read Revelation again."

"Revelation? Uh. All right. But sir, I have been in similar situations before. We'll get crushed to serve others' purposes. The powers that be will—"

"No, Win. You've never been in a situation like *this*, not even close. This is much bigger than what you are thinking.

"I'm serious. Stop everything else and read Revelation again."

Christopher paused, looked heavenward, and grinned. "And I'll let you in on a secret often lost in the imagery of Revelation ... We win!

"Things are gonna get much worse before they get better. Hastening the day comes with a unique cost. But God promises that in the end it's all worth it.

"Now remember the mission objective—No Place Left. 2025. Reassemble the forces, and let's get to it."

EPILOGUE

"The forces against you are great. In your own strength, you will never succeed. You are not sufficient. You need a deeper transformation."

"This is ludicrous. I'm above the law. No one need ever know about The Ten. Their evil plans must come to an end. Why can't I crush them now?"

Larson Sayers put both hands on Michael Wroth's shoulders, transfixing him with his gaze.

"On the contrary, Michael, you must proceed a different way," he said, gently pushing him to his seat. "By the way, has anyone ever told you the meaning of your name?"

Director Wroth wondered at the sudden shift in conversation.

"Uh, something about ... it was the name of an archangel?"

Sayers smiled, then chuckled with a faraway look in his eye.

"Well, yes, that is his name. But the name itself has a meaning in Hebrew. It means who is like God."

"Who is like God. Is that a statement or a question?"

The Saga continues in *Rebirth*

In the second book in the *No Place Left* series, Christopher Owen inspires a growing movement in the quest for No Place Left by 2025. The Ten assemble an international coalition to thwart these efforts and usher in a global rebirth. The dramatic showdown unfolds against the backdrop of apocalyptic events and life-giving sacrifice. The saga culminates with a finale that will leave you in tears.

Rebirth paints a picture of what can become reality if God's people rise up to finish what Jesus started.

For up-to-date publication information, quantity discounts, etc., **sign up at eepurl.com/beXiv9**

YOUR Response

Has **God** spoken to **YOU** through *Hastening?*
If so please prayerfully consider taking action:
Find active links at NPL2025.org/respond

- Join the NoPlaceLeft2025 movement
- Share a portion of *Hastening* with friends
- Review *Hastening* on Amazon
- "Like" NoPlaceLeft2025 on Facebook
  - Post there how *Hastening* impacted you
  - Share your post with Facebook friends and *encourage* them to read *Hastening*
  - Invite Facebook friends to *Like* this page
- Review *Hastening* on Good Reads
- Follow Steve Smith on Twitter
- Follow NPL2025 on Twitter
- Buy discounted copies for friends
  Read *Hastening* together and discuss its implications. (And share a copy with your pastor.)
- Set a daily alarm for 9:38 or 10:02 to pray:
  Lord of the harvest, I beg You earnestly to send laborers into Your harvest. Start with me as you did with your first disciples.
- Pray daily for UPGs with the *Global Prayer Digest*
- Train to make disciples who make disciples
  (apply this right where you live).
- Request *Rebirth* (the sequel to Hastening)
- Order *T4T* (Steve's manual on starting CPM's)
- Attend *Kairos* (a simplified *Perspectives* course)
- Attend a full *Perspectives* course (local or on-line)
- Contact an agency pursuing movements in UUPGs
- Help the *No Place Left 2025* movement
- Reread *Hastening*, seeking the Holy Spirit's guidance for **your role** in hastening the fulfillment of Matthew 24:14.

Author's Postscript

This story has been in the hopper for well over two decades, and I have worked on it off and on for much of that. The idea started in my spare time as a church planter in Los Angeles, was released in an early preview while I was in Asia as a strategist working on finishing the task among the unreached peoples of Asia, and was finally completed as I am in a new role coaching a global network of movements. The plot did not come out of a vacuum, but from my own work rubbing shoulders with ministry giants.

During the early writing I admired several other books, especially John Piper's *Let the Nations Be Glad* and Bob Sjogren's *Unveiled At Last* (re-released in 2014 as *God's Bottom Line*). These books resonated deeply as they were saying in non-fiction similar things to what I was trying to convey with fiction. I heartily recommend these books to you.

However, I chose fiction to coax many who would never pick up a "missions" book into becoming enthralled with the Great King's highest goal: bringing all the nations to worship His glory. Wherever this story accomplishes that, I have succeeded.

This story was never intended to be another end-times thriller, but an account of God's mission—including by necessity the end times. For years it has been my personal aspiration to be part of the generation that welcomes Christ's return and to do so by bringing the gospel to every remaining people group. My timeline has developed from my straightforward reading of Scripture.

Several novel series have been written in recent years on the end times. I have very intentionally avoided them. Primarily, I have not wanted to subconsciously plagiarize anyone else's ideas. Any resemblance to another such work is purely coincidental. Secondarily, I am not that interested in outlining an end-times scenario; this is simply an element of history integral to my main plot of the gospel going to the nations. Perhaps now I'll sit down and read someone else's end-times books just to see how differently we view it all.

The one certainty we have is that Christ will come, every eye will behold Him, and His judgment will be final!

None of the characters in this story represent actual people, and many of the people group names that figure significantly are fictional. This is to protect the dear workers who toil among these people as well as the people groups themselves.

In my years of teaching and counseling, I have discovered that the greatest question one can ask is NOT "What is God's will for my life?" but rather "What is God's will—His purpose in this generation—and how can my life best contribute to it?"

Talk with your pastor, your local church's missions committee, your denominational missions agency, or an independent missions agency. Find out where you can best be involved. For your reference, find a growing number of like-minded initiatives at **NPL2025.org/networks**. The end of the task has already begun, and we're not stopping until there is no place left!

For one of several widely-embraced approaches to working with God in initiating church-planting movements, see my book *T4T: A Discipleship Re-Revolution* (2011, WIGTake Resources). This approach, T4T, is bearing fruit all over the world.

God has an unstoppable plan to fulfill His unchanging purpose (Hebrews 6:17). My prayer is that our generation will choose to stand up and embrace it and remove the remaining obstacles to Jesus' return so there is no place left where Jesus is not named.

To Him be the glory forever and ever!

About the Author

Steve Smith trains and coaches believers on how to cooperate with the Spirit of God to see church-planting movements emerge among the nations.

His education includes: B.A. in New Testament Greek, and M.Div., M.Th., and Th.D. in missiology. The first few years of his ministry were spent pastoring both in rural situations and in the urban core of Los Angeles. He and his family started a church in L.A. very similar to the one described in this book.

For 16 years, the Smiths labored in Asia, and were privileged to be personally involved when God started a church-planting movement among a previously unreached people group in Asia. After that they moved into training and leading missionaries in Asia and beyond. They live overseas in their current role of training globally.

As a student of the Word and works of God, Steve seeks to help fellow believers live out the timeless principles of God's kingdom wherever they serve. He (with Ying Kai) is author of *T4T: A Discipleship Re-Revolution* (2011, WIGTake Resources).

Steve is married to the wonderful Laura Nesom Smith and has three incredible sons, Cristopher, Joshua, and David. For almost three decades they have worked together as a family to see all the remaining people groups of the world fervently bow the knee to the Lamb who sits on the throne.

Steve's aspiration is to be in the final generation, the one that welcomes the return of the King.

Learn More

To learn more about cooperating with God in initiating church-planting movements at home and abroad, read Steve's book *T4T: A Discipleship Re-Revolution*. It is available in hard copy from **ChurchPlantingMovements.com** and in Kindle format from **Amazon.com**.

T4T presents the clear, biblical explanation of how God is initiating discipleship revolutions all over the world today which result in multiplying churches. It includes numerous modern day case studies to help you adapt the timeless biblical principles to your particular context, in cooperation with the Holy Spirit, to see His Kingdom come fully in your community.

Unprecedented Kingdom progress is being made, and the facts and figures in this story about the enormity and feasibility of finishing the Great Commission were current as of July 2015.

Steve Smith has posted a variety of reference materials and short articles at **KingdomKernels.com**

Follow Steve on Twitter **@kingreigncome**

Lists of the unreached can be found in many missions circles. Joshua Project (**JoshuaProject.net**) and the Southern Baptist International Mission Board (IMB) research department (**IMB.org/globalresearch** and **PeopleGroups.org**) both keep well-documented lists publicly available. Global Mapping International (**GMI.org**) provides additional mapping and research resources.

Rapid progress is being made, and the facts and figures in this story about the enormity and feasibility of finishing the Great Commission were current as of July 2015.

It is these undeniable facts and the clear commission of God's Word that I hope will propel you out of a cozy reading chair and onto your knees to evaluate where the Father wants to involve you in His plan to save the nations.

The Creation to Christ Story

Would you like to learn a summary of the whole Bible you can share in ten minutes?

What follows is simply that. It explains the gospel as the power of God to bring salvation in a way someone with no knowledge of God can understand. This is the message George preached in Yijing's village in Chapter 24.

This story can help you in two ways:

1. If you have never personally put your faith in Jesus Christ as your Savior and Master, this explains how you, too, can come to God, receive new life as His son or daughter, and find the life you were meant to have. You can make that decision right now.

2. This is also a simple way to learn and present the good news in a story format that anyone can understand. It's easy to learn one part at a time. And when you've learned all the parts, you can tell the whole story in ten minutes!

This gospel presentation is bearing fruit in cultures around the world through people putting their faith in Christ, learning, and sharing this story as part of a discipleship process. We invite you to become part of this story by learning and sharing it with others in your own words.

Hear the author narrate an illustrated video of this same *Creation to Christ* story at **NPL2025.org/c2c**.

This is a story that is changing the lives of people all over the world.

PART 1—True Story from the Bible

It is a story of the Most High God's relationship with the world. It is from a book called *The Bible*. People did not make up *The Bible* but rather it is the Word of the Most High God. The Most High God is more powerful than any ancestor, person, government, or god that people worship. He is all-powerful. This story is true and reliable because it is the Word of the Most High God.

PART 2—Created for a Relationship with God

There is only one God, and He is the Most High God. He existed in the beginning before there was anything else. The Most High God is the Creator. He created everything we can see and cannot see. He created things we cannot see such as angels. They are beautiful spirits who worship and serve God. He also created everything we can see—the sky, land, water, mountains, oceans, sun, moon, stars, and all plants and animals. Finally, He created a man and a woman according to His image. When God began to create things, He spoke and everything came into being. God created everything and saw that it was good.

God placed the man and woman in a beautiful garden to live. They had a very good relationship with Him and with each other. He told them to take care of the garden and enjoy everything. He gave them a special command: they could eat from every tree in the garden except one. If they ate from that one tree, they would be punished and die. The man and woman listened to God and had a wonderful relationship with Him in the garden. **God created us to have a wonderful relationship with Him forever!**

PART 3—People are Separated from God

However, do you remember the angels God created? One of the angels was very smart and beautiful. This angel became very proud. He wanted to be like God and to have the other angels worship him instead of God. Only God deserves all worship and service. Therefore God cast the disobedient angel, the devil, and the other angels who listened to him out of heaven. These evil angels are known as demons.

One day, the devil tempted the woman to eat the food from the tree that was forbidden. The woman listened to the devil and ate the fruit. Then she gave it to her husband to eat. Both of them disobeyed God's command. **Sin is any time we disobey God's commands.** God is righteous and holy. He must punish sin. Therefore God cast the man and the woman out of the garden, and their relationship with God was broken. Human beings and God were now separated forever.

Like the first man and woman, all of us since then have sinned by not listening to God's commands and are separated from God. The result of sin is eternal punishment in hell. **We cannot live forever with God as we were designed.**

PART 4—People Can't Come Back to God

Over time, the number of people on earth multiplied. Yet God loved them very much and wanted them to have a relationship with Him. He gave them ten commandments to follow. These ten commandments teach people how to relate to God and how to relate to people. Some of the commands were: do not worship other gods or make idols; honor your parents; do not lie, steal, murder, commit adultery, or covet the things other people have. However, no one was able to obey all of these commands.

So, each time they sinned, God allowed them to repent of their sins and offer a blood sacrifice to take the place of their punishment. This sacrifice was shedding the blood of a perfect animal like a lamb. If they would repent and offer the blood sacrifice, God would forgive them and let the animal die in their place. **Only by the shedding of blood can a person's sin be forgiven.** However, people kept sinning and the sacrifices became empty rituals rather than something from their hearts. God became tired of their insincere acts. People were still separated from God. **People could not come back to God on their own no matter what they did. What could be done?**

PART 5—Jesus Comes to Earth

God still loved us very much. Therefore, at just the right time, He gave us a perfect way to reconnect to Him. God sent Jesus to show us the way back to Himself. Who is Jesus? Jesus is God's one and only Son. Around age 30 he was baptized and then began to minister in the power of God's Spirit.

When Jesus was on earth, He was a wise teacher. Many people would come to hear Him teach about how they could return to God.

Jesus was also a powerful **miracle worker**. On one occasion over five thousand people came to listen to Jesus teach about God. When evening came they had not eaten and were hungry. Altogether they only had five loaves of bread and two fish. Jesus held up the loaves and the fish, blessed them, and then passed them out. Jesus used the five loaves of bread and two fish to feed over five thousand people. **Jesus has the power to meet our needs.**

On another occasion Jesus and His followers crossed a large lake on a boat. While Jesus was sleeping, a powerful storm arose on the lake. Jesus' followers were very afraid. They awakened Jesus and said, "We are about to die!" Jesus rebuked the wind and spoke to the waves, "Quiet! Be still!" Immediately the wind and rained stopped. **Jesus has power over the natural world.**

When they got to the other side, Jesus saw a man with many demons inside him. The man was powerful and dangerous. People were very afraid of him. Yet Jesus loved the man and spoke, casting the demons out of him. **Jesus is more powerful than the evil spiritual world.**

Finally, on another occasion Jesus' good friend became sick and died. Several days later Jesus arrived at His friend's house. Jesus felt very sad and wept. His friend was already in the tomb. Jesus went to the front of the tomb and said, "Friend, come out." His friend rose up and walked out of the tomb alive! **Jesus has power over death.**

Jesus did all these things because He loves people and wants us all to come back to God.

PART 6—Jesus, The Perfect Sacrifice

Unlike us, Jesus never sinned. He obeyed His Father in heaven perfectly. He alone never deserved to be punished.

Most people loved Jesus. However, some religious leaders were jealous of Jesus. These men arrested Jesus and decided to kill Him. They placed Jesus on a large cross—two large pieces of wood shaped in a "t." They took His hands and His feet and nailed them to the cross. His precious blood flowed from His hands and feet and dripped to the ground. Jesus suffered much pain on the cross.

On the cross, Jesus became the perfect sacrifice. Jesus died for all mankind. God loves us and allowed Jesus, His only Son, to die on the cross in our place to take our punishment. Only through the shedding of Jesus' precious blood was God able to forgive our sin. Jesus death demonstrates God's love towards us.

After Jesus died, He was placed in a secure tomb. However this story doesn't end here. On the third day Jesus rose from the dead and proved He was Who He said He was! Then He returned to His Father in heaven but will come back one day as Judge to make all things right. *Jesus took our punishment and now provides a way for us to come back to God!*

PART 7—The Wandering Son

Before He left the earth, Jesus told a story to his followers about a father and his sons.

The father had two sons. The younger one said to his father, "Father, give me my share of the inheritance." So the father divided his property between his sons. The younger son got together all he had, set off for a distant country, and there wasted his wealth in wild living. After he had spent everything, he began to be in need. So he went and got a lowly job feeding pigs. He longed to fill his stomach with the pods that the pigs were eating, but no one gave him anything.

One day he came to his senses. He said, "How many of my father's hired men have food to spare, and here I am starving to death! I will set out and go back to my father and say to him: 'Father, I have sinned against heaven and against you. I am no longer worthy to be called your son; make me like one of your hired men.'"

So he got up and went to his father. But while he was still a long way off, his father saw him and was filled with compassion for him. He ran to his son, threw his arms around him, and kissed him. The son said to him, "Father, I have sinned against heaven and against you. I am no longer worthy to be called your son."

But the father said to his servants, "Quick! Bring the best robe and put it on him. Put a ring on his finger and sandals on his feet. Bring the fattened calf and kill it. Let's have a feast and celebrate. For this son of mine was dead and is alive again; he was lost and is found." So they began to celebrate.

PART 8—How to come back to God

We are all like the younger son. We have left God and are forever separated from Him. We must repent of our sins and return to God. Only Jesus can lead us back to God's side and make us His son or daughter. Only then can we live the life we were meant to live here on earth and with Him forever in heaven.

Only Jesus can bring us back. He said, **"I am the way the truth, and the life. No one comes to the Father except through me" (John 14:6).**

We must all go through Jesus to return to God. How can you go through Jesus? You must admit to God that you have sinned against Him. You must believe that Jesus died in your place. You put your trust in Jesus to bring you back and give you eternal life as God's son or daughter. From that point on, you let Jesus be your Master and obey His Word.

Do you want to let Jesus bring you back to God?

The whole Creation to Christ story is summarized in one verse: **"For God so loved the world that he gave his one and only Son, that whoever believes [trusts] in him shall not perish but have eternal life" (John 3:16).**

To come back to God, you must put your faith (trust) in Jesus. To do that, you must turn from our old sinful life and ask God to forgive you. **"If we confess our sins, he is faithful and just and will forgive us our sins and purify us from all unrighteousness" (1 John 1:9).** He is a treasure worth joyfully giving your life to gain!

Therefore, to return to God you must repent *(turn from) your sins and* believe *in Jesus as your new Master.*

God wants you, your family, and your friends to return to Him. To return, you must believe in your heart and confess ...

> **"God, I know you love me, but I have sinned against you.**
>
> **However, Jesus is the perfect sacrifice for my sin. I believe and trust in Jesus to take my punishment.**
>
> **I confess I have sinned and am sorry. God, please forgive me.**
>
> **I put my trust in You, Jesus, and ask You to lead me back to God.**
>
> **I agree to joyfully obey You as my Master from this moment on.**
>
> **Thank You for my new and eternal life as Your child."**

You can speak to God out loud or silently right now and He will hear you. .

If you truly turned back to God, you are now God's child. You have a brand new life—forgiven of your sins and a new creation! God's Spirit now lives in you. The Bible says:

"I write these things to you who believe in the name of the Son of God so that you may know that you have eternal life" (1 John 5:13).

No matter what happens, you are now God's child forever! He wants you to rest assured that you have a new life and nothing can separate you again!

It is important now to meet with other believers, read God's Word, and pray to Him regularly to grow in your new relationship with God.

God's plan is not only to bring you back but also to bring back your family and friends through you. God is waiting for your whole family to believe in Him. Go home and tell your family and friends this good news. God loves them too!

Write down the names of people you want to tell this story to this week. Who do you think would most like to hear it?